Until I Find You

Also by Rea Frey

Because You're Mine
Not Her Daughter

Until I Find You

Rea Frey

St. Martin's Griffin
New York

First published in the United States by St. Martin's Griffin, an imprint of St. Martin's Publishing Group

UNTIL I FIND YOU. Copyright © 2020 by Rea Frey. All rights reserved. Printed in the United States of America. For information, address St. Martin's Publishing Group, 120 Broadway, New York, NY 10271.

www.stmartins.com

Designed by Gabriel Guma

The Library of Congress Cataloging-in-Publication Data is available upon request.

ISBN 978-1-250-24158-0 (trade paperback)
ISBN 978-1-250-24159-7 (ebook)

Our books may be purchased in bulk for promotional, educational, or business use. Please contact your local bookseller or the Macmillan Corporate and Premium Sales Department at 1-800-221-7945, extension 5442, or by email at MacmillanSpecialMarkets@macmillan.com.

First Edition: 2020

10 9 8 7 6 5 4 3 2 1

for my daughter, Sophie,
the brightest light
I will ever see

THERE IS NO SUCH THING AS PARANOIA.
YOUR WORST FEARS CAN COME TRUE AT ANY MOMENT.

—Hunter S. Thompson

1

BEC

∴

SOMEONE'S COMING.

I push the stroller. My feet expertly navigate the familiar path toward the park without my cane. Footsteps advance behind me. The swish of fabric between hurried thighs. The clop of a shoe on pavement. Measured, but gaining with every step. Blood whooshes through my ears, a distraction.

One more block until the park's entrance. My world blots behind my sunglasses, smeared and dreamy. A few errant hairs whip across my face. My toe catches a crack, and my ankle painfully twists.

No time to stop.

My thighs burn. A few more steps. Finally, I make a sharp left into the park's entrance. Jackson's anklet jingles from the blistering pace.

"Hang on, sweet boy. Almost there. Almost." The relentless August sun sizzles in the sky, and I adjust my ball cap with a trembling hand. Uncertain, I stop and wait for either the rush of footsteps to pass, or to approach and attack. Instead, nothing.

I lick my dry lips and half turn, one hand still securely fastened on my son's stroller. "Hello?" The wind stalls. The hairs bristle on the back of my neck. My world goes unnaturally still, until I choke on my own warped breath.

I waver on the sidewalk and then lunge toward the entrance to

Wilder. The stroller is my guide as I half walk, half jog, knowing precisely how many steps I must take to reach the other side of the gate.

Twenty.

My heart thumps, a manic metronome. Jackson squeals and kicks his foot. The bells again.

Ten.

The footsteps echo in my ears. The stroller rams an obstacle in the way and flattens it. I swerve and cry out in surprise.

Five.

I reach the gate, hurtle through to a din of voices. Somewhere in the distance, a lawn mower stutters then chugs to life.

Safe.

I slide toward the ground and drop my head between my knees. My ears prick for the stranger behind me, but all is lost. A plane roars overhead, probably heading for Chicago. Birds aggressively chirp as the sun continues to crisp my already pink shoulders. A car horn honks on the parallel street. Someone blows a whistle. My body shudders from the surge of adrenaline. I sit until I regain my composure and then push to shaky legs.

I check Jackson, dragging my hands over the length of his body—his strong little fingers, his plump thighs, and perpetually kicking feet—and blot my face with his spit-up blanket. Just when I think I'm safe, a hand encircles my wrist.

"Miss?"

I jerk back and suck a surprised breath.

The hand drops. "I'm sorry," a woman's voice says. "I didn't mean to scare you. You dropped this." Something jingles and lands in my upturned palm: Jackson's anklet.

I smooth my fingers over the bells. "Thanks." I bend over the stroller, grip his ankle, and reattach them. I tickle the bottom of his foot, and he murmurs.

"Are the bells so you can hear him?" the woman asks. "Are you . . . ?"

"Blind? Yes." I straighten. "I am."

"That's cool. I've never seen that before."

I assume she means the bells. I almost make a joke—*neither have I!*—but instead, I smile. "It's a little early for him to wear them," I explain. "They're more for when he becomes mobile, but I want him to get used to them."

"That's smart."

I'm not sure if she's waiting for me to say something else. "Thanks again," I offer.

"No problem. Have a good day."

She leaves. My hands clamp around the stroller's handle. Was she the one behind me? I stall at the gate and wonder if I should just go back home. I remind myself where I am—in one of the safest suburbs outside of Chicago—not in some sketchy place. I'm not being followed.

It's fine.

To prove it, I remove my cane, unfold it, and brace it on the path. I maneuver Jackson's stroller behind and sweep my cane in front, searching for more obstacles or unsuspecting feet.

I weave toward Cottage Hill and pass the wedding garden, the Wilder Mansion, and the art museum. Finally, I wind around the arboretum. I leave the conservatory for last, pulling Jackson through colorful flower breeds, active butterflies, and rows of green. My heart still betrays my calm exterior, but whoever was there is gone.

I whisk my T-shirt from my body. Jackson babbles and then lets out a sharp cry. I adjust the brim of his stroller so his eyes aren't directly hit by the sun. I lower my baseball cap and head toward the playground. The rubber flooring shifts beneath my cane.

Wilder Park is packed with last-minute late-summer activity. I do a lap around the playground and then angle my cane toward a bench to check for occupants. Once I confirm it's empty, I settle and park the stroller beside me. I keep my ears alert for Jess or Beth. I think about calling Crystal to join us, but then remember she has an interior design job today.

I place my hand on Jackson's leg, the small jingle of his anklet a comfort. Suddenly, I am overcome with hunger. I rummage in the diaper bag for a banana, peel it, and reach again for Jackson, who is playing with his pacifier. He furiously sucks then knocks it out of his mouth. He giggles every time I hand it back to him.

I replay what just happened. If someone had attacked me, I wouldn't have been able to defend myself or identify the perpetrator. A shiver courses the length of my spine. Though Jackson is technically easy—healthy, no colic, a decent sleeper—this stage of life is not. Chris died a year ago, and though it's been twelve months since the accident, sometimes it feels like it's been twelve days.

Jackson's life flashes before me. Not the happy baby playing in his stroller, but the other parts. The first time he gets really sick. The first time he has to go to the emergency room, and I'm all alone. The first time I don't know what to do when something is wrong. The first time he runs away from me in public and isn't wearing bells to alert me to his location.

Will I be able to keep him safe, to protect him?

I will the dark cloud away, but uneasiness pierces my skin like a warning. I fan my shirt, swallow, close my eyes behind my sunglasses, and adjust my ball cap.

The world shrinks. I try to swallow, but my throat constricts. I claw air.

I can't breathe. I'm drowning. My heart is going to explode. I'm going to die.

I lurch off the bench and walk a few paces, churning my arms toward my chest to produce air. I gasp, tell myself to breathe, tell myself to do something.

When I think I'm going to faint, I exhale completely, then sip in a shallow breath. I veer toward a tree, fingers grasping, and reach its chalky bark. *In, out. In, out. Breathe, Rebecca. Breathe.*

Concerned whispers crescendo around me while I remember how to breathe. I mentally force my limbs to relax, soften my jaw, and count to ten. After a few toxic moments, I retrace my steps back to the bench.

I just left my baby alone.

Jackson's right foot twitches and jingles from the stroller; he's blissfully unaware that his mother just had a panic attack. I calm myself, but my heart continues to knock around my chest like a pinball. I open a bottle of water and lift it to my lips with trembling hands. I exhale and massage my chest. The footsteps. The panic attack. These recurring fears . . .

"Hey, lady. Fancy meeting you here." Jess leans down and delivers a kiss to my cheek. Her scent—sweet, like honey crisp apples—does little to dissuade my terrified mood.

"Hi. Sit, sit." I rearrange my voice to neutral and move the diaper bag to make room.

Jess positions her stroller beside mine. Beth sits next to her, her three-month-old baby, Trevor, always in a ring sling or strapped to her chest.

"How's the morning?" Beth asks.

I tell them both about the footsteps and the woman who returned the bells, but conveniently leave out the part about the panic attack.

Beth leans closer. "Scary. Who do you think was following you?"

"I'm not sure," I say.

"You should have called," Jess says. "I'm always happy to walk with you."

"That's not exactly on your way."

"Oh, please. I could use the extra exercise."

I roll my eyes at her disparaging comment, because Beth and I both know she loves her curves.

"Anyway, it's sleep deprivation," Jess continues. "Makes you hallucinate. I remember when Baxter was Jackson's age and waking up every two hours, I literally thought I was going to lose my mind. I would put things in odd places. I was even convinced Rob was cheating."

I laugh. "Rob would never cheat on you."

"Exactly my point." She turns to me. "Have you thought about hiring a nanny?"

"Yeah," Beth adds. "Especially with everything you've been through."

My stomach clenches at those words: *everything you've been through.* After Chris died, I moved in with my mother so she could essentially become Jackson's nanny. And then, just two months ago, she died too. Though her death wasn't a surprise due to her lifelong heart condition, no one is ever prepared to lose a parent. "I can't afford it."

"Like I've said before, Rob and I are happy to pitch in—"

I lift my hand to stop her. "And I appreciate it. I really do. But I'm not ready to have someone in my space when I'm just getting used to it being empty. I need to get comfortable taking care of Jackson on my own."

"That makes sense," Beth assures me.

"It does." Jess pats my thigh. "But you're not a martyr, okay? Everyone needs help."

"I know." I adjust my sunglasses and rearrange my face in hopes of hiding the real emotions I feel. "What's new with both of you?"

"Can I vent for a second?" Beth asks. She situates closer to us on the bench. Thanks to the visual Jess supplied, I know Beth is blond, petite, and impossibly fit—and is perpetually in a state of crisis. She's practicing attachment parenting, which, in her mind, keeps her glued to her son twenty-four hours a day. I've never even held him.

"Vent away," I say.

"Okay." She drops her voice. "Like, I love this little guy, truly. But sometimes, when it's just the two of us in the house all day, I fantasize about just running away somewhere. Or going out to take a walk. I'd never do it, of course," she rushes to add. "But I just have this feeling like . . . I'm never going to be alone again."

"Nanny," Jess trills. "I'm telling you. Quit this attachment parenting crap and get yourself a nanny. And if she's hot, she can even occupy your husband so you don't have to."

I slap Jess's arm. "Don't say that. You'd be totally devastated if Rob ever did cheat."

"Would I though? One less thing I'd have to do at night," she mumbles.

"That's not attachment parenting," I assure Beth. "That's how every new mom feels sometimes."

Beth bounces Trevor, her voice vibrating. "But am I a terrible human? Are you both sitting there judging me?"

"We don't have time to judge you," Jess jokes.

"You *never* complain, Rebecca," Beth says.

"Who, me?" I ask. "I complain."

I imagine Beth and Jess giving each other a look. "You don't," Jess says. "Ever. Which makes zero sense, considering . . ."

Considering your husband and mother died and you're raising a baby all by yourself.

I shrug. "I learned a long time ago that complaining doesn't change anything, so why bother?"

"Complaining is my hobby," Beth says. "And I realize I don't have anything to complain about. I mean, not really."

I roll my eyes. "Beth, you're allowed to feel however you want. Don't compare your life to mine. For your own good."

"But your baby is perfect," Beth whines. "If you ever want to trade, just let me know."

I laugh. "I'll let you know." I tune in and out as they gripe about their babies and husbands. I add in my two cents, wanting to tell them my deepest thoughts on the subject, but decide against it. Their voices come and go. My eyes flutter—closed, open, closed, open—and before I know it, I've accidentally fallen asleep.

2

BEC

⠃⠑⠉

AFTER THE PARK—AND MY UNEXPECTED NAP—I LISTEN FOR OTHER PEOPLE crossing the intersection and begin the grid-like walk back toward the house. I think of the chores I need to finish and the dinner I will prepare: steak, salad, and roasted rosemary potatoes. The steps I will go through. How I will set the table. How I will rely on timers and taste.

I approach the front of the house and fold my cane. Sweat has cropped up along my forehead. I wick away the moisture and fish my key from my back pocket. I bring it to the lock, but it smacks air. I reach forward and find the lock with my fingers.

The door is open.

I recoil, stunned. For the third time today, my pulse begins to race. I fumble for my phone, drop it, then retrieve it from the grass. Who can I possibly call? I spin around in an agitated circle, edge a few steps back, and stop. Am I being robbed? Are my earlier fears of being followed coming true?

Don't go in. I heed my own warning and pull Jackson's stroller to the edge of the driveway. Someone is always in the house, or crouched in a closet, or, God forbid, in the shower. I think about the alarm. Did I forget to set it?

Think, Rebecca. Think. I stall on the driveway and call Jess.

"Miss me already?"

"My front door is open."

"What?"

"I just got home and my front door is open." Saying it out loud makes me take another few steps toward the street.

"Don't move. I'll call the police."

"You don't have to call the police."

"Rebecca, I'm calling the police. Do not go into the house. Do you hear me? I'll be right there."

I exhale and push and pull Jackson's stroller in a lulling motion until Jess arrives.

"God, I hate running," she pants. Her tennis shoes thud to a halt. She hitches forward and rests her hands on her knees. "It's for the birds." She grunts then straightens. "Police still aren't here?"

I shake my head. A curl of hair brushes my cheek as she loops a sturdy arm around my shoulder.

"Keeping things interesting in old Elmhurst, huh?"

"Where's Baxter?"

"Nanny. Told you they're helpful." She drops her arm as she continues to catch her breath. "Do you really think someone broke in?"

"I hope not." I think of my cello, my computer, any valuables I have scattered about.

"Maybe you just didn't shut the door all the way?"

"Maybe." *I always shut the door.*

After a few anxious minutes, police sirens bleep and stutter along our street. My fingers tighten on the stroller as I imagine neighbors straining on their front porches, whispering behind cupped hands about the paranoid blind lady. This is not a neighborhood where cops do regular drive-bys. The red and blue lights pierce the blurred veil of my vision, and I squint behind my sunglasses.

A car door opens and shuts and then a lone officer approaches. "Ma'am?"

"Hi, I'm the one who called," Jess says. "This is Rebecca Gray. She lives here. She's . . ."

"I'm blind," I explain. "When I got back from my walk, my front door was open. And I'm positive I shut it before I left."

"Officer Toby." He thrusts a hand in my direction. "Do you have an alarm?"

"I do." I consider the possibility that I could have forgotten to arm it, but it doesn't add up. "I always set it before I leave."

"And the alarm hasn't gone off?"

I shake my head. "No."

"Have you gone into the home, ma'am?" His radio squawks with a string of garbled commands.

"No."

"Good. I'm going to check the perimeter of the property and the interior. Please stay out here until I've completed the search."

"Thanks, Officer." Jess whistles when he walks away. "Who knew Elmhurst had such hot cops?"

I laugh and elbow her. Another cop name floats through my mind. To distract myself until Toby returns, I blurt: "I used to date a cop."

"What? When?"

I shrug and shush Jackson as he fusses in his stroller. I reach around for his pacifier and pop it back into his mouth. "A lifetime ago. Before Chris." Just saying my husband's name sends a pang of fresh grief through my gut. "I met him when I still had my sight. I was twenty-five. He was a cop trying to make detective with CPD. Both of our careers were flourishing."

"So what happened?"

"He got transferred to Florida," I say. Though we both assumed we'd get married, have kids, and live in the city, when he got an offer to lead a narcotics unit, he took it.

"Ugh. Florida? No wonder you broke up."

I playfully slap her arm.

"That wasn't it, but I couldn't leave the symphony. And he couldn't miss out on such a great opportunity." I shrug. "We were both realistic about long distance. Once he left, my sight got worse. I met Chris when he was volunteering at the Chicago Lighthouse."

"What in the hell is that?"

"It's a community center for the visually impaired."

"Then Chris was a rebound."

I roll my eyes. "Chris was not a rebound."

"Chris was *totally* a rebound."

"No, he was just there when I needed him." I smile. "Chris was always there for me. He was dependable."

"Like a minivan."

"He was a bit like a minivan." My heart lifts just joking about Chris. *This is what I want to do more of,* I remind myself. *Talk about him as if he's right here.* Before I can say anything else, Jess leans in.

"Hottie approaching."

"Ma'am, the perimeter and interior are secure. No sign of forced entry. Nothing suspicious in or around the property. I'm happy to do a walk-through with you to make sure nothing is out of place."

"That's not necessary." I remove my ball cap and run a hand through my sweaty hair. "I'm sorry about this."

"No problem. You ladies have a great day, okay?"

"Thanks *so* much, Officer." Jess lightly touches my elbow. "Want me to come in with you?"

"No, I'm fine. Thanks for coming over." I hug her, wave good-bye, and head inside. I shut and lock the front door. "Is Mama paranoid or what?" I remove Jackson from his stroller. His body is sticky as I settle him on one hip. I peel off my T-shirt and invite cool air to flow in from the gap. "It sure is hot out there, huh? I'm ready for fall. Are you?" We walk to the kitchen, and I open the freezer and stick my head in and play peek-a-boo a few times. His hearty chuckle squeezes my heart until I think it might explode.

"Okay, let's get you settled so Mama can make dinner." I walk the few steps to deposit him in his Pack 'n Play by the kitchen table, except it's not where I left it. I rotate, inch by inch. Chills stud the back of my neck. I stall in the kitchen, moving methodically to retrace my steps. I round the corner and shuffle toward the middle of the living room, until I bump into something: his playpen.

My nerves sizzle. I would never put the Pack 'n Play in the middle of the living room. Because of my sight, I place most furniture on the perimeter of every room, leaving a wide open space to pass through. I'm certain it was by the kitchen table this morning. Could the cop have moved it?

I retreat slowly from the room, as though the playpen might detonate. I call Jess's number again, fit Jackson back in his carrier, and leave the house as fast as I can.

3

BEC

⠃⠑⠉

SOMETIME IN THE NIGHT, JACKSON WAKES ME. I OPEN MY EYES AND FIDDLE with the baby monitor, but his cries stalk the hallway. I don't bother checking the time and instead throw the duvet back and sit up.

My thoughts ping around as they do each night, when I lie awake for hours and wait for Jackson to signal he's hungry. Ironically, he's only been waking a few times per night. Now, I travel the hallway toward his nursery. The absence of morning light is like wading through ink.

At his door, the cries grow more urgent.

"Hold on, little guy. Mama's here." I cross to the crib. I lower my arms in, but he's not where he usually is. "Did you roll?" I scoop again, but my grip comes away bare. I rub my hands across the sheets and frantically scour every inch of the crib. "Jackson?" I traverse and skim again.

Nothing.

The cries intensify, but they aren't coming from the crib. Now, they're behind me. I whip around. "Jackson?" I rush out of his room and down the hall. The cry shifts again, as if bouncing freely through the house. I fumble for the baby monitor on my nightstand and knock over my water glass. It thuds against the carpet. Back in the hallway, I strain to hear exactly where he is.

Downstairs?

"Oh my God." I ignore the logical part of my brain that knows a three-month-old can't escape his crib, and I sprint downstairs anyway. My toe bumps into something. I crouch down and connect with a tiny nose, mouth, and chin. But it's not flesh I feel—it's plastic. A baby doll? I check to make sure. The doll cries harder, and I drop it and spin around in my foyer. "Jackson?" I call his name again, and mid-cry, he cuts off. The house grows deathly quiet, except for my chaotic breath.

A crack of lightning brings me out of it. I jolt awake, drenched, my heart a jackhammer. I lie in my bed, queasy with nerves. "It's just a dream," I reassure myself. "You're okay." I reach for the glass of water on my nightstand and suck down the last remaining drops. I collapse back in bed. Thunder rolls outside, then another flash of lightning.

The nightmares are becoming so real.

I snake a shaky hand over my face and wipe away the sweat. The events from yesterday drift into focus: the footsteps. The open door. The moved playpen. Last night, Jess worked hard to reassure me that my exhaustion is to blame, but I'm not so sure.

I gauge the empty space beside me and run a hand over the sheets. A sob catches in my throat. I squeeze my eyes shut until the outline of Chris's face fires in my memory—the slightly crooked nose, broken twice from college rugby, the large amber eyes and impossibly thick lashes, the tiny cleft in his chin. I reach out as though I can still press a finger into the dimpled flesh. My hand fists around air, drops, resettles.

I roll back over. Nights and mornings are always the worst. I can keep myself busy during the day, but at night, when I settle into bed, his absence is the loudest thing in the room. That, coupled with all of these terrors about Jackson—Jackson crying, but I can't find him; Jackson tumbling from my arms down the stairs; Jackson floating away in a river—it's enough to make me want to boycott my bedroom entirely.

I press the button on my alarm clock to tell me the time. It's only 4

A.M. I sit up, slip on my robe, and listen for Jackson at the top of the stairs. His white noise machine whooshes on low from his nursery down the hall.

It's still odd that I live in my mother's house, a dusty old relic on one of the best streets in Elmhurst, Illinois. Its drab interior, leaky windows, and outdated roof made me think about selling, but I was too tired to pack, sort, and figure out where to move again after her funeral. Plus, it had once been my home too. I was ready to make it that way again.

Now, I carefully navigate down the stairs, my fingers cruising over the worn banister. At the bottom, I pass the sitting room I never actually sit in—badly in need of paint and fresh curtains—the monstrous dining room, the open foyer, and the cozy living room with the sailboat wallpaper. I used to stare at that wallpaper for hours as a child, until my eyes grew blurry and the boats blended together into a deep ocean blue.

Later, as an adult, when I found out I was going to lose my vision, I'd walk to Lake Michigan, sit on the beach, and stare at the water. I'd let the calm wash over me and commit the exact hue to memory—the same blue as my childhood wallpaper—and focus on how the water glittered and churned. I'd close my eyes and get used to hearing, not seeing. When my vision worsened, Chris continued to bring me to the water every Sunday. He didn't talk. He didn't ask questions. He just let me be.

Since his death, I haven't been back even once.

I turn the corner into the kitchen, fill the kettle, and flick on the burner. Updating my childhood home will be the very first renovation project I tackle with Crystal, an interior designer I met at a grief group. Six months after Chris died, I'd waddled into the group with my pregnant belly, instantly wanting to leave, and that was when Crystal helped me find a seat. She didn't ask about my vision or why I was there, and I didn't ask her either.

We talked about other things: our careers and living in Elmhurst, though we had both lost our husbands. It was over a month before I even knew she had a daughter. I quickly learned she didn't like talking about her life—as if the mere mention of the people who composed it would somehow alert the universe to take them all away too. Not many people understood that, but I did. There, in that room full of Kleenex and anguish, was the most connected I'd felt to anyone in a really long time. We'd been on a steady incline to genuine friendship ever since.

Upstairs, the baby cries. My body tingles as he calls. I shake the electricity from my limbs and wait to see if he will settle back to sleep, but he continues to cry.

I walk the hall again and trek upstairs: fifty-five steps. From land-ing to nursery: thirty-five. It is amazing how important math has become in daily life. How angles and steps can mean the differ-ence between a smooth transition from room to room or a smashed nose or stubbed toe. While all visually impaired people have their blindisms—some people rock back and forth, some people listen with their mouths open, intent on absorbing every word—mine is counting steps. I don't *need* to count steps. I am oriented to our home and neighborhood and am blessed with a photographic memory, but it is my tic.

I crack the door and ease inside. My mother helped me decorate. She picked the Pinterest-worthy wallpaper. The elephant decals. The Crate and Kids dresser and changing table. I walk toward the large crib and stare into it.

The room is black. The shape of my son seizes my heart. His little body plumps beneath his onesie—a foggy halo—but a gaping hole appears where his head should be. I picture his exquisite gray eyes, like twin marbles bobbing beneath water. *Where are they?* My breath-ing intensifies. I place my hand gently on his belly. He jerks awake in the inky darkness.

There. There's my baby.

I slap a hand to my heart. The air escapes in an audible whoosh. The ugly black hole recedes as his face hardens in my mind. My hands traverse his body—the creased palms, the wiggly legs, the warm belly. It takes a moment for him to register in my brain first, then spring to life in front of me. *He is here. He is real.* I step back.

My eyes are playing tricks again.

It's an unwelcome side effect of Stargardt disease—besides losing my central vision, I also see shapes shift in the dark with what little sight I retain.

I scoop his pliable body out of the crib and find the rocking chair. He hunts for my breast. His tiny fist works against my chest as he drinks. I cast a map of his face in my mind and caress every feature. The fuzzy forehead. His thick lashes and squishy nose. His tiny scoop of a chin. Love fills my hand, my body, this chair, my world. I remember when he was placed into my arms at the hospital, I'd memorized every part of him. The wrinkled hands and impossibly compact feet. The down-turned lips. His crazy fingernails, which were so long, I had to cover his hands with socks to keep him from scratching himself. A surge of grief flattens me. Chris was supposed to be here. Chris was supposed to become a father. He and I spent so much time discussing our future, making plans for time we'd never have instead of just enjoying the moment.

What a waste.

I let the feelings come—now knowing that resisting grief only makes it worse—and wait until they pass. "Who's a good boy?" I stroke Jackson's cheek and mess with the bumpy skin close to his right ear. The pediatrician explained how to feel for rashes, how to differentiate between eczema, psoriasis, diaper rash, or even chicken pox. This is eczema.

I take inventory of the rest of his skin—all clear—and wind my fingers through his wispy hair. He drains my left breast, then my right. I resist the urge to fall asleep. So many times during the day, I try to nap and almost get there, but something happens: the phone rings. The baby cries. He's wide awake and wants to be entertained. But the sleeplessness is worth it for moments like these.

I rock Jackson until he is milk drunk and lay him back in his crib. I leave his door cracked and pad back downstairs to the kitchen, not even realizing the kettle has been whistling. The angry steam hisses from the spout. I flick off the burner and pour myself a cup.

I sip my tea. The silence consumes me. I ask Google Home to play my Spotify symphony playlist and briefly conjure my younger, sighted self in the Chicago Symphony Orchestra, followed by vision symptoms I could no longer ignore, which inevitably led to a diagnosis of Stargardt disease and Charles Bonnet syndrome. As my vision went, it was like staring at a painting whose center had been wiped clean. It was manageable at first, like having really bad vision and forgetting your glasses. And then, everything finite slipped away.

My career died with my vision, which was a catastrophic loss. I can still play, of course, but after pregnancy, Chris's death, and moving to the suburbs, I gave in to the reality of my condition. Now, it's about me alone in a room, practicing. Not me on the stage, performing. Thank God for my photographic memory and the music I keep in my head.

I walk to the front door and open it to get the paper. Sprinklers rhythmically sputter from neighboring lawns. I clutch the paper in my hands, now soggy. I haven't had the heart to stop my mother's subscription.

Inside, the door clicks shut and the humidity leeches from the room. I toss the paper on the entry table. The silence briefly roars again between songs, deafening, then slowly, sound bleeds back in: the ticking clock, the hum of the fridge, the whiny floors beneath my socked feet, the slow crescendo of a violin. I twist the lock. We live in a family-friendly community, but fears mount anyway: a midday break-in. A madman on the loose. A rapist.

"Stop it, Rebecca." My voice bounces off the walls, a dull echo. Inside my head, a single word repeats until I want to cry.

Alonealonealonealonealone.

I pivot, slide the chain into place, then remember I have grief group soon. I hesitate before unlocking the door and then release the chain.

I'm safe.

4

CRYSTAL

⠏⠄ ⠡⠄ ⠕⠄

CRYSTAL GRABS BOTH COFFEES AND JOINS REBECCA IN THEIR USUAL BOOTH near the back. It's their routine to get coffee after grief group each week. They download, process, and talk about everything.

Bec arranges her cane and wallet on the table. Today, she is wearing all black: black skinny jeans, black sneakers, and a fitted black V-neck T-shirt. She looks chic and urban, not homely and suburban. She thanks Crystal for the coffee and takes a tentative sip. Jackson sleeps in a stroller beside her. "Cecil's really made progress," Bec comments.

"He has." Cecil's seven-year-old daughter just died from leukemia. "I can't even imagine."

Rebecca gazes out the window and sadly shakes her head. "Me either." Her auburn hair catches the light. She absentmindedly twirls a silky strand around her finger. "It's so hard."

Crystal doesn't have to ask what she means. She stirs sugar into her coffee and wipes the granules from her fingers. "It is. It makes it impossible to go through life the same way."

"It does." Rebecca spins her cup on the table. "Question."

"Shoot."

"Why didn't you tell me about Savi when we first met?"

Guilt taps on Crystal's shoulder, but she knocks it away. "I guess that's my coping mechanism. I feel like if I don't talk about the people in my life, then they're somehow safe."

"Denial?"

Crystal nods, then self-corrects to verbalize her response— something she is still getting used to doing, even after all these months of friendship. "Yes. Savi aside, I'm really good at skipping over things I don't like talking about."

"Protection," Rebecca affirms. She lifts her chin and tilts it toward Jackson's stroller. "I cope by protecting him. As long as he's safe, then I'm safe. But lately . . ."

"Lately what?" Crystal leans forward as if Rebecca is about to reveal a secret.

"Lately, I just feel like something is off. Like I'm being followed or someone's watching me."

"Do you think it's because your vision is getting worse?" Rebecca recently confided that her condition is worsening, that the small bits of peripheral vision she retains are starting to slip away too, and it's making her feel unsteady, scared.

Rebecca has explained it so vividly to her—the early days of banged-up shins and bruises, the way everything appears milky and smeared, never sharp. How losing your sight bit by bit is like losing limbs. Bec once described it to Savi like throwing a bunch of paint on a canvas, mixing the colors until they are all soupy and impossible to distinguish, then dunking the painting in a pool. Her world is like that. Blurry, dreamy, uncertain.

"Maybe . . . Jess thinks I'm just overly tired, but I don't know. I just have this weird feeling."

"When you live alone, it's easy to feel scared. Especially with a kid." Crystal thinks about Savi, about what she would do to protect her. "But you're doing great."

Bec smiles. "Remains to be seen."

"I've had a weird feeling too, lately, if I'm being honest."

Bec cocks her head. "How so?"

"Just some weird things happening around the house."

"Like what?"

She hasn't mentioned it, but some of her dead husband's belongings have gone missing: his vintage Rolex, a few Navy medals, a journal, a business ledger. "Some of Paul's things."

Bec takes a sip. "Savi?"

"I don't think so. She knows she can have anything of his, if she just asks."

"Then who? The nanny?" Bec jokes.

She hired Pam a few months ago, and though Crystal isn't a naturally trusting person, she is even less so with a bubbly millennial on her hands. But Pam is exceptional with Savi, which is what matters most. "I can't bring myself to ask her, but I think I might have to."

"And you're positive it's not Savi just wanting something of her dad's?"

Crystal shakes her head. "No, we had a long talk about it."

"Maybe you could get one of those nanny cams. Spy a bit."

"I should get a nanny cam," she laughs. "Though, if it is Pam, that means I'll have to find another nanny, and I'm way too tired for that." Plus, she can't imagine taking another person away from Savi.

"I get that." Bec glances toward the stroller and turns serious. "I have to say, the one silver lining in all of this? That Jackson won't remember losing Chris."

"That is a silver lining," Crystal says. Savi wasn't so lucky. "I was a terrible mother when Savi was a baby." Her cheeks flush from the admission. Inwardly, Crystal cringes thinking about Savi as an infant. She suffered from postpartum depression and didn't feel attached to Savi the way a mother should. Looking back, she still marvels that she got through it in one piece. It's why she never wants to hold her friends' babies or talk much about them. She's not good with babies. Once Savi could walk and talk though, she knew just what to do.

To her surprise, Rebecca laughs. "You mean, you didn't enjoy sleep deprivation, leaky boobs, and being hormonal? What's wrong with you?"

Crystal laughs too. That's why no one else gets her. They can't possibly understand how two women who've lost so much can sit here, making jokes. Everyone thinks it's their obligation to help her heal instead of just being her friend. But she still wants to smile. She still wants to laugh. And she can do those things with Bec. "Well, I literally can't admit that to anyone but you. I feel like it automatically shoves me into the bad mom group."

"Oh, please." Rebecca waves one thin wrist in the air. "Savi is well-behaved, kind, and an absolute musical prodigy. You did something right."

"Don't forget about her budding magician skills." Crystal rolls her eyes.

Rebecca laughs. "She'll outgrow that."

"Here's hoping," Crystal says. Savi's musical talent definitely didn't come from her or Paul. *Paul.* His name cracks through her chest. Savi loves playing cello more than she loves playing outside or trying to make friends. It's become her entire world, and she's so thankful Bec can give her lessons.

"I've got big plans for her," Bec says. "So get ready."

Crystal smiles and pays their check. "Cool if I come over in a bit to go over the kitchen designs?" Though Crystal hasn't been in Elmhurst a long time, she's already booked several interior design jobs, and Bec's is one of them.

"Of course." Bec fingers her watch and then downs the last of her coffee. "Want to say an hour or so? It will give me time to put him down for a nap."

"Sure."

Outside, they go their separate ways. Crystal refrains from asking Bec if she wants her to walk her home. Bec knows these streets better than she does, and Crystal's learned it's a source of pride to be able to navigate on her own.

Rather than go home, Crystal decides to take a walk. Savi is at the library with Pam, and all of her design plans are already in her car, which is parked a block over. She takes her time downtown, waving at moms and shop owners.

When she and Paul were looking to move from Chicago, he'd immediately set his sights on Elmhurst. Once she'd glimpsed prices, she'd told him no way, but he'd made it work. He always made it work. They'd only moved in a few weeks before he died. He'd never even gotten to enjoy the house.

Crystal mulls over what they discussed in group today—emotional wounds. They had to write them down, put them in a hat, and draw one to discuss. What was Crystal's emotional wound?

What wasn't?

She takes a right behind a row of buildings and steps toward a clearing. There's a bench and a few skateboarders and dog walkers. She sits and tips her face up to the sun. There's so little time to process these days. Even though it's summer and Savi hasn't started her new school, Crystal's been trying to get the house in order, set up enough jobs to cover their mortgage, foster her friendship with Bec, attend counseling with Dr. Gibbons, go to grief group, and deal with her demons . . . but it's all so much. At the end of every day, she's so exhausted, she can't even think straight. She has too much to do at home, but she never wants to be there. Home reminds her of Paul. Home reminds her of . . .

She slaps her thighs and stands, picking up the pace as she loops around the park. A few cyclists shout "on your left," and she hugs the corner of the path. Why did she pick Rebecca to be her friend? Most people would say grief, but she wonders if it's because Bec can't *really* see who she is.

Crystal can hide and Bec will accept her anyway. She pumps her fists and grinds her teeth, a terrible habit that's given her TMJ. She makes a few more loops and then checks the time. It's already been forty-five minutes. She hustles back to the car, blasts the air-conditioning, and drives to Rebecca's house, which is a lovely—if not quaint—midcentury two-story home. She parks, gathers her supplies, and makes mental additions to her design plans to bring in a landscaper and slap on a fresh coat of paint to the shutters. She'll throw it in for free.

On the way in, she still can't shake the conversation in group today. The emotional wound she pulled from the bunch was *betrayal*. She'd almost choked on the word: betrayal.

She knows a little something about that. Luckily, no one else does. She's determined to keep it that way.

5

CRYSTAL

∴ ∴ ∴ ∴

"KNOCK, KNOCK." CRYSTAL EASES OPEN THE DOOR. "BEC? IT'S ME."

"Come in." Bec appears around the corner in her bathrobe, hair in a messy bun. She's already changed out of her "real" clothes and replaced them with pajamas, even though it's midday. "More coffee?" She raises an oversized white mug that says I BLEED COFFEE.

"You know me so well." Crystal shuts the door and wipes her shoes on the mat. She absorbs the open foyer that spills into the rest of the house, making mental calculations of their design plans. The finished product forms in her mind—a beautiful, midcentury-modern masterpiece with muted colors and spectacular art—and she walks to the outdated kitchen.

"Did you go home?" Bec turns. Her olive skin radiates around tired, unfocused eyes. Her smile cracks her face wide open, and Crystal marvels at it—this superpower her friend will never again glimpse.

"I didn't, actually. Just went for a nice, long walk." She crosses to the coffeepot and pours herself a cup. "Jackson asleep?"

"Yes, ma'am." Bec slips onto a bar stool. "When he stops napping an hour after he's awake, I don't know what I'll do."

"Is he sleeping through the night already?" Crystal leans against the counter.

"Mostly."

"I don't think I've ever even heard him cry."

Bec laughs. "Oh, he cries. Trust me."

"I've never heard him." True, she hasn't been around Jackson a lot, but if he's with Rebecca, he's always asleep in his stroller or snug against her chest. She probably hasn't even seen his face more than one or two times.

Crystal sweeps her hair over one shoulder. This morning, Savi brushed her mother's hair and told her how much she looked like Elsa from *Frozen*. After she was done, Crystal had offered to brush her daughter's hair, which was always tangled and tossed in a scruffy ponytail. As usual, they argued about it until Savi threw the brush on the floor and stormed off.

Bec moves her head to the side until it gives an audible pop. She rolls her shoulders a few times, her muscles knotted from playing cello. Savi does the exact same thing after practicing. Bec gently pats her thighs, her pale pink pajama bottoms nearly swallowing her. "Okay, plans. What do we have?"

Crystal almost thinks about picking up their earlier conversation and diving a little deeper. There are so many things she wants to know: Is Bec used to sleeping on her own yet? Does she still find herself doing Chris's laundry or calling for him in the next room when she needs to ask a question? Does she pick up her phone to text him? Because Crystal does.

Instead of losing herself to that steady downhill battle of depressing questions and answers, she unrolls her designs across the kitchen counter. She takes her time explaining every detail and runs Bec's fingers over different samples she pulls from her bag. She lets her choose cabinet finishes, knobs and handles, and the appropriate type of quartz.

"I love it all." Bec taps blunt, unpainted nails on the blueprints. "Do you know how long I've wanted to change this kitchen?"

Crystal assesses the brown cabinets, the scuffed countertops, the gummy tile under her shoes. "I'm guessing a while?"

"Almost thirty years. I remember going to friends' houses as a child and wanting kitchens like theirs. This one is just . . ."

"It's the bones that matter. It's got good bones."

Bec nods, slips off the stool, and expertly crosses to the refrigerator. Her fingers travel over the bottles on cold shelves and bump over organized Tupperware until she finds a smooth white bottle. She lifts the creamer in an invisible question.

"No thanks, I'm good." Crystal rolls up the plans and rummages in her bag. "Do you mind if I just retake a few measurements?"

"Knock yourself out."

"I'll try and be quiet so I don't wake Jackson."

"Oh, he's fine. Noise machine."

Crystal walks through the dining room off the kitchen and into the formal living room that wraps to the base of the stairs. Her hand snakes along the worn banister. She makes another mental note to check for sales with her wood guy. Bec should have something sleek and modern.

At the top, she turns left toward the master bedroom. Is it strange to sleep in your mother's old room? She couldn't imagine. She tentatively steps inside. But it's probably easier than staying in her old marital room. Once Paul died, she'd made their master bedroom the guest room and transformed their office into the master. She couldn't lie there night after night and think of him. No. *Massive action.* That was what it took to change a life.

That's what she is going to do to help Bec change hers too. She is going to change the interior of this house so it will feel like Rebecca's home—not her mother's. Not her childhood home. A new, fresh start for a new life.

She rolls her eyes at the cheesy affirmations she's plucked from grief group and turns to the task at hand. In the bedroom, she measures the windows and adjusts her last calculations. She winds down the hallway and pauses outside of Jackson's room. His noise machine whirs. She remembers when Savi was so tiny. She used to watch her sleep and marvel at how she'd made something so delicate, and then she'd wait to feel what she was supposed to feel. She didn't even want to touch her or pick her up. She was afraid she'd break.

Paul was the one who'd done most of the heavy lifting during the first year of Savi's life. He never made her feel bad about it. Instead, he'd just loop an arm around her shoulder and say, "It will get better. You'll see." Every week, every month, every season. Until she'd woken up one day and that gaping hole in her chest had hardened into something else: motherhood. This was her child. It was her job to protect her. Through it all, Paul had never given up on her. Once she was safely on the other side, he'd kiss the nape of her neck and whisper, "See? I knew you'd make it."

She lightly touches her neck now, her fingers grazing that spot that used to drive her crazy. She hastily pulls her hand away. If she'd known all that was coming, she would have tried harder. She would have told him how much she appreciated him every single day.

Where had the time gone? Savi is already ten, her childhood punctured by the grief that comes from unexpectedly losing a parent. It devastates her now to realize she and Paul had been so busy working to make ends meet, that what they'd really missed was spending as much time together as a family as they could . . . before they weren't.

She bypasses Jackson's room and opens the door to the guest room. Dust dances in front of the naked window. It smells musty, like there might have been a water leak at one point. How did she miss that? She checks the ceiling for stains and spots one on the far corner, a rusted brown patch she'll have her contractor check out. She measures for drapes and then leans against the window.

Down below, a few moms distractedly follow kids on bikes. Two neighbors water perfectly emerald lawns, waving and chatting over the spray. A young girl in a watermelon bathing suit sprints through a sprinkler and giggles. She thinks of Savi at that age, how simple life seemed. She thought she'd gotten through the hard stuff—Savi's first year—and it would be relatively smooth sailing from there.

Wrong.

The Metra train rumbles past a few streets away. The setting down below is so idyllic. There's no room for grief in a town like this, and yet she's drowning in it. *But so is Bec,* she reminds herself. Even though she puts on a brave face for the world, Crystal knows what she must feel in her quietest moments. Those moments reserved for the widowed. And yet they still have to get up every day, get dressed, make money, and take care of their kids.

She steps away from the window and rolls her own shoulders in an attempt to relax. She longs for a time when she is no longer getting through something but will instead be on the other side of it.

On the way back down the hall, she stops at the landing. This time, she closes her eyes. Her world tilts. She reaches for the banister. *Vertigo.* She toes the edge of the stairs and second-guesses gravity as she lowers herself inch by inch. She descends until she misses a step and opens her eyes before she falls.

"Jesus," she whispers. She turns to look at the battered staircase. She's always had a thing about stairs: a fear of falling down them, a fear of dropping Savi as a child, a fear of being pushed. What must this be like for Bec to go up and down *blind* with a baby? Crystal rounds the corner. Bec is audibly perusing emails. Crystal clears her throat and stabs a finger behind her.

"Have you thought about the stairs?"

She stops what she's doing. "What about them?"

"I mean, for safety. With Jackson."

She shrugs. "I'm used to them." She closes her laptop. She scoots forward on the stool. "But it's crazy you just said that, because lately I've been having nightmares about those stairs." She shakes her head. A few strands escape her bun. Her shocking green eyes slide back and forth under the harsh kitchen lights.

Crystal waits for her to explain, but she doesn't. She sips her coffee, now cold, and tops it off. "I used to have the same fear about the stairs," she offers. "The spiral staircase we have now . . ." She shivers. "Let me come up with some creative ideas for you. Some safety features at least. It would make me feel better to know you have a better system in place."

"Sure." Bec smiles. "And I'd still love to come to your place sometime. I'm sure you're tired of coming over here."

No one has been to their house except Pam. "When I get the place set up, we'd love to have you over. It's just such a mess right now."

I'm such a mess right now.

From upstairs, Jackson begins to cry. Bec fingers her braille watch. "See? He does cry." She waits for him to quiet, and miraculously, he does. "Did you get what you need?"

Crystal nods. "I did. Thanks." She checks the time. "I'll get out of your hair." She walks toward the door and re-shoulders her purse. On her way out, she turns. "Are you still okay to give Savi a cello lesson tomorrow?"

Bec winks. "Highlight of my week."

"I'll be sure to tell her that. Have a good one. Call me if you need anything." Crystal pauses before leaving, the hairs on the back of her neck pricking to attention as she passes the stairs.

"Bye, Crystal."

She ignores the eerie feeling and waves. "Bye, Bec."

6

CRYSTAL

∴ · ∷

AT HOME, CRYSTAL SLIDES THE KEY INTO THE LOCK. THE HOUSE IS MUCH TOO large for her and Savi without Paul, but she wants Savi to grow up in a good neighborhood with good schools. As if the goodness could somehow erase her daughter's grief.

Their grief.

She calls for Savi and then sees a note from Pam taped to the fridge.

Gone to the park! XOXO

She opens the fridge and uncorks a bottle of white wine. Never too early, right? She pulls down a stemless glass from the open shelf. She completely gutted the kitchen before they moved in, and now it's minimal, clean, and organized. It looks out onto the pool and manicured scrap of lawn. Paul had argued the yard was too small, but she'd disagreed. Neither of them wanted to spend their Saturdays mowing or obsessing over the lawn. In hindsight, she's glad she stuck to her guns. She sips the crisp drink and walks back through the house and pauses outside the living room.

A row of moving boxes takes up the entire back corner. She lowers her wine to the hall table and approaches the stack. She trails a finger over the cursive Sharpie: *Paul study. Paul bedroom. Paul garage. Paul office.*

Though a few of Paul's personal items are scattered around the house (some of them now missing), most of his items are here. Six months have already passed since the accident. *Why haven't I unpacked them yet?* Though they are a constant reminder of loss, she can't make herself slice open the tops and dig into the remainders of his life. She doesn't want to hold each personal memento in her hand and decide how it will be handled. It's too much. So she pretends they don't exist.

She's so good at pretending.

Crystal walks past the spiral staircase and heads out back. She sits at the edge of their rectangular saltwater pool, next to her favorite azalea bush, removes her sandals, and dangles her feet into the cool water. She needs to work, but it's so rare she's alone in the house. She leans back and cocks her face to the sky for the second time today. A steady breeze lightens the summer heat.

Her phone buzzes at her hip: Pam.

"Hey, what's up?" she asks. "Everything okay?"

"Savi fell."

She sits up straighter. "What do you mean? Is she okay?"

"She fell off the monkey bars. She was trying to skip a rung, and her hand slipped."

Crystal immediately thinks of Savi's cello lessons—more specifically, her wrist and fingers. "Where are you guys?" Pam tells her which park. Crystal rushes inside, grabs her keys, and laces up her tennis shoes.

She drives the short distance to Butterfield Park, heart hammering. Crystal frantically searches the area, shielding her eyes from the sun. She charges toward the playground.

"Crystal!"

She pivots. Pam waves one frantic hand from the far park bench, her plump wrist outfitted in her brand-new Apple watch. She ignores Pam and skids to a stop near Savi's feet. Her daughter sniffles and cradles her elbow. Her face is pasty white, her brown ponytail unruly and matted. Her dress is lightly smeared with dirt.

"Hey, sweetie. Can I see?"

She extends her arm. Crystal braces for the worst. A fracture? The tip of a bone angling through purple skin? Instead, she finds her daughter's normal arm. No broken bones. No punctures. She exhales in a rush, bending, flexing, and straightening Savi's wrist—accessing the few nursing classes she'd taken in college before switching majors. She searches for bulges or swelling. "Can you move your fingers?"

Savi rotates her wrist in a circle, slowly at first, then makes a tight fist.

"I think you're fine. Let's go home and put some ice on it." She tries to smooth Savi's ponytail, but she jerks away.

"So sorry," Pam says. Lines crease her freckled forehead. "I was sitting here and—"

"It's fine," Crystal snaps. "I'm going to take her home."

"Do you want me to come?"

Crystal assesses the nanny, this sweet young woman with her expensive sunglasses perched on her mop of curly red hair. "In a bit. I just want to get her settled first."

"Okay. I'll text you."

Crystal nods. With one arm around Savi, they cross the park to her car. "You okay?"

"I'm fine." Her daughter's voice is more certain. "Can I still play?"

"I think so." Crystal knows she's not talking about playing outside. On the way home, Savi is quiet from the back seat, and Crystal doesn't push her to ask what happened. At home, Savi rushes ahead of her.

"Why don't you go take a shower and then we'll ice it?"

"I want to play first." The dried tears have made brown tracks down her face.

"You're filthy, Savi. Just go rinse off."

Savi rushes ahead of her. "No, I'm going to play!"

Crystal sighs. Lately, everything is an argument. If Crystal makes a suggestion, Savi negates it almost instantly. If Crystal has a personal problem though, Savi tries to help. She's talked to Dr. Gibbons about it, who's explained that often when kids lose a parent, they will do anything to make their other parent happy.

Except brush their hair. She laughs to herself and refills her wine, her nerves still crackling from the unexpected adrenaline rush.

From upstairs, the cello thunders through the cavernous house. Crystal takes advantage of the gap to unload the dishwasher and check client emails. She forgets all about Pam until an hour later, when the front door opens and shuts.

"Is she okay?" Pam sets a bag down by her feet.

Crystal nods upstairs, distracted by work. "Hasn't stopped playing since we got home."

Pam exhales. "Thank God. Mind if I just . . ." She points upstairs.

"Please."

She disappears from the kitchen, and Crystal sits back, removes her reading glasses, and rubs her strained eyes. She checks the time and texts Bec.

Coffee?

They just saw each other, but suddenly, she wants out of this house. Savi is fine. Pam is here.

What, do you have ESP? Bec texts back. **Literally meeting Beth and Jess now. Come join us!**

Bec texts which coffee shop and Crystal smiles and sends a happy reply. She's about to call up to Pam that she's leaving for a bit when Savi screams.

Crystal drops her phone and sprints upstairs. She pushes her daughter's door open and finds Pam on the floor, scooping at something. Strips of construction paper? Her eyes travel up to her daughter, whose hair is lopsided and hacked in an uneven bob.

"Savannah Isabelle Turner!" Crystal searches for the scissors. "What have you done?"

Savi looks at her feet. Pam's arms are full of her daughter's tangles and a pair of shears that she guiltily drops.

"Did you do this?" Crystal asks Pam. "Did you just cut off her hair?"

They are both eerily silent. "She asked me to," Pam says. "But then she freaked out when I started, so . . ."

"Out." Crystal points toward the door, and Pam rushes to collect the rest of the hair. Once Pam is in the bathroom across the hall, Crystal firmly shuts the door and crosses to the bed. She silences the urge to scream and instead motions for Savi to sit. "What happened?"

Savi stares at her lap and shrugs.

"No, Savi. I want to know now."

"You always tell me it's a rat's nest. And I didn't want to wash it."

"So you asked Pam to cut it off?"

She nods. "So we wouldn't argue anymore."

Crystal listens to her logic, but knows the more likely scenario is that Savi started cutting her own hair, only to have Pam wrestle the scissors away, which caused Savi to scream. There's no way in hell Pam would cut Savi's hair without her permission. "Savi." Her heart twists. She pulls her into a hug, and Savi begins to cry.

"I'm sorry." Savi pulls away. "Do I look like a boy?" The reality of her rash decision clicks in her ten-year-old brain. The uneven bob will have to be straightened. Crystal thinks of where she can take her. "Come on. We're going to the salon."

Savi wipes her nose. "Really?"

"Yep. Get your shoes on and meet me downstairs."

In the hall, Pam rushes toward her to explain, but Crystal cuts her off. "I'm taking her to the salon. We'll talk when I get back."

"I'm so sorry. I should have asked first."

She doesn't know why Pam is covering for Savi. That, coupled with the missing items and the fall at the park . . . it's a problem. She takes a cleansing breath and walks down the spiral staircase. Once she retrieves her phone, she texts Bec that she's not going to make it after all.

She washes her hands in the guest bathroom and catches her reflection in the mirror. Her eyes are weathered, but they are still her most prominent feature. Her ice-blond hair and nearly translucent eyes make her look like an alien sometimes. Savi is the total opposite: olive skin, dark hair, dark eyes. *Paul's eyes.*

She flips off the light. "Savi, let's go!" she calls. Crystal grabs her keys, then walks back outside, her glass of wine lost in the earlier commotion. She catches her wavy reflection at the edge of the pool. She stares, unblinking, then dips her toe in and distorts it.

Gone.

7

BEC

⠿⠿⠿

AFTER MEETING THE GIRLS, I PUT JACKSON DOWN FOR A NAP AND FILL THE bath with bubbles and overpriced salts. I drag the baby monitor into the bathroom, undress, and slip into the scalding steam.

I slide lower into the water and replay the conversation with the girls today. Jess seemed a bit cold when I told her I'd invited Crystal. Beth and Jess haven't spent much time with her; in their tiny worlds, they are most comfortable with women who have young children too. They say they can't relate to moms with older kids. While that has some validity, I want friends like Jess and Beth *and* friends like Crystal. I lower myself even farther into the water.

Tonight, Jess is throwing a Hollywood-themed party and inviting the entire neighborhood. Though I don't feel like going, I know it's important to socialize, to rally around my community and keep busy. She begrudgingly told me to invite Crystal too—not wanting to seem snooty—but I know she won't feel like going either. At least we'll have each other at the party.

I close my eyes again and think through the contents of my closet. The last party I attended was in Chicago for one of Chris's work functions. He knew how disorienting it was to acclimate in a large group of strangers. But he would firmly tuck my arm into his and lean in. "I promise not to let go." And then he wouldn't. A man of his word. I open my eyes and press my hand to my heart.

"I miss you so much." The words empty into the steamy room as tears drip into the bathtub. Yes, it's been a year, but I don't think missing him will ever lessen. Chris was so easy, so kind. He would have made a wonderful father. Correction: he *is* a wonderful father. He will always be Jackson's father, and I will make sure Jackson grows up knowing that.

Much to my mental protestations, familiar images float to the surface: Chris and Jackson playing baseball in the backyard. Chris walking a five-year-old Jackson to kindergarten or taking him to a Cubs game. Chris and Jackson surprising me on my birthday with a homemade, lopsided birthday cake. All things I would never be able to *see* but can feel as if they have already happened. Like it's an alternate universe that I can step into anytime I want.

A footstep. The water slaps the porcelain as I hurriedly sit up.

"Hello?" I strain to hear and half stand in the bath. Silence. I wonder if I imagined it. I'm ready to settle back into the cocoon of water when the wood groans again. But there's no wood in the bathroom. The realization smacks me in the face: it's not coming from my bedroom. It's coming from the baby monitor.

Run.

I manage to explode out of the tub without slipping, throw on my bathrobe, and hustle toward the nursery. I step toward the cracked door, except I ram right into it. I falter. I left Jackson's door cracked.

I *always* leave it cracked.

"Oh my God." I fumble with the doorknob. It slips in my damp palm. I twist it again and charge into the room. "Jackson?" I slap the empty space and hurry over to his crib. "Please be okay, please be okay." I gently lay my hand on his chest. The measured rise and fall of his breath is a comfort. I sweep my trembling fingers over his cheek, step back, and open his closet. I plunge my hands under his hanging onesies to make sure no one is hiding. I stab the corners of the empty room with a bare hanger, and after a few minutes of listening, I waver between carrying him downstairs without his carrier, or just locking his door with the spare key at the top of the door frame. If there's an intruder in this house, I don't want to announce that I have a baby. I close and lock the door, drop the key in my pocket, and hurry toward the stairs.

I take them too fast and hurtle down the final few steps. The unforgiving wood jams into my tailbone. Crystal's warning flickers and dies. I pull myself to standing and massage my lower back. The front door is secure. The door leading to the garage is too.

In the kitchen, I listen for lurking dangers. To be safe, I slide a serrated knife from its block and silently pad down the hallway toward the dining room. I extend the knife in front of me and enter and exit each room with more authority than I feel.

At the back door, I check the lock, then lurch backward and drop the knife. It clatters on the tile as I rotate in a circle. It's unlocked. I fall to my hands and knees and search for the blade. I made *sure* to lock it before I left to meet the girls. That horrible sense that someone is watching crawls over my skin like a rash. I grip the blade's handle in my hot palm. "Who's there?"

My phone rings. I jump and almost drop the knife again. I retrace my steps to the bedroom and answer.

"I just had a quick question about the party." Jess's perky voice slices through my fear.

"I think someone is in my house," I whisper.

"What?"

"I was in the bath, and I heard footsteps on the baby monitor. I went to Jackson's nursery and the door was closed, not open. I always leave it open. And the back door is unlocked, but I know I locked it before I left. I'm . . . I'm really scared."

"You need to get out of your house right now and call the police, Rebecca. This is the second time something like this has happened in less than a week. Can you activate your alarm from the inside? Like a panic button?"

"I'm not sure."

"Do you want me to call Officer Hot Pants?" She's attempting to keep her voice light, but I sense panic beneath her snarky tone.

"No, no. Don't call him. Just let me finish walking through the house with you on the phone." I hold the knife in one hand and the phone in the other. I open and shut every door, check all the windows, locks, and even reach under the beds. Everything is secure. Back upstairs, I unlock Jackson's door, check on him, relock the door, and collapse on my bed, drained from the unexpected adrenaline surge. "Holy shit. Am I losing it?"

"Maybe you just forgot to lock the door? I do that all the time."

"And then I accidentally left the front door open the other day?" I think about the moved playpen too. "I don't think so." I replay everything in my mind, but all the logistics crash into one another until they're a muddled mess in my brain.

"Are you okay? Seriously?"

"I don't know." I slow my breathing and swallow a few times.

"I still think you should call the police to be safe."

"No, I'm not going to drag them out on two false alarms. I'll be the girl who cried wolf." I roll to my stomach. "It's probably just the house. It makes all kinds of noises. Always has."

"Maybe it's haunted." She hesitates. "Is there anything I can do?"

"Are you putting away your own dishes?" I joke. "I thought you had a maid."

"Today's her day off."

I sit up, approach my dresser, and waver between putting on actual clothes or pajamas. I reach for my yoga pants and a T-shirt. "So, what can I bring tonight?"

"Just Jackson. Got the nanny on call." She rambles off a question about the Hollywood theme, but my mind is on the footsteps and unlocked door.

"Why don't you come over early and get ready here?" Jess finally asks.

"No, I'm fine. Sorry to freak you out. I'll see you tonight, okay?"

I hang up and absorb the deafening silence of my bedroom. I do another walk-through—this time without the knife—and once I'm satisfied that no one is in our house, I pass by the front door to lock it when the doorbell rings.

I freeze behind the door, before a vaguely familiar voice calls: "Mrs. Gray? It's Officer Toby."

"Dammit, Jessica." I unbolt the door and wear a tight-lipped smile when I open it.

"Ma'am? I got a distress call from your neighbor about another possible break-in? May I come in?"

I recognize his voice, so I know it's Toby. I open the door wider and gesture inside. "I can't believe she called you."

"She was worried. What happened?"

I take him through every detail.

"Mind if I do a walk-through? Is your son sleeping?"

"He is. Here." I hand him the key. "I locked the door when I thought there was an intruder. I just haven't unlocked it yet." I cringe even as I say it. Who locks an infant in his room? How will this look?

After what feels like an hour, Toby comes back through. "Ma'am, I would strongly suggest surveillance cameras on the perimeter since you live alone."

I motion toward my eyes, accustomed to people forgetting that I can't take the same precautions they do.

"Pardon me, ma'am. Is there a visually impaired equivalent?"

"Probably."

"Thought about getting a dog?"

I nod. Chris had begged me to get a guide dog, but I always refused. I didn't want one more thing to take care of, but now . . . maybe. "I have. There's a lot of training involved and with everything that's happened, I just haven't had the time."

Just one more thing to possibly lose, I think.

"Of course. I'll tell you what." He shifts and his handcuffs and baton bump and clash on his hip. "Why don't you let me park a patrol car outside the next few days? It sure would make us feel better to keep an eye on you."

My face reddens, and I correct my posture. "I appreciate that, but it's not necessary. I think I just need to get some sleep. I appreciate you coming by though." I cross expertly to the door and open it.

"That's my cue." He chuckles and steps onto the front porch. "Have a good day, Mrs. Gray."

"Thanks."

I shut the door and realize I still have my towel clenched in my fist. I toss the towel in the laundry and head upstairs to check on Jackson. Still sleeping like a champ. I prepare to go back downstairs, then make a left into the office. I open the closet, reach an arm in, and swat past old coats and bins to find what I'm hunting for: the sleek handle of my cello case. I gently tug it closer. The familiar heft immediately placates something deep inside me.

I close the door, hoping not to wake Jackson, and hoist the case onto the sofa. I run my fingers over the cognac exterior, unlatch the buckles, and stare down into the blurred bowl of my beloved instrument. A great heaving sigh escapes my chest. I pick it up with the same care I show Jackson. I sit on the worn sofa, which is much lower than a chair would be, and separate my knees to allow the cello space. The spike pivots on the rug. I rest it against my chest. The instrument barely clears my left ear.

My fingers hurry to their position—left hand on the strings, right hand clutching the bow. I slick wet hair behind my ears and knot it into a bun. I reposition my four fingers on the bow—pinky finger on the button, ring finger on the metal, middle finger on the hair, and the first finger resting in space. My thumb curls into the butt of the bow.

The first note shudders through my body. The defining sound thunders like a ship entering the dockyard, and I try to contain myself. I warm up, and the bow drags lower to the bridge, so that the notes are a different color entirely.

My elbow cuts the air in a precise angle. My wrist stabilizes the line between elbow and shoulder. I play the next note and the next. The familiar horn amplifies and injects the room with life. I chop the strings into separate notes.

I transition to scales, the notes as familiar to me as the shape of my son's face. I close my eyes and let the whole tones and semi-tones captivate and transport me somewhere else. My left hand springs to life. I stretch to reach different tones—I stretch to forget. The dormant muscles shake awake.

I channel a different memory. I'm in my finest black dress with ample slits that let the fabric slither up my thighs. I wear earrings, delicate diamond studs that twinkle under the blinding symphony lights. My lips are full and red, my eyes obsessed with the notes on the page.

I am not in my pajamas, my breasts heaving with milk, in a home office in Elmhurst, Illinois. I am on stages in New York, London, Paris, Chicago. I am a traveling cellist who is defined by what her hands can do—not what her eyes don't see.

I launch into Prokofiev's Sinfonia Concertante. My breath comes hard and fast as my body detaches from my brain and knows just what to do. I finish, gasping. I open my eyes and the hazy landscape returns, the images of my real life here, as a mother. A widow. A cello teacher.

After running through scales once more, I put the cello away and go to my computer to check emails and Facebook. I sift through the various messages and junk and pause on a Facebook request. Voice-Over says the name: Jake Donovan. My body responds before my brain. My fingers hungrily navigate to his page and scroll to a recent photo. I wait for the audible description. "May contain man, tattoos, motorcycle, tree." In spite of myself, I smile as an entire world comes crashing back: hotel rooms; long, romantic dinners; kisses that made my knees weak; the promise of forever; then the crushing grief of our sudden breakup when he got transferred. Over the years, I wondered if he'd ever get in touch, but Jake is chivalrous. If he knew I'd gotten married, then he would respectfully keep his distance. And he had.

Before I know what I'm doing, I audibly like the photo, then log off and do a quick cleanup of the house. I lose myself in a podcast. I feed Jackson and put him in his Pack 'n Play. When I open the fridge to grab a bottle of wine to bring to Jess's, something bites into the edge of my palm.

"Ow." I retract my hand. I carefully reach in and remove the serrated knife from earlier, my fingertips gliding over the handle. I turn in a slow circle, knife in hand. Did I mistakenly put it in the fridge? I mentally retrace my steps then slide the knife back into the butcher block. The blade zips into the slotted wood.

I walk around the counter to Jackson and lift him into my arms. I kiss his soft cheeks. "Mommy's just tired," I insist. "Right?" I bounce him until he laughs, my thoughts scattered, my pulse erratic. I gingerly put him down and continue with my pre-party dinner. I scoop noodles into a bowl and pour the meat sauce on top, but I can't mute the worry.

I crank up the podcast, slide my bowl to the edge of the bar, and get lost in someone else's world, but I can't answer the single question that hammers my mind:

What is happening to me?

8

BEC

∴ ∴

TWO HOURS LATER, I RING JESS'S DOORBELL. THE SYMPHONY OF BELLS trills through the house before someone opens the door.

"Holy hell." Rob whistles. "You look sensational."

"Thank you." On a whim, I'd gone into Kie&Kate Couture a couple of hours ago and let the store owner, Hailey, dress me. She picked a gorgeous hunter-green satin gown and even offered to do my makeup. I self-consciously pinch close the deep slit in the front.

"Want me to take Jackson?" Rob removes the diaper bag from my shoulder as I step into the foyer. The air-conditioning studs my skin.

"I'm good." I swing Jackson to my other hip. "Is the nanny upstairs?"

"I'll take you."

I follow Rob. My fingers skid over the cool wood of the banister. My high heels click on the hardwood floors. Upstairs, the raucous noise disappears as we turn right toward the nursery.

"Candace, this is Rebecca," Rob says. "And this big bundle is Jackson. Bec, we have another crib for him."

"Great."

"It's lovely to meet you, Rebecca," Candace says.

Her palm finds mine and she gives it a firm pump. I run through what's in Jackson's diaper bag and tell her about his favorite stuffed animal—Eliot the Mouse—if he wakes.

I sweep a hand over his head and then hook my arm through Rob's as we retreat toward the landing. Downstairs, the doorbell chimes, and I release Rob in the foyer. "Go be a host. I know where the kitchen is." I wink at him and count my steps. Voices rise and cluster, and I attempt to get my bearings.

"Larry and his wife look like the typical corporate drones," Jess narrates in a deep, steady voice behind me. Her lips almost tickle my right ear as she leans in. "His wife wears yellow—perfect for summer—and he's in a charcoal blazer. Just in case you want to freak them the fuck out."

"I'm still mad at you," I say.

"Me? Why?" She deposits a champagne flute into my fist.

"Toby?"

"Who?"

"Officer Hot Pants. You sent him to my house after I asked you not to."

"Oh." She takes a swig. The bubbles foam and sizzle. "That."

"I appreciate it, but I'm fine."

"If you say so."

I cock my head toward Larry and his wife. "So who are they?"

"Head of the Elmhurst neighborhood watch. It's a *thing* around here. Hey." She nudges me. "Maybe you can talk to them about your house scare. Come on."

I let out a dramatic sigh. I hate small talk, especially in crowds of people I don't know—and I definitely don't want to bring my recent string of mishaps into the conversation. I approach anyway, pass the glass to my left hand, and extend my right. Larry's rough, calloused palm enters mine, and then his wife's small, delicate one with a rock the size of an inflamed knuckle. I flash what I hope to be a dazzling, lipstick on tooth–free smile.

"My dear, this dress. You are an absolute vision," Caroline says. "I'd ask you to spin, but that seems inappropriate. Larry, isn't she a knockout?"

Larry clears his throat and resumes chatting with another neighbor, Bruce. Caroline engages me about the dress, how I'm enjoying Elmhurst, and my days as a cello player. "And you're a new mother too? Are you getting any sleep at all?"

If she only knew. My laugh says it all.

"I'll take that as a no." She squeezes my hand. "It gets so much better. I promise."

She doesn't know I'm a widow, or that I'm on my own, but I cling to her words like some sort of promise. *Things will get better. They have to.*

"What gets better?" Jess asks.

"Sleeping," I say. "Caroline assures me that one day I will sleep again."

Jess snorts. "That's not the worst of it. Tell them about what's been happening."

I shoot her a warning look.

"What's been happening?" Caroline asks.

"Nothing. I think my sleep deprivation is just getting the best of me."

"She thought someone broke into her house. Twice. Wait, no. First, you thought you were being followed to the park, then you heard footsteps on the baby monitor while you were in the bath, of all things. And doors have been unlocked when they should have been locked too, right? Oh, and then her son's playpen was moved. I think it's a ghost."

"My dear." Caroline grips my wrist. "Larry, are you hearing this? We can offer you some extra protection or set up a specific neighborhood watch if you need it?"

"We called the police and Officer Hot Pants came by," Jess explains.

"Officer Toby," I correct. I realize I don't even know his last name.

"Officer Toby is right over there." Caroline motions somewhere off in the distance. "Takes himself a little too seriously, if you ask me. He's Chief Holbrook's pet. On the fast track to being promoted."

"It's really okay," I say. "Probably just exhaustion coupled with an overactive imagination."

Jess butts in. "They offered her surveillance, which I think is a good idea."

"It's not necessary," I say.

"Hi." Beth wanders over and joins the conversation, and I'm thankful for the distraction. Beth introduces herself to Larry and Caroline, and then introduces Trevor, who begins to cry.

I swallow my champagne in one fizzy gulp. "Excuse me." I venture toward the backyard, eager to abandon the conversation. Someone cuts me off near the patio. "You're the cello player, right? Suzie, come here! I found her!" A gaggle of women close in until I am drowning in demands to give cello lessons to their brilliant offspring.

"Do you need saving?" A familiar voice hovers near my ear before I'm steered away. Crystal addresses the group. "Sorry, ladies. I'll bring her right back." She leads me to a quieter area. If I recall right, it's near the study.

"My savior," I joke.

Crystal laughs. "What did they want?"

"My soul, apparently." I giggle. The champagne has clearly gone to my head. "Or cello lessons. But mainly, my soul."

"Rebecca Gray." Crystal assesses me. "Are you drunk?"

I mash my thumb and finger together. "A smidge." I squint at her. "Tell me what you're wearing."

"I feel like an idiot. But I'm wearing a white maxi dress, very Marilyn

Monroe without the curves. It's been hanging in my closet for years. This house is insane," she adds.

"Isn't it?"

"What's insane?" Jess asks. She takes the empty champagne flute from my hand and replaces it with another one.

"Your house," Crystal and I say together.

Jess laughs. "Thanks. Crystal, can I get you anything?"

"I'm good, thanks."

Jess turns back to me. "Why did you leave?"

"Because I didn't want to be the topic of conversation."

"But you're a great topic of conversation. Come." She tugs me toward the pool. I turn to say something to Crystal, but we're already gone. Her fingers, though cold from pouring champagne, are still a guide. "Let's get you properly drunk."

"Too late," I say.

Neighbors mingle outside as she situates me at a patio table. "Then I'm going to get you some food. Stay."

My eyes are thick, my head heavy. How long has it been since I've had two glasses of champagne? For some reason, Jake enters my mind. The events we used to attend together, all the boring symphony dinners or cop galas he was always too pleased to attend. I recall him by my side, sharing a drink. One muscled arm slung around my shoulders or cradling the slope of my ass. The heat from his body. Our insane chemistry. The public bathrooms we'd often slip off to . . . The sudden craving for my old, exciting life—before I lost Chris, before I lost my vision—slices across my heart like a blade.

"Hey," Crystals says. A champagne flute plinks against the tabletop. "There you are."

"Here I am." I reach for my flute and accidentally knock it over. Crystal rights it. The bubbles sift across the table and I slide back a few inches to avoid the slick result.

"You okay?" Crystal mops up the mess with a napkin.

"I'm great." I lift my flute into the air as though it will inevitably refill itself and then gingerly set it back down. "Will you excuse me? Ladies' room." I stand too fast and grip the edge of the table.

"Bec, why don't you sit?"

"No, I'm fine." I take a few unsteady steps toward the swimming pool. My green dress trails behind in a silky train. The blue water runs parallel, pungent with chlorine.

I rotate a few steps and make out a blurred shape walking toward me with a bundle in her arms. Candace? My heart leaps. I begin walking at a fast clip. I just want to be with my baby. I want to take Jackson out of here, go home, and get some sleep.

"Oh!" Candace screams. A dark mass flies from her arms and splashes into the pool. It bobs on top of the water and begins to sink. Fear detonates like a bomb.

Jackson's name is on my lips. Candace screeches again and careens toward the pool's edge. It all happens in slow motion: she is walking toward me, baby in arms, then she is tripping, and the bundle goes flying. Before I know what I'm doing, I kick off my heels and dive into the water. The ominous, unexpected splash steals a collective gasp from the crowd. The water's icy fingers asphyxiate my lungs, but I claw toward the object. My satin gown gathers moisture and drags me down.

The water makes everything even darker, but I will drown before I come up without my child. I trace the trail of the fallen object in my mind and listen for chortled cries. I wait for someone to jump in after me, but no one comes. My lungs bite for air. I open and close my hand and plunge deeper into nothingness. Just when I think my lungs will explode, my fingers bump into something gritty. I yank and realize it's not Jackson. What is it? I loop a strap around my wrist and tug. My hands close in on something large and full of lumps: his diaper bag.

The humiliation propels me toward the surface, the bag heavy and last to rise. My lungs scream, and I break free just as I run out of breath.

"Rebecca!" Crystal is at the pool's edge. She reaches for my drenched arms. "Oh my God. Are you okay?" She helps me out of the pool. The crowd has grown impossibly silent. I turn toward Candace, who profusely apologizes. The wet silk clings to my body like a second skin.

"Oh my God, Rebecca. I'm so sorry," Candace says. "I dropped the diaper bag. You thought . . . I feel so awful. He woke up and wouldn't take the bottle, so I just thought I'd find you and see if there was anything else I could do . . ."

Jess approaches with a fluffy towel and wraps it around me. "Let's get you upstairs."

I ignore the dramatic murmurs from the neighbors. Candace follows behind, her apology on repeat.

"Just take him to the nursery and we'll be right there, okay? And here, take this." Jess hands Candace the sopping diaper bag. "Get the baby settled and see if you can salvage what's in here, please."

Jess ushers me to her bedroom, strips the dress from my body, and rummages in her closet. "Well, that was interesting."

I shake my head, bewildered. "It was honestly a mistake. I could have sworn he was drowning. I thought . . ." *Once again, I thought I sensed something that wasn't there.*

"You really need to get some rest, Bec."

"I know." My voice sounds defeated, even to my own ears. "How will I go back out there?"

"You're not." Jess presses some clothes into my hands. "You're going to change into these, feed Jackson, take a sleeping pill, and go to bed. No explanations. No apologies. You just need a good night's sleep. I'll take care of this."

"I don't have sleeping pills."

"I do. I'll be right back."

I slip into her T-shirt and oversized pajama bottoms and wring my dress out in her bathtub. I locate her shower rod, drape the dress over it, then pad down the hall to get my baby. I push open the door and hear a voice singing a nursery rhyme—not Candace. My skin bristles.

"Beth?" I push into the room. Jackson is cuddled in her arms, smashed next to Trevor.

"Sorry. I came up to see if you were okay, and I heard him crying," she whispers. "Are you alright?"

My body deflates. I consider her question and think about lying, about saying I'm okay, that it was all a mistake. Instead, I shake my head. "No." I find the rocking chair and sink into it, and Beth kneels beside me. Jackson coos in her arms. I stroke the top of his head and pull him into my lap.

"I can't believe that just happened."

"You did what you had to," Beth says. "Anyone would do the same."

Someone else hovers in the doorway. "Hey."

I shift in the chair. "Come in."

"I'll let you two talk," Beth says. "Let me know if you need anything, Bec." She grabs Jackson's bare foot and shakes it. The bells tinkle. "And you, little man. Be good for your mom." Beth eases out the door and makes room for Crystal. The sound of gathered, swirling fabric bunches in Crystal's fist as she crouches beside me.

"I may be overstepping my bounds here, but I have a therapy session tomorrow. Why don't you take it? I'll call Dr. Gibbons and tell her you can take my place. I think it would do you good." She pats my arm. "To talk to someone. I know it always helps when I go."

I swipe a hand to clear my tears. "I don't see you making a public fool out of yourself."

"Because I go to therapy," she jokes.

Immediately, I open my mouth to say no. But what would be the harm in talking to someone? In sharing all of these recent fears? Though the monthly grief group is helpful, it's not tailored to *my* grief. My mother just died, for God's sake. And I haven't even taken a couple of days to grieve her death properly. "Are you sure?"

She takes my hand. "Consider it done."

"Thank you." I clasp her palm in response and rock back and forth in the chair.

"There you are." Jess enters the nursery.

"I'll leave you to it." Crystal releases my hand. "Call me if you need anything."

"Thanks." I let out a sigh and adjust Jackson in my arms.

"Let's go to my room so we don't wake Baxter," Jess whispers.

I replay the events in my head and wonder who else saw my little stunt at the pool. What must they all think of me? I carry Jackson to Jess's bedroom and sit on the edge of her bed.

"Pills are in your bag. Do you need me to walk you home?"

"No, I'm good. I'm so sorry about this."

"Stop apologizing. Stay here as long as you like, okay? I'll just be downstairs."

I nod in her direction and free my still damp breast to feed Jackson, who paws the bulging flesh with tiny palms. What a night. No, what a *week*. The incidents stack up until they lead me to one clear conclusion: I need help.

"Knock knock." Officer Toby steps into the room and clears his throat, embarrassed. "Sorry, ma'am. Do you want me to come back?"

I grasp for the towel I left on the bed and drape it over my shoulder to shield Jackson. "It's fine. Come in." To lighten the mood, I smile. "Can't seem to get rid of me, huh?"

He laughs. "Apparently not."

"I'm fine."

"Ma'am, I don't mean to pry, but . . ."

"Rebecca."

"Rebecca. You can understand my concern here. Three incidents in a couple of days." He whistles. "Quite the week."

I motion to my face. "Well, these incidents wouldn't have happened if I could see." I focus on Jackson, but inside, worry sounds like a siren.

"I asked around a little about you." He hesitates. "You've been through quite the ordeal. I'm sure it's difficult. Grief is long, isn't that what they say?"

Thanks, Yoda. "Yes, it is," I say instead. "It's been a really tough year. Toughest year of my life."

"The chief knew your mom. Nice lady."

"She was. She grew up here." Emotion lodges in my throat.

He steps forward and places a card in my hand. "If you need anything, please call me, day or night. I mean it. My offer still stands about the patrol cars outside. Might help you feel safe."

"I appreciate it."

"Do you need an escort home?"

I shake my head. "I just live down the street. I'm fine."

"Have a good night, Rebecca." The door clicks shut. I don't tell him that having his card is pointless, though I can use Voice Dream, a software program that scans and reads the information, just like I do when I need to read food labels. I pocket the card, burp Jackson, and bring him to eye level. "Okay, little guy. Enough is enough. Mama needs to get her shit together before everyone thinks I've really lost it. Deal?" I gather his drenched diaper bag, my dress that's now been shoved in a dry-cleaning bag, and carefully descend the stairs.

At the bottom, wild laughter and music drift from the other rooms. I imagine all of my neighbors out there, dressed up and tipsy. Now they have something exciting to discuss. They will run home to tell friends or partners about the blind woman who thought her child was drowning. There will be a story attached to this night, attached to me. I pause with my hand on the doorknob and finally open it. The air is still thick and muggy, even though it's late.

I don't want to go back to my house alone, but I don't have a choice. I think of the sleeping pills in my bag. I could take them and actually get some sleep. It's been so long since I've slept through a whole night.

No matter how tired I am, I fidget mercilessly, my life playing out on a relentless loop. When I do sleep, it's punctured by nightmares.

Get some sleep. Jess's words beat out a sensible anthem in my head. My fingers itch to pop the pills, if only to experience temporary relief. But I don't have the luxury of another partner being there if the baby wakes. *No.* I'm not someone who takes pills.

Instead, I'm someone who faces her demons in the dark.

9

BEC

⠃⠑⠉

THE NEXT MORNING, I WAKE TO A THROBBING HEAD. MY FINGERS CHECK THE time. *Too early.* The party flits through my mind and I stuff a pillow over my face.

Did that really happen?

"It doesn't matter," I say out loud. I toss the pillow to the side and get up. At the closet, my fingers rush past hangers and then slip over Chris's lone tie I can't bring myself to donate. I pause and traverse the slick fabric. It slides through my fingers with ease. I'd given him this tie on our first Valentine's Day together, a memento from Marshall Field's. It was red silk, and I loved putting it around his neck, or sometimes letting him find me after a long day at work in the tie and nothing else. I smile from the memory. I push past the tie. It's the little things that get me the most these days: a whiff of his cologne on a passing stranger. A similar laugh. His last voice mail.

I'd listened to that message so often those first few months after he died that I had it memorized. I'd only just found out I was pregnant. I close my eyes and replay it in my head. His voice is as clear as if he's standing right next to me. "I know you're still sleeping because that little monster is sucking the life out of you, but just know this: I love you both and will see you tonight. And little monster, if you're listening, go easy on your mother, please. She's not as tough as she looks. Bye, Bec."

Bye, Bec.

His very last words, and I hadn't been able to tell him good-bye too. My fingers hesitate on a blouse and return to the tie. I tug it free from its hanger and wrap it around my neck, expertly tying a full Windsor knot. I close my eyes again, remembering. The morning Chris died, he'd kissed me good-bye. I'd not shaken myself fully awake, which is one of the greatest regrets of my life.

His breath smelled like coffee, his skin clean and freshly shaven for work. He'd called me on the way to the bus stop just a few minutes later. Even a year after his death, I try to make myself change the outcome. It's a dangerous game I play when I'm feeling particularly sorry for myself: if I had woken up when he kissed me, would it have made a difference? If I'd answered the phone when he called, would he have stepped just a few feet to the right and missed the car that hit him? What if he'd not taken the time to kiss me good-bye or leave that message? Would he have arrived at his stop in time to catch the previous bus?

These questions always threaten to rattle the normalcy I'm trying to tether into place. And I know they're not questions, not really—they're torture devices aimed to keep me paralyzed by grief.

Suddenly, the tie is too tight. I hurriedly unknot it and let it slip from my fingers and sink to the floor. A sob hurries up my throat but I suppress it. I miss him. God, how I miss him.

After the accident, I'd called my mother, and she'd never really left. She stepped in to fill those empty spaces, except she was small and manic, where Chris was large and calm. She'd helped me pack, sell the condo, box, donate, sort, and ditch all of Chris's belongings. She'd held my hand as I was flat on my back and pushed my way into motherhood. Even with her bad heart. Even when all the doctors told her that her time was limited.

When she insisted I move in, I didn't want to bring much with me beyond the tie, his watches, and a few items I'd pass on to Jackson someday. Now I wish I'd held on to more. Why had I been so eager to leave it all behind before I was really ready to say good-bye?

I drive my knees to my chest and press my cheek against their knobby tops. Is it normal to have this much loss in a single life? First Jake, then my vision, then my career, then my husband, then my condo, then my mother? Mom's wasn't a total shock. Her heart condition had put her in and out of the hospital so many times, I'd lost count. The doctors constantly warned her that she needed to change her diet and drinking habits, but she told them that if she had a limited amount of time on this great big earth, she was going to listen to herself, not them. She enjoyed every day, I'll give her that. And she'd gotten to meet Jackson.

Her death wasn't grisly like Chris's, the wreckage of my beautiful thirty-eight-year-old husband displayed on Milwaukee Avenue like roadkill. Only his tie was clean, blown neatly over one shoulder, as if he'd placed it there on purpose.

Dignity in death.

I take a deep, cleansing breath, hold it until I feel dizzy, and exhale completely. "Enough." I abandon those memories, place the tie carefully back in the closet, and ponder what to wear. When I was first losing my sight, I used ColorTest, a gadget that actually alerted me to what colors to wear. Now, I buy clothes in muted shades of gray, black, and white so everything matches.

I drop Jackson with Jess for my therapy session. I kiss him goodbye and hesitate. I've only left him with Jess one other time, but I tell myself he'll be fine, and continue toward the train. Today is like any other day, except I am going into the city. This is about my first therapy session with Dr. Gibbons. It's not about the life I used to live with Chris, or as a musician, or with Jake. My fingers tighten instinctively around my cane at the mere thought of Jake in the city—*our* city—alive and well.

This is your life now, I remind myself. *This is who you are. You are a mother.* There is no pretend reason to go into the city anymore. No husband. No condo. No rehearsal to get ready for. No past lovers to avoid. No agenda. I am going in for therapy. Period.

I concoct the markers in my mind: the thin sidewalks that out-line tidy yards; the sharp left turn at the end of our street onto Park Avenue. The white vinyl fence I drag my fingers over like water; the divot in the weed-choked sidewalk. I maneuver over the holes and watch for unassuming objects—cones, rocks, a feral cat—and loosen the grip on my cane. The parallel Metra tracks, surrounded by groomed pits of gravel, bisect the town into distinct halves. A train barrels to the right. To the left, Glos Memorial Park, another spot I often walk to, blossoms past a cluster of mammoth trees. The bridge ahead bows in a slight incline and is always decorated for each season. I pull these details from memory—from updated descriptions my friends feed me, from long walks I used to take with my mother, where she'd indulge me in the latest Elmhurst gossip.

Delicious scents of baked bread seep from Courageous Bakery. I sidestep rows of yellow plastic chairs fanned in front to facilitate morning loitering. Five steps, then Lou Malnati's. Ten steps, then Kimmer's Ice Cream. Twenty-five steps, then Brewpoint Coffee.

At the station, I fish out my card. The announcer's voice fades as our train thunders to a stop. The doors hiss open, and I use my cane to step on. I settle in a window seat, remembering how much I used to love trains, how endless rolling green hills would whip by, the lush, changing landscapes making my life seem so insignificant. One of my greatest pleasures used to be in watching the world from a win-dow and pondering my place in it. What I would do to glimpse even one more meadow. One more hill. One more tree.

I plug in my headphones, shuffle through emails on my phone, and open up Facebook again. I check the Chicago Lighthouse page, a fo-rum for the blind. I miss my vision-impaired city friends. There used to be a small group of us who met up at the Chicago Lighthouse once a week. After Chris died and I decided to move in with my mother, it was like suffering yet another loss.

Having other vision-impaired friends was a lifesaver in countless ways. We didn't talk about our disability—we just talked about life. But they understood my need to be in the suburbs.

When I left, a few of them warned me how hard it would be without vision-impaired friends, but I'd knocked away their concerns. I didn't want to admit to anyone how hard it was to prove myself to a world of people who took their vision for granted. Hell, I used to be one of them.

But they were right.

However, it was on my to-do list—to find a vision-impaired community in the suburbs—but life seems to keep getting in the way. I navigate away from the Chicago Lighthouse page, but before logging off, I'm notified that a direct message has come through from Jake. Did I will him to contact me just from thinking about him? I dismiss the ridiculous notion, but my heartbeat quickens as I hold my finger over it to listen.

Hey, Bec. I know it's been a long time, and I didn't know if you had the same cell. I heard about your mom and your husband . . . I'm so sorry. I'm back in Chicago and would love to see you and catch up. Here's my cell: 773.858.7663. I miss you.

I hike up the volume and replay the message. Jake is back in Chicago? Jake misses me? Eleven years have gone by, and he still misses me. I close the message and drop the phone in my lap. I obviously shouldn't respond.

I pick up the phone again. I have a book queued up on Audible but suddenly am thick with fatigue. I close my eyes and don't open them until the train rumbles into Ogilvie station.

My limbs rebel when I stand, joints stiff and bones like lead. My sleep-starved body demands more. We exit and the familiar city smells hit me, like hot cat piss and a thousand dirty gym bags. But then I think about what's outside: energy, nature, steel, possibility, memories . . . *him.*

I maneuver through the tight spaces and mumble my apologies to people in massive hurries. An elbow jabs my ribs. Sweat already dampens my clothes, and it's still morning. I huff up the stairs, erecting my cane and sweeping it over the concrete. Finally, I explode outside to a slight chill from the lake and a blast of buttery sunshine I'd give my left arm to see.

I head the few feet to Le Pain Quotidien and someone holds the door open for me. I fold my cane. "Thank you."

I step toward the front and inhale fresh croissants and strong, rich coffee.

"Table for one?"

I nod. I attempt to follow the hostess's footsteps, but my hip rams into a table's edge. I massage the sore spot, settle onto a bench, and order coffee and avocado toast. When I'd first gone blind, everything had been a land mine. Stepping foot into the city not only seemed like the scariest thing on earth—it was. I was terrified of potholes and traffic. Too many times, I'd miscalculated a turn and literally dropped off the curb into the street. I'd had so many horns blared at me, I thanked God drivers hadn't been using cell phones as often as they did now, or else I'd be dead.

Like Chris.

I sip my coffee, eat my toast, and shift gears to think about anything other than my dead husband or Jake's message. Despite my better judgment, I pull up Facebook and listen again. Before I can think too much about it, I issue a verbal response and attempt to keep my voice low so as not to disturb the other patrons.

Jake, my God, it's been too long. Thank you for the kind words. It's been a really tough year. I do have the same cell and would love to catch up. I'm actually in the city right now for a noon appointment. Let me know if you can grab coffee after?

I send it and immediately regret it. Have I opened a dangerous door? A few minutes later, his message comes through:

I'd love to meet. Want to do Big Shoulders Coffee?

He provides the address and I tell him I will text when I'm on my way. I swipe sweat from my hairline. I immediately rethink my outfit, my appearance, my choice to say yes.

I remember the last day I saw Jake. I'd walked him to the orange line so he could head to Midway Airport. I watched him board the train and knew I'd never love anyone else the same way I loved him. And despite how much I loved Chris, how stable Chris was, what a good husband . . . it was and had always been different than what I shared with Jake.

I sip the last cold remnants of coffee and wonder what would have happened if I'd moved to Florida. But I'd had my career to think about, my mother, my friends.

I tinker with my small ceramic pot, now empty, but my mind is sucked back to Jake.

"Another cup of coffee?"

"Yes, please."

The waitress clears the dishes and brings me a fresh cup. Jake and I met when he'd come to one of my performances with a group of friends. He was the only one dressed down, in jeans and a leather jacket. It's what drew me to him. He didn't give a shit about prestige or proper etiquette.

I'd come outside after the performance, the Chicago wind icy and sharp. He'd taken a drag off a cigarette and pushed away from the brick wall he'd been leaning against. I was instantly attracted to him—so much so, I didn't even mind the cigarette.

Jake told me he'd missed the entire performance because I was distracting him. I'd bought right into it and asked why. He'd exhaled smoke into the air, and I found myself wanting to lick his Adam's apple. I'd somehow pulled my eyes back toward his face and he'd said, "Because I realized I was staring at the woman I was going to marry. Which is a pretty important moment in a man's life, don't you think?"

"I don't know. I'm not a man." Though I was making a joke, I'd never had a man say anything remotely that serious the first time meeting me. We had an instantaneous connection—the kind that crackles through your entire body like a sparkler.

"Hungry?" His piercing eyes looked right through me, and I decided right there on that street that I was all in.

"Starved," I'd replied.

We'd made love that very night, even though he was a virtual stranger. But Jake never felt like a stranger. Not on the first night I met him and not now, eleven years later without a word between us.

I once again banish the thoughts, finish breakfast, and pay. Outside, I check the time: too early.

I hesitate, then call a Lyft, and verbally enter the destination. I make small talk with the driver, and five minutes later, we've arrived. "Thank you," I say. I pull on a sweater from my bag as the wind from the lake picks up. I steady my cane until it bumps into sand, then I fold it and almost run toward the water's edge. Random voices and barking dogs fill the periphery, but I easily claim my old familiar spot on the sand.

At my feet, the water crashes and lands, churning against the shore. I sit, wrap my arms around my legs, and listen. Why has it been so long since I've been back? I realize I've been avoiding it because it reminds me of Chris and the life we shared.

My fingers sift through the sand. I remember so many days of sitting here, thinking about the trajectory of my life. Feeling sorry for myself. Feeling proud of myself. All the hopes, fears, worries, and accomplishments. All the unknowns. I should have invited Chris to sit right next to me. I should have held his hand and never let go.

I shouldn't have stayed away so long.

Much too soon, a timer goes off, alerting me to my upcoming appointment. I stand, wipe the sand from my jeans, and call another Lyft. Back downtown, I gather my thoughts and clear my mind.

Entering and exiting new buildings is one of my least favorite activities, especially in the city. There are so many variables: ladders with workers. Construction sites. Throngs of people who won't move out of the way for a cane.

Chris was always impressed by how I handled myself on the street once I got the hang of things. My photographic memory was my sharpest tool in the toolbox. It allowed me to see without seeing . . . a godsend, really.

I press the button for the handicap door and wait for it to open. Someone ushers me to the front desk.

"Take the elevator to the eleventh floor. Here, I'll help you." I thank the front desk man for his kindness and exit on the appropriate floor. I memorize the path to Dr. Gibbons's office and check in. After only a few minutes, I'm called back. Her office smells like fresh pine.

"Come in, Rebecca. Make yourself comfortable."

Dr. Gibbons—Jan—has a soothing voice, one of those voices that makes you want to fall asleep. I wait for her to show me to the couch.

"Oh, right. Forgive me. Let me just . . ." She takes my arm and points me toward the couch. "Can I get you water, tea?"

I situate myself and set my purse by my feet. "No, thank you."

She sits across from me and takes a sip of something herself. "So you know Crystal."

I nod. "I do. We met in our grief group."

"I'm so glad you two have each other." She flips a few pages of a notebook. "I'm sure she told you this is solutions-based therapy, so I'd love to just give you the quick spiel about how it all works. And how it might be different from other types of therapy you may have tried."

"Well, I've tried exactly *no* therapy, so . . ."

She laughs. "Well then, this should be easy." She clears her throat.

"In these sessions, what we're here to do is to figure out how to cope with your loss and then come up with a plan of action. You're not going to think about what you're going to do. You're going to actually do it."

"Basically the opposite of regular therapy then," I joke.

Dr. Gibbons chuckles. "It's very effective, if that's what you mean." She clears her throat. "So tell me why you're here."

I think about my litany of recent concerns: last night's party, being followed, feeling afraid in my own home. Then, I think about the bigger issues: Chris's death, my mother's death, insomnia, the move, and even the stress of the impending renovation. "My friends don't think I'm grieving properly."

"And what does proper grief look like?"

"I'm not really sure." I pull a throw pillow onto my lap. "Some days, I think I'm okay and other days, I can barely get out of bed. Except I have to get out of bed. I have to keep moving. Stasis is death, right?"

"Sure, that's what they say."

"My friends also think I'm becoming paranoid." I remove the pillow and toss it aside.

"Paranoid about what?"

"Paranoid about being followed." I tell her about the walk to the park, the unlocked door, the moved Pack 'n Play, the footsteps on the monitor, that sense of someone watching me, and the party. "I literally feel like someone is toying with me."

"Why would someone be toying with you?"

"I don't know. Sometimes I even wake up in the middle of the night, and I swear I can make out the blurred shape of someone just standing there, watching me. I know there's no one there, but it's unnerving at times."

"I'm sure. This feeling of being followed . . . did you have it before your husband and mother died?"

"No." I think back to my insulated city life. "Only since I moved."

"Do you think anything else is contributing to this sense of paranoia?"

"Maybe." I chew on my bottom lip. "I'm not sleeping very well. I have a three-month-old son."

"How's that been going?"

"Parenting?" I smile. "Amazing. Jackson is easily the best thing that's ever happened to me. It's just . . ." I lean forward slightly. "Lately, I've been having these nightmares about him."

"What kind of nightmares?"

"I can't find him. He's not in his crib, but I can hear him crying. That sort of thing."

"Well, given your condition and what you've been through, Rebecca, I think that's a perfectly natural nightmare to have."

"They're just so real," I confess. "My friend gave me some sleeping pills. She says if I just take them and get caught up on sleep, everything will be different."

"Do you think sleep would help?"

"I do." I nod. "I'm desperate for it."

"Then your friend might have a point."

"I just hate the thought of Jackson needing me in the night and being too out of it to help him." I fiddle with my Bradley watch, fingering the raised markers and magnetized ball.

"That's a legitimate concern."

"There's something else." I sigh. "There's this guy—my ex—Jake." An involuntary warmth spreads through my body. "Before I lost my sight, we were very seriously involved." I swallow. "Long story short, he was a cop. He got transferred to another city, and I didn't want to move, so we broke up."

"And?"

I absorb her shape, the pieces of her coming through like an abstract painting. "Well, he's back in Chicago. He reached out to me on Facebook."

"Did you respond?"

"I did. And now I feel guilty."

"Why?" There's a rustling of fabric, and I imagine her crossing and uncrossing her legs.

"Because I just lost my husband. It's too soon to even think about anyone else, isn't it?"

"Do you think it's too soon?"

"I don't know." I work something out in my head, maybe for the first time. "I honestly think I fell for Chris because he was so unlike Jake—or anyone I'd dated, for that matter. I was scared of being alone. I needed stability, certainty, someone who could handle my diagnosis. Chris wasn't scared by what was happening to me."

"Do you think Jake would have been scared?"

I shake my head. "Probably not."

"How does that make you feel?"

"Sad that I didn't give him a chance or reach out when I was diagnosed." The words slip out before I can rein them in.

"Have you talked to him since you broke up?"

"No. Once he moves on, he moves on, but I don't know . . . I miss him. I want to know how he's doing, how his life has turned out. On the way here, he sent me a direct message and I answered him." I shift uncomfortably. "We're meeting for coffee right after this."

"How are you feeling about that?"

I hesitate. "Excited . . . like a part of me that's been buried is about to come alive again."

"Because you feel like Jake knows you?"

I nod. "For so many years, I've only been 'Rebecca-who's-losing-her-sight' and Chris was the guy who loved me anyway. But Jake knows a different version."

"The sighted version?"

I nod. "I know I was only twenty-six, but I feel like a part of me died when he left. As dramatic as that sounds, considering everything that's actually happened."

"That doesn't sound dramatic at all. That sounds honest." Dr.

Gibbons leans forward. "Here's what I think. Have the coffee. See how you feel."

"But isn't that dangerous? To project all that grief or loss on an ex-boyfriend?"

"Are you projecting? Or are you simply reconnecting with someone you once loved?"

Love. I fold my hands on my lap. "Then why does it feel like a betrayal?"

"Because you still love your husband. When a partner dies unexpectedly, it's confusing. There's no end to the relationship. You didn't *choose* for your marriage to be over, right? There's no finality there." Dr. Gibbons scribbles something on a pad, then leans forward again, so much that I can smell spearmint on her breath. "But it's not an either-or situation. Chris knows you loved him, but he's gone, Rebecca. As painful as that is to hear. You can honor his memory and still have future relationships. Maybe not now, but someday." She rests her pen on the pad. "The only person you harm in not moving on is yourself."

"That makes sense." The words echo in my ears: *he's gone.* Chris is gone. So many things have been taken from me, but here's something I can give to myself.

"What are you thinking?"

I don't rush to fill the silence. Finally, when my thoughts are gathered, I speak. "I'm thinking I really do want to see Jake."

"Then go see him. You owe it to yourself."

We quickly make another appointment, and as I rise from my chair and find the door, I turn. "Thank you. I needed this."

"You're welcome," she says. "Now go have some fun."

10

BEC

∴·.

I EXPLODE ONTO THE STREET WITH RENEWED PURPOSE. I EXPECTED TO TELL
Dr. Gibbons my plan to meet Jake and for her to give me a lecture
about the past. Instead, I somehow got the permission I didn't know
I needed.

I call a Lyft, voice text Jake, and anxiously wait. I ask the driver's
name as soon as I climb into the car. I slick on some lip gloss, blot my
forehead and nose, and take deep, yogic breaths. For the first time
in eleven years, I'm going to see my ex-boyfriend. Scratch that: not
ex-boyfriend.

The love of my life.

Like all past relationships, I'd filed away my time with Jake. When
I got married, I knew it wasn't fair to Chris to mentally obsess over
an ex-boyfriend, so I never brought him up. He was like a secret I
hoarded for myself, but the emotional baggage would stalk me in the
quieter moments, alone. Only then would he invade my heart like a
disease.

After a short ride, the Lyft driver grinds to a stop. I thank him, ask
which way to exit, and unfold my cane. Will Jake be inside or out?
We didn't get that far via text. My limbs pulse with adrenaline as I
gather my bearings on the sidewalk.

"Rebecca."

My name floats from Jake's lips, and my entire body freezes. I'd

forgotten how much I missed his voice. I turn in his direction, suddenly self-conscious about the cane and the dark glasses, but he
crushes me against him before I can even take a step. His smell in-
toxicates me. His battered leather jacket and familiar aftershave give
me a visceral reaction, and I let out a surprised cry. My lips smash
into his neck, and I hold him tighter than I've ever held anyone. City
sounds echo around us, but time threatens to stop.

We stay like that for minutes, embracing each other, remembering.

"I've missed you so fucking much," he whispers against my hair.

I finally extricate myself from his arms. "Me too."

"Haven't aged a day," he says.

"Neither have you," I joke.

"Still a smartass, I see."

"Would you have it any other way?"

"Never."

I take Jake's elbow and he guides us inside to a table by the window.
"Coffee, black?"

"Sure. Let me . . ." I fish in my purse for my wallet.

"Don't insult me, Bec."

His words send a flush of heat to my chest. A few minutes later, he
slides my coffee across the table and sits. God, how I want to drink
him in and admire every square inch: muscles, tattoos, scruff, piercing eyes that can level me with a cursory glance. I lean forward and
do something I never do. I ask to touch his face.

"Of course you can." He cocks forward in his chair and leans ten-
derly into my palms. My fingers tremble as they traverse his flesh. I
linger around the new web of laugh lines, the slight stubble on his
jaw, the inky lashes that tickle my palms and illuminate gorgeous
blue-gray eyes. I travel toward his hairline. His head is still buzzed.
I run my hands back toward his ears and neck before releasing him.

He sighs and drums his fingers on the table. "I feel like I need a
cigarette."

I laugh. "Still smoking?"

"In case of emergencies only."

"With your line of work, I'm assuming there are a lot of emergencies." I take a sip of coffee and burn my tongue. I blow on the brew and twist my paper cup. "Tell me everything."

"You first."

"No, really." I nod at him. "Yours is hopefully far less depressing than mine."

He tells me CPD had been asking him back for years, but he'd just recently moved home. He lingers on the word *home*. Does he mean me? Memories of our life together surge to the surface; memories I've kept buried for so many years.

"It's been a grind working homicide, but I love it. They keep me busy."

I attempt to focus on the current conversation. "Which station?"

"Riverside. Little bit of a haul, but not too bad."

I falter before asking the next question and intentionally keep my voice light. "Married? Kids?"

He's silent, and I realize he's probably nodding or shaking his head.

"Verbal, please."

"Right, sorry. No, I never got married." He pauses. "But you did."

The words are a betrayal. I'm thinking what he's thinking: how in the world could I have ever married someone else, even if that someone died? "I did."

"I'm . . . so sorry. About what happened." Something passes through his voice, but vanishes. "How long now?"

"A year. Hard to believe sometimes."

"And you're a mother?"

I smile. "I am. Jackson. He's three months old."

"So your husband—"

"Chris," I supply.

"Chris. He never got to meet him?"

"No, he didn't." I clear my throat to keep from crying. "Life." I shrug, such an insignificant movement to contain my sorrow. "And you heard about Mom?"

"I can't believe it." His voice lowers.

"She really loved you."

"Because I loved her daughter." The confession bullets into the room.

My heart literally skips a beat, and I realize I'm holding my breath. There are so many questions I want to ask. Is he happy? Has he thought about me over the years? Has he been in love since our breakup? Has he shot anyone? Has he been shot? I decide on the first question, but my phone interrupts. "Excuse me," I say. "I need to get this."

"Hey." Jess's voice is calm, but I immediately bristle.

"Is Jackson okay?"

"He's fine. Rob left an important client file here and needs me to run it to him. Candace is off today, and I can take Jackson, but I don't have an extra car seat."

"I'll be there as fast as I can." I hang up, exhale, and return to the table. "Sorry, I have to go."

Jake scratches his jaw. "Need a ride?"

I shake my head, because I'm afraid if I speak, my voice will betray me. "I'm just going to grab a Lyft."

"You sure?"

"Positive."

We walk outside. I call a Lyft. He steps closer.

"To be continued?"

I nod. "Definitely."

When he leans in and whispers—"It's been so good to see you, Bec"—I don't pull away.

He's gone before I can catch my breath.

11

CRYSTAL

⠿⠁ ⠿⠇⠁

"Is that my superstar?" Bec opens the door in jean shorts and a crop top, a yellow kimono trailing her thighs.

"I cut off all my hair!" Savi exclaims. "Mom was always telling me to brush it, so now it's short. Want to feel?" She bumps into the foyer with her cello case and accidentally rams into Bec.

"Savi." Crystal snaps at her daughter—both for the admission and banging into her.

"She's fine." Bec laughs. "Let me feel this amazing hair." Her fingers outstretch and playfully land on her face. She squeezes her nose. "Hmm, feels a little rough if you ask me."

Savi giggles. "Ms. Rebecca, that's my *nose*."

"What?" Bec tents her hands on her hips. "That can't be your nose. That's your hair. I'm sure of it."

"No!" Savi jumps up and down and then guides Rebecca's hand to her hair.

Bec smiles and ruffles the ends. "Oh *here's* your hair. Silly me." She inspects the cut. "My goodness, this is so glamorous! Maybe I should get a haircut too? Good job, Mom." Bec directs a smile her way.

Crystal doesn't tell her the truth, though not knowing exactly what happened has sparked something grim in her gut.

"Now I look like a more serious mugician *and* masician," she says.

"Wait! I mean a magician and a musician." Savi's scrambled words make her laugh so hard, a tiny toot blasts into the room. Rebecca erupts into uncontrollable laughter and hitches forward, holding her stomach until tears smear her cheeks.

"A mugician!" She laughs again and finally straightens. "Oh my God, Savi. You have no idea how bad I needed that today." The laughter keeps coming and going until they both compose themselves.

Once they're quiet, Crystal clears her throat. "Sav, why don't you head upstairs to get ready?" Crystal suggests. "I've got something for Bec."

"Okay." Savi takes off toward the staircase, hoisting her case overhead like a pro.

"Holy shit," Bec says, once Savi is out of earshot. "That kid is medicine."

At least someone finds her recent behavior amusing, Crystal thinks. She retrieves the gift at her feet. "I brought you something."

"You didn't have to do that. Coffee?"

"Sure." Crystal lugs the piece into the kitchen and carefully lays it on the counter while Bec pours her a cup. "How are you doing . . . since the party?"

"Well, I've not jumped into any pools or made a public fool of myself, if that's what you mean." Upstairs, Savi's bow begins to work. Bec smiles, closes her eyes, and tilts her chin up until her throat is exposed. Her hair cascades down her back in a brown river. "Listen to that. What a gift."

"She definitely has a natural talent."

"As a mugician and a masician," she jokes. "I hate the word *prodigy,* because it gets tossed around in the musical world, but she"—Bec stabs her finger upstairs—"is a true prodigy. You need to know that."

"It's a lot of pressure," Crystal suddenly blurts. "To know what to do with that much talent, I mean."

"Oh, I know. That's why you have me." She searches for her hand on the Formica, and Crystal slides it forward to help. "So what did you bring? More blueprints?"

"No." Crystal studies the piece of art. "I'm sorry I didn't wrap it. I figured I didn't have to . . . is that insensitive?"

"Oh, please. Waste of wrapping paper. May I?" Crystal guides her hands to touch the piece. "Is this . . . ?" Bec's fingers connect with the braille and tread expertly over the steel balls that dot an entire hunk of painted wood.

"I saw this in a shop when I was getting a few things for another client," Crystal explains excitedly, "and I remember thinking how remarkable it is because you never see braille in public. I thought it could be a great piece for the dining room."

"It's miraculous." Bec's hands hungrily read the words.

"It's called *The Travelers*," she explains. "It's made of painted board and copper. They're—"

"Quotes," Bec finishes. "'An eye for an eye only leads to more blindness. Margaret Atwood.'" She moves on to the next. "'It is a terrible thing to see and have no vision.'" She swallows, her face overcome with emotion. "'Helen Keller.'" Her fingers hum across the piece, faster and faster. "'Do not follow where the path may lead. Go instead where there is no path and leave a trail. Ralph Waldo Emerson.'" She looks up, eyes moist. "Crystal, this is one of the most thoughtful gifts I have ever received. I don't know how to thank you."

Crystal feels an expansion in her chest. "I'm so glad you like it."

She flattens both hands on the braille. "Where did you find it?"

"Lake Geneva," she says. "There's the cutest little gallery there. I couldn't resist."

"Which one?" Bec traces each quote again. "I love that place."

"Malloy's, I think?"

"Well, it's inspired. I'll treasure it."

"Ms. Rebecca, can we play now?" Savi's voice echoes from upstairs.

"Where are her manners today?" Crystal worries about Savi waking Jackson.

Bec pulls her into a hug. "She's fine." She moves back and studies Crystal. Even though she can't see her, it seems like she's able to look right through her. "Thank you. This art means so much to me." She turns to go upstairs. "Are you staying?"

"Do you mind? Thought I'd get some prep work done for the kitchen. And then I wanted to talk about your studio."

Bec claps. "I can't believe I'm going to have my own music studio. A dream come true." She squeezes Crystal's arm as she passes. "All thanks to you."

Crystal prepares everything for the contractors, listening to the toggling chords above. She unlocks the patio door off the kitchen and steps into the rectangular yard. Not too big, but perfect for a pre-fab studio dropped right on the perimeter. Her contractor has already sectioned off the yard. She retrieves her designs and makes sure everything's set.

On her way back inside, Crystal catches a glimpse of Savi and Rebecca upstairs. The window is open, and their music drifts down. Even from this distance, Crystal sees Savi's face set in concentration and how she's totally tuned in. Rebecca's brown hair hangs loose around her shoulders, the breeze lifting and pushing it across her face, while Savi's now sits perfectly under her ears. They look like mirror images of each other—the young and grown, the student and teacher.

The two of them are caught in some sort of musical trance, sharing a bond Crystal not only doesn't understand but can never have with Savi. Her heart fills with gratitude that her daughter can have that after so much has been stolen from her. She deserves it.

Crystal stays until the music stops and her phone vibrates in her pocket. Pam. She sighs. She and Pam had a long talk, and she stuck to her story that Savi had asked her to cut her hair. But judging from the absolute hack job, it was Savi who grabbed those scissors—not Pam. She doesn't know what bothers her more: that Savi did it or that Pam is lying for her.

Instead of answering, she silences the call. Inside, Crystal carries the art to the dining room. After some finagling and serious leveling, she hangs it and steps back to admire her work. "Perfection."

"Mom, did you hear? I learned a new concerto today! Did you hear?" Savi rounds the corner and notices the art.

She closes her tape measure. "I did hear. It was mesmerizing. Are you done already?" Crystal checks her watch.

"Ms. Rebecca says I can stay a bit longer. Please? Can I stay a little longer?" She bobs up and down again on her toes. A spray of freckles, highlighted from summer, dapples the bridge of her nose. Crystal pushes back her daughter's thick fringe of bangs and almost tugs on her now nonexistent ponytail. "Only if Ms. Rebecca really doesn't mind."

"Yay!" She rushes back upstairs. For the next half hour, Crystal loses herself in work and then heads upstairs to retrieve Savi. She pauses on the landing.

"Being an only child can be fun," Bec says.

Crystal knows from their many conversations that Bec is an only child. She's told Crystal about her cocoon of books, her forts made from tattered sheets, her mounds of stuffed animals, her treehouse built by a neighbor with pieces of salvaged wood.

But what has Crystal really shared with her?

"How?" Savi asks.

"Well, let's see. You never have to share," Rebecca explains. "You get to play with your friends and then send them home. You don't have to argue or get in fights. Your room is your safe space. You get more attention. It's quiet."

"That's true, I guess." Savi plays a few chords, and Crystal marvels at the smooth vibrations that erupt into the silent room. "Though it's never quiet in my house."

"Oh yeah?"

"Yeah." Savi sighs. "I just want everything to be how it was before."

"Before what?"

"Before my dad died."

"Oh, sweetie, I know. It's so hard."

"My mom was so much happier then."

"Well, losing a husband can be really hard."

"I keep trying to fix things to make her happy, but nothing works."

Bec is silent, and something cracks inside Crystal.

"You know what would make her so happy?"

"What?" Savi asks.

"For you to be happy."

"That doesn't work either."

"Hmm. Well, what do you think is making her the most unhappy?" Bec finally asks.

"That's easy."

Before Savi can answer, Crystal pokes her head into the room. "Savi, honey? Time to go." Savi is curled up next to Bec, as though she's going to hear a bedtime story. Bec stretches her legs and prepares to stand.

"But you said I could stay."

"And you have. Now, it's time to go." She keeps her voice neutral so as not to be combative.

"Fine." Savi grumbles and packs up her cello.

"See you soon?" Bec says.

"But I'm already here now."

Bec laughs. "That's true, but you don't want to get in trouble." She drops her voice to a mock whisper. Savi scowls at her mother and moves carefully down the stairs with her cello case.

"I'm going to be in for it during her teenage years, huh?"

Rebecca laughs. "Without a doubt."

They say good-bye. Outside, Crystal loads Savi's cello into the trunk, and her phone vibrates again. She hesitates, silences it once more, and gets in the car.

"Hungry?" she asks.

"Starved," Savi answers.

She reverses onto the street and drives downtown.

"Why did you make me leave?" Savi says. "We don't even have anything to do now. I could have played longer."

"Well, because you'd already taken up a lot of Ms. Rebecca's time, and I'm just trying to be sensitive since she has Jackson. And other lessons."

Savi crosses her arms and pouts. "Jackson isn't even like a real baby. He *never* cries."

She shrugs. "Some babies are better than others." As she says it, she backtracks. "I don't mean better. Just less fussy." On their drive, she points out a few new sights to Savi—the middle school and high school she'll go to someday. While she talks, a thought worms into her mind, one she can't seem to shake.

You can't outrun the truth.

12

BEC

AFTER THEY LEAVE, I TRY TO DISTRACT MYSELF WITH HOUSE CHORES AND emails. I have no more lessons for the day. I think about texting Jake, then decide against it. I'm not ready to open the door to the past. Not yet . . . maybe not ever.

Even though it was so good to see him. Even though I could have sat there all day and listened to him talk. I text Jess and Beth and we plan to meet at Wilder. As I lock up and leave the house, I worry that my life is already becoming like Groundhog Day—park, lessons, home, repeat.

I bump over the cement, take the appropriate turns, and think about my last solo walk to Wilder. Already, I feel silly—like maybe I did imagine being followed. On the way, Jake pops into my mind again. The way he leaned in, how his lips whispered in my ear. The way he felt in my arms.

Home.

That word sends a stab of guilt through my heart. Is it a betrayal to Chris's memory to even talk to Jake? To reconnect so easily with someone I was once so passionate about? Though I've thought of Jake over the years, I haven't allowed myself to go down that rabbit hole of memory besides a cursory thought or two. I wasn't available. He'd moved on. I was always busy. He wasn't in Chicago. I lost myself in the cocoon of domesticity while I could, and though life with Chris was always good, it was never wild or passionate. It was warm, comfortable, safe. And after talking to Dr. Gibbons, I'm realizing I have the freedom to now compose my life the way I choose. It doesn't all have to be a product of circumstance.

Once at the park, I pick up my pace to nab the same park bench.

"Bec! Over here!"

I slow to a chorus of hellos, some from moms I know and some from moms I don't.

"Lucky you. You get the last spot," Jess says.

I tug the stroller toward her voice and she helps me wedge Jackson's stroller in with the others behind the bench. My hands bump over the other strollers. There are five. Mine fits in the second space from the right. I grab Jackson's ankle and give the bells a gentle shake. I picture his sweet smile and my heart swells. I sit on the bench.

"Hey, girl."

I smile at Beth. "Hey."

"I just want to say how badass that was at Jess's party the other day. Seriously."

"Hardly." My face warms as I adjust the top on my travel coffee mug.

"What was badass?" asks Ramona, a mom I've met a few times. A few others chime in, and I want to disappear into the turf. They call me brave. They say they would have done the same thing. They tell me I'm their hero.

I wonder if Chris were alive, would he have the same reaction, or would he have thought I'd finally gone off the deep end? I wait for the subject to change. Eventually, one of the women starts talking about Mother's Day Out programs. I listen as they volley suggestions back and forth. I check on Jackson a few times and then move to throw away a wet wipe.

When I do, a batch of silver stars explodes across my vision's smeared black veil. My ears ring. I open my mouth to speak, but nothing comes out. I attempt to sit right back down, but my body won't cooperate. My legs hyperextend, then bend, and I crumple foot-by-foot. A collective gasp escapes from the group. I am up one moment and down the next. My cheek cracks against a rock that's wedged into the rubbery earth.

Everything goes inky. I allow myself to be pulled under. Visions clash in my mind: Chris, Jake, my mother, Jackson, the red tie being carried away by the wind. I surrender to it, to how right it feels to be still and give in. Children's voices screech and whine—a reminder of reality. Bells trill in the distance.

My baby.

I open my eyes, roll to my back, and blink into the bright sky. My sunglasses must have flown off. I reach for them, but my fingers close on air. I finger the spongy knot on my cheek and sit up. The playground turf burns under my legs.

"Give her room," Jess says.

"Did she just faint?"

"Someone call nine-one-one."

Park mothers fret over what to do, their voices thin and muffled, like I'm trapped underwater. I sit up, my palms hot against the scorched rubber. Finally, I locate my sunglasses and clutch them to my chest. The sharp tang of blood fills my nostrils. I touch my face again. This time, my fingers come away slick.

I blink until the fizz-pop of stars fades, but the ringing in my ears sticks. I yawn, wiggle my jaw, try to get them to pop.

Jess's sturdy hand hoists me onto the bench. I reach for my tri-fold cane and my diaper bag. Both are right where I left them.

Jess taps my shoulder with a bottle of water, which sweats onto my bare thigh. "Drink."

The plastic seal cracks apart, and I drain the bottle until it crinkles in my fist. I attempt to recount what just happened: I stood and then fainted.

"That's a nasty cut," Jess says. She almost sounds impressed. "We should wash that out."

"I will." I make no attempt to move or hunt for the first-aid kit in my diaper bag.

After questions and murmured concerns—the second time in a few days—the other mothers disband. The air thins, and I try to clear my head.

What just happened?

Their footsteps squish over the earth, their trilling voices wrangling unwilling kids and tossing used-up snack baggies and juice boxes into trash cans. My head jerks behind me toward the stroller, something primal kicking in. When I fainted, I could have sworn I heard the tinkling of Jackson's anklet: bells.

"He's fine," Jess insists. "Are you?"

Am I fine? What a loaded question. I almost laugh. Instead, I nod. "Let me just sit for a second."

"Take your time." Jess's hand connects with my back and rubs repetitive, soothing circles.

"Ms. Rebecca!" A voice calls behind me and I turn my head too sharply. My world tilts again.

"Ms. Rebecca!" Savi is breathless and smells like bubble gum. "I just saw you fall! Are you okay?"

I nod. "Where's your mom?"

"Right here." Crystal rushes over. "We were just walking to the music store. Are you okay?"

I nod. "I think so."

"Bec, you need to lie down. Or go to the doctor. She fell pretty hard," Jess says to Crystal.

"Can she come rest at our house for a second, Mom? Please?" Savi hops up and down, and all the commotion makes my head pound.

"That's okay, Savi. I can walk home." To prove my point, I stand, but my legs buckle. My heart beats in a strange, labored way.

"Come." Crystal drapes a firm arm around me and guides me toward her house. Jess grabs my diaper bag, cane, and stroller. Jess chats with Savi in an attempt to lighten the mood and warp the truth: *I need help.*

As we navigate the short path through a thicket of trees to Savi's house, worry spreads through my chest—a physical ache that darts straight to my back.

"This is the backyard," Savi explains. Metal groans as she runs ahead to open the latch. "It gets stuck sometimes. And there's a pool to your left."

I attempt to orient myself and struggle for breath.

Crystal's hand clasps my waist, this time tighter. "Bec?"

Jackson.

She says my name, but it's my son I'm thinking of. The son I've been having nightmares about: how he's missing or crying, but I can't find him. The son I work so hard to prove I can take care of, even though I'm a fucking blind widow with zero help. The son who has no living grandparents left. The son I pull along now, like an afterthought.

"I'm fine. I just need to sit."

"Here." Crystal hurries ahead to open another door. "We're coming in through the back, but let's go to the living room."

Savi grabs my hand, which is sticky and warm. "Careful."

I turn to grab Jackson's stroller, but Jess shoos me away. "I've got it. Just go rest."

Once Jackson's stroller is secure and out of the way, Crystal and Savi help me to the living room, which—from what Savi tells me—is enormous, with two couches, a baby grand piano, and an entire wall full of books.

Crystal lowers me to the couch. "Savi, go get her some water, please. And go tell Pam we're here." Savi runs off. "Now, this"—she whips a blanket into the air before it cascades gently over my body—"is my favorite blanket of all time. My mom sewed it for me when I was a little girl."

As the blanket hovers and lands, I'm instantly reminded of Saturday mornings when my parents used to change the sheets and I would sit cross-legged on the mattress as they lifted fresh, warm sheets over my head. The memory shocks me with longing.

Savi returns with the water.

"From what this little one says, your house is beautiful." I take a greedy sip and hand it to Crystal.

"It needs some work, but it's a pretty special house. Now, let me see that cut."

I reluctantly show her my cheek.

"Hey, Sav? Will you go upstairs and grab the first-aid kit? It's under the guest bathroom sink. Pam can help."

"On it!"

When she's out of earshot, I whisper: "How's it going with Pam?"

She grunts. "Conversation for another day."

Jess walks into the room. "How ya doing, kid?"

"Never better."

Jess's cell shrieks through the room, her personalized ring tone of Ginuwine's "Pony" lightening the mood. "Shit, Bec. I need to take this. Charity stuff."

"I'm fine. Go."

"Jackson is sound asleep. This will be quick." She slips out the front door.

"I'm just going to go grab a couple of washcloths and see where Savi is with that kit." Crystal pats my knee. "Sit tight."

I sink back against the cushions, close my eyes, and make promises to the universe. I promise to get more sleep, to eat a more balanced diet, to go see Dr. Gibbons a few times a week if I need to, to figure out a way to afford help. To forget about Jake. To do whatever I need to in order to focus *solely* on my son. On cue, Jackson fusses from his stroller.

I sit up, but he instantly quiets.

"Okay, back." Crystal sits next to me. "Turn."

"You don't have to do this," I say.

"Don't be silly." She dabs my face with something cold. "I thought about studying to be a nurse."

"Why didn't you?"

"Oh, you know . . ." She dabs my cheek. "Life." In just a few minutes, my wound is clean and bandaged. "Voilà."

"Thanks."

"Of course." She balls up the materials and snaps the lid shut.

"I think I'm good."

"You're welcome to stay."

"That's okay. I appreciate it though."

"Let me drive you at least," she insists.

I place my arm on Crystal's hand. "I'm fine. The fresh air will do me good."

"Okay. Call me later?"

"Promise."

"Let me tell Savi you're leaving." When she's out of the room, I stand. I pray the room doesn't spin, and luckily, it doesn't. I extend my cane and find the front door. I grapple with the fancy knob.

"I'm ready to go," I say to Jess.

Jess finishes her call and whistles. "Look at you. You look like you went a few rounds with Mike Tyson."

"Who won?" I joke.

"Remains to be seen." She slips past me into the hall, Baxter snug in his carrier on her chest. "Let me grab the stroller." I follow her into the foyer.

"Are you guys going already? No fair." Savi's disappointment is clear. "I hope you feel better, Ms. Rebecca."

"I will. Thanks for your help."

Outside, Jess insists on walking me home.

"Gotta hand it to old Ice Queen," Jess comments. "That house is money. Kid seems a little lonely though."

"The curse of being an only child." I know how often Crystal works just to make ends meet, but I'm confident Savi will make fast friends once school starts. At my house, I refold my cane on the porch steps, fish the key from my bag, and stick it in the lock. Jess helps roll the stroller to the door.

"Still got those pills I gave you?"

I nod. "Yes."

"You're going to take two and get some rest. That's an order. Give him a bottle if you need to. Actually, do you want me to take him for the afternoon?"

I shake my head. "No, that's okay. You're right. I just need to rest."

Jess rummages in my diaper bag and opens my hand. The two pills land. She fishes another water bottle from her diaper bag. "Here. Take them now."

"I can't take medication. What if Jackson needs me?"

"That's why I'm here."

The fatigue washes through me. I hesitate, then toss them back. I need sleep. My head throbs and I finger the cut. "Is it okay to go to sleep after I just fell?"

"Oh shit." She hesitates. "I didn't even think about that."

"Technically I hit my cheek, not my head."

Jess's voice sounds strangled. "Is there a difference?"

"I'm sure it's fine."

"Rebecca."

"Seriously, I'm fine." I unlock the door. My knees involuntarily buckle.

"Okay, that's it. You, upstairs now. I'll feed Jackson and put him down."

I think about protesting, but I'm too tired. I point weakly toward the kitchen. "There are a few bottles of milk in the fridge."

"Got it." She adjusts Baxter and wheels the stroller into the kitchen. "Nighty night!"

"Night," I mumble. The word is thick on my tongue, all of my senses turning gluey. My eyes are gritty. My hand grips the banister as I drag myself up the stairs. I practically crawl to my room and climb under the crisp, cool sheets.

I'm asleep before my head hits the pillow.

13

BEC

⠃⠑⠉

I WAKE TO PRESSURE ON MY SHOULDER. JESS'S VOICE GENTLY URGES ME awake. I come to, peel my eyelids apart, and find my voice thick with sleep. "What time is it?" I claw my way to sitting. My head pounds and my mouth feels like it's been stuffed with sand.

"Drink this. It's seven."

"Seven?"

"You needed the rest."

"I slept all afternoon?" My cheek throbs, and I lightly touch it. "How's Jackson?"

Jess shifts. "A bit fussy."

Worry pricks through my drugged haze. "Where is he?"

"Already fed him and put him down."

I collapse back against the pillow and massage my temples. "Thank you for staying." My world spins, and I suck down the glass of water Jess thrusts into my palm.

"What are friends for, right?" She takes the empty glass.

"Not this." I pile my hair in a ponytail and heave myself out of bed. I stand for a moment and let a fresh wave of dizziness pass before escorting her to the bedroom door. "Sorry to take up your entire day babysitting. Both of us," I add, embarrassed. "Has Baxter been okay?"

"He's fine. And seriously, it's no big deal. I got some much-needed

Netflix binging out of the way." She adjusts Baxter and kisses me on the cheek. "Let me know if you need anything."

"I will." I pat the top of Baxter's head and wait until the front door has closed to walk down the hall toward the nursery. I press my ear against the door, but all is silent. I resist the urge to sneak Jackson a kiss, but I don't want to wake him, especially if he's been fussy. Downstairs, I ransack the fridge. I make myself a quick dinner and check my phone before browsing Netflix myself. I listen to my options, wanting something mindless and easy to consume.

I rest my head against the couch cushion. Today was a major wake-up call. How can I be expected to take care of an infant if I can't even take care of myself? I continue the plan I concocted earlier: sleep, therapy, healthy food, a possible nanny, and absolutely no thoughts of ex-boyfriends.

Suddenly, a cry from the nursery cracks the complex web of my inner dialogue. My body charges to attention. My breath stalls. Silence follows, but that cry sears into my memory. I press mute on the television and wait.

Again, the cry smacks me between the ears. I wade through the murky darkness. The wood groans under my socks as I climb the stairs.

At the end of the hall, I nudge open the nursery door. The blueprint pulses in my head: dresser, crib, rocking chair, changing table. The baby cries again, a raspy, dry thing. It is cawing, achy, awful.

I reach into the crib and pick him up, but he cries harder. I sit in the rocking chair and run my fingers over his face—cupping the shape of his chin, his chapped lips, his smooth ears, his hair. I search for the notch in his collarbone where he got stuck during labor and find only a smooth blade of bone. He cries so hard, he starts gagging, and I shush him until I am breathless.

An unfamiliar scent invades my nostrils, and I stop rocking.

There's a baby in this room: a baby who feels like Jackson, who looks like Jackson, who could probably pass for Jackson if someone wasn't paying close enough attention.

But I am.

I yank a terrorized breath, but it does little to calm my nerves. My mind sparks, terrified. There's only one thing I know: this baby is not Jackson.

This child is not my son.

14

CRYSTAL

⠠⠉⠗⠽⠎⠞⠁⠇

ON THE WAY HOME FROM A CLIENT'S HOUSE, CRYSTAL TEXTS BEC TO CHECK in. She's been worried about her all day and didn't even have time to process what happened before she was back at work with a client.

As the streets drift by one after the next, she waves at neighbors. Though she's been living here for months, she's not really stopped to appreciate her new life or the friendly people in it. Between the grief group, therapy, motherhood, and work, she has little time for relationships. Her grip on the wheel softens. Except for Bec. She's beyond thankful for their friendship and how good she is with Savi.

She puts on her blinker and waits to turn left. So many people have told her she should get back out there and date. But there's no such thing as "casual" dating when you have a kid. Rebecca is the only one who really gets that. They've both joked about joining Bumble, and one drunken night, Crystal made a fake account and described all the guys so Rebecca could tell her which way to swipe. She couldn't remember the last time she'd laughed so hard. Neither of them were ready for that next step, and Crystal couldn't imagine a time when she would be. Not because Paul was dead . . . but just because she is too exhausted to put herself back out there in any *real* way. It is all just too much work.

At home, she kills the engine and eyes the exterior of her house, sometimes still floored that this palatial home is all hers. Though this house wasn't her style when they bought it, she's managed to marry its traditional bones with her more modern aesthetic. Inside, the house is quiet. She checks her phone, but Pam didn't say anything about going out tonight.

She drops her bags and glances at the living room out of the corner of her eye. "What in the world?" The room has been cleared. No boxes.

Something in her gut tumbles and drops. Did Pam do this? She would never move Paul's boxes without permission. But what about her recent concerns with some of Paul's missing belongings? She walks through the kitchen and opens the garage door. Nothing there either.

Suddenly, in the absence of Paul's boxes, her fingers itch to open each one and hold her husband's possessions. His old blazers. His tennis rackets and trophies from high school. His military medals. His notebooks full of goofy drawings. Keeping them tethers her to who she was then—a clueless wife, a distracted mother—but the sudden thought of not being able to say good-bye robs the breath from her lungs. She needs to see the faded Sharpie. She needs to open those boxes *now*.

She circles around toward the kitchen and pulls open the blackout shades from the glass doors that lead to the pool. "Oh my God!" Reams of smoke drift horizontally across the backyard. They curl over the privacy fence and evaporate into a stream of gray. Crystal fumbles with the glass doors and steps outside to assess the fire.

Where is Savi? And where the hell is Pam? Though they've built fires before, they've always been contained to the fire pit. As she nears the scene, she realizes the source of the fire. It's not piles of leaves or sticks that are burning: it's her husband's boxes. *All of them.* She watches the last letters of his name disintegrate and burn, just like her memories.

Crystal stands, dumbfounded, as the fire roars. She ransacks her brain for signs of pyromania. Sure, Savi likes playing with hot candle wax or using the gas stove to cook eggs, but this? It's too much. Not to mention, her daughter could never drag these boxes out here by herself.

That leaves just one person: Pam.

The hostile black smoke curls higher. First things first. She moves to the side of the house and cranks the hose. She extinguishes the fire, which takes more effort than she would have thought. She gazes at the mangled mess of her husband's life, now melted and too hot to touch.

Good-bye, Paul. The sorrow strangles her heart. Once the fire is out, she looks over her shoulder, expecting to see Savi or Pam waiting to confess, but no one is there. She cleans up the mess as best as she can, wearing gloves and scooping all of the charred remnants into the trash. She washes her hands and climbs the stairs, checks and rechecks each room.

Where are they? She sends Pam a frantic text and waits.

In Savi's room, she searches for other culprits that could have started this: a crumpled piece of music, perhaps. A shredded bow. Her cello, angrily—but carefully—placed facedown on the carpet. A failed magic trick. But all looks intact. Unable to help herself, Crystal snoops through her daughter's belongings, searching for the missing watch and medal. Nothing. Finally, Crystal crosses her arms and leans in the doorway. Her phone dings.

Almost home. Went for pizza!

Crystal stares at the message. How in the world could they have gone for pizza *and* started a fire? Nothing adds up. She walks through the house, searching for other clues, but there are none. In the living room, she stares at the empty void again, knowing that while the boxes needed to be cleared, now she'll never really have closure.

Just one more thing snatched away without permission.

A few minutes later, Pam rushes through the door, plastic bags knotted in her fist. "Hey. Let me just put this stuff down." She motions to the bags then disappears down the hall.

"Hi, Mom," Savi says as she removes her shoes. "Bye, Mom."

"Stop right there, young lady," she barks. Savi freezes in her tracks. Crystal waits to say more.

When Pam returns, she ruffles Savi's hair affectionately. "What's up?"

"What's *up*? What's up is this." Crystal motions to the living room. "Who did this?"

Savi and Pam look at each other. "The boxes?" Pam asks. "Um, I did. I cleared them for you. I know you haven't had time, so . . ."

"So you dragged them outside and set fire to them?"

"What?" Pam's perfectly shaped eyebrows arc into twin half-moons. "Of course not."

Crystal turns to Savi, hands on her hips. "Did you do this? Did you set fire to Dad's stuff?"

Savi looks just as shocked as Pam. "Why would I do that?"

"Answer the question!" Crystal screams. She yanks Savi to the back, opens the doors, and points to the charred earth. "Did you do this? Did you? Because I just came home to a blazing fire that could have burned our entire house down!" She grips Savi's elbow again and shakes. "Why would you do this?" Crystal's body vibrates with rage.

Pam rushes forward and steps between them. "I can explain. Savi, go inside."

Savi massages her sore elbow and obliges. Once she's out of earshot, Pam takes a breath. "I'm sorry, Crystal. I cleared the boxes earlier, and I was just going to put them in the garage for you. But then Savi got really upset and said she just wanted them to disappear. She found the matches and lit one. I extinguished it, but then she must have lit one again right before we left."

Crystal takes a step closer and Pam actually flinches. "So you're telling me that you dragged my husband's boxes *outside* for no particular reason, and then Savi set a fire without you knowing?" She cocks her head and studies this young girl's face. "Why are you lying for her?"

Pam stays silent.

"Have you also been swiping Paul's stuff? His watch and medals?"

She looks at her toes. "I'm so sorry, I—"

"You're fired. Pack your belongings and get out of my house." Crystal motions for her to leave.

Pam turns and tears spill from her eyes. "Can I say good-bye at least?"

"No. Go." Crystal knows the damage that will come from yanking Pam away without explanation, but this is too much. Whether she did it by herself or she's covering up for Savi, both are unacceptable.

"Crystal, please . . ."

"Leave!"

Inside, Pam gathers her purse and turns to say something. Crystal stabs her finger toward the front hall and then, when she doesn't move, stalks past her, opens the front door, and waits until she's on the other side.

"If I could just explain—"

Crystal slams the door and stands in the foyer, stunned. *What in the world just happened?* All of the recent mishaps pile onto each other until she can't make sense of anything. Finally, she climbs the stairs to Savi's room. She doesn't even knock. Savi sits cross-legged on the bed, reading a book.

"Why did you do that?" she asks.

"Do what?" Savi asks.

She looks so innocent, Crystal is almost fooled. "Drag all those boxes outside. Start that fire. Ruin all of your father's possessions. Tell me the truth."

She closes the book. "I didn't. I promise."

Crystal waits for more. When she doesn't say anything, Crystal has to remind herself that she's the adult here.

"Where's Pam?"

"Fired."

Savi's eyes grow wide. "Fired?" She jumps off the bed. "Is she already gone?"

"Yes, she is." Crystal almost hesitates but forges ahead. "You won't see her again."

Savi turns in the door. "But you can't fire her! She's my only friend!" Savi's voice rises as she rushes down the stairs. "Pam! Pam!"

Crystal sighs and follows her. "She's gone, Savi."

Savi whips around in the hallway, and her eyes are fierce and dark. "You can't fire Pam. I need her. Please."

"You should have thought about that before you set fire to your father's things." Crystal folds her arms.

Savi nervously opens and closes her fingers. "Fine. I did it, okay? I was tired of looking at the boxes, and you were never going to do it, so I did."

"Savi."

"I did! I swear. Now can you hire Pam back, please?" She runs to the front door. "Pam!" She screams into the open night and Crystal gently pulls her inside.

"Savi, stop. Stop it right now."

Savi bucks, and Crystal wraps both arms around her little body while Savi fights against her. "You can't fire her! You can't! I need her." Her sobs escalate then muffle against Crystal's middle. "Please. I need her."

"Just calm down. Take some deep breaths."

Savi sucks big breaths and Crystal waits until she stops crying. She guides her to the couch. "Talk to me."

Savi looks up. "You're never happy."

Crystal forces herself not to react. "What does that mean?"

"I know those boxes make you sad. I wanted them to go away too."

"So you dragged them out there all by yourself? How is that even possible?"

She shrugs. "Pam was napping. She was tired. It didn't take long."

"You cannot set fires, young lady. Do you understand me? You could have died."

She swipes her nose. "I know."

"Do you, Savi?" She scratches her forehead. "Are you not getting enough attention?"

"I just want Pam back. Please hire her back. It wasn't her fault."

She sighs. "It *is* her fault if these things keep happening and she's the one taking the blame."

"She's only doing that so I won't get in trouble. She's my friend."

Crystal stands. "No, she's not your friend. She's your nanny. She's an adult, Savi. There's a difference." Crystal senses another tantrum coming, and she quickly backtracks. "We'll talk about it tomorrow, okay? Go brush your teeth and get ready for bed."

"But—"

"Savi, *go*."

She nods.

"And there are going to be some serious consequences for what you've done," she calls simply before her daughter disappears upstairs. She doesn't want to negate her feelings or make her feel worse by forcing false remorse or an apology, but her actions have pushed things into new territory. She locates her phone and sends Dr. Gibbons a frantic text to see if she can squeeze both of them in for an appointment tomorrow.

She thinks about pouring herself a giant glass of wine but wants to wait until Savi is in bed. While Savi brushes her teeth, she grabs the laundry and puts it away. Upstairs, she hears Savi humming while she changes into pajamas. Down the hall, she enters the last room on the left.

She puts away laundry in the extra dresser and stares out the window that overlooks the pool. She attempts to grasp at her thoughts, but they are slippery. Her child is lying. Her child chopped off all her hair. Her child set fire to her father's possessions.

Her child could have died.

She knows this is a massive cry for attention. When is the last time they'd spent real quality time together? Crystal pulls up her calendar on her phone to check her schedule and realizes just how difficult that will be over the coming weeks. She has so many jobs to do, Bec's kitchen renovation being one of them. She can't disappoint her clients. But Savi comes first. Her daughter always comes first.

On her way back down the hall, she peeks into Savi's room, but she's already asleep. She pulls her comforter over her shoulders and kisses her forehead. Despite all that's happened, Savi is still the best thing in her world.

Nothing lasts.

The truth is harsh and quick and sends a physical stab of pain through her heart. Tears quickly splash onto her lap at the thought of losing Savi—of something tragic happening to her too. While all parents have that fear, it used to be a hypothetical worry. Now, after what she's been through, that worry has roots.

"I love you," she whispers. "No matter what." She tiptoes back downstairs. In the kitchen, she pours herself a glass of wine. Outside, the heat is still stifling. The ugly charred earth stares back at her, and the stench of burned plastic and cardboard lingers in the air. She'll have to re-sod that area or do something creative to cover it up. The dollar signs collect in her mind.

She doesn't want to think about that now. On a whim, she sets her glass down on the table, undresses to her bra and panties, and dives into the tepid water. She stays under until she's straining for breath. She thinks of Rebecca—how terrifying it must have been to dive into a pool because she feared her child was drowning. And then she thinks of Savi—how unhappy Crystal must really appear for her own daughter to set fire to her father's belongings just so she can move on.

My dear girl.

Crystal claws to the surface and once again bursts into tears. She swims to the edge of the pool and clings to the hard cement. Parenthood is so hard, swinging constantly between joy and terror . . . all of this pressure as the only living parent. While she worries about something happening to Savi, what if something happens to her? Who would take care of Savi? She cries harder, not knowing if she's crying for Savi, herself, her poor, dead ex-husband, or the uncertain future.

Paul.

She squeezes her eyes shut. All of Paul's boxes, gone. His memory, gone. They've been sitting in her living room for months and now they literally went up in flames.

Agitated, Crystal pushes off the edge of the pool and plummets to the bottom. She doesn't want to think about Paul. She has to move on.

After a minute, Crystal resurfaces and begins swimming laps. Her breath is choppy and unpracticed, but she doesn't care. She keeps swimming—five laps, then ten, then fifteen. Her shoulders burn, her lungs scream. Her thighs quiver from the exertion.

At twenty laps, she hoists herself up on the pool's edge, her heart rate dangerously high. Her chest shudders, but she wants to capture this feeling of being so very alive and wet.

"Mama?"

She turns, suddenly embarrassed to be caught in her bra and underwear. Savi hasn't called her Mama in years. "Yeah, baby?"

"What are you doing?" Savi rubs her swollen eyes. Apparently, she's not the only one who's been crying.

"Swimming." She laughs. She's still breathless and is afraid she might burst into tears again. "I was hot."

Savi looks at the water and back at her mother, gauging if she's still in trouble or if the storm has temporarily passed. "Can I?"

Crystal thinks about saying no, that they need to talk, but honestly, she doesn't feel like talking. And isn't this why they have the privacy fence? "Sure."

Savi excitedly strips down to just her flower underwear. "Can I jump in?"

"Wait." Crystal stands, legs aching, and trots over to join her at the deep end. She grabs her daughter's small hand. "On the count of three."

Savi's face lights up in a way she hasn't seen in months. In that single look is the little girl whose spirit could never be diminished. Not by death. Not by crushing disappointment. Not by anything.

"One," Crystal counts.

"Two," Savi says.

"Three!" They jump into the pool together, their hands clasped.

They plummet down and then break to the surface, spewing, treading, and giggling.

"Can we do it again?" she asks. She slices her arms in a sloppy freestyle toward the edge. She's already pulling her light body to the surface and waiting for her mother. A real smile overrides the incident from earlier.

She joins her daughter and doesn't let go of her hand.

15

BEC

⠃⠑⠉

THIS IS NOT MY CHILD.

The truth sizzles inside my skull. I lean over the crib again. My
fingers reach for him, but the baby shrieks and his entire body arches
backward, as if he's been poked in the spine. I travel his small body
again, double-checking for differences. His skin flushes under my
touch. He wails and bucks against me like an agitated bull. I edge a
few steps away. The recent fears . . . they weren't paranoia.

They were warnings.

The baby quiets, whimpers, then screams. Milk leaks inside my nursing bra. I hurry back downstairs to the kitchen, absentmindedly fingering the irritated knot on my cheek. I drink a full glass of water, take a
clotted breath, and calm my racing mind. Maybe I'm mistaken. Maybe
something in those sleeping pills—paired with wine—is making me
hallucinate. But every rational thought is clipped by the hard truth that
this baby is not Jackson. I *know* it.

I slowly return to the nursery. My fingers skim the wall to help me
stay upright. His unfamiliar cries nip my nerves. I rack my brain
for other babies' cries—the cries of my friends' children, or random
strangers at the park—but I don't know this cry. I don't know *him.*
I slide the baby into my arms, his diaper heavy and hot, and a gut-
wrenching realization overrides this screaming infant: *Where the hell
is my son?*

I almost capsize. Could someone have purposefully swapped my child? Or is this some sort of mistake, *my* mistake? I could have grabbed the wrong stroller. I calculate that possibility, but know it's not likely. I'm obsessive about identifying my own objects, especially his stroller. I also made sure of its precise location in relation to the others.

I retrace my steps back to the moments after I fell. Did I check Jackson thoroughly once I was awake? Hold him? Feed him?

No, I didn't.

I shush the baby and bounce him, but he only cries harder. What do I do? My brain feels cloudy as I attempt to grasp next steps. Jess! She was with him the entire afternoon. She would know the difference between my baby and someone else's.

I pat the baby's back and wonder if he's hungry. I walk to the kitchen and find a bottle of milk in the fridge. I thrust the plastic nipple into his mouth, and he sucks it all down in one greedy gulp.

While he's placated, I place him back in the crib and call Jess. Her phone goes straight to voice mail. I try again. I then send a frantic text to call me immediately and pace the living room. I need to think, but my mind is jumbled, all of the pieces not fitting together just right. The panic threatens to render me useless.

The phone fractures my turmoil. I pick it up and issue a breathless hello.

"Everything okay?" Jess asks. In the background, a door shuts.

"This baby isn't Jackson," I hiss.

"What?" Her voice springs to full attention. "What do you mean?" She starts to speak again and then stops. "I'm confused."

"When Jackson started crying tonight, he sounded different. It's not him."

"Whoa, back up. What? How in the world would that baby not be Jackson? I was with him all day."

"Exactly." My voice catches, fills with dread, and releases enough for me to speak. "You're positive it was him?"

She's quiet for a moment. "Yes."

"At the park, you don't think I could have grabbed the wrong stroller?"

"Of course you didn't. I was with you."

"But you said he was fussy."

"So? Babies are fussy."

"Not like this. Not Jackson."

Jess is silent. I know it's not fair to impose the same frantic energy on her because she's not his mother. No matter how well she knows Jackson, he isn't hers. If I was sighted, would I know the difference between Baxter and another baby? The answer comes in an instant: of course I would.

When Jess speaks again, her voice has changed. "Bec, I think you need to go to the doctor. You fell and hit your head. I gave you those pills, which I realize I shouldn't have, but I think you really need to get checked out. I think you need—"

"Jess, listen to me! This child is not mine." My throat burns from the outburst, which causes the baby to scream louder.

"Rebecca, listen to what you're saying."

"I know what I'm saying. I know it sounds . . ." I don't dare say the word *crazy*. I'm not crazy.

"It's been a stressful couple of days." Her voice lowers. "Maybe when you hit your head, you got slightly concussed, or I don't know—maybe something with the pills. Just drink some water, try to flush them out of your system, and then reassess, okay? Do you need me to come over?"

I don't know what to say. She's wrong, but I can't drive home the point. I can't *make* her believe me. "No, I've bothered you enough. I'll call you back."

I throw the phone in disgust and listen to the baby wail.

A stranger.

I walk toward where I threw the phone and drop to retrieve it. After fruitless swatting, I find it by the leg of the dining room table.

All I need is validation, for someone to see what I already know. I think about calling Crystal, but I don't want her to drag Savi over here too.

I climb the stairs back to the nursery. The baby quiets slightly. I lift him into my arms and gently rock him. My heart shatters at the thought of my sweet baby boy in someone else's arms, being held or—God forbid—harmed. *Stop it.* This has to be some ridiculous mistake. Jackson is fine. He has to be fine. There can't be a God cruel enough to take away my baby too.

No.

I question what to do next. Should I call 911 or Social Services? Officer Toby? I know where the local precinct is—I memorized the location when we first moved. I could be there in less than ten minutes. Yes, that's what I'll do. The police will help.

Once the baby is fed another small bottle, I change him, strap him to my chest in the carrier, and make sure the door is locked and the alarm set.

The night is quiet, save for a few vocal crickets and barking dogs. Suddenly, I wish I had taken Chris up on his offer to get me a guide dog. The dog would be able to tell this child isn't Jackson, just by smell alone.

As I walk, a protective hand slides to the back of this little boy's head and behind his right ear, where I find a patch of smooth skin. No eczema. Yet another difference. I log all of the ways this baby is not mine. He must appear similar enough to Jackson if Jess didn't notice. Though, to be fair, how often does she really spend time alone with Jackson? She doesn't hold him or study him the way I do. I'm sure, at this age, that most babies really do look the same.

At the precinct, I hesitate and then tug open the door. Musty air hangs, stagnant. I acclimate, trying to detect if I'm in a big or small space, if there are many people or few. I clock disgruntled voices. Phones. No echoes. I've been in enough stations with Jake to know there's usually a front desk or partition. I take a few steps forward. Eventually, someone asks: "May I help you, ma'am?"

A muffled voice behind a partition. Ballistic glass, maybe? I track the voice: female. I fold my cane and stop before I accidentally ram the little boy into the chest-height counter. I gather the words but then hesitate. My visually impaired friends' cautionary run-ins with the police give me pause. Sarah got mugged, but the police didn't help because she couldn't identify the perpetrator. Gary's house was broken into while he was inside, but again, the cops could do nothing. Lucy got into a man's car who claimed to be an Uber driver, but he wasn't. She was assaulted and left on the side of the road, but they never caught the guy because she couldn't give any details—not even the make or model of the car or license plate.

"Ma'am?"

I open my mouth to explain myself, but I already know the way my confession will sound to a stranger. I rock the baby against my chest. What if they take him and then I am left with nothing? No leads to get Jackson back. No . . . *leverage*?

"I'm sorry. I think I'm in the wrong place." I backtrack with my cane, push through the door, and press my back against the cool brick wall outside the station. If I tell them my suspicions, they'll either give my story the benefit of the doubt because I'm blind—issuing me a report and ID number—or they'll think I'm 10-96.

10-96. Crazy. Nuts. A loose cannon. The common cop lingo resurfaces, and I push off the wall. Of course. Jake. Why didn't I think to call him first? The baby coughs, and I pat his back and hunt for fever with my cool hand. Where is Jackson?

At the thought of my son out there somewhere, a cry hurries up my throat and spills into the night. The baby stiffens, but I can't stop. I take off down the sidewalk, wanting to scream his name and not stop until he's found.

I hurry home, unlock the door, and place the baby in Jackson's swing. I crank the mobile, turn the chair to vibrate, and hope to God he will fall asleep.

A text comes through and I read it. Worried about you. Are you okay? Let me know if I can do anything.

I wish Jess believed me, but a mother *knows* her child. A mother always knows.

I decide not to text her back. There is only one person in this world who can help me—one person who might believe me and help find Jackson. I dial the number from memory and wait.

Jake answers before the second ring.

16

BEC

"WHAT'S WRONG?"

I know a homicide detective is probably used to calls at all hours of the night, but I'm still uncertain of what he might think—his ex-girlfriend whom he just saw now thinks her child is missing? Even I'd have a hard time believing that. I tell him what happened and about my visit to the station. He collects all the basic information—time, where I was, when I realized Jackson was gone—but background movement makes his questions terse and punchy. I concentrate on the sounds: arms being stuffed into stiff leather. Keys scooped from a table. Shoes tugged on, laced, double knotted.

"Stay there."

He's coming.

I hang up and feel a modicum better. Now what? I replay every missing child's case I've ever heard about, stories a dime a dozen in a city as big as Chicago. But not in Elmhurst. This isn't just a simple missing child case though.

This is a *swap*.

I walk to my computer, open a web browser, ask for information on baby swaps, and listen. Moments later, I am immersed in folklore. Instead of real stories about swapped children, I quickly learn that a changeling is believed to be a fairy child left in place of a human child. The main reason for the swap is because the infant is sickly, has developmental disabilities, or is afflicted with unexplained diseases.

On cue, the baby starts up, coughing and crying in tandem. Did someone switch my baby because something is *wrong* with this one?

Upstairs, I run my hand across his cheeks: warm but not hot. Only his chortled snores stutter through the nursery. I pick him up and strap him in the carrier. Worst-case scenarios about Jackson slice through my mind. I grip the sides of my head and bite back a scream.

I replay Jake's request—*stay there*—but I'm already defying it. Downstairs, I pull on my shoes again, grab my keys and cane. The earlier fears of being followed in broad daylight are child's play compared to walking alone late at night. But I have no choice.

The baby quiets with movement. He jostles against my chest, arms and legs bouncing from my brisk pace. Crickets and belchy frogs display their nightly calls, a few sprinklers hissing from obsessive neighbors' desires for pristine lawns.

I scrape the cane across the sidewalk. I can't get too lost in thought or I could trip. I grip the baby and think about turning around. I can't put us both in danger in order to what? Go sit on the park bench and cry?

But there could be a clue or some spark of memory that helps me find Jackson. I force my legs to keep moving, taking a left and then another left. My heart beats in my ears, and I feel the baby's forehead again. I remind myself to take his temperature when we get back. I stop near the entrance to the park, all of the nighttime nature free to vocalize. The trees sway above me, their leaves already crisping from the insane August heat. I take a deep breath and head toward the playground. I sweep my cane along the earth like those people who look for buried treasure at the beach.

A few feet ahead, it bumps into something. I crouch down to get it, knees popping, and retrieve a shoe. I toss it to the side and wipe my hands on my pants. The turf is buoyant. I stop at the edge of the bench I sat on earlier today, hoping a bum isn't sleeping or waiting to attack.

"Hello?" I whisper. I tap my cane on the surface and confirm it's clear. Instead of sitting, I walk around to the other side. My fingers curl around the bench's back. I inch forward and replay the scene from earlier. All of the other strollers were situated in a neat row right here—the smooth, curved hoods, the wide, open bassinets practically touching. I stop where Jackson's was and then drop to my hands and knees. I swipe under the bench, cradling the baby in the carrier with one hand, and plunge my hand across the sticky turf. I don't know what I'm searching for, but my hand closes on nothing. I sit back on my heels and think.

Even though I fainted, I was still aware of sounds . . . the sounds of the park. Children. Mothers. *Bells.*

That's it. I brace a hand against the turf and re-extend my cane. I recall where I heard the sound—off to the left, toward the trees—and set off in that direction. I hunt for the bells, knowing what a longshot it would be to actually find them, but that would be proof. Proof that someone took him. Proof that my baby took off with a stranger and I'm not imagining that this child in my arms is different. To confirm, I feel this baby's ankle, which is bare.

Or proof that the bells just fell off again before I made it to the park. I sigh, defeated at my own logical thinking, but I keep searching anyway. I walk around the playground in a tidy grid, tears dampening my cheeks. If I could just see, I'd know exactly what I was looking for. If I could just see, I could prove to the world this child isn't Jackson.

My phone buzzes in my pocket, and I activate VoiceOver.

I'm here. Where are you?

"Oh shit." I turn back toward the entrance of the park and rattle off a text.

\ **Be right there.**

The walk back is quick and hot. The baby is surprisingly quiet the faster I walk. I'm sweating when I reach the driveway.

"Bec?" Jake seems confused.

I lift my hands, drop them, and fumble with my keys. "I know you said to stay here, but I had to go to the park. I had to see if there was something I missed from earlier." The tears aren't even dry on my cheeks before a fresh round comes. "A clue. Something to explain what's happened."

He pulls me into his arms and shushes me, careful not to crush the baby. "Let's go inside and we'll figure this out, okay?" He removes the keys from my hands, but before he unlocks the door, he tilts my chin up to the porch light. "Did this happen when you fell?"

I self-consciously touch my eye. "It did."

He turns and unlocks the door. All of the earlier adrenaline disappears as I haul myself up the steps and inside. I unlatch the baby and turn him toward Jake, also pulling a few photos of Jackson from my phone for comparison. I don't take many photos, but I try and document as much as I can so he can see them someday.

He studies the photos and then the baby. "Bec, it's hard to tell. We'll have to get others to verify that this isn't Jackson. We'll file a report at the station. But, I'm just going to warn you. This isn't a regular situation. It will be up to the chief to see how they handle this, and from what I know, he's conservative. Doesn't pull the trigger unless warranted."

I pull the baby back into my arms. "What does that mean?"

"It means he's not going to jump to issue an Amber Alert unless he has definitive proof."

"Bullshit." Anger tangles with my fears. Rather than argue, I excuse myself to put the baby back in Jackson's vibrating swing in the nursery. Downstairs, Jake is filling the coffeepot. "Coffee?"

I shrug. I can't think about coffee. I can't think about anything other than my child.

He works silently in the kitchen, not making any comments about the house or how many times he's been here for dinner with my mother or fixed things around the house after Dad died. Once the coffee is brewing, he extracts a small notepad, the pages crisp as he flips them. "I know you filled me in on the phone, but tell me again."

I walk him through exactly what happened from the time I got up to the time I realized Jackson was missing.

He scribbles notes. The coffee gurgles its last drops into the pot. The air conditioner kicks on. Fear screams inside my skull.

He pauses writing. "I ran a check on the way," he says. "No missing child reports for the area."

"What?" My hand freezes in midair as I reach for a mug.

"It's not unusual."

"What's not unusual?"

"Babies don't have identification, Bec. They can be tough to identify."

"If some other mother accidentally took Jackson home, she'd know. Trust me."

"I hear you. But there's a protocol for these things. You know that."

My jaw twitches, and I grind my teeth so hard, I fear they might crack. "No, I don't *know* that. I don't know anything other than the fact that I've been having this . . . *feeling* like I'm being followed and now my son is missing."

"I get that. But if you walk into any station and explain what happened without evidence, then you'll be laughed out of there. Or worse."

"That's why I called you."

"I know. We have time."

I know he's bullshitting me. Jake has taught me the dire statistics of child kidnappings. If a kid isn't found in the first few hours, then he's not coming back. I ask Siri the time. Twelve hours missing.

What if I never see my son again?

I clear the defeatist thought from my brain—it will do nothing to help—and collapse over the counter, bracing myself on my elbows. "What do we need to do? Get DNA or something?"

"DNA is tricky. Labs take forever. And it's gotta be an exceptional case. They don't do it in some of the highest-profile cases."

"You're kidding."

He adjusts on the stool, and the leather cracks over his sturdy body. "Wish I were. Chicago's a big city, lots of crime. They can't accommodate all cases, especially ones without firm evidence."

"What evidence do we need?"

"Bec, even with evidence, a DNA test can take months."

"Months?" This can't take months. Jackson has hours at best. "But we're in Elmhurst. This isn't Chicago. There's hardly any crime here."

"While that's true, technically this isn't my jurisdiction. And as I said, the chief's tough. I'm going to have to call in some favors if you want me to look into this."

"Can we alert the neighborhood at least?"

"Look, you're asking all the right questions. We'll get there. You just have to let me do this part first, okay?" His hand finds mine and briefly squeezes.

In the nursery, the baby screams.

"That child is not my son. Doesn't even sound like him," I say. "What proof do I need beyond that?" I rummage in the fridge again, but I'm out of pumped milk. "Shit." I close the fridge and walk upstairs to the nursery. The walk stretches before me— interminable stairs, endless hallways, a nursery with another baby instead of my own.

I take him out of the vibrating chair, my breasts aching for relief. He settles against me and hungrily tracks the smell of my milk. I hesitate and then lower into my rocking chair, replaying such precious time spent here with Jackson—my favorite moments.

"Who are you?" I whisper. I rock and attempt to get him settled, but he's hungry. Finally, I lift my shirt to offer him a hard, engorged breast. He fusses but doesn't latch. I brush the nipple back and forth over his lips, and my whole body jerks as he finally connects. Even his latch is different, sloppy and unpracticed. The letdown comes quick. A gush of milk explodes into his mouth and with it, physical relief tangled with anguish for my missing son. I close my eyes and pinch off the thoughts. My only focus needs to be on finding him, not mourning him.

Once the baby's full, I burp him and change him, wiping over and over again until I can tell he's clean, then figure out how best to put him to sleep. What works for Jackson doesn't work for him. I clock the differences, categorizing them in my brain one after the other. When he's settled, I rummage in the dresser and remove the thermometer. I take his temperature and wait for the audio reading: 99.1. I exhale. A little high, but nothing dire. Once he's asleep, I tiptoe back downstairs.

"What distinguishing marks does Jackson have?" Jake launches right back into questions. "Birthmarks? Moles?"

Sadly, I shake my head. "He just has a bit of eczema behind his right ear. But no birthmarks." I hand him my phone again, queued up to photos. "The nurse described every square inch when he was born. His pediatrician updates me at every appointment."

"Speaking of the pediatrician, something we could do immediately is the footprint examination. Most hospitals use a digital footprint now instead of ink. Enters each child into a national database. I'll see if I can access the police fingerprint analyst to check if he's a match."

"That's perfect." I exhale, turn, and rake my hands through my hair. "But what if this baby doesn't have a digital footprint?"

He rubs his head. "Hopefully he's in the system. If we can somehow get him rescanned, all his information should be there. We need to get Jackson's footprints too, so we can have the comparison done immediately."

Tears spring to my eyes and I slap a hand to my chest. "Thank God."

"That still doesn't mean much though," he explains gently. "It just proves this child is not yours. It doesn't lead us to Jackson. But it could lead us to this kid's parents at least."

"Right." I squeeze my hands together. "So what now?"

"We'll visit the park first thing in the morning, talk to moms. I'll see if one of the neighboring businesses has any surveillance footage. And we need to talk to your friends—friends who know Jackson." He pauses. "You went to your friend Crystal's right after you hit your head, correct?"

"Yes."

"Did you hold Jackson?"

I shake my head. "I didn't. Crystal helped me with my face. He stayed in his stroller."

"No one picked him up."

"No."

"I hate to say this, but because you're visually impaired, it's going to make protocol more challenging." He hesitates. "Not impossible, but it's critical that someone can confidently confirm that this child isn't Jackson. That's step one."

I nod. "Of course." Inside, I panic. None of my friends, except for Jess, have held Jackson in the last few weeks. At this age, babies change on an almost daily basis.

"I'll need a list of your contacts."

"Sure." I ask Siri to open VoiceOver and bring up contacts. "It's all yours." I swallow. "What should I do?"

"Let me do my job. Without a missing child report, proper police procedure, or the footprint, we're going to have to approach this a bit off the books."

"Okay." I hate feeling like a victim. I want to ask him to knock on every door, to be as riled up about all of this as I am, but without any evidence, all I have to rely on is protocol. I don't dare ask him if he believes me. While I know he's giving me the benefit of the doubt, I don't think I could handle anything other than yes.

"I'm just going to do a little digging. Why don't you go upstairs and take a cold shower?"

"I don't want to take a shower."

"It will clear your head, shock your system. Go. I'll let you know if the baby wakes up."

I stare stubbornly in his direction, suddenly taken back eleven years. What else am I going to do? Pace the kitchen until he's done? "Fine."

"It's going to be okay, Bec. I promise."

I shrug off his words, walk upstairs to the bedroom, and click the door shut. I crank the water to cold and do as I'm told. I undress and enter the icy spray. Instead of standing under a hot shower and crying, I gasp for breath and think of nothing else but staying put. After a full minute, my skin adjusts and I focus on breathing in and out.

I stay until I can't take the cold, then quickly dry off, redress, and wrap my hair in a towel. Jake is in the kitchen. He pours another cup of coffee.

"Better?" he asks.

No. "Did you find what you need?"

"Kind of." He swallows. "I hope you don't mind, but I logged onto your computer and saw the open browser." He drums his fingers on the table. "What's all this stuff about the changeling?" His tone is light, but concern smarts underneath.

I shrug. "I went to Google 'baby swaps' and that came up." I keep my voice steady, my eyes as focused as possible. "I just wanted to see what it was about."

He doesn't respond and I wonder if I should keep explaining. I wish I could see his face to tell what he's thinking. I unravel the towel from my damp hair and busy my hands with soaking up the excess moisture.

"Do you have any enemies? Anyone in Chris's life who wants to get back at him?"

I bristle at his question. Chris didn't have enemies. And I don't, as far as I know. I shake my head. "Everyone loved Chris."

He hesitates. "No past lovers or affairs that you're aware of?"

I almost laugh. The idea of Chris cheating seems as ludicrous as this alleged baby swap. "Chris would never cheat." I know my words must sound cheap, but I'm certain. Yes, Jake has seen it all—humans doing unspeakable acts, breaking all kinds of promises, lying to save face. But Chris was different. "I'm positive," I say, to drive home the point. Sensing I don't want to explore that subject further, he changes tactics.

"Your friend Jess." He scratches his jaw, his fingernails grinding on sandpaper. "Let's start with her since she was with the baby all day."

I nod. "Should I call her?"

"It would be helpful, yes."

I cringe at what I assume to be a highly inappropriate hour, but I make the call anyway. She doesn't answer, and I send her a text. "She might be asleep."

"Let's just see if she responds." He hesitates. "I'm going to push this—even though it's out of my jurisdiction—to see what I can get done tonight. I'll probably be at the station most of the night, but if I need to crash . . ."

"Of course." I exhale the breath I didn't realize I'd been holding. I retrieve the sheets, pillow, and blanket from the ottoman.

"Let me."

"It's a pullout," I explain, motioning toward the couch.

The coils groan as he unfolds the mattress and dresses it. I don't want to be here without my baby. I can't sit in my room all night, thinking. I'm Jackson's mother. I need to be out there, doing something.

"Look, Bec." He moves right in front of me so that I get a whiff of his skin: clean, like soap. "I'm working a few other cases. I'm going to fight to be here for you, but if my unit calls, then—"

"Then you have to go. I know the drill." I pray that Chicago can have one crime-free night to spare its lead homicide detective. "There's this guy, Officer Toby." I turn and walk to the small dish by the front door. I retrieve the entire dish and extend it toward Jake. "His card's in here somewhere. He told me to call if I needed him." I explain about Officer Toby's two visits a few days ago, and our conversation at the party. "Do you know him?"

"I don't, but let me give him a quick call, okay? See if he can get down to the station and get a jump on this."

"Okay."

He moves into the dining room to make the call. Not knowing what else to do, I walk back to the nursery. Outside the door, I bury the irrational fear of finding the baby lifeless or not breathing—an unsuspecting victim of SIDS or allergy to something in my milk. I push open the door and immediately hear his labored, snotty breathing. At the crib, I lower my hands to where his body should be, but find that he's positioned himself all the way to the edge of the rails. I gently palm his body—still warm.

"Poor little guy." The words are out of my mouth before I realize it. Though he's not mine, he's *someone's* child, and I'm still a mother. I press my hand against his forehead and then down to his cheeks. I trace small circles over his back. I decide something in my son's room, comforting another woman's child. While this baby is here, I will make sure he's okay. I make the promise to myself, to Jackson, to *us*.

My phone rings. My heart does an irrational lurch and I back out of the room before it wakes the baby. I issue a breathless "hello." Could it be whoever has Jackson? Maybe this nightmare will be over before it's even begun.

"Hey. Are you okay?" Jess's voice is clogged with sleep, and I feel guilty for waking her.

"Is there any way you can come over?"

"Now? Is the baby okay? Are you—"

"The baby is fine, but a detective is here."

A door shuts. "Already on my way."

I hang up. I walk back downstairs to tell Jake, but he's still on with the precinct. I sit on the bottom stair, drop my head into my hands, and wait.

17

BEC

JESS LETS HERSELF IN MOMENTS LATER. "BEC?" SHE WHISPERS INTO THE
hallway. Jake and I meet her in the foyer.

"This is Detective Jake Donovan," I explain before she can ask.

"Hi." Jess's voice is confused. "Where's Jackson?"

I steel myself and sigh. "Let's go into the kitchen." Once there, I
turn toward her. "I know you think I'm confused, but I'm not. I don't
know what happened from the time I fainted until the time we left
the park, but somehow I made it home with a different baby."

"Rebecca." Jess's tone borders on condescending. "I was right
there. You fainted for like twenty seconds."

"Didn't every mother turn to see what was happening when I
fainted? Someone could have switched him."

Jess remains silent.

"Look," Jake interjects. "I know this all seems confusing. And it
is, but we'll get to the bottom of it, okay? Jessica, can I ask you a few
questions?"

Jess sighs and slips off her stool to pour herself a cup of coffee.
"Shoot."

"Bec, would you mind if we talked alone?"

I balk at the suggestion but realize that Jess might not be completely honest in front of me. He probably wants to gauge her genuine
reactions on his own.

"I'll go check on the baby." *The baby.* The words send irrational chills down my spine. I want *my* baby. I step into the hallway but linger as Jake begins his questioning. I flatten myself against the wall and listen.

"So you know Bec pretty well?"

"As well as someone can know another person in less than a year, sure."

"And you've spent a lot of time with Jackson?"

"I have."

"Would you say you'd be able to recognize him just from sight alone?"

"I would."

"Any distinguishing marks you can recall—birthmarks, scars, that sort of thing?"

Jess is silent for a moment. "I know he has eczema. And a little dent in his collarbone. At least she told me that. I've never felt it."

My stomach tightens at the way she's talking, like what I've told her might not be true.

"Can you take me through what happened today? You and Rebecca walked to the park together?"

"No, we didn't walk to the park together, but I saw her once she arrived. All the moms had their strollers lined up behind this park bench—we do that sometimes, just so we can sit and chat. I made space for Jackson beside my son's stroller—Baxter."

"How many strollers were there?"

"I don't know . . . five? Maybe six?"

"Did you get a good look at Jackson?"

"I peeked into his stroller to say hello, but we were already talking. I wasn't paying close attention, if I'm being honest."

"How did Rebecca seem? Normal? Tired? Off?"

"Nothing seemed off. She was tired but in a good mood."

"Okay, then take me through what happened."

"Well, we were all just talking for a while, and then Rebecca stood up too fast and fainted. It was pretty scary actually."

"And you rushed to help?"

"We all did."

"How many other mothers?"

"I don't know . . . again, maybe five or six? I was just focused on helping. I told everyone to give her some room because they were all pushing in on her. Even I was getting claustrophobic."

"During this time, was anyone watching the strollers? Did you notice any commotion going on behind the park bench? Anyone out of the ordinary?"

"I didn't. I was one hundred percent focused on making sure Rebecca was okay. I didn't even check my own son." Jess takes a slurp of coffee. "But Elmhurst is safe. We all watch out for each other."

"I understand." Jake pauses, and I wonder if he's taking notes. "So then what happened?"

"I helped her sit up and walk to the bench. She actually said she should check on Jackson, but I told her he was fine."

"How did you know he was fine?"

"I . . ." Her voice fades. "Well, I mean I guess I didn't *know* he was fine, but it had only been a couple of minutes and his stroller was still there and he was in it. Like I said, nothing looked different. I assumed everything was okay."

"At what point did you check the strollers?"

"Once I got her settled, her friend Crystal offered to let her rest at her house. We decided to walk there since it was closer. I was the one to get the stroller."

"When you got the stroller, nothing appeared out of place?"

"Not at all. Everything was just as we'd left it minutes before."

"Did you pick up Jackson?"

"I didn't."

"Did Rebecca pick up the baby?"

"No."

"Then what?"

"We walked the very short distance to her friend's house. I told

Rebecca I would watch Jackson and I situated his stroller right by the back door."

"Does this friend have children of her own?"

"Just a daughter, Savi. She's older."

"No other children?"

"No."

"And you were with Jackson the whole time?"

"Yes." She hesitates. "Actually, I had to take a call outside, but no one picked him up. He stayed in the stroller the entire time."

"So no one touched Jackson from the time she fainted until the time you walked her home?"

"That's correct."

"What happened once Rebecca got home?"

"When we got to the front door, I—now I feel bad—but I insisted that she get some rest and that I would watch Jackson for the afternoon. I also gave her two sleeping pills so she could sleep. I wasn't even thinking about the fact that she'd hit her head."

"Rebecca consented to let you watch the baby? Did she feed him or pick him up once she was home?"

"No."

"But you stayed with him here while she slept?"

"I did. All day."

"And how did the baby seem?"

"Well, like I told Rebecca, he was really fussy. Normally, Jackson is easy, but he seemed agitated. He cried and he didn't want the milk she'd left. He just seemed like maybe he didn't feel good."

"During this time, you didn't register anything different in his appearance?"

She's quiet. "People don't switch babies. That's not a thing that happens."

"Just answer the question, please."

She lets out a shaky breath. "I mean, I don't think so. I was also trying to juggle Baxter and I was watching a show, so I wasn't one hundred percent focused on Jackson. He just seemed a bit more work than usual."

"Do you think the baby upstairs is someone else's, or do you think Rebecca is mistaken?"

My heart hammers so hard against my ribs, I fear I'm going to be sick.

"She's been through a lot." She drops her voice so much that I strain to hear.

"Yes, she has." This time, I can hear him scribbling something.

"But to answer your question . . . I'm not sure. My gut says the baby upstairs is Jackson—just given the way Rebecca has been acting lately. It's true I hadn't held him for quite some time until today, but it's just a feeling. She's a brand-new mom. I remember being that tired. But I don't want anything bad to happen to her or for anyone to question if she's a good parent," she rushes to add. "Because she's a great mom."

Her admission—even though partially complimentary—devastates any lingering hope that she believes me.

"Would you be willing to take a closer look at him to see if you might have a different opinion now?"

"Sure."

Feeling caught, I push off the wall and wait in the hallway.

Jake rounds the corner. "Bec, do you mind if we check out the baby?"

"Sure. I'm going to get some air." I grab my sweater off the hook in the foyer just in case the temperature has dropped and step outside. The air is crisp and reminds me of the autumn days ahead. All of the things I wanted to do with Jackson mock me: raking piles of leaves, making huge pots of chili, hay rides, carving pumpkins, settling into our new life as a twosome. I wanted to use these next few months to create a new normal between the two of us. How could all of it fall apart so quickly?

From upstairs, the baby screams and starts to cry. I half stand, so conditioned to rush to Jackson's aide, but then I remember they are examining him. He's not just a little boy I can placate. He's *evidence.*

Evidence of what? The question plagues me, but I attempt to stay focused. A few minutes later, he quiets. I pace the front yard. The grass tickles my feet. I tip my face up to a sky full of stars I can't see and pray for a miracle.

"Bec?" Jake opens the door. "Can you come inside?"

I brace myself for the verdict. "So?" I shut the door behind me.

"Bec, I'm sorry, but I still maintain what I said before," Jess says. "I really do think it's Jackson."

Jake stays quiet. *They don't believe me.* "Now what?" My voice is resigned, even to my own ears.

"I can take you down to the precinct," Jake says. "Toby is expecting us. And then we'll handle the footprint with the hospital. We'll need to take some statements from your friends as well."

"How'd you get him to stop crying?" I ask.

"Swaddle," Jess says.

"Jackson hates to be swaddled," I say. "*Hates* it."

"Do you need me to come to the station too?" I don't know if Jess is directing that question to me or Jake.

"Yes, but not tonight," Jake says. "I'll call you if I need anything further. Thank you for your time."

On the way out, Jess grabs my hand. I resist shaking her off. "Get some rest, okay? It's all going to be fine."

When she leaves, I bite back the millionth scream of the evening. "Should we go?"

"Hey, come here." He wraps his arms around me, and I cling to him: his smell, the familiarity and strangeness of him, and the slim hope that he understands I'm telling the truth. He opens his mouth, probably to say something generic, like, "It's all going to be okay," but I stop him.

"Don't," I say.

"Don't what?" he asks.

"Don't give me some bullshit line about everything working out. It won't be okay until I have Jackson back."

"I know," Jake says. "That's not what I was going to say."

"Then what were you going to say?" I peer up at him, wishing this was all a bad dream.

"I was going to say—" His phone cuts through the charged moment and he extricates himself from me. "Donovan." His clipped tone turns right back to business. "Copy that. On our way."

"Toby?"

"Yep. He talked to the chief." He sighs. "Because Toby's already had three run-ins with you, he's on high alert. Just a warning."

"What does that mean?"

"It means they're prepared not to believe you. It's your job to prove otherwise. With statements like Jess's . . . if your other friends say the same thing, it will be detrimental to your case. We need someone to corroborate your story. It's the only way we'll get traction. Want me to grab the baby?"

I nod, suddenly too tired to walk back upstairs even one more time. I gather the diaper bag—Jackson's diaper bag—and loop it over my shoulder. A few minutes later, Jake hands me the baby.

"Ready?"

I nod, too afraid to speak. I'm not ready. But I have to be. I have to be strong. I have to believe what Jake said. I have to trust my friends to help me out and not sabotage me.

I have to trust myself.

18

BEC

THE STATION IS QUIETER THAN BEFORE, AND I FEEL BETTER HAVING JAKE BY my side. He won't let anything bad happen. He won't let them confuse me or make me admit to something I didn't do.

The baby burrows against my chest, and I place a protective hand on his back while Jake meets with Toby.

"This way," Officer Toby says. I grab Jake's elbow and let him steer me to what I assume will be an investigation room. I remember Jake and I once made out in one of these rooms in Chicago. He'd pressed me against the two-way glass, and secretly, I'd hoped someone was watching from the other side. He'd told me all about what happened in these rooms; how inmates cleaned them, how often scare tactics were used or bullshit deals were made.

Now, it's me sitting here—not some convict—being watched and judged.

How did I get here?

I ignore the question and focus on the mission at hand: find Jackson. Get my son back. Return this child to . . . wherever he came from. My hold tightens as I think of handing this baby over to whatever monster left him in the first place. I remember hearing those stories about mothers dumping their children in toilets, garbage cans, or leaving them on doorsteps. But whoever did this had an agenda. They took what wasn't theirs to take.

"Rebecca, it's nice to see you again. Though I wish it was under different circumstances," Officer Toby hurriedly adds. His voice is tired. I wonder if I've taken him away from his own family or small children, but I know it comes with the job.

"Me too." I clear my throat.

"Let's start from the beginning," Toby says. "See what we can figure out, okay?"

"Okay." I answer the questions honestly, going back over the incident, the days leading up to the incident, all the way to this very moment. I have to confirm that Jess doesn't believe me and that I don't have anyone else close to me who can confirm this child isn't Jackson . . . except maybe a few of the other moms I'm friends with, like Crystal or Beth.

"That's fine. We'll get their statements."

"What can we do tonight?"

"I understand how nervous you must feel, Mrs. Gray, but there's a protocol here. I'm under the chief's strict orders, and as much as we'd like to believe you, we can't just take your word for it. If we believed everyone who came in here, we'd be in all sorts of trouble."

I look toward Jake to help—I can always sense where he is in the room, a magnetic charge that pulls me right to him.

"Listen, I've offered to extend my services here, maybe speed things along a bit. Can we speak privately?"

"Sure."

The two men step out of the room and I think about eavesdropping for the second time tonight. I press my ear against the door. "Look, the chief doesn't want to pull the trigger on announcing this unless we have proof. I've had three encounters with Mrs. Gray in less than a week, and none of them have been accurate. She's paranoid, Jake. I've seen it a million times." I pull my head away. I don't want to hear the rest.

I walk in a circle and thrust my fingers through the baby's hair and gently bounce him up and down. For the first time, he seems content. As if on cue, he lets out a tiny satisfied sigh that tugs at my heart. "Who wouldn't want you?" I whisper. "Who in the world . . . ?"

The door opens, and I wait for further instructions.

"Bec . . ." The way Jake says my name makes me nervous. "We're probably going to need to wait until morning. We need to verify a few things—talk to witnesses—before we can go further. We've done another scan and there are no missing babies reported. Not in Elmhurst or the surrounding areas."

"If someone did this on purpose, I'm sure they aren't going to alert the authorities that their baby is missing," I snap.

"We understand that, but again, without some sort of finite proof, we have to go with protocol. We'll get the digital footprint, talk to witnesses, and go from there. Okay?"

I laugh, a short bark that echoes in the dull room. "So I'm just supposed to wait until morning?" I look between them. "And do what exactly?"

"I know this is hard," Jake says.

"No, you don't. You have no clue." I'm talking about Jackson, but I'm also talking about everything else. He doesn't have any idea. No one does.

"Mrs. Gray," Officer Toby begins.

"It's *Rebecca*," I say. "I'm not a Mrs. anymore. My husband is dead." I bounce the baby, who has started to fuss once I raised my voice. "And what happens to him?"

"He stays with you tonight, unless you want us to call Social Services."

"Don't be ridiculous," I say.

Jake lowers his voice and whispers something to Officer Toby, who straightens papers on the table. "I'll just let you two talk. We'll be in touch in the morning, Rebecca." He slips out the door.

"Can we go now?" I ask. I'm already reaching for him, having forgotten my cane when we left the house so fast. He guides me outside, and I'm incensed that the police aren't helping. This is a missing baby we're talking about.

We're silent on the walk back. For the second time tonight, I assess the sounds of nature—loud and persistent.

"What time is it?" I finally ask.

"Two," he says.

I calculate the hours missing: fourteen. Too long. At the door, I unlock it and almost stumble into the entryway.

"Rebecca." Jake is instantly beside me.

I clutch his jacket as though I'm drowning. "I need my baby," I cry. "Please, I need him. I need him." My pleas grow louder. As my voice strengthens, the baby cries. I can't be in this house. I can't stay here, staring down at an empty crib. I press to standing, but my throat constricts. "I can't breathe," I whisper. Suddenly, I'm back in the park, feeling like I'm going to die. "Jake . . ." I pitch forward and fall to my hands and knees. The baby jostles against my chest and cries harder. I roll to my back. I'm dizzy. I'm going to faint.

"Jesus Christ, Rebecca. Here, sit up." Jake gathers me in his arms, but I refuse to sit. I don't want to sit. I don't want to breathe. I don't want to do anything without Jackson. "Rebecca!" He shakes my arms, unlatches the baby, and takes him somewhere else. His cries pierce my ears, and I lay back against the cold wood. My black world spins, slows, grows dreamy. But before I give in, I hear the groan of pipes upstairs, a shower running.

Then, Jake is back downstairs, and tosses me over his shoulder. I'm too weak to protest. He hikes the stairs, kicks open my bathroom door, and dunks me in the bathtub fully clothed, the icy needles instantly jolting me awake for the second time tonight. I scream, but he presses me down until I'm gasping and crying.

"Stay," he orders. His hands restrain while I fight against him, my tiny fists banging his sturdy muscles. "Stop it. Just stop it." His voice is gentle, though his meaning is firm.

And finally, too tired to do anything else, I give in and wrench his body against mine. He soaks his own jacket, his shirt, and his entire body, but he holds me there, not moving, until the water makes me numb, and I'm drained of tears.

19

B E C

⠃⠑⠉

LIGHT CRACKS THROUGH THE BLINDS AND ALERTS ME TO MORNING. I SHOOT
up in bed. I must have fallen asleep sometime early this morning. *Oh
God, the baby.* I launch out of bed, rummage for my robe, and hurry
down the hall to the nursery. I tiptoe just in case he's still sleeping, but
the crib is empty. Movement echoes from the kitchen.

"Jake?" I take the stairs and round the corner. "Where's the baby?"

"Morning. It's okay. He's right here."

I check the baby, who is in Jackson's playpen. Last night sears into
focus. I've never been so unglued—not even after Chris died—but
Jake was there every second. I shake away that version of Rebecca,
the unglued woman who's lost everything. Today, there will need to
be a new version in her place: strong Rebecca. Resilient Rebecca. A
mother who will do virtually anything to find her son. "What time
is it?" The same question I asked on our walk home from the station.

"It's only seven. No new reports on my end. Here." He thrusts a
cup of coffee in my hand. "Drink up." The cup heats my palms. I
take a tentative sip, a heavy breath. It's been almost twenty hours
since I've fed Jackson—despite the reluctant feeding yesterday, my
breasts hang like heavy boulders on my chest. I set the coffee on the
counter, grab the pump, and excuse myself to the bathroom.

As I sit and ponder what might happen today, my body involuntarily
responds to the pump and fills each freezer bag almost to bursting. I

know it will be too early for the mothers to be at the park, but I am desperate to get there. Someone has to know something or have seen something. I think about Beth and Crystal. Have they already heard through the grapevine what's happened?

I label the bags, give the baby a bottle, and get dressed. I steel myself for the day—and inevitable judgment—ahead. Jake helps change the baby, packs extra bottles, and lowers him into the stroller.

"Are you okay with work?" I ask.

"For now." He opens the front door and maneuvers the stroller to the driveway.

As we head toward the park, I mourn the circumstances. This is a scenario I'd often envisioned in my twenties with Jake: sans missing baby, dead husband and mother, and blindness. I text Jess to let her know we're headed to Wilder. I wanted to put out a group post on the Elmhurst Moms Facebook page last night, but Jake advised against it. "In case there is someone behind this, we need to be discreet. Don't announce yourself."

The day is perfectly warm without an ounce of humidity. The baby fusses from the stroller, and the longing for Jackson takes me off guard. Jake steadies me with his arm. "You okay?"

"I can physically feel him out there somewhere."

"Just stay focused," he says.

We take a left into the park. It's quiet, and I sag with disappointment. "What now?" I ask.

"Now we wait." We sit on the park bench. I take myself back to yesterday morning: the path I walked, how I stopped behind this bench, how my fingers trailed over the edges of each stroller so I knew exactly where Jackson's was. How Jess slid Baxter's stroller to the right so she could make room for him. How I sat in front of my baby and arrogantly thought the bells would alert me if something was wrong. I was so engrossed in conversation—in feeling normal, in blending in, in making friends—that I didn't pay attention. What if it happened while we were all just sitting there? What if the swap happened *before* I fainted, not after? As I calculate possibilities, a few women finally straggle in. Sensing the shift, Jake leans in.

"Let me do the talking, okay?"

I nod and squeeze the stroller handle tighter.

"Excuse me, ladies? I'm Detective Jake Donovan." Jake's voice is steady as he approaches the moms. "My friend Rebecca Gray was here yesterday with her baby, Jackson." I imagine him turning to gesture toward the bench.

"Oh yeah, you fainted! Are you okay?" A woman's voice I barely recognize—Ramona?—speaks up, and then another woman joins in. I offer up a smile, but it's fake. This whole thing is a lie—sitting here with another baby in my son's stroller, depending on my ex-boyfriend to get to the bottom of this when *I'm* his mother. This is *my* job, not Jake's.

"So you were both here yesterday?" Jake continues. "Anyone else?" He cases both benches and gathers the women to talk, take statements, and ask questions. I avoid trailing him like a huntress and instead stay glued to the bench, retracing my steps before and after I fainted. I play the dangerous *what if* game. What if I hadn't gone to sleep when I got home? What if I hadn't let Jess stay with him? I would have known immediately and could have done something about it then. Instead, I slept all day and gave whoever it was hours to escape. I smother a sob with my hand as the baby starts crying. I rock the stroller and shush him. My head pounds. My heart hurts. I dab my tears and adjust my sunglasses.

"Hey, any luck yet?" Jess slides in beside me.

"I don't know. He's asking questions." My voice falls flat.

She sighs. "Look, I know I wasn't a great friend last night, but I'm going to be here for you, okay?"

I nod, unable to say thanks. Because if she doesn't believe me, then I don't really want her help.

"I'm going to go see if Jake needs anything. You okay here?"

I nod again. Suddenly, someone thrusts a flyer into my hand. "Big end-of-summer parade today. You should come!"

I almost say thanks but no thanks and then stop. I've often heard people who commit crimes stay close just to see how the victim reacts. What if the kidnapper shows up in a large group? I know it's unlikely, but it seems logical. "Excuse me. Can you read this to me?" I lift my cane. "I'd love to come, but I'm assuming you don't have flyers in braille?"

"Oh, sorry. Sure. It's right in downtown Elmhurst from two to five today. Fun for everyone and free to the public. Lots of cool things for the little ones too."

I thank the woman and wonder if I can talk Jess and Jake into coming with me to scout things out. I fold the flyer and tuck it into my pocket.

"Okay." Jake approaches. "I got a few names of women who were here yesterday. I can start with them." He flips a page on his notepad. "Bec, I'd suggest we call Prentice Hospital for the footprint. Since this child doesn't have identification, you're going to have to see if they will scan him."

Suddenly, I have an idea. "What if I take him to Elmhurst Hospital? It seems likely that he would have been born here, not in Chicago."

"Worth a shot. Let me finish up here and we'll head over there." He retreats for a few more questions.

I listen to all the happy children—just not mine. Jess clears her throat. "I know this must be excruciating."

"You have no idea," I whisper. I unfold the flyer from my pocket. "I want to go."

"Why?" She takes it.

"Jackson could be there. Some crazy person could be playing house and bring him out in public."

"Rebecca, you won't be able to see anything."

"You will."

Finally, she sighs. "Let me check with Candace."

"Okay, I've got the names of all the women with strollers." Jake returns and rattles off the names of the other women here yesterday:

Jess and me, of course, then Lanie Jenkins, Ramona Thompson, Barbara Wang, and Sandra Phillips.

Jess confirms. "You know what, I think that's right. A few were on the other benches, but I remember their strollers. They have the top-of-the-line stuff: thousand-dollar strollers, all the fancy models."

My heart drops. "So what you're saying is that no one could have taken mine by mistake."

"Look, we're doing our due diligence," Jake says. "Jess, can you get their addresses and I'll pop by for questioning? Meanwhile, let's hit the hospital." Suddenly, Jake's phone buzzes. "Shit. Hold that thought. Donovan." He answers and barks orders in short, professional clips. The phone call is all of thirty seconds, but I know, even before he hangs up, that he's about to leave me. "Bec, I'm so sorry . . ."

"Go." I know murder is more important than a missing child, but it feels like I'm the one who's dying.

"I'll be back as soon as I can. Let me know what you find out at the hospital." He kisses my cheek and he's gone. My anxiety peaks as he walks away. Before I can catch my breath, I'm hyperventilating. "I can't do this without him," I gasp.

"It's okay. Let's just do what he said, okay? I can go to their homes if you want to do the hospital? I know where they live. Unless you need me with you?"

I shake my head and begin to tug the stroller behind me. "No, go. It will be faster if we split up."

"At least let me walk you there."

On the way, I try on different scenarios: one of the women from yesterday saw something or knew something. Someone wants a ransom. Someone is angry. I think about what Jake suggested about a scorned lover who might want revenge. A small seed of doubt blossoms, even though I know to the depths of my being Chris would never cheat.

But you couldn't see him, a small voice reminds me. He could have done anything, and I wouldn't have known. Am I positive he never cheated?

Yes.

I dismiss those ugly thoughts and mull over other possibilities, but nothing sticks. We stop in front of the sliding glass doors.

"Text me once you find out," she says.

I take a breath and step inside, wandering forward until I locate an information desk. "Pediatrics?" I ask.

I'm directed to the third floor. I work out my story in my head and then have a paralyzing thought. They'll need his name. They'll need my name. I flatten myself against the wall as I come out of the elevator. How the hell will I get records if I can't tell them this baby's name? I rush into the bathroom and extract my phone to call Jake.

"You okay?"

"I have a problem." I relay the conundrum.

"You're going to have to get creative, Bec. See if they can scan his foot and find him in the system. Make up a story if you have to. He was left on your doorstep, whatever. Just get that footprint." Jake slams on the horn and curses. "Let me know how it goes, okay?" He punches the horn again. "I'll be in touch."

I hang up and steady myself. I can do this. I just need to get the footprint.

20

CRYSTAL

⠊⠀⠉⠀⠊⠀⠑

SAVI KNOCKS ON BEC'S FRONT DOOR AND WAITS. "WHERE IS SHE?" HER daughter turns, confused. Her cello case bangs dejectedly against her legs.

"I'm not sure," Crystal says. She dials Bec again, but it goes straight to voice mail. "Let me check that I got the day right." She did. "Maybe she forgot?"

"So I'm *not* doing cello now?" Savi's disappointment is written all over her face.

Crystal attempts to backtrack. "I'm not sure. Maybe she had an emergency?" Crystal peeks in the front windows, but it's dark. She dials again and looks at the driveway. She can't check for a car, because Rebecca doesn't have one. But it's not like her to not get in touch if she had to cancel. Bec never cancels. "Want to drop your cello back home and we can go do something fun?"

"Shouldn't we wait first in case she comes back?"

"Well . . ." She doesn't want to give her false hope, but she also doesn't want to keep bothering Rebecca.

"What about Pam?" Savi asks.

"It's fine," Crystal affirms. "Let's just have some mother-daughter time."

Pam had come over last night and they'd had a real heart-to-heart. She'd admitted to Crystal that Savi had been vying for attention, and promised that what happened with the haircut and the fire wouldn't ever happen again. She continued to take the blame, but it was clear that Pam wasn't responsible for all of it. Crystal agreed to keep Pam on a very strict probation period—partly to help her out until she could find someone else and partly to placate Savi so she didn't do something else extreme.

Once she heard the news that Pam would stay on, Savi promised she would be on her very best behavior. While she couldn't know all of the emotions Savi was juggling, she did know a skipped cello lesson on top of everything else wasn't going to bode well for her spirits.

On the way home, Crystal spots flyers tucked under the flags of every mailbox. At theirs, she plucks one free. "Hey, Savi. Want to go to a parade today?" She presses it into her hand. "It's downtown."

Savi's mouth loosens from its frown. "I guess," she mumbles.

Crystal tosses Savi the house keys so she can put away the cello. She checks her phone again for missed calls or texts from Bec. She dials again and leaves one last concerned message. When Savi comes back, she pockets her phone. "Hungry?" she asks.

"Not really," Savi says.

"Not even for ice cream?"

Savi's head lifts. "But it's not even lunch."

"So?" Crystal says. "Let's be crazy. One scoop or two?"

"Two!" Savi jumps up and down. "Can I get sprinkles?"

"Why not?" Crystal walks hand in hand with Savi toward downtown. She's committing the ultimate parenting sin—trying to cheer her kid up with sugar and bribes—but it won't kill her.

On their walk, Crystal absorbs how lucky they are to live here. The town is small, but safe. Kids can still ride their bikes and run to each other's houses. Though they live in a modern world, Savi can still cling to a bit of that childhood freedom Crystal had when she was younger. Savi just needs to make some friends first.

At the ice cream shop, Savi presses her nose against the window. "Yum!" She pulls open the door and is gone before Crystal can even comment. She catches her reflection in the glass and is surprised to find herself smiling.

She steps in after her daughter and inhales the delicious buttery scent of fresh waffle cones and indulgent flavors. Savi asks for samples, straining on tiptoes. Crystal admires her daughter, her palms splayed on smudged glass, hair smooth and straight, eyes alight with an exciting childhood tradition. Her tanned calves flex, the peach fuzz more evident in her prepubescent years. A bright Band-Aid covers the side of her knee. Crystal memorizes this version of her daughter on a perfect summer day.

"Mom, what are you getting?" Savi turns, her gorgeous spray of freckles on display.

Crystal shakes out of her reverie. "Let me see." She rubs her hands together and joins her to peruse the endless flavors. "What are my choices?"

A few minutes later, they sit outside, eating their ice cream cones. The heat melts the sickly sweet scoops, and Crystal hurries to lick hers before it makes her hands sticky. Parade participants prepare at the end of the block: dancers, band members with clunky instruments, oversized floats, even the mayor, dressed in a funny top hat and bright suit to match. Neighbors line the streets, their viewing spots solidified. She wonders where they should watch.

In her pocket, her phone buzzes. It's Pam. She hesitates, then ignores it. She wants to sit with her daughter, enjoy the parade, and eat ice cream. *A normal day.*

She smiles at Savi, but a knot of worry sprouts while she continues to eat. Though she's trying to create a new sense of peace for her family, what she's really doing is biding her time until something—or someone—tears it all apart.

21

BEC

⠿

"DO YOU HAVE AN APPOINTMENT?"

I keep my sunglasses on at the reception desk and try to plaster on a friendly smile. "I don't, but I was wondering if you could help me." I take a breath and keep my voice as steady as I can, despite the panic rotating in my chest like a ceiling fan on maximum speed. "I delivered my son at Prentice in Chicago, but I live in Elmhurst now. He had the digital footprint done there, but their system got hacked and he's no longer showing up." I play my trump card. "I'm blind, so having the digital scan is critical in case something were to ever happen. I was just wondering if I could get him scanned and entered into the system since this is our primary care?"

"You'll have to make an appointment." The woman taps a few computer keys. "Our next available is . . ." More pecking. "September twentieth."

"That's over a month away," I say.

"That's our earliest available." She stops typing.

I weigh my options. Why didn't I just start with some version of the truth? "I actually don't need an appointment. I just need the scan."

"I understand, but we don't do the scan in this office. That's actually done by a nurse when the baby is born—not at checkups. They can do it if he's here for a well-child visit, but that's all. You might try maternity?"

"Thanks."

I back out of the office and ask someone in the hall which way to the maternity ward. In the hall, I extract my phone and research the company who actually does these scans: CertaScan. I think about calling them to see if they could access the database but decide to try maternity first. I locate the floor and suite number and figure out where I'm going thanks to a woman in the hallway. Memories terrorize me as I recall Jackson's birth only three months ago. I rip away the anguish and approach yet another front desk.

"Hi." I replay the same story I told pediatrics.

"Have a seat and let me see what I can do."

The lies are just getting started, but I tell myself it's what I have to do to get proof. An idea blooms while I wait. After twenty minutes, I'm called back and a kind nurse—Beatrice—leads me into what I assume to be a standard exam room. I've left the stroller by the front and have the baby on my hip, the cane announcing my impairment so I don't have to.

"Just have a seat." She closes the heavy wooden door, and I bypass what I know to be the crinkly paper to have a seat in the chair against the wall. "So what brings you here today?"

Just get through it. "I just moved here from Chicago. I had my baby at Prentice and the nurse used the CertaScan . . . except something happened with the technology and I don't think it was saved properly."

"Can you give me your baby's date of birth?" The click of the computer buttons fills the silence. "All of these are saved in a database . . ." she says. "Yep, here he is. Jackson Gray?"

"Yes." I continue. "The thing is, I was told that something happened with his scan and that it wasn't accurate? Would you mind scanning him again . . . just for peace of mind?" I add quickly. "Seeing as I can't verify the information myself." I give her my very best I'm-blind-and-everyone-is-out-to-get-me look.

"Give me a minute."

When the door shuts, I shift the baby, who has gone miraculously silent. I hold him a little tighter until he lets out an uncomfortable cry. "Sorry, little man," I whisper.

The nurse knocks and then enters. She wheels a cart into the room and clicks more buttons. "Alright. Let me just . . ." Her voice fades and then she asks for the baby's right foot. I pull off his small sock. She flattens something against his sole and presses a button. "Okay, it's just scanning. It should bring up your son's former footprint. Hmm."

A rush of blood roars through my ears. "What?"

She clicks a few more buttons. I wonder if he's already in the system, if the child's name is going to pop up so I'll know who he is and part of the mystery can be over. "Hold on a minute." She removes the paddle from his foot and presses it back. "Would you excuse me for a second?"

"Sure." My entire world shrinks until I feel I might disappear. My voice is a forced whisper. I don't want to wait even one more second.

The door clicks shut, and I exhale. Validation is coming. I'm certain of it. Once I have the scan, I can prove to Jake, Jess, and the whole world that this child is not my son. I bounce the baby on my knees and calculate what my next move will be once I have proof.

The door opens again, and a new voice speaks. "Hi. I'm Dr. Chen. I hear we might have an issue with our machine?" She taps a few buttons and speaks in a low voice to the nurse.

The machine?

"You see that? There." She clicks a few buttons. "Same issue." The doctor stops speaking to the nurse and directs her attention toward me. "I'm so sorry, but we're having some technical issues," she explains.

"Do you have another one you could try?" *My son's life depends on it,* I want to scream.

"There's been a recall on this model. Same issue at Prentice. The good news is"—she groans as she leans down to pick something up— "this technology is really only needed for a missing child. But we'll have the front desk call you as soon as it's fixed, okay? Or you can try Prentice if they get theirs back sooner."

Panic slices through my abdomen, a steady, sharp blade. "Do you know of other hospitals in the area who might use the same technology?"

"Just us and Prentice. We're beta testing, helping them work out the kinks. Sorry we couldn't be more help."

"Thanks." My voice is hollow. The entire exchange takes less than twenty minutes before I am on my way. I locate the elevator and stab the cold, round button. When I step on, I ask if someone could press the lobby. I don't have proof. Without proof, I don't have anything.

I call Jess as soon as my feet hit the pavement.

"Where are you? My search was a bust. Every single mother has her baby with her . . . I just don't know what to tell you, Bec."

"The machine is broken."

She's silent on the other end of the line. "What do you mean?"

"They tried to scan him, but it didn't work. Apparently, there's a recall or something." Hysteria creeps into my voice, but I tamp it down.

Jess takes a breath. "Okay, don't panic. Do you want me to drive you to Prentice?"

"Same issue."

"I still think you should call them. Do you want me to call them?"

"Would you?"

"Yes. Just stay in front of the hospital and I'll be right there."

I nod, hang up, and breathe. I call Jake, but it goes straight to voice mail. I suddenly realize I might not be talking to Jake for days, depending on the case he's working. He could be undercover, he could get shot, or worse. The thought makes me flinch. I leave him a message.

I sit on the grass beside the stroller and edge back against the brick wall. I drop my head into my hands and think about Jackson. The baby fusses on my chest, and I lightly rock him and hum a lullaby. A few minutes later, Jess arrives. "You okay?"

I smear away my tears. "Did you talk to Prentice?"

She sits beside me. "I did. They don't have any machines either. I told them it was an emergency. They're doing what they can."

"I just don't understand why this is happening."

"Have you heard from Jake?" Jess asks.

"No." What I really mean is: *I'm on my own.* For the first time in my life, I'm truly on my own.

"What should we do?"

"I'm not sure." Every movie, book, or TV show says I should let the cops handle this. Authority figures handle cases. Mothers and fathers sit in rooms, being questioned, with their hands tied. Not me. Not today. "I still want to go to that parade."

Jess checks the time. "It doesn't start for another couple of hours."

I pull myself to standing. "Then I'm going to research these machines and harass every hospital within a fifty-mile radius until I can find one."

"Want me to help?" Jess asks.

"No. Be with your family. I'll call you about the parade, okay?" I say good-bye to Jess and check my phone on the way. I've been so consumed, I didn't even realize I'd missed calls. I scold myself for being so careless. What if someone has information about Jackson? I listen to my messages while I walk and wince when I realize I missed Savi's cello lesson.

"Shit." I fire off an apologetic text and tell Crystal an emergency came up, but I'll call her later. I feel horrible bailing on Savi. I know, more than anyone, how important consistency is for her right now.

At home, I check the mail and head inside. Such ordinary movements—checking the mail, unlocking the door, disarming the alarm—when an entire world of inner turmoil lurks beneath the surface.

I shut and lock the door. The house is too quiet. I stand in the middle of the foyer. The baby fusses, and I shush and rock him. "Are you hungry?" I grab a bottle, feed him, change his clothes, and put him down for a nap. Jackson's noise machine seems to work wonders, and he's out in minutes.

Drained, I check the time on my watch. It's already noon. Noon! Jackson has been gone a full twenty-four hours. So where is the Amber Alert? Where's the neighborhood notification, the support I know this community would put forth if they only knew?

I do a little digging on the technology for the digital scans, but the doctor was right: no other hospital in the vicinity uses it. I make call after call and hit a dead end every time.

I bring up a new browser and open Facebook. My fingers itch to post something on the Elmhurst Moms page. I know Jake said not to do it, but I literally can't sit here with my hands tied. I'm just creating a post when the doorbell rings.

"I didn't think you should be alone." Jess pushes into the house and thrusts a to-go cup of coffee in my hands. "Drink this. Then we are coming up with a plan." She moves past me into the kitchen. I cradle the steamy drink and follow.

"If Jackson really is out there somewhere, we're not waiting on the police—or anyone else—to find him. If this were Baxter . . ." Her voice fades. "Suffice it to say I'm here to help, okay? You're not alone."

Her words loosen the gigantic weight in my chest. Tears spring to my eyes, but I clear my throat.

Stay focused.

"I just wish there was something I could actually do."

"There is." Jess slides my computer toward her, and her fingers expertly traverse over the keys. "We're going to make up a missing-person flyer. I know, I know—super old-school. But this community talks. If someone local is behind this, we'll figure this out. Do you have a photos folder? We need a clear shot of Jackson, preferably in the last week or two."

I direct Jess to the proper folder and trust her judgment. Even if we don't do anything with the flyers, it will make me feel better. It's proactive.

An hour later, we've printed fifty copies. I've woken the baby, strapped him in the carrier, and he instantly settles—already used to me. I make a call before we head to the parade—not to Jake, but to Officer Toby.

"Toby." His voice is clipped.

"Hi, this is Rebecca Gray. I'm just checking in."

He sighs. "Mrs.—Rebecca," he corrects himself. "Like I said, we'll call you once we have further information."

I know Jess has already given her statement, but who else have they talked to? I fill him in on the scan.

"Keep me posted," he says noncommittally.

"Can you issue the Amber Alert?"

He's silent. "Not yet." He doesn't elaborate.

"What more do you need?"

"Look, Rebecca. I'm under strict orders from the chief. We're doing our best. Once we have something concrete, I'll let you know. Keep your phone on." He ends the call and I grip the cell in my hand, shocked.

"I bet even if I had the footprint, he still wouldn't believe me."

"He's just doing his job," Jess says. "You know how many whack jobs they probably see every day? They have to go by the book. But"—she straightens the stack of flyers—"we don't. Not yet anyway. Ready?"

I nod, lock up, and reset the alarm. She's right. We can't rely on the police. Finding Jackson is up to me.

Silently, we walk to the parade.

22

BEC

⠃⠑⠉

DOWNTOWN ELMHURST IS MANIC. JESS USHERS ME TO THE EDGE OF A sidewalk. "Sure you don't want to use the cane?"

I shake my head. "It will just slow us both down."

We stand on the precipice of the action while she scans the crowd. "I'm pretty sure all of Elmhurst might be here," she says. She takes a deep breath. "Sure you're up for this?"

I nod. In order for Jackson to be found, I have to spread the word.

Excited bodies consume every available inch of space. Expensive perfume, sizzling meat, and funnel cakes smack my senses, and despite the moment, I'm shuttled back to my own childhood. My parents lived for days like these, when the few city blocks jammed with bodies and booths, and children were free to roam without fear of street traffic. I cling to those memories—a girl in a dress with an ice cream cone— watching a parade from my father's shoulders, or buying myself a beautiful necklace with allowance gained from raking leaves. Watching my mother and father hold hands or kiss. Emotion gathers in my chest—for my parents, for never being able to do this with Chris, for my sweet boy.

"You okay?"

"Fine." I compose myself. Jess helps me step onto York Street. I anchor my cane in my fist, as though it can bring me protection. "Don't let go," I warn.

She hugs my elbow tighter to her rib cage. "No chance."

I extend my free arm. "Give me some."

She hands me a stack as we navigate to the center of the street. The papers shake in my hand, and I falter. *Do I say something as I hand them out?*

"Please keep your eye out," I hear myself saying to strangers. "Have you seen this boy?" People bypass without taking any. I wave them in front of me as though I'm a panhandler shaking a cup for change. The baby fusses in his carrier, and I attempt to shush him, but he kicks into high gear and screams so loudly, the flyers slip from my fingers and flutter away in the wind.

"Oh!" I yell, but Jess grips my arm.

"I'll get them. Come with me." She leads me to a bench. "Just take care of him. I'll hand them out." She turns back, stops. "Stay here, okay?"

I unlatch the baby and rock him, then transition him to a football hold, his limbs draped and dangling around my forearm. He quiets marginally until I flip him over and he roots around my chest. My body responds, but I can't feed a baby who's not mine in public. I try and distract him, but he grows more desperate. I wick the sweat from my forehead, willing Jess to come back. I just need to get home. This is too much.

The happy cries of the neighborhood intensify around me until tears slip down my cheeks. What I wouldn't give for a normal day— just *one*. A sob flies out of my mouth, and before I know it, I begin to cry louder than the baby. I'm sure passersby are staring, but I can't seem to stop. I drop my head toward my knees, the baby firmly against my chest.

"Okay, okay, it's okay." Jess's arms are around me. I shake her off, the baby still in my arms, and move a few feet away.

"Get me out of here." My voice is a whisper. "I need to get out of here. I can't . . . it's too much. I just want Jackson."

"Hey, I know. Come here. Let's get you home." She helps fit him back into the carrier. Her free arm is firmly around me. Finally, I collapse against her.

"I'm so tired," I say. "So tired."

"I know." Jess's voice isn't sarcastic, happy, or full of disbelief. In it, I hear only empathy.

She believes me. This small thing suddenly feels so big. As we leave the parade, the street grows eerily quiet. My cell cuts through the silence, and I jump.

I remove the phone from my pocket and show Jess the screen.

"It's Jake," Jess says, breathless.

I swipe to answer.

"Rebecca." His voice is certain.

Everything in me charges to attention. I hold my breath, wait.

"I've got something."

23

CRYSTAL

⠠⠉⠗⠽⠎⠞⠁⠇

CRYSTAL AND SAVI WALK PARALLEL TO THE PARADE, WHICH IS ALREADY IN full swing.

"Look at this." Crystal can't help but smile. "It's like stepping back in time."

Savi crunches the end of her ice cream cone and wipes a hand across her lips. "There are so many people."

The parade drifts by. The local high school marching band blows their horns slightly off tune. She claps and assesses the crowd. There are so many neighbors she hasn't yet met, so many fun things they need to do.

"Hey! Crystal, right?"

Crystal turns to find a familiar-looking woman, but she can't remember her name.

The petite blonde motions to her chest. "Beth," she says. "A friend of Jess and Bec's?"

"Yes, right. Good to see you."

Beth motions toward Savi. "Is this your daughter?" Beth leans forward and smacks her hands against her thighs like she's talking to a five-year-old. "I'm Beth." She extends her hand and Savi reaches a palm, sticky with ice cream, into hers and pumps it up and down in a firm motion like she's been taught.

"I'm Savi," she says. "Nice to meet you."

"That's quite a handshake you have there, Savi." Beth extricates her hand and inconspicuously wipes it on her yoga pants.

Crystal sighs and turns to Savi. "Savi, give it back."

Savi looks up at her innocently, her expression pleased. "Give what back?"

Crystal holds out her hand. Savi rolls her eyes and places Beth's watch in Crystal's hand.

"What in the . . . ?" Beth touches her bare wrist. "How did you do that?"

Savi displays both hands, still sticky with chocolate, and waves her fingers. "Magic."

"Well that's quite the talent you have," Beth says as she clasps her watch.

Crystal searches for Beth's baby . . . Trevor, if she's remembering right. Bec has filled her in on the attachment parenting thing. She looks at her, confused. "Where's your little one?"

Something flashes across Beth's face, then vanishes. "Oh, he's at home. I didn't want to subject him to all the noise." She looks between them. "Are you meeting Bec?"

Crystal shakes her head. "I haven't heard from her, actually. Have you?"

"Not today." Beth dabs her forehead. "Hot, huh?" She turns toward the parade and waves at someone. "I'm going to meet up with some friends, but it was great to see you! And you, Savi. I've got my eyes on you." Beth motions to her own eyes and then at Savi. She squeezes Crystal's forearm and then bounds off down the street to join a fit group of women in matching yoga pants. They all carry lattes. Crystal watches their easy banter and longs for the same. How long has it been since she's belonged to a group? Since she's met up on a weekend to grab brunch and just enjoy the company of other women?

She brushes aside the pointless thoughts and turns to Savi. Except Savi isn't there.

"Savi?" Fear constricts her breathing. "Sav?" She scans the street left to right, but there's no sign of her. She steps off the curb as the last of the parade rushes by. Suddenly, everything's too loud. She attempts to get her bearings. She turned away for what—maybe a minute? She searches the stalls around her, full of trinkets and local finds. Savi is good at hiding, but she wouldn't just run off in a parade unless there was a reason.

Crystal reads the names of the shops across the street. What could have caught Savi's eye? That's when she sees it: the music shop on the corner. Without paying attention, she charges through the middle of the street, ramming into a tuba player who almost loses his balance. His feathered hat goes flying and she stoops to pick it up. "Sorry!" she yells behind her.

She yanks open the door and spots the back of Savi's head before the door even closes behind her. She calms herself—*it's all okay, she's okay*—before laying into her daughter. Savi is pushing limits lately—the hair, the fire—but running off is never okay. Crystal is still her mother. There are still rules, even in grief.

"Savi Turner, what do you think you're doing?"

Savi pivots, her eyes wide and seemingly innocent. Smeared chocolate sticks to the corners of her mouth, making her appear younger than ten. Her hand hovers above a shiny cello. "I wanted to look at the instruments."

"I understand that, but you should have asked. You do not run off in a crowd of people. What if I couldn't find you?" She thinks about scaring the shit out of her with kidnapper stories or missing child statistics.

Savi shrugs. "You found me, didn't you?" She turns back to the cellos. "I want a new cello."

That's it. Crystal grabs Savi's elbow, ignoring the owner's inquisitive stare, and steers her toward the open door and onto the sidewalk. "Listen to me, young lady." She shakes her arm. "I am still your mother and there are rules to follow. Do you understand me? I don't know what's gotten into you lately, but you are not allowed to act this way."

Savi peers at her shoes, and Crystal gives her another tentative shake.

"Did you hear me?"

Her head lifts and tears threaten to spill. "I just want to feel *normal*." The words are tiny, but the effect is immediate.

Crystal releases her arm. The anger evaporates. She gathers her daughter into her arms. "Oh, sweetie. I know." The festival crescendos, people sidestepping around them. "I know you do," she murmurs in Savi's hair. She's been in such a rush to feel better herself that she didn't realize she might be rushing Savi too. Of course her daughter is going to act out. Of course she's going to be upset. It's been *months* since the accident, not years.

"Do you want to go home?" She holds her daughter at arm's length.

Savi swipes a hand over her nose and shakes her head. "Can we stay?"

"Of course." She looks around at all the booths and brightly decorated tables. She spots a short line for face painting. Savi sees it at the same time.

A peace offering. "Face painting?" When Savi was little, she and Paul used to wait in endless lines to get Savi's face painted. After they'd shell out the money, Savi would sweat or wipe all the makeup off in less time than it had taken for the artist to paint it. It was their running joke every time they went to a carnival or festival. Avoid the face painting station! They'd each distract Savi so she'd never see the booths. Suddenly, the need for Paul wedges into her heart. She hasn't thought about them in happier times in so long. It's always him after he changed, him after he betrayed her, him after he died.

Crystal extends her hand and Savi takes it to walk toward the booth. On the way, she makes some mental notes to bring up at her next session with Dr. Gibbons.

"Isn't that Ms. Rebecca?" Savi sniffs and points across the street at a woman rushing away.

Crystal lifts her sunglasses and squints. "I don't think so." The woman disappears from sight.

"Can you call her so we can have another lesson soon?"

"I will."

Savi diverts her attention back to the face painting and the many options on the cardboard stand. "I want a tiger!"

Crystal glances at her phone again and sees two missed calls from Pam and a short text from Rebecca, but it's cryptic. She suppresses the urge to immediately call her back. Rebecca will call when she can. She doesn't want to come off as needy or desperate.

"Look, Mom." Savi lifts her hands and roars. "I'm going to be a tiger." Savi's face has already been painted a bright orange with a giant dirty makeup sponge.

"Vicious." Crystal laughs.

Savi closes her eyes and lets the artist continue.

Crystal makes polite conversation with the girl and glances over her shoulder, to where Savi thought she saw Rebecca. But no one is there.

Only shadows from the trees.

24

BEC

⠏⠗⠑⠎⠎⠥⠗⠑

I PUT JAKE ON SPEAKER. MY HANDS SHAKE AS I AWAIT HIS NEWS.

"Alright, so there's a nearby museum that has a surveillance camera. I've requested the tapes, which should give us a pretty clear shot of the park and maybe even show us what happened. I'm also going to check street cameras."

"That's good," Jess offers. "When do you get the footage?"

"Not sure. Working on it."

Bated breath drains from my lungs. "Did you get my voice mail about the footprint?"

"I did. I'm looking into that as well. Maybe another hospital we can try outside the area, but it looks like a company issue, not a hospital one."

I tell him about my calls to the other hospitals and the flyers, even though Jess slaps me on the arm.

"Rebecca." His disappointment is swift. "You can't do things like that. There's a reason we don't put out an immediate blast. It's strategic. You could have just compromised this case."

"I had to do something," I say.

"I know you feel that way, but that's not helping." Something muffles his voice, then he's back on. "Look, I'm on a pretty intense case, but I'll keep you updated. Keep your phone on."

I look toward Jess. "Now what?"

"We do what he says. Keep your phone on. We'll keep hunting on Facebook. We might not know where your kid is, but we can try and find out who this one belongs to. I'll look at all the forums, photos of women in the area with their babies. See if we can do some digging."

I nod. The baby's cry stalks the charged silence, and we keep walking to placate him. I ignore the part of me screaming that these early hours are critical. And here I am, walking home from a parade, taking care of another baby like I don't have a care in the world.

Coward.

"Rebecca! Jess!"

We both turn. Beth trots up to us, breathless. "Hey! Were you just at the parade? We had a huge group of moms there. All without the kiddos, for a change." She pauses. "You're a brave soul, Bec. Did all that noise not bother Jackson?"

Though I can't see Jess, I know a look passes between us. How much do I say? I know Beth well enough to realize she's a perpetual gossip.

"We're actually just heading back now because Jackson's so exhausted. Coffee this week?" Jess gently ushers me in the opposite direction. Suddenly, I'm so deflated, I can barely stand.

"Wait, what's going on?" Beth's bubbly persona drops. "Did something happen?"

I turn to her. "Why would you ask that?"

"Because you both look like shit. No offense. What's up?"

I dab my tearstained cheeks, desperate to tell someone, but then I think of what Jake said. I remember so many days of brutal cases when Jake would come home, crack a beer, and wear that glazed look that said: *you can't possibly understand this.* He was never allowed to talk about his cases, but he never shut me out either. He was one of those rare breeds who could separate work from home. I'd never forgotten that—all the many kindnesses he'd shown me without even being aware of it. The least I can do is obey his wishes now. Before I can speak or Jess can concoct some story, the baby starts crying.

"Whoa, the baby who never cries is crying." There's almost glee in Beth's voice. "I guess he is human after all."

I want to twist him around to face her, to ask her if he looks different. Instead, I walk away to bounce him while she and Jess talk. I can't possibly explain myself. How can I? No one can grasp the gravity of this situation, especially if it appears I'm just out for a stroll at the parade with my child.

"Let's go," Jess whispers.

"What about Beth?"

She stops. "Wait. I knew something seemed different about her."

"What do you mean?" I ask.

"Trevor wasn't with her. I wonder if she finally got a nanny or something."

"Trevor's not with her?" I ask, surprised. I've never been around Beth when that baby wasn't glued to her. We continue walking, but I glance over my shoulder.

Where is Trevor?

I crane my neck to witness the hazy canvas of my world and turn back to keep focused on my steps. It's not like I can see if she's still there, but the hairs prick to attention on the back of my neck.

I can feel her watching us.

25

BEC

⠃⠑⠉

arms—literally. He jerks me into a tight hug and crushes me so hard, my back cracks.

"Easy, babe. There are bones in there," Jess reminds him. She takes the baby from me and disappears to get both boys situated in the nursery.

"Drink?" he offers.

I shake my head but walk to the kitchen anyway. I reach for the bar and sit on an available stool.

"Man, Bec. I don't even know what to say."

"I just feel like no one is *doing* anything." I rip my hands through my hair. "Don't communities like this rally together with signs and go knocking on doors or something?"

"When the police say you can, sure." He pours me a glass and slides it over. "Your friend Jake—does he have any leads?"

I shake my head. "Not yet. He's working a case right now so he can't give it his full attention, but he's looking into surveillance cameras. And Officer Toby, who was at your party, is helping too."

"Toby's good police."

I know he's spent a lot of time working cases with local cops, since it's a close-knit community and he's the only criminal defense attorney in town. I rotate the glass in my hand. "Let me ask you a question. You know criminal behavior. Take me through this. What would be someone's motive?"

"Plenty of reasons. One parent or relative wants custody or guardianship. In your case, this doesn't make sense, of course, because there's another child involved."

"This isn't an act done by a relative." My mother floats to mind. If she were here, she'd go to the ends of the earth to bring Jackson back. If she were here, he wouldn't have gone missing in the first place. I smack away that loss and focus on this one. This is the one I have to get through. This is the one to survive. "What about a stranger's motivation?"

He sighs. "Where do I begin? Extortion, ransom, legal adoption, sex trafficking. The list is endless."

He must register the horrified look on my face because he quickly backtracks.

"Those are just the typical reasons someone would take a child. I have to say though, babies aren't as common. And to leave another child in his place?" I hear him scratch his head. "That's a new one for me. Probably why Elmhurst PD is a bit slow to start. They may not have seen it before. Chief Holbrook is notoriously—"

"Conservative. Yes, I've heard." I groan and drop my head in my hands. "Or they just don't believe me and are biding their time until this all blows over."

"It's possible." He takes a swallow of the brandy he's poured.

Jess enters the kitchen and pulls another glass down. "What are we talking about?"

"Chief Holbrook."

"Pussy," Jess says. Her foul mouth warrants a reprimand from Rob. "Don't say that about the chief."

"What? It's true. He's so concerned with Elmhurst's reputation that he overlooks most things."

I almost remind her that she's overlooking her own feelings to help me, but refrain.

"We need to know whose kid this is," she continues. Jess situates her laptop on the island.

"What are you going to do, Google 'Elmhurst babies' and hope he turns up?" Rob asks.

"What do you think Facebook is for?"

"Not that."

"Okay, genius. Do you have a better idea?"

"This is so ridiculous," I say.

The two of them stop bickering. "What is?" Jess asks.

"That we're sitting here, in your kitchen, on a laptop, when someone has Jackson." My voice shakes, but I center it. "How do parents just sit and wait? No, I can't do this." I slip off the stool and grab my purse.

"Rebecca, what are you doing?"

"I'm going for a walk to clear my head, okay?" I head upstairs to the nursery, grab the baby, and strap him in.

"I'll be quick," I call to them in the kitchen and then retrace my steps toward the front door, unfold my cane, and hurry down the porch steps before they can stop me. Where to?

I falter on the sidewalk. I could go home and wait. I could take the Metra into Chicago, bang on Jake's door, and demand he help me instead of his unit. I could go to the Elmhurst police station and beg Officer Toby to just issue the damn Amber Alert. I could call Dr. Gibbons and ask for an emergency session. I could paste flyers throughout the entire neighborhood, get a band of mothers together, and go door-to-door until I find Jackson.

The baby coos on my chest and yawns, and I reach down and automatically kiss the top of his head. "What should I do?" I whisper.

"Bec!" Jess swiftly approaches, her feet pounding pavement. "Rob is on the phone with Toby right now."

"Can he get the Amber Alert issued?"

"He's trying." She hooks an arm around me to guide me back, but I pull away. "Come inside," she insists.

I waver on her front porch—if I go inside, I'm waiting on the police. If I go on my own, I'm what? Walking in circles? The impatience sears my brain, but I do as I'm told because I can't think of a better option.

Jess holds the door for me. I step inside. Rob's booming voice expands through the entire kitchen. I sit on the sofa, my fingers digging into the cushion. After a few interminable minutes, he appears.

"Let's go," he says. "We're heading to the station."

26

CRYSTAL

⠠⠉⠗⠽⠎⠞⠁⠇

BY THE TIME THEY'RE DONE WITH THE PARADE AND BACK AT HOME, CRYSTAL'S legs ache, and they are both sweaty. "Can I go play?" Savi asks before they're even inside.

"Of course." Crystal shuts the door and glances at the empty living room. They haven't talked much about the fire, but now that Paul's boxes are gone, she has to admit the room feels better.

Cleansed.

Crystal checks her phone again like an obsessive teen waiting to hear back from a love interest, but there's nothing new from Rebecca. She wants to know what's going on, but she also doesn't want to bother her if she needs space. She remembers those dark days—the days where you don't want to talk to anyone. She still has them.

There's also a new text from Pam that says she's on her way over. Good. That will give her some time to run errands and get on with her day.

The music begins, and though it is now as familiar to her as breathing, she still revels in it. Crystal imagines Savi up there with her smeared tiger paint, window open, totally in the zone. Paul didn't get to see the depth of his daughter's talent. He'd only attended a few recitals these last few years, always so busy with work. Because he was a no-show on more than one occasion, Crystal made it a point to show up no matter what. She's never missed a single performance. Again, the terror of so much solo responsibility bears down.

What if you make promises you can't keep?

The bow stops, and Crystal waits. The unexpected silence startles her, and her heartbeat quickens.

"Crystal?" Pam lets herself in. Dust particles float around her head. *Jesus. When was the last time I vacuumed?*

"Sorry I didn't call you back. We were at the parade."

"You were! When?" Pam sets down her bag.

"Just a little while ago." Crystal stares at Pam distractedly. The house is too quiet. Everything is too quiet. "Everything good?"

Pam offers a tentative smile. "Yes. How about here? Savi okay?"

"Hi." Savi appears around the corner and waves her bow in the air.

"Hey, you. I brought you something." Pam turns her attention to Savi.

Another peace offering, Crystal thinks. Pam extracts something big and bulky from her bag. "I saw you eyeing this the last time we were out."

"Yay!" Savi rips it from Pam's hands.

"What is it?" Crystal asks.

"It's a magic kit with a disappearing cloak!" She hugs Pam around the middle. "Thank you!" She runs back upstairs to tear into the kit.

"You shouldn't have done that," Crystal says. She doesn't remind Pam that presents will only reinforce bad behavior.

Pam shifts uncomfortably. "Look, I'm so sorry things got so messed up. I promise we're turning over a new leaf."

Crystal waits for more, but Pam doesn't elaborate. The silence roars through her ears. Her phone slices through the tension. "Sorry, I've been expecting this call." She steps onto the front porch and answers. "Bec? Are you okay?"

There's only rustling on the other end. She looks at the phone as if that will give her an answer and tries again. "Bec? Can you hear me?" Bec's voice muffles in the background, and Crystal realizes she must have accidentally called her. She listens for a few minutes, then hangs up. At least she's okay.

Inside, Pam has already disappeared. She walks up the spiral staircase. In Savi's room, Savi excitedly takes Pam through her latest magic trick. Pam *oohs* and *ahhs* in all the right places. To her relief, Savi doesn't seem agitated, annoyed, or frustrated. Maybe it's the boxes being removed. Maybe it's the fact that she was finally honest with Crystal about wanting to feel better. Talking helps. Maybe it's . . . She walks down the hall as snapshots corkscrew her conscience. Paul. The crash. What came after.

She shuts the heavy door and collapses on the floor. The images come. The more she pushes them away, the more they close in. She blinks. There's Paul, at the end of the aisle, waiting for her. She remembers the giddy swell in her chest of being a carefree, young bride. Then the day Savi was born and Paul's tears of happiness. Their first house outside of Chicago with the wraparound porch and duck pond . . . a house she thought they'd grow old in. But as Savi grew up, they grew apart. She was the idiot wife who truly had missed all the signs: how he'd carry his phone with him wherever he went. The made-up work events. The stories that every clichéd husband told, and yet she *really* hadn't known. She'd been too consumed with Savi, preschool, violin lessons, then cello, and reconstructing her interior design career from a years-long gap.

She rolls to her back and blinks at the ceiling. The first day of Savi's kindergarten, Paul had called from a work trip. She'd been prepared to ask him if he'd lost his job or had some secret gambling addiction she hadn't known about. Instead, he shocked her with his confession. He said that name—*Evelyn*—and everything unraveled quickly after that. What he'd been hiding. What she didn't want to hear.

"No." Her answer was clear. "We have a daughter. We have a life. No. You can't do this."

"It's not a request, Crys."

She bristled that he could use her nickname at a time like that. She sorted through their recent issues: finances, business, the logistics of parenthood, work stress, their shitty sex life. She knew divorce wasn't a novelty, but was it foolish to think they really *would* stay together for the long haul? Not because they were madly in love anymore—she was no longer a young, naïve bride—but because they needed each other to keep Savi's little ship running smoothly. They weren't just husband and wife. They were parents. And parents needed to stick together, because she couldn't do it alone. And neither could he. But now he wanted to insert someone into their lives, someone who didn't belong.

No.

Again his statement slammed into her with enough force to knock the phone from her hand. She stared at her cell on the carpet, thankful that the screen hadn't shattered. She picked it up. "I said no." Her tone was firm, even though her mind spun wickedly. Over the years, she'd wondered which women could possibly insert a crack into their family dynamic: his secretary. Women from work. Strangers from the gym. Her friends. But he'd chosen someone else.

Evelyn.

"She needs me," he said.

She inhaled so sharply, she choked. "*We* need you." It was Evelyn or them. He had to choose.

"Crys, I'm sorry, I . . ."

Her blood ran cold. Her head hurt. Fuck that. It wasn't her head; it was her heart. She didn't give him a chance to continue. Though he came home that night at seven on the dot, like usual, in a single moment, she went from loving her husband to not trusting him. She'd always balked when women told her similar stories—how they could kiss their husbands one day and then look at them like strangers the next.

At her age, she'd witnessed most of her friends go through divorces, custody battles, and nasty alimony arrangements. Now, despite her best efforts, she feared she would become one of them.

Crystal closes her eyes, remembering. *Guilt.* If only she'd put her foot down. Said no and meant it. He'd still be alive. He'd still be with them.

The door opens behind her and she moves out of the way.

"Oh, sorry. I didn't know where you were. Are you okay?" Pam drops to her knees, her face flushed.

Crystal prepares the usual statement—"Yes, I'm okay"—but for some reason, the words get stuck. She's tired of lying. She's tired of hiding the truth. She sits up and then sags against this young woman who does what she's told but can't possibly grasp the enormity of what's on Crystal's plate. All she has to prove. All she has to get through. All she has to hide.

"I know it has to be hard, but it's getting better. It's all getting better," Pam affirms.

Crystal doesn't know exactly what she's talking about, but she chooses to believe her. It's all getting better because it has to.

They've already been through worse and survived. That's something. She wipes her eyes and pulls away, embarrassed. Pam's curly red hair smells like strawberries. This close, she can see ill-placed makeup caked under a set of hazel eyes. She wants to demand she go home and scrub her face. She's too young and pretty for makeup. She doesn't need it.

"I'm sorry. I think I'm just going to go rest for a bit. Is that okay?"

"Of course." Pam's face remains kind, open, but she can tell she wants to say something more. Crystal realizes her mistake. Pam has now seen her at her worst. She has lost a bit of her power as the employer, but she can't think about that now.

Crystal steps across the hall to her room and shuts the door. She silences her phone, flips on her fan, and crawls under the covers, fully clothed. Pam fusses in the next room then heads down the hall and says something to Savi, probably some nicer version of "Don't bother your mother for a while."

She waits for sleep. Finally, the whirring of the fan takes her away, but in the back of her mind, a warning scratches:

The truth is closing in.

27

BEC

⠠⠃⠑⠉⠀⠀⠀

NIGHT HAS FALLEN.

I find myself at the local precinct for the second time. They don't have a suspect. They don't have the make or model of a getaway car. They don't have a true physical description of the supposed kidnapper.

Women are called like cattle into the interrogation room. Not women. My close friends: Jess and Beth. Acquaintances: Ramona, Lanie, Barbara, Sandra. I wonder why Crystal isn't here and then remember it's all the women from the park they want to talk to first. They huddle and wait their turns, entering and exiting the sterile room wordlessly. I can tell they don't know what to say. Neither do I. I'm normally so conditioned to fill silences to make others feel comfortable.

Not today.

I squeeze my eyes shut. The last police station I'd visited was in Chicago after Chris died. I'd come in to collect his belongings and to decide if I would press charges against the man who hit him. I wanted to, but I didn't. The man hadn't been drunk, as I'd suspected. He was texting, and by the time he looked up, it was too late. His life was already ruined—he'd killed a man. I didn't want his money or for him to suffer a worse fate. I just wanted my husband back.

"Jessica Peters?"

"Be right back." Jess heads into the interrogation room, which makes space for another woman to sit and wait her turn. These women will decide Jackson's fate. How many have been back? Three? Four? I review my own behavior over the past months, weeks, days, hours. Would I believe me?

The baby relaxes against my chest, content. He's not mine. I remind myself that he will be given back, taken, or worse. I cup the back of his head. A few of the women whisper. I drop my hand.

"Rebecca?" The bench groans beneath the weight of a new person. It's Beth. "Can I see him?"

I twist his warm body toward her. Her inspection is quiet, thoughtful. "Are you sure . . ." Her sentence fades and with it, her certainty. "Bec, he looks exactly like Jackson." Her voice is smug, like her.

"But it's *not* Jackson." The words crack too loudly into the overrun station. It's as if the phones, conversation, and rampant dialogue in my head ceases with my son's name. No one will say his name but me.

It's *not* Jackson. *Not* my son. *Not* him.

"I'm sorry. I'm not trying to upset you," Beth explains.

"You're not." I pat the baby's back. "I don't expect anyone to get it . . . but I'm telling the truth. I am."

If I say it enough, they will believe me.

A few minutes later, the door opens. Jess files out and sinks into the chair.

"Beth?" Officer Toby is official, detached.

"How'd it go?" My voice is neutral as I turn toward Jess.

"You know how it goes. They ask stupid fucking questions, try to trip you up."

"Does it look . . ." *Good? Bad? Am I going to jail?*

"Not good, no."

My jaw settles. If my mother were here, she'd flip a damn table. If Chris were here . . . Chris makes me think of Jake. I haven't heard from him in hours. I sigh. I know Rob called in this favor, gathered all these women after word spread and the flyers were distributed, but it seems fruitless. None of these women *saw* anything. None of them believe me. Is Jake right? Is all of this doing more harm than good?

"Do you want me to stay with you tonight?"

I think of walking into my mother's house, alone. I think of putting this stranger baby to bed again in my son's crib and pretending it's all going to be okay in the morning. I've been running so hard for so long, but grief has found me. I'm caught.

Yes. The word burns at the back of my throat, but instead, I resist. I can't keep taking Jess away from her husband and child. "Thanks, but I'll be fine."

Jess sighs so loudly, the baby rouses. "What is it going to take?"

"For what?"

"For you to realize that help isn't a bad thing, Rebecca. You have people who care about you, but you push us all away. And now look what's happened. You want to be alone? Fine. Be alone." She huffs off, leaving me speechless. Jessica has never talked to me like that. Her words sting, partly because they're true. But she isn't me. It's so easy for her to say those things when she's surrounded by money, family, friends, her husband, her son.

After a few uncomfortable minutes, I wander to where Rob stands in the corner, in a heated debate with Jess. "Am I allowed to get some air?"

"Sure." He claps a hand on my shoulder. I step out of his grip, extend my cane, and head outside. I don't know what time it is. Eleven? Midnight?

Thirty-six hours missing.

I pace out front, a few people smoking cigarettes. I sidestep the stench, rake my fingers to clear the air, and walk in the same small grid on the sidewalk.

"Rebecca?" Officer Toby finally steps outside.

"What?"

"I'm sorry to keep you waiting," he says. "Listen, we've reviewed everything. Taken statements from your friends. We've accessed Jackson's footprint scan, but without a comparison I'm . . . I don't know how to say this, Rebecca, but I'm afraid we just can't issue the Amber Alert. We don't have enough evidence to build a case, and your friends . . ."

"My friends what?" I brace myself for the truth, the words I know but haven't said out loud. The words that will force me into a different path of action.

"They all believe you're mistaken." He says it as nicely as he can, I'll give him that.

"So what does that mean?"

"I just think we need to make sure you're thinking clearly—that you remember what actually happened. We're happy to get Social Services to take the baby for a few days, if need be."

I take a step back and clamp a hand over his back. "Social Services will not touch this baby."

"I'm not saying they will. It's just an option."

"That's not an option for me." I pace back and forth, then stop. "What now?"

"Jake is coming in. We'd like to interview you one more time, if that's alright. Then you can go for the night."

I nod and he heads back inside. A few minutes later, the women exit in a tangled, vibrating cluster of dramatic conversation. When they see me, their excited chatter ends. "Get some rest, Rebecca." Someone's voice I don't recognize says good night. I stand there, dumbstruck. My whole world has imploded while they get to go home to their friends, families, and overpriced houses.

I stand on the sidewalk for what feels like hours. I don't want to go inside. I don't want to go home. I don't want to go anywhere.

"Bec." Jake's arms climb around me before I can take a breath. "You okay?" He kisses the top of my head.

I reluctantly extricate myself from his arms and fill him in on what's happening. "Did you get the surveillance tapes?"

"Passed them to Toby a few hours ago. No clear shot of the park. Nothing suspicious or out of place. I'm sorry, Bec."

No evidence, no Amber Alert, no Jackson.

"Let's get this over with then," I say. We head back inside. I'm already drafting a new plan, one that has nothing to do with the police. It's not up to them anymore. It's up to me what happens next.

28

BEC

⠿⠀⠿⠀⠿⠀⠿⠀⠿⠀⠿⠀⠿⠀⠿

AFTER OFFICER TOBY ASKS ME A SET OF RIDICULOUS QUESTIONS AND
explains that after talking to the chief, they do want me to leave the
baby for the night, I storm outside for the second time. Jake eventually joins me. "I'm not leaving this baby here." I say it softly, but my
intent is clear. "Not until we know who he is." I hesitate. "He trusts
me. He does."

Jake scratches his neck. "Let me see what I can do, okay?"

I nod, those words *let me see what I can do* losing steam every passing
second. The closer he gets, the further away Jackson's return seems.
All the waiting, the questions, the protocol. When it's a human life,
shouldn't those types of rules go out the window?

Not when they think you're lying.

Again, the truth digs in its heels. That's why there's no Amber
Alert. Because they don't believe there's a crime. Outside, the baby
falls asleep on my chest. I sing him a lullaby and rub his back.

"Bec." After another few endless minutes, Jake's hand finds my
shoulder. "I'm so sorry, but you have to leave him here. Just overnight."

"Who says?"

"The state."

"No. He's not going into some crazy system. I'll never get him back
again. That's not happening."

I can tell he's calculating odds in his head, but so am I. "So what do you want to do?" He knows what I'm thinking by the way I look at him. "Bec . . ."

I exhale and let go of all this police nonsense. "I have you, right? I mean, as long as you can help me. I just can't . . ." I motion to the police station. "I can't hand him over. Like you said, if we can just figure out who he is, then I can find his parents. It could lead us to Jackson." I blink up at him, concocting a crystal-clear image in my head. "Even if you don't one hundred percent believe me, what if I'm right? Think about that, Jake. What if I'm right?" I tug on his sleeve like a child. "I have to do this. I can't waste any more time."

"Dammit, Rebecca." Finally, he speaks, and I know I've got him. I know he'll help. "You want to keep this baby for the night, then you're going to have to lie. You're going to have to say you were confused. You're basically going to have to hang yourself."

I nod. "I don't care." But I know the ramifications. I know what it will seem like to the community. But this is about more than the community. This is about getting Jackson back above all else—and the police not taking this baby away too.

"You realize Toby will see right through this," he adds.

"But he can't legally take him, right? If I'm claiming he's mine?"

"No, not legally." He slaps his palm against the automatic door button. "Come on, Dead Man Walking. Let's get you inside."

The door stalls then cranks open. On the walk to Toby's office, I rewrite my story. I'm a widow. I'm confused. I must have been mistaken.

"Toby?" Jake knocks on the door. "Rebecca has something she wants to say."

I open my mouth, but I'm not sure where to start. Do I just come right out and say it? I refrain from drumming my fingers on the desk. Air-conditioning pours in cold, recycled air from ceiling vents. The mood shifts in the room while he waits.

I channel every bit of high school drama I can remember and

rearrange my face to a look of sheer remorse. "I made a mistake." A stab of fear inserts itself right between my ribs. I lick my lips, swallow. I lightly touch the baby. "This is Jackson." The lie twists deeper. My voice is robotic, flat. "I think . . ." I look to Jake, this new plan concocted on the fly. "I think I just wanted attention. I just wanted to . . ."

"Wait." Toby's voice is tinged with skepticism. "Are you trying to say your son isn't missing now?"

No, no, no. Don't say it! My conscience rebels against my plan, but I close my eyes and nod. "I made a mistake."

Officer Toby is quiet, and for a panicked moment, I wonder if they're going to take the baby anyway. Lock me up for lying to authorities. He clears his throat. "Say no more." I imagine Toby lifting his hand. Instead of challenging me, relief replaces the skepticism. Relief to be through with this nonsense. Relief to go back to important matters that aren't make-believe. Relief to alert the chief that it's all been handled. "Look, none of us can imagine all that you've been through," Toby continues. "But I do think you should have a psych evaluation to make sure everything's good," he adds.

"Already on it. I'm taking her now." Jake speaks up before I can make an indignant retort. "I'm handling it from here. She'll get the help she needs. Toby." Fists pumping in a firm handshake signals the meeting is over.

We turn to leave, but Toby stops me. "I meant what I said when we first met. Let me know if you need anything."

I bite my lip so hard I'm afraid it might split. We are out of the station before I can change my mind about what I've just done.

"Jesus Christ," Jake mumbles. He smacks the automatic door and it opens into the steamy night.

"Now what?" I grab Jake's elbow in place of the cane.

"Now we get you home." There's a new tone in his voice—urgency, frustration, or fury—I can't tell. The walk is brisk, the hour late. It seems all my insomnia has prepared me for this very situation. Being "on" when everyone else is asleep.

At my door, I hand Jake the keys. The baby sleeps snugly against my chest.

"I'm just going to put him to bed," I whisper.

"Rebecca." Jake stops me. "What you said in there about wanting attention."

"Don't flatter yourself," I say. "I would never pull a stunt like that for your attention. I'd hope you know me better than that."

"No, that's not what I meant. I just wanted to make sure there wasn't any truth to that. I mean, I'd understand it, but I need to know."

"I'm going to pretend you didn't just say that." I take the stairs so he can't see the flame of my cheeks. At the nursery, I pause at the door. Though Jackson isn't here, his scent still fills the room. I unstrap the baby and gently lay him in the crib, sweeping my hands over his little body to make sure he's comfortable. I flick on the noise machine and get lost in the staticky roar.

My motherly instinct has kicked in for this child. It's been less than two days and already, I can't imagine him not here. The questions start up again—who would do this? What's wrong with this baby for someone to swap him?—but I stop myself. I fan my shirt and prepare to leave. My foot bumps into something. I reach down to retrieve a plush toy. "Eliot." I run my fingers over the mouse's nose and floppy feet.

I sink to the ground and come undone, this stuffed animal ripping me apart. Wherever Jackson is, he doesn't have me and he doesn't have his favorite toy. I place Eliot over my mouth and scream into his stuffed belly, my anguish muffled enough not to disturb the baby. How did Eliot get in the middle of the floor?

Once again, I retrace my steps the day of the swap. I got Jackson dressed. I put him in the stroller. I wheeled him to the park. But I'm missing something. I close my eyes and go over it again. I replay finding this baby upstairs, examining every inch of him to confirm he wasn't Jackson. How shocking their similarities and differences.

They were even both in onesies . . . I sit up straighter. That's it. His onesie.

I move toward the hamper in Jackson's closet. When I changed this baby, I remember thinking it odd that a onesie would have such a rough tag instead of one printed directly on the material, like Jackson's. I'm overly sensitive about materials and am careful to always cut Jackson's tags out. I rummage through the clothes until I'm sure I've found it. As if clutching a prize, my fingers find the tag. I stuff the entire onesie in my pocket and leave the door open as I hurry back downstairs.

"Jake!" I shake the dirty onesie in my fist. "The onesie this baby came home in. It's different than Jackson's."

He doesn't ask what I mean. He knows. "The tag. Jesus, could they make the print any smaller?" He mumbles to himself and strains to read.

"What does it say?" I ask impatiently.

"Have you ever heard of a store called Cornerstone?"

I try to remember all the shops in Elmhurst: Kie&Kate, Diana and Nicky Baby Clothing Boutique, Hazyl Boutique . . . but not Cornerstone. "I haven't. Which is good, right? It means it's not just a generic purchase from Target."

"It's something."

I slide my computer over to him in the kitchen and get us something to drink.

"Okay, we're going to have to narrow our search. That's a popular name." We try Cornerstone Kids, Cornerstone Clothing, Cornerstone Boutique, but there's nothing. We case Elmhurst online, but only a church pops up.

I drum my fingers on the table, the same movement I avoided at the police station just an hour before. "It's got to be somewhere close, right? What about Chicago?"

He types it in. "Just more churches and community centers. I'll call Pat." While he calls Pat, his go-to research guy, I obsessively check my phone again. Another text from Crystal. I hesitate. I want to talk to her and tell her what's going on, but I don't want to burden her. I send her a quick I'm okay, call you later text and wait for Jake to get off the phone.

As I stand in my kitchen, listening to his clipped conversation, I'm transported back to another time and place. Jake would often come to Elmhurst after my dad died. My mother was a capable woman, but she struggled with certain chores due to her heart condition.

Jake would wordlessly tackle her to-do list while Mom and I made dinner to reward him. We'd eat and then sit out on the patio to drink whiskey and talk. Sometimes we'd crash in my old room, making love quietly so as not to wake my mother. Back then, I couldn't imagine ever loving another man. Even now, I can't believe it was something as insignificant as distance that tore us apart.

How did we end up here?

"Okay, he's on it." Jake brings me back to the present.

I nod. "So what now?"

"Now we wait." He exhales. "Except that's not going to work for you, is it?" His hands find my shoulders and squeeze.

I shake my head. "If I wanted to wait, I would have done what Toby wanted."

"Roger that."

Instead of stepping away, I move into his arms. His hands hover, then slide lower and tighten on my lower back. I rest my head against his chest. His heart thumps beneath my ear and gains momentum. My fingers tighten instinctively and glide up and down his studded spine. My breath deepens. I tilt my face toward his.

"Rebecca." His voice grows husky.

In his arms, I want him to erase it all. My past. Chris. Jackson's disappearance. My mother. The truth. I just want to feel something other than this pain that threatens to destroy me at every turn. His fingers wander up my hips and ribs and hesitate on the outer curves of my breasts. My body goes limp as his fingers dance on my neck, then up to my jawline. My body pulses so hard it hurts.

"Please." The word is a demand. I close my eyes. His mouth moves closer. The memory of us resurfaces and grips me around the throat. I can't breathe, but I lean in.

His phone slices through our moment. He recedes and the mood shifts. The passion instantly drains from my body.

"Yep, got it. Thanks, man." He hangs up. "Got three hits on the kid's boutiques. Chicago's the closest. We'll go first thing?"

I nod. Hope surges. There will be a next step. Though he doesn't speak, I know the apology he's already forming in his head.

"Bec . . ."

"Don't." I straighten my clothes and attempt to calm my nerves. "I'm going to head up, okay? Let me know if you need anything."

His fingers encircle my wrist when I pass him. "Are we okay?"

I nod. The baby starts crying, and I extract my hand. "We're fine."

I remove a bottle from the refrigerator and climb the stairs to tend to a baby that's not mine. Downstairs is a man who was once mine and now isn't. And yet here we are, caught in a tangled web where we almost just kissed. Life keeps tricking and challenging me with its hardships, tragedy, and time. But grief doesn't stop a life. It doesn't cause the whole world to stand still with you, because there are still bills to pay, friendships to keep, and relationships to forge. There's school, work, grocery shopping, and health crises. Emergencies. More loss, even when you think you can't possibly bear it.

I pick up the baby, sit in the rocking chair, and feed him from the bottle. Jackson used to be my reprieve from all the heaviness of life. Even in just a few short months, I could sit still with him in this chair—just the two of us—and we were independent of our losses. He wasn't a son without a father. I wasn't a wife without a husband. We were just mother and son, bonded.

I adjust the bottle and the baby's head. My heart breaks for this little unwanted boy. I check his temperature again, but his forehead is cool, his breathing already better than it was. It makes me feel good—however ridiculous—to know that I can take care of someone who needs it.

I pause mid-rock and wonder: who will ever take care of me?

You will. The words are hard but true. My eyes snap open. Jess is right. Every time someone has attempted to help, I rebuff them or they disappear. Crystal pops into my head again. She's the only one who really gets this level of grief, who clings to it but then also has to let it go because life marches on regardless.

I reach into my pocket for my phone, but it isn't there. I must have left it downstairs. The baby works on draining the bottle. I sing to him. My voice is soft, but he seems to enjoy it, because he falls asleep while eating. I gently burp him and lay him back in the crib. Another tear slips down my cheek as I crank the mobile and step silently from the room. On the landing, I hesitate.

I know what will happen if I go downstairs. I take a step anyway. The wood groans. One drink. One touch. One kiss. Chris flashes through my mind, my amazing husband who will never again get to have a drink, touch, or kiss. My conscience surfaces. I can't. However much I want to, I can't. I retreat to the bedroom and sit on the edge of the bed, overcome with memories of Jake and Chris, all clashing for space in my brain.

I stare at the vast, dark space. I remember my first kiss with Jake, wild and unbridled, and my first kiss with Chris, sweet and unsuspecting. My brain dims. My eyes grow heavy but my mind isn't kind enough to let me sleep.

I think of the first motorcycle ride with Jake, slicing through the city streets and feeling on the brink of death. My first walk without my sight felt similar—every Chicago block offering an uncertain land mine just waiting to detonate. In one experience, my fingers had wrapped around Jake. In another, Chris. I'd needed something from both men—love and adventure from Jake, comfort and security from Chris. When had I stopped relying on myself? Why had I always relied on a man for help?

The questions trample my brain until I'm desperate for a break. But still, sleep eludes me. Sometime, hours later, when my memories are raw, the sun cracks through the blinds. I stand, shower, and prepare myself for the day ahead.

29

CRYSTAL

⠠⠉⠠⠗⠠⠽⠠⠎⠠⠞⠠⠁⠠⠇

SAVI SHAKES HER MOTHER AWAKE. "YOU SLEPT THE ENTIRE NIGHT. ARE YOU sick?"

"What?" Crystal rolls over and rubs her eyes. "What time is it?"

"Seven. You missed dinner and everything!" She bounds out of the room.

Crystal checks her phone. Pam had texted last night to say she'd stay the night and also that she was now downstairs making breakfast. Crystal rolls her eyes at the amount of emojis in one text.

She uses the extra time to shower, brush her teeth, and get dressed. She can't remember the last time she slept so long. What was that, twelve entire hours? Instead of feeling rested, she's groggy and desperate for coffee.

Downstairs, Savi and Pam laugh about something. Crystal wraps her damp hair into a topknot and pauses at the entrance to their sleek, white kitchen. Pam flips a piece of bacon and scoops some eggs onto a plate for Savi.

"Morning." Crystal slides behind her for a cup of coffee.

Pam turns, cheeks flushed. "Morning. Did you get good sleep?"

"I did. I'm sorry to have kept you overnight."

"Don't apologize." She waves the spatula in the air. "I was happy to help. Right, Savi? We braided each other's hair and watched a movie. It was awesome. So quiet."

Crystal bites her tongue. Pam is the oldest of four children and loves to feel needed. It's why Crystal hired her, but she doesn't want to blur the lines of Pam being Savi's buddy versus being paid to watch her. Especially with their recent string of issues. She clears her throat and takes a sip of coffee.

"Busy day today?" Pam asks cheerily.

Crystal checks her calendar and realizes she's supposed to start Bec's kitchen renovation tomorrow. Today is prep day. "Yes." She scrolls through her texts again and finds one from Bec that says she's okay and will call later. But she hasn't called. She wonders if she's forgotten about tomorrow.

"Savi and I already have our day planned, don't we?"

Crystal peers at them and waits for either of them to elaborate, but they don't. "Are you going to tell me what you're up to?"

"It's a secret." Savi giggles. "But it does involve magic!"

"Okay, Houdini. I'm going to finish getting ready," Crystal jokes.

Fifteen minutes later, she's laden with bags and materials for her meeting at Bec's. The contractor is set to meet at the house later today, but on the way, Crystal calls him to explain there might be a delay.

Bec's house is dark. She peers in one of the windows and then checks her watch. Bec should be here. She shoots her a text and decides to check Wilder.

At the park, she makes sure her supplies are locked in the trunk and does a quick loop. Once again, Crystal marvels at the fact that Bec does this so many days per week by herself. As an experiment, she closes her eyes and walks a few steps on the sidewalk. Just like on the stairs, her world tilts and she almost steps on the back of someone's shoe.

"Sorry." She apologizes to a bewildered mother who gives her a hostile stare. A leaf detaches and brushes her shoulder. The crunch is satisfying under her shoe. She can't wait to attend the fall festivals with Savi. Halloween is her daughter's favorite—the whole season, in fact. Carving pumpkins, dressing up, finding spooky activities—it's all part of the package as Savi's mom. She's been told that Elmhurst allows kids to run lawless through the streets. Neighbors transform their homes into makeshift haunted houses. Crystal appreciates the trustworthy nature of this town, but there's no way in hell she'd ever leave Savi alone to run through the neighborhood without her.

At the playground, she searches for Bec. Not here. She glances around for any familiar faces and sees a few women on the park benches. She hesitates. She doesn't want to seem creepy, but she's also just curious about her friend. Rebecca comes here almost every day. Surely, someone has seen her.

She takes a deep breath, feeling like a new kid at school, and approaches. "Hi." She offers a wave.

Two moms stop their conversation and look up. One bounces an infant on her knee and wipes his face with a wet wipe.

"Sorry to interrupt, but I was just wondering if either of you know Rebecca Gray?"

They look at her blankly.

"She's . . . blind." Her face heats at the admission, as though she's exposing her disability for some sort of benefit.

The woman smacks her friend on the arm. "That's her. That's who everyone's talking about."

Fear detonates like a bomb. "What do you mean?"

"Here." The other one reaches into a bag at her feet. A few bracelets slide down her wrist. She extracts a folded flyer and presses it into her hands. "These were being handed out yesterday. I also heard some other rumors, but you know how people talk."

Crystal slowly unfolds the paper. Jackson's face stares back with the title: HAVE YOU SEEN THIS BOY?

"Holy shit." Crystal's heart beats so fast, it clogs her ears with sound. She scans the flyer. There's not much information. Just facts about Jackson and when he was last seen. She lowers it. Is this a joke?

She thumbs back through their texts. There's no way this can be real. Rebecca would have called her. She wouldn't be so flippant in her texts. She wonders if this is a prank someone is playing on her. Maybe Rebecca got wind of it and is furious, embarrassed, or ashamed.

She interrupts the women on the bench, already deep in another conversation. "Sorry, but where did you get this?"

"At the parade yesterday. Two ladies were handing them out."

"I thought it was for free yoga." Her friend snorts.

"Has he been found?"

The one with the bracelets waves her arm. "Oh, no. It was a false alarm. The woman was mistaken. Everyone's talking about it. She thought her baby was missing or swapped or something, but then she changed her mind. I mean, she *is* blind, so . . ." She shrugs. "All babies look alike, right? Isn't that what they say?"

Crystal's face heats once again and she fans herself with the flyer. "Thanks." She turns and speed walks back to her car, starts it, and blasts the air-conditioning toward her flushed face. She voice dials Rebecca, this time leaving a serious message. "Rebecca. It's Crystal. I just saw the flyer. Tell me where you are. I want to help."

She ends the call and drums her fingers on the wheel. Who would know what's really going on? Jess?

She puts the car in gear and drives to Jess's house. Her heart breaks thinking that Rebecca didn't come to her first. But she understands. She probably thought she'd be bothering her. Both women hate to ask for help. *Well, you're going to get it whether you want it or not,* Crystal decides. Bec has done enough on her own. It's time to be there in the way she wishes someone had been there for her.

It's time to help her friend.

30

BEC

⠃⠑⠉

JAKE AND I ARRIVE IN CHICAGO AFTER A MADDENING RUSH-HOUR CRUSH.
The baby sleeps the whole way in Jackson's car seat. The store isn't
yet open, but Jake pulled some strings and the manager is getting
here early to let us in. We park on a side street and Jake feeds the
meter an exorbitant hourly rate with a credit card. "Chicago parking.
Taking over the world," he mutters.

I fit the baby into a sling and offer a tight-lipped smile. It's one of
the things I'm thankful for—not shuffling my car from place to place
in the city, though I would do that any day of the week if it meant I
could get behind the wheel again. He guides me toward the shop,
which is in Wicker Park.

City energy buds around us, even this early in the morning. It
brings me a sense of peace. No matter how long I stay away from the
city, it's always like coming home.

"Detective?" A hesitant voice approaches us. Male. Young. The
click of dress shoes on concrete.

"Thanks for meeting us, Dan."

"Sure." Dan shuffles keys and sticks one into the lock. He turns and
the dead bolt releases. "Come in." A few lights flip on, and I immediately smell cleaning supplies covered up by some expensive fragrance.

Since I can't see what I'm looking for, I extract the onesie. "I'm
trying to see if this onesie was bought here."

He tuts as he takes it from me and mumbles to himself. "Same name, but this isn't one of ours, I'm afraid. Let me just check to be sure." He rummages through a few racks and returns to the checkout area. "Nope. Not ours."

The disappointment is a swift kick in the gut. Another dead end.

"But," he adds and leads us to the computer. "I've seen this brand. Not necessarily for onesies, but they make children's clothing too." He types hurriedly and then cranes the screen toward Jake. It squeaks with the effort. "Were these stores on your list?"

Jake jots down the names and addresses and claps him on the back. "You did good, Dan. Thanks again for meeting us."

In less than five minutes, we're back on the street. "What did he say? What are the other stores?"

"They happen to be the two on our list," he says. "One in Oak Brook and one in Lake Geneva, Wisconsin."

I calculate the odds of finding this needle in a very large haystack. "So if we can narrow it down . . ."

"Then we can maybe trace it back to recent purchases, a sales receipt, and if we're lucky, a credit card. But that would mean pulling some major strings. No store manager is allowed to offer up that information."

I tighten my ponytail and drop my hands. "I feel like we're on a wild-goose chase."

"Because we are." Jake unlocks his car. The quick chirp of the alarm disables. He opens the door and helps with the baby. "But it's the little things that solve cases. Trust me."

I make sure the baby is secure and climb into the passenger seat. I rest my head against the headrest. I know he's right, but it seems like we're grasping at straws.

When Jake gets behind the wheel, I cringe from embarrassment. Here I am with one of Chicago's lead homicide detectives, chasing onesies in hopes of solving a case. This must be laughable for him. I almost tell him so as the car revs to life.

"Oak Brook? Or Lake Geneva?"

"Jake." I find his arm and rest my hand on it. "You don't have to do this. I know you have to work. Can't we just call them or scan a photo in? I feel like . . ." I scratch my head and point to an invisible solution beyond the windshield.

He twists in the driver's seat to look at me. "You feel like what?"

"I feel like you're just indulging me. Like you are in this with me but you might not really believe me. You might not *really* think this will lead anywhere." My insecurity is out, and I await his easy reassurance. But he's silent.

"Honesty?"

This used to be our thing. "Honesty?" we'd ask when either of us wasn't sure how to articulate something we wanted to say. We'd have to drop whatever we were doing to listen. They were our naked moments where the other person couldn't get defensive. It had pushed our relationship toward an amazing trajectory of honesty and openness. Even though we weren't together, I needed that from him now. I nod, afraid of what he's going to say but also somehow knowing.

"I'm not sure if I believe you."

The words hurt more than I'd anticipated. My eyes water, and I adjust my sunglasses and clear my throat to keep the tears at bay.

"I want to believe you. And the ex-boyfriend in me does believe you. You know that. I'd follow you to the ends of the earth—*would* have followed you," he quickly corrects. "But the cop in me says that the evidence just isn't there. There's too much that doesn't add up. There are so many things mounted against you, Bec, and it's not your fault. It's just fact. And I'm trained to look at facts."

"And the facts don't look good," I murmur. "I get it. I do." I form my next words carefully. "While I appreciate you agreeing to help, I'm not going to waste any more of your time, Jake. You have real cases to solve. I've pulled you away from your life enough." What I really mean is: *I will find another way.* What I can't do is spend one more minute with someone who doesn't really believe me. I don't want any favors. I don't want anyone's sympathy or pity. I want to find my son.

"You can't get rid of me that easily, Bec."

"Watch me." I open the door of the idling car and remove the baby from the back seat.

"What are you doing?"

"I'm going to go see Dr. Gibbons for an emergency therapy session," I say. "Maybe she can help." To confirm, I ramble off a manic voice text to see if she's free.

"And how will you get home?"

"Train."

"Rebecca." Jake kills the engine and gets out of the car. "You're not going anywhere without me." He grips my elbow and I yank it free.

"I want to be alone right now. I just need space."

He's confused. I can feel it. Last night, I begged him to help. I had him lie to a police officer. I almost kissed him and then pretended it was all fine. And now, I'm insisting I'm going to do it on my own. But in this case, my stubbornness—easily one of my worst traits—will lead me to my son. I'm sure of it.

Rather than argue, Jake knows me well enough not to push. "At least let me drop you there."

"Fine." I put the baby back in the car and recite the address. We drive wordlessly to her office. I tune in to the smashing of horns, distant ambulances, and the fiery scream of fire trucks.

"I'll be waiting." Jake hits his flashers in front of the building, and I give him a look. "Don't challenge me, Rebecca. You'll lose." He crosses his arms—I can tell by the squeak of leather and the self-satisfied smirk he must wear on his face. "Meanwhile, leave the onesie here. I'm going to see what I can find out."

I nod and gesture to the back seat. "Should I . . ."

"Leave him. He's fine."

I know he is probably fine with Jake, but I can't let this baby out of my sight on principle. "No, I'll take him." I unstrap him and grab the diaper bag. "See you soon."

"Yep."

I shut the door and head inside. I'm not sure if Dr. Gibbons is even here yet or if she will be able to squeeze me in. But I decide right then and there to tell her everything that's going on. I want a professional opinion about what I should do. Not from a cop. Not from my friends, but from someone who is trained to give me the benefit of the doubt.

"May I help you?"

The front desk person—different than the last time—speaks up.

"Is Dr. Gibbons in?"

They press a few buttons. "Go on up."

I'm not offered help this time, but I remember my route to the elevator and that she's on the eleventh floor. My fingers glide over the buttons, adjusting for error, until I land on eleven. I count my steps to the door and approach the receptionist's desk. I'm told she's with a client.

"Dr. Gibbons has back-to-back clients today. It's not a drop-in situation," her receptionist explains.

"This is an emergency."

"I understand that, but she's booked."

"Is it okay if I wait until she's done?"

The woman must nod or shake her head, but I take a seat anyway, clumsily fumbling with the chairs. A few minutes later, the door opens.

I stand and bounce the baby on my chest. Someone shuffles past and says good-bye to Dr. Gibbons.

"Rebecca, hi. You're not on my schedule today. Are you okay?"

I open my mouth but I can't find the words. Her arm is around me in an instant. Dr. Gibbons addresses her assistant. "Push my next two appointments." She guides me into her office and I sit on the couch.

"Okay, what's going on?"

The words gather in my throat. I bat away the skepticism. *What if she doesn't believe me?* At this point, it's a chance I'm willing to take. "Someone swapped my son." My tongue sticks to the roof of my mouth. The words sound preposterous, even now, knowing that it happened. But I confide in Dr. Gibbons. She listens. The scribble of her pen scratches paper. The noise distracts me and I lose my train of thought. I stutter over my words.

"Rebecca." She leans in as she did the first time. "Take a breath. I'm here. You don't have to convince me of anything. You just have to talk."

I rub the baby's back. His limbs are warm and sticky. "Can you show me to the bathroom? I need to change him." She ushers me to the door, which is by the reception area. I change his diaper and collect my thoughts. Once he's situated, I splash some cold water on my face and flick off the light. I hesitate before opening the door. Dr. Gibbons whispers to her receptionist.

"Call Dr. Marley. I think she needs a serious psych evaluation. I'm not sure if the baby is safe. We can take extra precautions after if need be."

I press my ear against the door, certain I'm mistaken. I pull back, frantic. I root around the cool wood to listen for more, but she's stopped talking. My heart thuds against my ribs. The baby cries. Who is Dr. Marley? And what extra precautions could she be talking about?

It was a mistake to come here. Why did I think it was safe? I count to ten in my head, rearrange my face, and open the door.

"Dr. Gibbons is waiting in her office." The receptionist's voice drips with forced cheerfulness.

"I just need to make a quick phone call." My voice tapers as I fumble for the door. I trip on the edge of a chair. My knee throbs but I keep walking at a fast clip until I reach the exit.

"Are you okay?"

"Fine. I'll be right back."

I open the door and walk just out of sight. When I'm past the office, I jog back toward the elevator and stab the button.

"Rebecca!" Dr. Gibbons's voice floats down the hall.

"Come on," I whisper. I stab the button over and over, like that will force the elevator doors to part.

The swift clip of her shoes closes the gap between me and the eleva-tor. I stab the button one more time and the doors magically wrench apart. I step on and press a button—any button—to get the doors to close.

"Rebecca!"

Her voice cuts away as the doors shut. I exhale the breath I've been holding and resist sliding to the floor. In the lobby, I slink out and wonder if security is going to be waiting for me, but I hear the same crush of people as before. I find the handicap button, wait for the door to open, and push out into the Chicago day. I recount my steps to the car and knock on the glass. Jake stabs the door lock, and I pull open the back door and strap the baby in the car seat with shaking hands.

"That was fast," Jake observes. "Do you need help?"

I shake my head and listen for Dr. Gibbons. I get in the car, yank the door closed, and fasten my seat belt. "Just drive."

He puts the car into gear wordlessly. I close my eyes and lean against the window.

The simple, hard truth ignites my brain: *nowhere is safe.*

31

CRYSTAL

⠠⠉⠗⠽⠎⠞⠁⠇

JESS OPENS THE DOOR IN A DENIM JUMPSUIT, HER CURLY HAIR PILED HIGH on her head. Baxter balances on one hip, his chubby legs splayed and kicking. "Hey," she says, surprised. She sets him down and he takes off crawling toward the back of the house. "What's up?"

"I'm looking for Bec." Crystal keeps her voice calm, but inside, she's unglued.

"She's not here."

Crystal unfolds the flyer and thrusts it into Jess's hand. "What's going on? I haven't heard from her. She told me she had an emergency, but she won't answer any of my calls."

Jess sighs. "Come in." She hitches her head toward the foyer and opens the door wider. Crystal steps into the monstrous entryway. The air is cool and smells like cinnamon. "I'm baking," Jess says in response.

"So you haven't seen her?"

"Not today."

Crystal follows her into the kitchen and takes a seat on one of the bar stools. The island is covered in muffin tins and baking sheets, as well as dozens of pastries. "This is quite the spread."

"I know. It's for a bake sale. Can I get you something to drink?"

"Water's fine."

They descend into an awkward silence, but Crystal decides to get right to the point. "Tell me what's going on. I'm worried about her."

Jess slides over a glass of icy cucumber water in a crystal tumbler. "We're all worried about her."

She takes a cool sip. "Why is there a flyer with Jackson's face on it?"

"Because she believes someone took him when we were at the park."

"When?"

"Thursday morning."

"Thursday?" Crystal struggles to keep track of the days in her head, all of them running together in a hazy clump. "You mean after she fell?"

"Yes. She thinks from the time she fell to the time she went to your house, someone took Jackson." She lowers her voice. "It's fine. She was trying to get an investigation underway, but it's clear that no one believes . . . that everyone believes she's mistaken. She's tired. She's grieving." She shrugs.

"I'm confused." Crystal sorts through the information. "So Jackson wasn't taken?"

"No. But she believes he was. She thinks she has a different baby in his place."

A cold vise clamps Crystal's throat and squeezes. *Bec thinks Jackson was swapped?* "Wait, what?" Crystal replays their recent conversations. Has she been overlooking Bec's paranoia in favor of chalking it up to grief?

"She thinks it's another baby. Insists on it, in fact." Jess opens and shuts the fridge and sets a carton of fresh eggs on the island. She takes one, cracks it, lets it ooze into a bowl. "But I'm telling you. It's Jackson." She cracks two more and then whisks them together.

Crystal takes a sip of water. "So you've seen the baby?"

"I have." She pauses. "I mean, I don't spend every day with Jackson, and I haven't held him in a while, but it sure looks like him. I'm surprised they haven't called you to come in yet."

"I wasn't at the park," she says.

"But we went to your house, so . . ." She shrugs.

She takes another drink, and the cold shocks her system. "There's literally no one who can confirm it's him?"

"Not even her dreamboat of an ex."

"What ex?" Suddenly, Crystal feels completely in the dark. She ransacks her brain for information of Rebecca's ex, but they don't talk much about their lives before they became widows. They help each other. They fill in. They lean on each other. It's about the present. It's about *survival.*

"His name's Jake. He's a detective. Look." She releases the whisk and rinses it in the sink. "Bec needs someone who believes her. I'm not telling you to do something you can't or don't want to do, but if you could be there for her . . ."

"Of course I will," Crystal says. "But she's not answering my calls."

Jess raises her eyebrows and lifts her hands in surrender. "All I'm saying is she needs a friend."

"Funny because I thought she had some." Crystal hops off the stool, too furious to sit. These women parade around and pretend to be sympathetic until something happens that they don't understand. Isn't it their job to be supportive no matter what? *Maybe not to this extent,* Crystal reminds herself. "Do you have any idea where she might have gone?"

"I don't." Jess wipes her hand on a dish towel. "I haven't heard from her this morning. We were all at the police station late last night. I heard through the grapevine—aka Officer Hot Pants, aka Officer Toby—that she had a change of heart and said she made the whole thing up to get attention. It's a mess."

"How did you find that out?"

"Rob. He and Toby are friends."

Crystal processes this information and turns to leave. "Will you please just have her call me if you hear from her? I'd really appreciate it."

Jess nods and resumes baking. Crystal lets herself out and stands on the porch, contemplating her next move. The wealth of Elmhurst consumes her, all of these million-dollar homes and manicured lawns as far as the eye can see. This is a safe, respectable town, and yet something awful has happened to her closest friend.

And you weren't there to help.

She knocks away the voice as she climbs into the car. She glances at her phone. She could call Bec again, or she could just show up and wait. *That's what friends do,* she thinks. She puts the car in gear.

They show up.

BEC

⠟⠄⠮⠆⠒⠱⠒⠀⠦⠲⠒

JAKE PULLS INTO THE DRIVEWAY AND PARKS.

"Bec, what the hell happened back there? Are you really going to shut me out?"

After a few uncomfortable moments, I speak. "Dr. Gibbons thinks I need a psych evaluation. And I'm not shutting you out—I'm just trying not to waste your time."

As if on cue, Jake's phone rattles. He answers. I close my eyes and release something—some version I had of us reconnecting after so long. How it might turn out. Instead of another friendly coffee or a meal to reminisce about old times, I've sent him on a wild-goose chase for a child he doesn't even believe is out there.

He ends the call and sighs. "Well, you got your wish. I'm on a case." He presses something into my palm. "This is the address of the Cornerstone you need to go to. The Oak Brook location was a bust." He recites the address, and I pocket the piece of paper to be safe.

He walks me to the door and sets the car seat at my feet. "Let me know what you find." He kisses my temple. When his car reverses down the driveway, I head inside. The baby wakes and starts crying again, and I pull him into my arms. The regularity of feeding, rocking, and placating him is the only comfort I have left.

Once he's down for a nap, I concoct a new plan. I call Cornerstone in Wisconsin and see how long they're going to be open. I map it on my phone. At least ninety minutes in traffic.

Someone knocks on the front door, and I close the app. I listen cautiously, wondering if Dr. Gibbons got my address and sent someone to have me committed.

"Rebecca, it's Crystal. Are you home?"

Emotion surges as I pull open the door. I can sense her support even before she envelops me in a hug. "What in the world is going on?" Her familiar perfume—clean and light—instantly calms me.

"You wouldn't believe me if I told you."

"Try me." She closes the door and I motion toward the kitchen.

"How much time do you have?"

"As much as you need."

We sit at the dining room table, and I bring her up to speed. She listens silently. I wish I could see her face to judge her level of disbelief. I reach into my bag and hand over the onesie. "This store in Wisconsin is my last shot. If they carry it, then I might be able to get the receipt of the person who bought it. It's a shot in the dark, according to Jake, but it's really all I've got."

"Rebecca." Crystal's voice is clogged with emotion. "I'm sorry. I don't even know what to say. This is all just so unbelievable."

Annoyance builds. "I know it is, which is why I'm doing this alone."

"No, I'm not saying that I don't believe you. It's just *literally* unbelievable. I can't believe you're still standing."

"I'm not. I'm sitting." I make the small joke and it fires into the room. It's a betrayal to make light of the situation in any capacity. I drop my head into my hands.

"Okay, this is what we're going to do." Crystal uses her business voice. "I'm going to go to this store for you and see what I can find out."

"I can't ask you to do that."

"You didn't. I offered."

"What about Savi?"

"Pam," she says. "These days, she prefers her anyway." There's an edge to Crystal's voice, but I don't challenge it.

"I'm coming with you."

"You should stay here in case you hear anything."

A restlessness radiates in my chest. "I don't want to stay here. I can't sit here one more second."

Crystal seems to contemplate her choices and finally agrees. "Okay. Should we go now?"

"Do you want to see the baby first?" Though I'm not sure her taking a look at the baby will do anything to help. Even my friends with babies are as blind as I am when it comes to facial recognition. But I trust Crystal. And part of me wants the validation that she sees what I know to be true. But if she doesn't see it . . . I'm not sure I can handle any more skepticism.

Her phone shatters the tension. "Hold that thought. It's the contractor."

The renovation! In all of this, I'd completely forgotten that they were supposed to start tomorrow. I rewind back just a few weeks, when the hardest thing I had to contend with was sleeplessness and nightmares about Jackson.

I listen to Crystal talk to the contractor about pushing the dates back. I'd taken such joy in picking out cabinets, countertops, and hardware—as if having a nice kitchen would somehow make my life better. But isn't that a start? And now, all of it is irrelevant. My son is what matters. Not this house or the memories in it. I need to take action. I need to act *now*.

"Rebecca?" There's another knock.

I walk to the front hallway. "Jess?"

"Hey." She lets herself in. "I was worried when I didn't hear from you. Are you okay?" She pulls me into a hug, and my edges soften a bit.

"Sorry about that." Crystal walks to join us. "I told him we'd need to push out a bit. Hi, Jess."

"I'm so sorry," I say to Crystal. "You've worked so hard."

"Don't apologize." Her keys jingle in her hand. "Listen, you and Jess stay here. I'm going to Cornerstone, okay? I'll report back."

I shake my head. "No, I really want to come."

"What's Cornerstone?" Jess asks.

I fill Jess in and show her the onesie.

She examines it. "I feel like I've seen these before. Wait, I've been to this shop. The owner, what's her name?" She snaps. "Patty? Betsy? She's the best. I've been in there a few times."

"Can you come with us?"

Crystal is silent as Jess contemplates. "I guess, if you think it will help."

I nod. "I do. I'll go get the baby." I'm already heading for the stairs. I feel bad about putting him in the car yet again, but movement seems to placate him. I want Crystal to look at the baby, but she doesn't offer, and I don't force it. I buckle him in and sit in the second row of her car, while Jess takes the passenger seat.

"Hello, Suburban." Jess whistles. "This is huge."

"It's for business," Crystal explains. "When you're a designer, you transport a lot of stuff." She puts in the address on her GPS and the automated voice guides us out of the neighborhood.

Though I'm one of Crystal's clients, I'd almost decided not to work with her because I didn't want a stranger in my home. Since Jackson, I feel fiercely protective in a world that shares its children on social media as if they are shiny objects for sale. But because of that need for privacy, now no one can positively identify my son, and I'm left chasing ridiculous leads to get closer to him.

Crystal finds a playlist. "Music okay?"

"Fine with me," I say.

"So what are you hoping to find exactly?" Jess asks.

"I want to know who bought this onesie. It's what the baby came home in."

"Store owners aren't allowed to give up that type of information though, are they?" she asks.

I shrug. "Maybe she'll make an exception." I wish I could see the passing trees, the road below—the perspective of something other than the voices in my head. "I'm just going to close my eyes," I say.

Crystal turns the music lower, and the conversation dies.

My thoughts wander in various directions. I miss my son's face. I miss his smell. I miss being his mother. Memories of my precious baby rattle me to my core, while a hard truth wedges itself firmly in place: if I don't find him, no one else will.

Time is running out.

33

CRYSTAL

⠠⠉⠗⠽⠎⠞⠁⠇

LAKE GENEVA IS ONE OF CRYSTAL'S FAVORITE TOWNS. SHE STAYED HERE with Paul at the Grand Geneva Resort shortly after they were engaged. He'd regaled her with tales of the former Playboy Club Hotel. While Paul played golf and she'd indulged in the overpriced spa services, she couldn't shake the vivid image of Playboy bunnies straddling Hugh Hefner in their massive suite. She almost shares the amusing memory now but refrains when she senses the tense mood.

Jess busies herself with senseless scrolling on her phone. Crystal wants to break the ice with her—to find some semblance of common ground besides their joint friendship with Rebecca—but her mind is too caught up trying to figure out real ways to help Bec. It makes her nervous to think about being called into the police station to verify that this baby is Jackson, but she assumes they will. When Savi was born, Paul would constantly urge her to spend time studying her daughter's features, holding her, and bonding, but she just couldn't make herself get close. Honestly, she couldn't pick Jackson out of a lineup.

The audible directions interrupt her circuitous thoughts and tell her to turn right. She navigates the adorable downtown shops and parks in front of Cornerstone Shop & Gallery. She cracks the windows and they all exit. She waits for Bec to strap the baby in. Crystal averts her eyes until the carrier mostly blocks him from view.

"Ready?" Jess asks.

Crystal opens the door. A set of bells rattles as they enter. Bec takes a deep breath.

"What is it?"

"The bells," she says. "Makes me think of Jackson." Her fingers trail down to his bare ankles.

Crystal glances around. "Did you lose them?"

She nods. "That day at the park."

Jess waves at the shop owner, who meanders over. The two chat like old friends. Crystal takes in the strange mix of art, kids' clothing, and various oddities scattered about. Somehow, in all her visits to Lake Geneva, she's never come into this store.

"What can I help you ladies with?" the shop owner asks. She's an older woman with silver hair scraped back into a severe ponytail. She wears a gingham dress and cat's-eye glasses on a chain around her neck.

Crystal doesn't know where to begin. Luckily, Bec hands over the onesie. "Would it be possible to tell us if this was purchased here?"

"Well, let me see." The woman's voice is kind. She slides the readers up her nose, stretches the onesie in weathered hands, and peeks at the tag. "Yep. One of ours. Are you wanting to return it?"

Bec stands straighter.

Hope. She must be feeling hope.

"Not exactly." Crystal tries to form the right words again but falters. Jess steps in.

"I know this is a strange request, Betty, but we're trying to figure out who bought it."

Betty chuckles. "Well, without a receipt, that's going to be a tall order, I'm afraid."

"I know. This is a bit of an emergency." Jess smiles, as unthreatening as they come. "We think it would have been purchased in the last few months."

"Not necessarily," Crystal interjects. "It could have been a gift from someone too. A baby registry present, maybe?"

Bec chews her bottom lip. Her brow creases and her shoulders round as she absently rubs the baby's back. Crystal needs to be helping her, not making her feel worse. Betty assesses Bec: her cane, her sad face, the vacant eyes, the baby. Sympathy tugs the corners of her mouth until she smiles. "Alright, let me see what I can do." She waves them over to the computer. "We keep a backlog of receipts for up to six months before they're whisked off to the land of accounting." She laughs and pecks a few buttons on the computer. "I can put in the SKU number and see what comes up. If you ladies want some lemonade while you wait, please help yourselves." She motions to a small sitting area a few feet away with a big glass pitcher of lemonade, cups, and floral saucers.

"Thank you. That sounds lovely." Crystal steers Rebecca toward the antique chairs while Jess hangs back. A container of cinnamon sticks has spilled next to the cups and Crystal rights it.

"Is this impossible?" Rebecca glances at her worriedly while she sits.

"I'm not sure." Crystal arranges the cinnamon sticks and wipes her hands on a napkin. She almost asks to take a look at the baby, but he seems so content in her arms. She's such a natural mother—a *good* mother—even if it's for a son she doesn't believe is her own.

"Crystal." Jess says her name sharply and motions her over.

"Be right back." Crystal joins Jess and Betty, who points at the point-of-sale screen. "There've been quite a few of these purchased over the last few months." Betty scrolls through initials and partial credit card numbers. "Do you know who you're looking for?"

"Not exactly. Is there a way to print this?"

"I can't legally do that, I'm afraid." Betty points to the credit card numbers. "Privacy."

"Right."

"Hey Betty, while you're here. I was wondering if you could hook me up with a piece of art for my son's bedroom." Jess casually motions to the back wall, where a row of colorful paintings hang. "Are these new?"

"They are. Great line from a local artist." When Betty turns to describe the paintings, Jess signals to Crystal.

Crystal slides her phone from her pocket and takes a few photos of the screen. When Betty realizes she's left the computer unattended, she turns, but Crystal is already walking back toward Bec. "You've been super helpful, Betty. Thanks so much," Crystal says. Jess busies her with purchasing one of the paintings, which Betty struggles to get off the wall.

"Hank!" She calls someone from the back to help. Jess makes Betty laugh, and Crystal marvels at how Jess puts most people at ease. She's never been like that, instead wired so tight, she feels she might slice someone apart if she's not careful.

"Okay, got the list." Crystal thumbs through the names. "How do we even know who we're looking for?"

Bec is listening, but appears despondent. Her delicate fingers snake around her cup of lemonade. With her dark glasses and erect posture, she could pass for a statue. Except for the wriggling baby on her chest.

"How many names?"

Crystal hurriedly counts them. "Twenty."

"Any of them look familiar?"

She scans the last names. "Unfortunately, no. But I'm probably not the right person to ask."

"Do you mind texting it to Jake?"

"Sure." Bec recites Jake's number from memory. Crystal sends him a text and pockets her phone. While they wait on Jess to check out, Crystal leans in. "What can I do to help?"

Rebecca sighs and her face, usually filled with such optimism, crumples. "I don't know. I really don't."

"Well, that was easy," Jess says as she lugs a small painting of a giraffe toward them. "Ready?"

They walk outside. "Thanks for distracting her." Crystal pops the trunk.

"It's what I do best," Jess says.

Once she's behind the wheel, she starts the car and glances once again at the shop. Inside, Betty fusses with the front window display. She moves a vintage baby stroller. Its large chrome wheels take up most of the space. Betty pulls back the fire engine–red canopy, adjusts something, and tugs it back into place. Crystal continues to stare. She'd had a stroller just like that when Savi was little.

The color of cherries.

The color of blood.

She ignores the eerie feeling and starts the car. "Anyone hungry? Want to grab something before we head back?"

"I could eat," Jess says.

"Home." Bec leans her head against the window. She seems just out of reach, her emotions caught in a complex web Crystal can't possibly untangle. "I want to go home."

"You sure?" Jess asks. "There are so many great places around here. Maybe a good meal would—"

"I'm not in the mood. I have a child to find."

Crystal and Jess look at each other. She inputs Rebecca's home address into the system and pushes start. "Home it is then."

From the back seat, Rebecca's hair shrouds her pretty face before she sweeps it all back and knots it at the nape of her neck. "I swear on everything I've ever believed in that this really happened. I am not imagining it."

"I'm not questioning you," Crystal affirms. "You know your baby best."

"You would know if Baxter wasn't yours, right?" Bec asks Jess.

"Yes," Jess affirms.

"And you'd know if it wasn't Savi?"

"Of course." *Now* she would, anyway. Back then, no. But what if she were blind? In some ways, she'd probably be more aware of all her child's little quirks. But in other ways, she could never be sure. It would be a constant fear that plagued her. Was this a common fear for all blind mothers?

She takes a left onto the highway, and the boutique shops and quaint streets give way to flat, rolling reams of concrete and crisped corn fields. All this time, she'd thought she and Bec were so bonded—the same, even—but now she realizes Bec is having a solitary experience, and no matter how much grief unites them, she can't ever really understand what she's going through. But she doesn't want their differences to tear them apart either.

"No one spends as much time with him as I do," Bec continues. "I've memorized every square inch. I could pick him out of one hundred babies."

Crystal shifts in her seat and hits the horn as a car almost sideswipes them. "I believe you."

"Do you, or are you just saying that?"

Crystal glimpses her reflection in the rearview: green eyes searching, pained.

"I'm not just saying that." She sneaks a glance at Jess, who's gone conveniently mute. "You know, after Paul died, I was convinced it was all my fault. If I'd just been in the car with him. If I'd woken up before he left. If I'd called him before he got into his car, then maybe it wouldn't have happened. We've talked about that." The scene flashes in her head. The phone call from the police. Her husband's mangled car. His unrecognizable body at the morgue. Her love, eviscerated. "Everyone just kept telling me it would get better. That I needed to take time to grieve, but that life goes on. I swear, I didn't really start to feel better until I met you." Her cheeks pink at the admission. "So if you believe something, then I believe it too. Okay?"

Bec reaches forward and touches Crystal's shoulder. "Thank you for saying that. Truly." She collapses back in her seat, visibly relieved.

Surprisingly, Jess takes Crystal's hand, squeezes it, and mouths, *Thank you.*

And that's when Crystal decides: no matter what she doesn't understand, she will try . . . for Bec.

34

BEC

⠃⠑⠉

CRYSTAL AND JESS DROP ME OFF, DESPITE THEIR PERSISTENCE TO STAY. I promise to keep them both updated. I don't even have the baby situated again before I call Jake.

"Donovan." His tone is clipped. He must not have even looked at his caller ID.

"It's me," I say. I don't bother asking if he's busy because I already know.

"Bec." His voice softens. He closes a door and returns to the phone. "What's up?"

I'm surprised by the nonchalance. "You got the photo, right?"

"What photo?"

My heart hammers in my chest. "Crystal texted you a photo. We went to Cornerstone Shop & Gallery."

"Hold on." He takes a few moments and then comes back. "Here it is. I didn't recognize the number, so I didn't check it yet. Sorry." He clicks on it. "This is excellent." He types on his computer. "I'll send this to Pat and see what hits we get."

My hands shake. "This is something, right?"

"Could be. I'll call you if I have something, okay? And I'm not trying to be short. Working a big case."

"It's fine. Thanks."

"You bet." He disconnects.

What is he doing right now? Scribbling facts on whiteboards and casing murderers? I'd always wondered, even when we were together, how he erased all of the terrible things he saw when he went to sleep every night. So many times I'd thought about him over the years, especially when I heard about random cases in Miami. Why had I never reached out?

All of this is a reminder to keep people around that I trust. People like Crystal, Jess, Beth, and Jake. I pace the house, restless. I check the time, change and feed the baby, pop him in the stroller, and head to the park. Maybe, just maybe, there will be some sort of clue I missed.

On the way, I calculate how long it will take to go through each name on that list of receipts and if we will find what we're looking for.

"Rebecca?"

A hand on my elbow rips me out of my internal dialogue. The voice sounds familiar, but I can't quite place it. I turn, one hand on the stroller and one on my cane. "Hi . . ."

"Caroline Walker. We met at Jessica's party the other night. How are you, my dear? After . . ."

After you jumped into a swimming pool fully clothed and made a fool of yourself?

"I'm fine. You?"

"Waiting for this insane heat to break. I thought Illinois wasn't supposed to be hot. But climate change isn't real, right?" She laughs, and I attempt to smile. She steps closer. Her grip tightens. "How are you, really?"

I will myself to tell her I'm okay, but something pricks the recesses of my memory. Didn't she say she and her husband were part of the neighborhood watch? "Actually, do you have time for a quick cup of coffee?" I lick my lips and work out what I need to say. "I think I might need your help."

"My dear, I *live* for help. Brewpoint?"

Caroline falls into step beside me and chats about the weather, the upcoming fall festivals, and the latest neighborhood scandals around a few stolen trash cans. I want to ask what to do about stolen babies, but refrain.

We order our coffee and grab a quiet table near the back. I tuck the stroller next to me, and Caroline murmurs about how children grow so fast. Instead of making small talk, I launch right in. "Do you remember me telling you about the recent scares I'd been having?"

"How could I forget?"

I twist my paper cup in my hands. Wasn't I just sitting in a coffee shop in Chicago with Jake? Life, even with all of its complexities, seemed so much simpler only a few days ago. "Well, something happened after the party."

"What do you mean?"

"I know what I'm going to say is going to sound a little . . . out there, but mother to mother, I need you to hear me."

"I'm listening."

A dish crashes in the background. Someone claps and whoops. I scoot my chair even closer and give her the high-level rundown, as if I'm letting her in on a top-secret investigation. She listens intently and doesn't interrupt. Finally, I finish and sit back, awaiting the criticism.

"You mean to tell me that Officer Toby didn't take this seriously?"

"He didn't. And then I lied to him." I glance toward the stroller and bite my lip. "I didn't want this baby taken away too."

"You did the right thing." The table jolts as she scoots closer. "This is what we're going to do. We're not getting the police involved yet, because they'll come around once the community demands it. Chief Holbrook does things by the book until the neighborhood says otherwise. Trust me. It's just the way it goes. I'm going to hold a candlelight vigil for your little boy tonight, and we're going to get every last person there."

"But isn't a vigil for someone who's . . . ?" I can't bring myself to say the word *dead*.

She pats my hand. "No, no. This is just what we're going to do to rally the troops. Someone knows something, I can assure you of that.

People talk in this community. You have our support, Rebecca. I'm just so sorry you've gone this many days without it."

I want to cry from her kindness, but I also don't know what a vigil will really do. "How will this help?"

"Awareness. Awareness is the first step."

"What's the second step?"

"Catching the bastard who did this." She finds my hand, pats it again. "Which we will."

I nod, take a deep breath, and release it. With Caroline on my side and Jake looking into the receipts, I know we're moving in the right direction.

"Now, let's see. What time is it?" Her ring knocks against the wood. "I've got to get busy, my dear. Do you have any more of those flyers?"

"Of course." I fish one from my diaper bag.

"Perfect. Seven tonight. Wilder." She kisses my cheek. Her heavy perfume lingers long after she's gone. I don't even get to thank her for the coffee.

Wilder. I shudder to think we will be having the candlelight vigil at the place Jackson went missing. Even if I get him back, all of these memories—places I've grown up in, places I've come to know and love—will be tarnished. They will either remind me of my life before loss or my life after.

Anxiety presses in again until I'm suffocating from it. I extract my phone to call Jake, but he beats me to it.

"I was literally just calling you."

"Rebecca." He's breathless. "Where are you?"

"I'm at a coffee shop near home. Why?"

"I found something. Rather tell you in person."

"What is it, Jake?"

"Just get home. I'll see you soon."

I toss back the last of my coffee, maneuver the stroller and my cane, and thank someone who opens the door. I practically run home.

Will this be another dead end, or are things finally turning in my favor? In my hurry, I miss a crack in the sidewalk, and pitch forward. The stroller thuds behind me, and the baby gives a small laugh. I stop and turn. So far, I've only heard his cry or tiny sighs. His voice is sweet, soft, and knifes the mangled flesh of my heart. "Was that funny?" I run a finger over his cheek and miss my son with such ferocity, I feel sick.

You will find him, I remind myself.

By the time I arrive home, I'm breathless. I situate the baby in the nursery and wait for Jake on the front porch.

A few minutes later, his SUV powers into the driveway. "Rebecca." My name again. I hold my breath as he crosses the front walk. His hulk blocks the sun and dims the blurry landscape. I wait for the news—good or bad, pointless or useful—when the baby screams from inside. I listen to see if he'll quiet, but he doesn't.

"Hold that thought," I say. I take the stairs two at a time, almost dizzy from needing to know what he's found out. In the nursery, the baby is wet. I change his diaper, kiss his cheek, and lower him into the crib. I keep the door cracked and hurry back to the landing.

I don't even realize I've missed the top step until my foot closes in on air and I'm pitching forward into space.

35

BEC

EVERYTHING STOPS. TIME, BREATH, GRIEF. ALL OF IT EVAPORATES WHEN I step down onto nothing. I pull myself back so severely, my neck makes a sickening pop. My spine cracks against the top step. My body lique-fies and slides down the rest of the stairs. I give a sharp cry as I skid toward the landing.

I lie there, staring up at the ceiling, just as I'd stared up into the bright blue sky on Thursday. No sense of time, thought, or direction. Just me, flat on my back, in pain. "Jake." My voice is weak, as if I've been strangled. I try to sit up, but can't. "Jake!"

The front door opens. "Bec." Jake sprints to the base of the stair-case. His hands dance delicately over my bones. "Can you move?"

Wicked fingers of pain stab my spine. "My back."

"What the hell happened?"

"Gravity." I wince.

"Sense of humor intact, I see. Don't move." He resurrects his months of EMT training, back when he had thought about becoming a firefighter instead of a cop. He takes me through an endless array of tests with my fingers, toes, and other various movements, and then finagles an ice pack out of every frozen vegetable I have in my freezer. "Let's get you off the stairs." He tucks me into his side like a football and guides me to the couch. My toes tingle, and my back aches. He lowers me onto the stiff couch in the formal sitting room and arranges the veggies behind my back.

"You're shaking like a leaf." He leaves the room and brings back a glass of water and a blanket. "Drink." He drapes the blanket over my lap.

I drink the glass and place it on one of the thousand coasters my mom kept in random stacks throughout the house. "What did you find?"

He sits forward.

"What did you find, Jake?"

"Do we need to take you to a doctor?"

"Jake Foster Donovan, you tell me what you found right this instant." I attempt to give him my sternest look, but my voice breaks as my torso spasms.

"Here. Lie back." He arranges the pillows and props my feet up in a way that alleviates the injury. He adjusts the frozen vegetables. "Better?"

I nod and normalize my breathing. I close my eyes and just want him to get on with it, but the baby starts crying upstairs. I try to sit up again.

"Stay. Is he hungry?"

"Maybe. There's a bottle in the fridge." My words come out in angry little puffs, so annoyed by yet another interruption to a possible break in the case. I focus on Jake's assured footsteps crossing from sitting room to dining room to kitchen. The suction of the refrigerator door. "Do I need to heat it up?" he asks.

I take him through the instructions. He heats the milk, every second he's gone like a bomb on the verge of detonating. "Be right back." He takes the stairs, and a tear slips down my cheek at the thought of him up there, scooping that sweet baby from Jackson's crib, sitting in the same chair I rock my son in to feed a stranger.

Not our make-believe baby.

Not Jackson.

I turn my head to the side and sense the drowsiness working over my body as the adrenaline drains. I can't believe I just fell down the stairs. Twice in a week. After Crystal warned me. I've never had an issue with stairs before. Why now?

Because you haven't slept in months.

The truth nips at that vulnerable place in my heart that's been ravaged by so much grief. I think of the pills Jess gave me. If it hadn't been for those fucking pills, I would have my baby. Or at the very least, I would have known sooner that he was missing.

An eternity later, Jake returns.

I roll my head to look at him. "Did you burp him?"

"Shit." He retreats back upstairs and I let out a good-hearted laugh.

"Grab a baby blanket and drape it over your shoulder. Check if he needs to be changed while you're up there!" I cross my hands on my belly and revel in the help. No one's changed a diaper since my mother. Already, I've grown accustomed to doing so much on my own that I take a moment to enjoy it—despite the circumstances.

"Holy moly!" I hear him cry down. "It's like Armageddon in here!"

"Wipes are on the changing table!" I shout up. My back aches with the effort, but the silly banter lightens my spirits and almost detracts from why he's here.

I work my way to sitting and roll my shoulders and neck and then check for numbness in my extremities. My feet have stopped tingling. I situate the ice behind my back and gingerly tilt back.

He hurries down the stairs. "Garbage?"

"He has a Diaper Genie up there."

"For the love of God," he says. But I can hear it in his voice. He loves being needed. He loves taking care of any little thing that will bring me some sense of happiness or comfort. I hunt for the baby's cries, but all is quiet.

When Jake is back, I smile. "He likes you."

"He is a creator of crime scenes. What has that kid been eating?"

"Welcome to motherhood," I joke.

"How's your back?" He slides in next to me and adjusts the ice. The crunch of it tickles my spine.

"Sore." I lean back and look at him. "Talk."

He sighs and props my head up with a pillow. "Pat cross-referenced all of the cards on file and we narrowed it down to a few possibilities. We found one that traced to an address here."

I snap my head up and the pillow falls away. "Here where? Like in Elmhurst?"

"Yes."

My breath quickens. "Who?" My brain wraps around the outcome, of strangers I don't know, of neighbors I do.

"I don't know how to say this, Bec. It's someone you know."

Fear and anticipation flood my system and tamp down the pain from the fall. "Who?" My fingers constrain the fabric of the couch cushion until my knuckles ache. Blood fizzes in my ears. My mouth goes cottony.

"It's your friend."

Time reverses. A riot explodes in my head.

"Which friend?" I run through their names in my head, the ones I'm close with and the ones I'm not.

I hear the syllables form before the name is even out of his mouth:

"Beth. Beth Harrison."

36

CRYSTAL

"SAVI?" CRYSTAL CALLS HER NAME WHEN SHE ARRIVES HOME. HER STOMACH grumbles, and she passes through the house, already knowing it's empty. She checks upstairs anyway and texts Pam to see where they are. She makes herself lunch and attempts to sort through all of the information Rebecca provided.

Her mind drifts to Paul. When Paul was alive and Savi was a baby, Crystal was bone-tired. She was always weepy, hormonal, and unexplainably sad. She literally wouldn't have survived Savi's first year without Paul. If Paul had already been dead and she'd had no support, what might *she* think was real?

Someone knocks on the front door and interrupts that dark train of thought. Crystal swallows the last of her sandwich and wipes her hands on her jeans.

"Hi, so sorry to drop by unannounced. Caroline Walker." On the other side of the door, an elegant older woman with cropped hair, linen pants, and a cream top thrusts a flyer into her hand. "We're holding a candlelight vigil tonight at seven for one of our own. Please come. It's important." She's gone before Crystal can ask questions, leaving a trail of expensive perfume. A vigil? She shuts the door and glances at the paper. Her stomach bucks. It's for Rebecca. The flyer is vague, but the message is clear: a baby is missing and this community is going to find him.

After Paul died, people placed bouquets of flowers on the side of the road to commemorate the crash. They were hideous arrangements that reminded her of a funeral every time she passed by. The same for his grave. Tacky plastic flowers from his friends or co-workers, who insisted on getting bigger and better ones every few months.

How can you move on when everyone keeps reminding you?

A few minutes later, the front door opens. Savi steps through, breathless. Her cheeks are red. "It's still so hot!" she exclaims. She kicks off her shoes and scratches her calf with one socked foot.

"Just wait a few months and you'll be begging for sunshine." Pam closes the door and waves at Crystal and then moves around her to drop bags.

Savi tells Crystal about the latest tricks she was attempting from her magic kit, and she rotates her wrist in a circle. "I even healed my own wrist! See?" On cue, she produces a wand from thin air. "Ta-da!" She taps in her mother's direction. "You're healed too."

Crystal refrains from asking what she's supposedly healed from and tells her to go upstairs and wash her hands.

Once Savi is out of earshot, she turns to Pam. Before she can say anything, Pam starts talking. "That kid is hysterical. She had all the kids at the park mesmerized."

Though Crystal and Savi share the occasional sacred moment, it's Pam she likes to spend time with. It's Pam who takes her to do fun things. Crystal is just the mom who works too much and tries to keep it all together, erasing memories of her dead father, living in a fancy house, and still . . .

So many secrets she's kept.

A moment later, Savi bounds back down the stairs and holds up her hands. "All clean. Want to smell?"

Crystal shakes her head. "I believe you."

"What's that?" Pam interrupts her train of thought and her eyes travel down to the flyer still clutched in Crystal's fist. Savi snatches it before she can say anything. Her daughter's eyes grow large and fearful.

"This is for Jackson?" She looks between Pam and Crystal. "Are we going?"

"I am." Crystal wants to be there for her friend, of course, but it's more complicated than that.

Pam moves closer. "Can I see?" She peeks at the flyer, her full lips moving as she reads the words. "Is her son missing? Oh my God, how awful." Her hand clasps over her mouth. "Come on, Savi. Let's get you a snack." Pam steers Savi away distractedly and moves around comfortably in their kitchen. Has Crystal been too accommodating with her? Have the lines blurred between who's in charge and who isn't?

Before she knows what she's doing, she crumples the flyer and tosses it into the trash. "I'm going out."

"But we just got back!" Savi stomps back into the hallway. "Why do you always leave?"

Pam mindlessly bites into a carrot as she prepares lunch.

The statement smacks her in the chest. "Honey, I'm not always leaving."

"Yes, you are!" Savi balls her fists. "You never want to be where I am." Savi throws a carrot onto the ground. Pam picks it up and tosses it into the trash.

"Hey, Savi. That's not true." Crystal crosses to where she's standing and kneels in front of her. "Look at me. I always want to be where you are. I'm still just juggling work and home, okay? It's a lot. That's why we have Pam. She's our special helper." Crystal crushes her daughter in a hug and releases her.

She looks at Pam. "Can I talk to you outside for a second?" Crystal jerks her head toward the front door.

"Sure." Pam wipes her hands on a dish towel and smiles at Savi. "You've got to help me make a bunny rabbit when I get back."

"I'll get the dates and the cashews!"

Pam laughs as she steps outside. "We found the cutest recipes to make little bunny rabbits from this kid's cookbook. She's really enjoying cooking lately."

"What's going on?" Crystal interrupts.

"What's going on with what?"

"With you? With Savi? With . . ." She motions toward the house. Crystal folds her arms and glances toward the street to wave to Parker, an eighty-five-year-old who walks five miles per day, rain or shine. A sprinkler hisses next door. Crystal eyes their own lawn, desperately in need of watering, and drags her gaze back to Pam.

"Something's different with Savi." Pam verbalizes what she's been thinking. Something *is* different.

"What?"

Pam gathers her unruly hair in a bun then releases it. A few ginger strands flutter toward the front porch. "I need to tell you something." She takes a shaky breath.

Crystal holds her own breath, expecting her to confess something terrible.

"When you mentioned Paul's things had gone missing, I felt terrible." She lowers her voice and eyes the front door. "I didn't want to upset Savi, but I was putting her magic kit away, and I found them hidden in one of the compartments. The stuff you mentioned. There was a journal too. And a business book. I didn't want to get her in more trouble with everything going on, so I left them there." She stares at her feet like a child. "I can show you."

The truth lands like a fist. Not that Savi took Paul's items, but that her own daughter lied straight to her face. Before she can respond, the front door opens.

"Your phone." Savi wags Crystal's cell. She fingers her back pocket. Savi must have swiped it. She bites back a scream. "You have a text from Ms. Rebecca."

She shoves down Pam's confession and reads the text. "I've got to go." She dashes inside to grab her keys and brushes past Pam.

"Is everything okay?" Pam asks.

"Can I come too, Mom?"

"No, stay here," Crystal says. "I'll be back soon." She looks at Pam. "We'll talk later, okay?"

She stabs her keys in the ignition and hurries to Bec's house.

She hopes she's not too late.

37

B E C

I'M SURE I HAVEN'T HEARD HIM RIGHT. "BETH BOUGHT THAT ONESIE? FOR
Trevor?"

"Trevor is her son, correct?" Jake asks.

I nod. "Yes, and he's the same age as Jackson." I catalogue all of
our recent conversations: Beth, constantly complaining about her
child, wishing for a little space, making comments about Jackson
never fussing. I grab his forearm. "She just made a joke the other day
about us trading babies."

"Why didn't you mention that?"

I shake my head. "Because the baby upstairs isn't Trevor."

"How do you know that for certain, Rebecca?"

How *do* I know that for certain? I've not held Trevor, and I've never
scanned him the way I have Jackson, but I'm almost certain it's not
him from his cry alone. But in this situation, can I really be sure of
who's in that crib?

"When's the last time you saw her?"

I change positions, and my back screams. "I just saw her at the
parade."

"Was Trevor with her?"

I glance up, suddenly terrified. "No, he wasn't with her. Jess even
commented on it. Beth said he was at home. But she practices attachment parenting. He's always with her." I wonder if that's why

this baby loves to be held so close too? "Oh my God." My body goes limp. Does Beth have Jackson? As irrational as it is, the thought gives me some sort of strange comfort. Beth would never hurt Jackson . . . would she? "What do we do?"

"I'm going to talk to her. See if Trevor is there. I've got the photo of Jackson, so I can compare."

"Let me come." My legs still tremble from the fall. "Please."

"Bec." Jake sighs. "Stay here and rest. I'll call you."

I reluctantly nod. Once he's sure I'm placated and comfortable, he's gone. I sink farther into the couch cushions and replay every conversation I've ever had with Beth, deconstructing our relationship piece by piece. Our babies are just weeks apart. She constantly comments what a good baby Jackson is and how lucky I am. Why haven't I held Trevor? Plus, she bought a onesie from the store. The same onesie the baby upstairs came home in. Doesn't that prove something?

Or everything.

I grab my phone and text Jess and Crystal to come over. I say those four little words into the quiet house, as my voice translates it to a group text.

I need your help.

I dissect what I know about Beth. She's married to a wealthy surgeon. She belongs to several clubs: tennis club, country club, boat club. But since Trevor, she's been holed up in her house or out with a few friends and that's it. Why was she suddenly alone at the parade?

The timing is too uncanny. Every part of me wants to chase after Jake and break Beth's door down to deliver my own line of questioning. But I know I have to wait. After I work myself into a mental frenzy and ice my back until it's completely numb, the doorbell rings and interrupts my train of thought.

"Bec?" It's Jess. "What's going on? Are you okay?" She closes the door behind her. "Why are you walking like you're ninety?"

"I fell down the stairs."

"Oh my God, what? Are you okay?"

I wave my hand. "It's fine." I explain what Jake found out about Beth. "Remember at the parade? Trevor wasn't with her. That can't be a coincidence. It just can't be."

"Where's Jake now?"

"At Beth's."

Jess slides my hand in hers and then sighs. "Bec, you're forgetting one thing."

"What?"

"*I* know what Trevor looks like. Unequivocally. I see him all the time. It's not him."

The crushing disappointment holds me under. "But you see Jackson all the time too and you swore that the baby upstairs is him. And it's not."

"I haven't spent as much time with Jackson as I have with Trevor."

"Just go check again. Please."

She disappears upstairs. My head sags into my open palms. This can't be another dead end. I can't handle one more misstep, one more false hope.

"Bec?" Crystal knocks sharply on the door and enters. She rushes to my side. "What in the world is going on?"

I don't say anything. I attempt to form the words, but I can't. She walks me to the couch. To my surprise, I start to cry.

"Hey." Her fingers comb through my hair. "It's all going to be okay." I lower my head against her shoulder and for one agonizing moment, I miss my mother so much, I can't breathe.

Jess's footsteps sound on the stairs. I blot my tears with my T-shirt and sit up. The effort strains the muscles around my spine, and I wince.

"It's not Trevor," Jess confirms.

"Who's not Trevor?" Crystal asks. "What am I missing?"

"The receipt," Jess explains. "Jake narrowed it down to Beth. Beth bought the same onesie that the baby has."

"Wait." Crystal's voice changes. "I saw Beth at the parade, but she didn't have Trevor. When I asked her about it, she was weird."

"What do you mean weird?" I ask.

"Just . . . I don't know. Nervous or something."

"See?" Hope surges. "Where is he? If she has Trevor, then *where is he*?" I address Crystal. "You've seen him before, right?"

"Only a few times. Honestly, I'm not sure I'd be able to recognize him."

"Well, I can," Jess affirms again. "It's not Trevor."

"Because you think it's *Jackson*!" I scream. "And it's not!" My throat is raw. "I can't do this. I literally can't do this." I lurch toward my front door, pain throbbing from the base of my spine to my heels, and grab my cane. I leave my friends, the baby, even my phone.

"Rebecca!" They call after me, but I'm too quick. I disappear down the walk, make a sharp left, and press my body against a neighbor's garage in the back, next to a ditch. Even if they pass, they won't see me. I used to hide here as a kid, when our neighbors Nancy and Fred lived here. It was the best hiding spot in the whole neighborhood, and I'd sometimes fall asleep from waiting so long for someone to find me—which they never did. I sink to the ground and attempt to catch my breath. Crystal's voice calls for me, and I bite my lip to keep quiet. Though Jess insists I'm wrong, Crystal hasn't. But I haven't come right out and asked her either: does she believe someone is out to get me, or does she think I'm out to get myself?

When her voice dies, I hobble away from the wall. I hesitate with one hand still against the brick. A neighbor's dog barks and growls, and I pray he's behind a fence. Part of me just wants to turn back and go home. Without my phone, it could be dangerous if I take a wrong turn. But I need to see Beth and know that the child in her home isn't mine.

I make it to the end of the block and calculate directions in my head. I piece the street names together, imagining my neighborhood on a map. On the way, I channel every interaction with Trevor.

While I've held Baxter countless times, Beth is strangely possessive about Trevor and never lets him out of her sight. Until the parade.

I quicken my pace. What if Jake's already found something and is on his way back to my house? What if he has Jackson? The thought halts me in my tracks.

"Rebecca!" Footsteps pound behind me until a breathless Crystal joins me. "Where are you going? The baby . . ."

Guilt squeezes my heart. "I know. I just wanted to see . . ." I collapse against her shoulder, and once again, she's there to comfort me.

"I can't even imagine everything you're going through, but I know Jackson is okay. He has to be." Finally, she pulls away. "At least let me walk you there."

"You're not going to talk me out of it?"

"I don't think that's really an option, is it?"

In all the commotion, Crystal left without getting Beth's address from Jess, but I remember. I search for landmarks on the way and commit them to memory. I fumble only once, when we turn a block early, but Crystal tells me the street name and we turn back to find the correct one. My thoughts have caused the ultimate distraction, and when I step up to knock on the door, a woman answers and asks if she can help me.

"I'm so sorry. I'm looking for Beth Harrison's house?"

"Just one more over."

I motion to my left. "That way?"

"Are you blind, dear?"

I nod.

"May God bless you." Her screen door bangs shut. I don't know how to tell her that sometimes I think God forgot to check my limit on what one can endure.

"Is Jake's car here?" I ask Crystal.

"Unless he drives a Mercedes, then no."

"At least she's here." I know from our conversations that Beth's car is candy-apple red, obsessively waxed, and she bought it in cash after working for Rodan + Fields. Aside from Trevor, that car is her pride and joy.

Crystal guides me toward the front door. "What if Jackson really is here? What do I do?"

"We'll figure it out." Her voice cracks with tension. She slips her free hand through mine and squeezes.

I stab the doorbell and wait.

38

BEC

⠃⠑⠉

BETH OPENS IT ALMOST IMMEDIATELY. "REBECCA, MY GOD. ARE YOU OKAY?"
She pulls me into a hug. Her fingers press against my bruised spine,
and I wriggle out of her touch. "Your friend was just here. I can't
believe you think . . ."

I don't even ask to come inside or explain why Crystal is with me. I
ask her the single question I need the answer to: "Do you have Jackson?"

She sighs and opens the door wider. "No, I don't." Her cold fingers
clamp around my wrist. She walks me to her sitting room that smells
like freshly cut flowers.

"Then where's Trevor? He wasn't with you at the parade."

"I know. He wasn't." She sits beside me, and I twist my body to face
her. I'm not sure where Crystal is in the room, but she's silent. "I felt
guilty."

"Guilty about what?" I ask.

"Guilty that I couldn't handle the whole attachment parenting
thing. I needed a break."

"What does that mean?"

"It means that I hired a babysitter and went out and enjoyed myself." Her voice cracks, and I marvel over people's thresholds—what
will break some people and not others. "I know that's terrible, but it's
what I needed."

"Where's Trevor now?" I ask.

"Upstairs. Finally asleep, thank God."

"Did Jake confirm that?"

"He did, Bec." Her fingers find my knee. "I'm so sorry. I would never do anything like that to you. You have to know that."

"I don't know anything anymore." Hysteria creeps into my voice, but I steel myself. "Do you mind if I go up?"

"I'll go with her," Crystal says.

"How about we all ago?" Beth slaps her thighs and follows us upstairs. The wood doesn't groan under my feet as it does in my own house. Instead, a plush runner silences all of our footsteps as we reach the landing.

"Which way?"

"Left. First door to your right."

I hesitate outside the nursery. Part of me wants to go in and part of me doesn't. Beth breezes past. "So much for just getting him down," she mumbles.

I almost roll my eyes at her self-centeredness, but I also understand that she's just a mom going through her own rough spell too. And she's indulging me—I have to give her that, at least.

"Hey, little guy. Hey." She scoops him up and shushes him before he's even crying. "He likes to be bounced constantly. So unless you want a pierced eardrum . . ."

She hands him over, and I catch my breath as his weight lands in my arms. A tiny chasm of hope widens inside of me: he's the same weight as Jackson. I lower a hand over his face. My fingers skitter over his eyes, nose, and mouth as if singing him a lullaby. The hope eviscerates. His nose isn't the same. Neither is his chin. I search his collarbone: smooth.

He opens his mouth and begins to cry. Now I remember its exact sound, how it scratches and hunts for whoever's listening. It's why Beth is always so tired. For the second time, I know for certain: that's not Jackson's cry. I hand him back over to Beth, who starts shushing and bouncing him so loudly, I fear she'll pass out from lack of breath. Miraculously, he settles, and we tiptoe out the door.

"That's the only thing that puts him back down lately," she whispers. "I literally shushed so hard the other night, I almost fainted."

A raging disappointment overtakes my body on the bottom stair.

The three of us stand awkwardly near the front door. "I'm sorry, Beth."

"Don't be. I can't imagine what you're going through." She touches my arm. "Do you want a cup of tea or something?"

Beth isn't British, but she's watched enough BBC to think that a cup of tea really is the answer to all of life's problems, and that by continuously offering, all of her Midwestern friends will eventually convert. I shake my head and hesitate with my hand on the doorknob. "Wait." I turn back. "The onesie."

"The what?"

"The white onesie from Cornerstone. You bought one, right?"

"I did. I picked one up a while ago, but couldn't believe the price for a plain white onesie. But I loved that it wasn't just another generic find. I found the artist on Etsy and placed an order in bulk for the summer festival this June."

I shake my head. "You sold them?"

"I did some letter-printing. But I also sold some plain white ones."

"How many did you sell?"

"I don't know. Maybe thirty?"

"Would there be a way to get the receipts for who bought them?" I know I'm plucking at straws, but it's all I've got.

"I handed them over to the festival manager for their seasonal write-offs. I can look into it though."

"That would be great." Crystal finally speaks up and snakes an arm around my shoulder. "Thanks for your help, Beth."

"Of course." She opens the door for us. "I'd do the same thing if I thought . . . well, anyway. I'll see you at the vigil?"

I turn. "You're coming?"

"Friends show up for each other no matter what." She sounds like she's reciting something from a Hallmark card.

I don't remind her that my supposed friends are the very reason I had to lie to the police in the first place.

"Bye, Bec." Her door shuts, but I am still haunted by Trevor's cry.

Crystal's phone rings, and she drops her hand. "Hello?" She steps away and talks in hushed tones then hangs up. "That's odd. That was Officer Toby. He wants me to come in."

"Really?" If they've dropped any sort of investigation, why are they calling her in now? Suddenly, I feel horrible that all my friends are being subjected to questioning, but if it gets me even one step closer to finding my son, then it's a price I hope they're willing to pay. "I'm sorry, Crystal."

"Don't be. I'm happy to help." Her voice is strained. "The station is just a few blocks away. Do you want me to walk back with you first?"

I shake my head. "I'm okay. Let me know how it goes."

"I will." She pulls me into a hug, and I grimace. "I'll see you to-night."

She jogs away in the opposite direction. I'm alone on the street. I don't want to go home and face Jake or Jess—if she's even still there. The baby! I hurry back toward my house and attempt to calm my nerves. Jessica would never leave a baby at home alone. Though she's been leaving Baxter with the nanny to tend to my every beck and call.

Once again, I battle the guilt about taking my friends away from their children. I turn right, pick up my pace, but stop at the entrance to Wilder. Voices vibrate from the playground and prick my ears with curiosity. No matter how hard I try, this park keeps sucking me back like the scene of a crime.

Because it is, I remind myself. My clothes stick to my heated body, and I'm practically folded in half from how severely my back hurts. I go to ask Siri the time and remember I've forgotten my phone: such a stupid mistake. I finger my wrist, but I'm not wearing my watch either. When someone passes, I ask for the time: three.

I have four hours before the vigil. I wind through the path and stop at the bench. The same bench. What will I find this time? Life chirps around me, filling the lapses in thought. *The baby.* My chest feels naked without him.

Random conversation ebbs and flows. Moms so obliviously tired. Moms with their girlfriends. Moms with their children.

"I know, right?" A woman's bright, happy voice laughs and then another sound cracks against my skull like a hammer. Such a large impact for such a small thing. I gasp and crank my body toward the sound. I slide closer to the edge of the bench. My tailbone screams.

One woman continues to talk about bedroom organization, the mess of books versus toys, what to feed her youngest daughter who's just started solids. Hands plunge into a bag, fingers rummaging. I wait, but nothing.

Suddenly, something drops off the bench, and there it is again: the slightest tinkle. I lower to my hands and knees. "Let me help." My fingers fuss around random objects—tampons, lipstick, wipes, keys, a compact.

"Thanks, but I've got it." The woman scoops possessively at her belongings, but not before I find what I'm looking for. My fingers bump over the tiny bells, each of them as familiar to me as Jackson. I clutch them to my chest and almost weep. The tiny jingle is a welcome relief from all the uncertainty.

"Excuse me," I interrupt. A few of the women stop talking at the urgency in my voice. I dangle the bells like a Christmas caroler. "Where did you get these?" My voice is clipped, and I rearrange my tone, soften it to get the answers I need.

"They're my daughter's. Can I have them, please?"

"Are you sure they're hers?" I examine them again. "Did she find them somewhere, or . . . ?"

"No." The woman snatches them from my extended palm. "I bought them."

"They're so cute. They remind me of Christmas," one of her friends says. "Though they can be a choking hazard. Does she know not to put them in her mouth?"

"Christmas will be here before we all know it; can you believe it?" another woman comments.

That sets off a chain of commentary about how fast the years are going and how none of their kids need toys, and can they boycott the holidays this year like Vince Vaughn and Reese Witherspoon did in *Four Christmases*?

"Where? Where did you buy them?" My voice knots in my throat.

"Some boutique store downtown."

"Downtown Elmhurst?"

She doesn't confirm. "The thing is, my son has some just like those. He lost them in this park. I've been looking everywhere."

Someone smothers a laugh behind her hand.

"Well, I'm sorry he lost them. But these are *ours*." The woman continues talking to her friend. I can almost imagine her hair flip and eye roll. Apparently, I've stumbled onto the only mean girl group in Elmhurst, but at the moment, I don't care. I turn, grab my cane, and unfold it. The women silence as I follow the path to the sidewalk. That can't be a coincidence. How would his bells end up in her bag at the same exact spot? I wish I could glimpse the women—to see if there are any obvious clues.

Don't get your hopes up.

On the way home, I can no longer ignore the ache in my body. I need to sit down. I need to rest. In my driveway, Jake's car is still warm. "Hello?" I follow the sound of hushed voices in the dining room.

"Jesus," Jess rushes over. "Are you okay? We've been worried sick."

"I found the bells."

A chair scrapes. Jake crosses over to me in a few quick steps. "Where?"

"Wilder. A woman had them in her bag. She said they were her daughter's, but isn't that too much of a coincidence? I didn't get her name." Even to my own ears, I sound desperate, reaching. I take a step back and my foot catches on the edge of the rug. I right myself before I fall backward, but the way my body contorts makes me cry out in pain.

"Alright, that's it. Sit."

Jake ushers me to the couch, but I push him away. "I want to be alone."

"Rebecca." Jess's voice is firm, reassuring. "We're here to help."

"I want to be alone," I say again. "Please."

Jake whispers something to Jess and she sighs. She pauses on her way out. "Get some rest." The door clicks shut, and I cross my arms.

"You too, Donovan."

"I need to talk to you."

"Did you not hear me? I said I want to be alone."

"No. I need to talk to you," he says again. His calmness irritates me.

"Why? None of it matters, right? It's all just a wild-goose chase. The baby upstairs is *my* baby, and this has all just been some figment of my imagination, caused by my own grief."

"Sit *down*." Jake's voice is kind but firm.

I move around him like a petulant teen and gingerly lower myself onto the same couch cushion from only an hour ago. "What?"

"I went to Beth's."

"I did too."

"Of course you did." He almost sounds impressed.

"Is that it?" I lean forward to get up, but he stops me.

"No. I need to know you're okay." He struggles for words. "I'm really worried."

What is your point? I almost scream.

He scratches his jaw. "I got a call from Dr. Gibbons."

"And?"

"She thinks you might need an evaluation, Bec. And I hate to say it, but given all that you've been through, I think it might not be a bad idea."

"An evaluation for what?" He won't dare say it. He won't question my mental stability. He doesn't have the guts.

"I just think it would be wise to talk to someone. That's all I'm saying."

"You promised you'd help me."

Silence descends between us. He begins to speak, but then his phone buzzes. "Donovan."

I close my eyes. All this time and I'm not any closer to my son. What am I even *doing*? I think about Beth, the onesie, the vigil, the bells. Where are the real clues? The real leads?

"We'll be right there." He disconnects. "That was Prentice. They pulled some strings and got a working scanner. Not sure if it's as comprehensive as CertaScan, but it's something. Should be the same database."

"You mean . . ." My breath leaves my body. "We're going to actually get some answers?"

"Here's hoping. I'll get the baby."

The baby. I locate the carrier, car seat, and the diaper bag, and drop them in the front hall. I haven't even thought about the baby's real name, what it will be like to give him an identity.

Jake descends moments later. I gather the baby in my arms and realize I missed him the short time I was away. I close my eyes and breathe in this innocent child's now familiar scent.

"Will we be back in time for the vigil?"

Jake checks the time. "Gonna be tight."

On the way, Jake fills me in on the details about this particular technology as if reading from a brochure. "Pat did some digging. Certa-Scan is compliant with the latest NCMEC's Instant Security Guidelines and even mitigates hospital risk by preventing baby switches with the strictest infant safety guidelines available. Ironically, it's literally built to prevent things like this from happening."

"Only if your baby is switched in the hospital," I conclude.

I know he senses my despondency, because he sounds upbeat and positive—a tactic he used to employ for his most unhinged suspects. He forgets that I know him. The calmer he gets, the worse it really is. He continues to spout off facts.

Now that he's talking about it, I remember one of the nurses going over the same information after Jackson was born. But I was in such a blissed-out state, I wasn't paying attention. I didn't think my baby could ever get taken. Even with my vision impairment. Even though my husband was dead. When Jackson was placed in my arms, I experienced such an overwhelming protectiveness, it was . . . instinctive. Certain. He belonged to me.

Some of Jake's positivity starts to creep in as we inch closer to the city. Maybe this single piece of technology will be the very thing to bring my son home. If this baby is in the system too, then it will prove he's *not* Jackson. The world will know. People will start looking for him instead of just looking at me.

At the hospital, we take the elevator up. He verbally guides me down the hall, even though I remember where to go. Chris used to make jokes about my photographic memory—how only *I* would be able to navigate the world without sight and still be able to see. He wasn't entirely wrong. The images from memory play out almost like reading a book. Everything unfolds as if on a screen.

We reach the maternity floor. I remember coming here for my very first maternity class, where I held a lifelike doll and had to change a diaper. My fingers were clumsy and unpracticed, and I felt like all the other parents were watching me. It wasn't Chris in the class with me—it was my mother. I channel the strength she instilled in me now, because I'm going to need it.

Jake holds the door open and a blast of cold bites my skin. Suddenly,

I'm frozen with nerves. What if this is another dead end? If their machine somehow doesn't work too? I touch Jake's elbow. "If he's not in the system . . ."

"Then we'll scan him now and move onto DNA analysis. It will take some time, as I said before, but we need definitive answers. *You* need definitive answers."

At the desk, Jake flashes his badge, and things move quickly. No signing in. No waiting. We're immediately ushered back to one of the small, sterile rooms in under two minutes.

Jake does all the talking. I'm glad I don't have to lie, pretend, or rely on my other senses. Jake is here. Jake will tell me what happens. The nurse introduces herself, and Jake provides a high-level rundown.

"Well, let's see what we can do then," she says. She's soft-spoken. "This little machine is like an insurance policy against any sort of kidnapping or switches after birth. Which is why they're working so hard to get all the kinks out." Jake informs her that we're aware of all the machine's advantages. She messes with some cords. "Ready?"

I rearrange the baby on my lap. "Ready."

"Okay, little guy. I need that foot," she says. I settle him on his back so she can press the sole of his foot against the flat screen.

"So, I'm just getting his foot in position," she explains. She clicks a few buttons and turns a monitor. Jake walks me through it step-by-step.

"Once we scan him, it will bring up his electronic medical records on the computer, okay?"

"Okay." I can barely breathe, I'm so nervous.

The scan begins. There's a loud beep, then silence.

I draw a bottomless breath and await my fate.

39

CRYSTAL

⠠⠊⠀⠠�... (braille decorative text)

THE PLAYGROUND AT WILDER IS TRANSFORMED. SOMEHOW, IN THE SPAN OF a few hours, a small stage has been erected with twinkle lights hanging from a pergola. A podium with a microphone sits center stage.

Crystal checks her watch. It's only six-thirty, but people are already gathering. The excited buzz of neighborhood drama pulls people from their homes. It's like the parade all over again, as neighbors vie for their prime viewing spot. She hunts for familiar faces in the sea of strangers, ball caps, and high ponytails.

Caroline steps behind the podium. She folds her thin hands in front of her pressed mulberry pants. She leans in and the crowd hushes. "We will get started in exactly thirty minutes. Thank you all *so* much for coming." Her voice booms across the playground. She presses her hands to her lips in an invisible kiss and opens them in a gracious thank-you. Diamond-encrusted bangles travel up her wrists toward her elbows. The jewels twinkle as they catch the last remnants of sun. Caroline's eyes reveal nothing behind her Dior sunglasses. Is she wondering where Rebecca is too?

Crystal scans the crowd again, but she doesn't see her. After she left Bec this afternoon, her mind spun on a continuous loop. The station had been quick. She told Officer Toby exactly what happened when Bec arrived at her house and that Jackson had been in his stroller the entire time. It had made her uncomfortable how much Toby had probed her about Rebecca's character, but she told them what an amazing mother she is. She left the station feeling like she'd done something wrong—like they weren't pumping her for information to *find* Jackson—more like they were building a case to take him away. She almost called Bec to warn her, but she didn't want her to worry about one more thing.

Back at home, Crystal had looked at her daughter with fresh eyes. She wasn't angry about her stealing Paul's things. She just wanted to know why she felt the need to lie.

Instead of interrogating her daughter or getting lost in a sea of work emails, they'd made an early dinner and baked cookies, and then Pam had started a movie for Savi when Crystal had to leave. She'd ignored the knife twisting her gut. Was Savi right? Did she always leave?

Crystal walks the perimeter of the park and sits on a bench. The crowd grows and strengthens. The collective buzz of *something happening* builds. She watches neighbors wave and chat like it's just a casual gathering. Groups form then separate. Crystal ignores that outsider feeling—the one where she's part of a community, but not included in what makes up the community. Friendships. Neighbors. PTA meetings. Bake sales. It's what she recognized in Rebecca too—that they are different.

Some unruly children break free from their parents to climb the monkey bars and zip down slides. A few dads lose sight of their kids and bark out names. Mothers shift and whisper behind cupped palms. If there's a kidnapper on the loose, then no one is immune, right? Speculation tumbles and ripples like a wave. Crystal adjusts her sunglasses and leans forward to pick up a book a little girl accidentally dropped.

"Here you go."

The girl secures it to her chest and doesn't say thank you. Stranger danger is in full effect, it seems. After glimpsing all the kids, she realizes she could have brought Savi, but she doesn't want to expose her to anything else that could create a sense of anxiety.

"Long time no see," Jess says behind her.

Crystal turns to wave. Jess's brown, curly hair has caught the humidity and expanded. Her curvy figure looks perfect in her denim jumpsuit and Vans. Jess offers her a sincere smile. Baxter is in his carrier. Rob stands behind his wife, hands thrust into both pockets.

"Where's Savi?" Jess asks.

"At home with the nanny."

Jess sighs as she sits. "What a day, huh?"

"That's putting it mildly," Crystal says.

"Ladies." Officer Toby approaches the bench, and Crystal inwardly groans. He garners a few looks and comments from the crowd, as he's still in his police uniform. He shakes Rob's hand and the two launch into light conversation. Jess leans in and runs her fingers through Baxter's curls. "Is she here?"

Crystal knows *she* means Rebecca. "Not that I've seen, no." Crystal takes another quick inventory of the playground. "Have you talked to her since this afternoon?"

"Won't return my texts."

Bodies crush and sway in the small space. If there was beer and a band, she could almost trick herself into believing this was some lovely summer concert and not a vigil for her friend's missing son.

"Do you think she'll come?" Jess asks.

"Of course she will." The words are out of Crystal's mouth before she can really think them through. *Will she come?* Would *she* come if she were in Bec's position?

"Beth! Over here." Jess spots Beth through the crowd. She carries Trevor in a ring sling. He's wearing red-and-white-striped socks and clutches a wooden teething ring. His gray eyes blink and twinkle in the sun. It's clear, even from a few feet away, that this child is not Jackson. Even she can recognize the difference now.

"Good lord. This is insanity," Beth says. "How did Caroline do all this so fast?" Her cheeks are pink, her tanned, toned legs on display in white shorts. She bounces Trevor up and down, and her quadriceps flex. She doesn't wait for an answer. "I just feel so awful that she actually thought I would ever take her baby." She fusses over Trevor. "It's honestly made me look at him in an entirely new way. I won't ever complain about him again, I can assure you of that." On cue, he drops his teething ring and gives out a sharp cry.

Jess rolls her eyes. "Oh please. I give it a week."

"You're probably right," she jokes. She brushes off the teething ring and hands it back. Beth waves to someone and mouths hello. "I think the entire town is here."

"Well, Caroline Walker is a force," Jess says.

Crystal is surprised by their light, flippant attitudes. Behind her, she catches tidbits of Officer Toby's conversation with Rob. "Mrs. Gray told us she made it all up, but clearly Caroline has other ideas." He lowers his voice. "The chief doesn't want Elmhurst to become a laughingstock, you know?"

She waits for a lull and butts in. "Are you going to be turning this into more of an active investigation after tonight?" She wants him to verbalize his intentions. But she knows he'd never admit to what he was really after: Rebecca. Instead, questioning Crystal maintained the appearance of the police doing their part. The half-assed questioning. The quick dismissal. It had all been for show.

Toby rocks back on his heels. His crew cut and clean face make him look much younger than he probably is. "No, ma'am, we're not. Unless there's actual evidence, then I'm afraid we don't have a case."

Except the case you're building against Rebecca, you mean.

"Caroline seems to think otherwise," Jess scoffs. "Police or no police, she's taking matters into her own hands."

"That's Caroline for you," Rob says. "When she believes something, good luck to the fool who tries to stop her."

Officer Toby bows his head and shakes it. His military cut reveals a shiny, pink bald spot on his crown. Paul flashes through her mind.

He was in the Navy years before they met. He kept his hair short like Officer Toby's, and she loved to run her palms over the stubble when he was fresh out of the shower. By the end of their marriage, his hair had grown longer and would often flop into his eyes. She hated it that way, but Evelyn loved it. Her stomach tightens.

"Here you go." Someone thrusts a fake candle into her hand.

"Where in the world did Caroline find so many of these on short notice?" Jess sounds impressed. She twists the candle in her hand and lets Baxter play with it.

"Definitely sets the mood," Beth says.

Jess wrestles the candle from Baxter's strong grip and waves her candle in the air, as if at a concert. Beth joins in.

Crystal ignores their childish behavior, removes her sunglasses as the sun prepares to set, and turns her attention to the microphone. Caroline waits for silence. Crystal glances at her watch. Seven on the dot.

Showtime.

Finally, the crowd settles. "Welcome, everyone. We are here to raise awareness about Rebecca Gray's missing son, Jackson Gray." Caroline holds a flyer in her hand. "Rebecca's son has been missing since Thursday morning and it's up to us to bring him back." She pauses to show the crowd. Behind her, a projector lowers, which startles a few spectators. Jackson's face expands to the entire width of the screen. Crystal strains to see, since it's not completely dark yet.

Caroline mentions more details but conveniently leaves out the part about Rebecca believing her son is swapped. She's leading with the direst facts first—facts that people will believe. A missing baby is serious and warrants all hands on deck. But a *swapped* child? No one knows what to do with that.

Crystal grows antsier with every passing word, murmur from the crowd, and question flung up to the podium. She turns to Officer Toby.

"Shouldn't you say something?"

He shrugs. "Not my event."

Suddenly, there's commotion in the crowd. Bodies part to make room. Crystal stands to see what's going on, and then Rebecca appears, red ball cap pulled low over her forehead, sunglasses on, her cane swatting the space in front of her. A baby is strapped to her chest. Jake is right behind her and helps her onto the stage.

Everything in Crystal seizes. Rebecca fumbles, then connects with the podium. She strips the ball cap from her head. Her brown hair tumbles loose and wild around her shoulders. She removes her sunglasses, and her green eyes flash as she stares blankly into the crowd. Crystal glances around her, but everyone is riveted, a few whispering about the baby.

"I've just come from Prentice Hospital in Chicago," she explains. Her voice is hoarse. She clears her throat and tries again. "When Jackson went missing on Thursday, another baby was left in his place. This baby." She places both hands on the squirming bundle.

A surprised cry ripples through the crowd and she waits for them to quiet. "No one would believe that another baby was left in his place. *No one.*" Her voice is hard. It's a punch to the gut, but Crystal listens.

"But I know my child," Bec continues. "I know Jackson. And now, we have proof." She extends her hand and Jake lays a piece of paper in it. "We've just had this baby's footprint scanned." She explains what CertaScan is and how Jackson was entered into the system when he was first born. "This is confirmation that this child is not Jackson. Their footprints don't match."

A surprised cry escapes Crystal's lips. Jess pushes in beside her. "No fucking way," she whispers.

"What's his name?" someone cries.

Rebecca leans in, both of her hands squeezing the sides of the podium. "His name is Oliver Watson. And he's not my son."

One unified gasp radiates through the crowd, Crystal included. Heads swivel and voices converge and clash. Her heart pounds so violently, she braces one hand against her chest.

"Holy shit, holy shit, holy shit," Jess mutters. She bounces Baxter up and down. Their eyes meet in shock. "I didn't believe her. All this time, I didn't . . ."

"Son of a bitch." Officer Toby practically jumps the bench to join Jake onstage. Caroline loops an arm around Rebecca's shoulders, and Crystal finds herself sucked toward the stage, as people murmur and figure out what to do.

Jess calls out to her, but it's as if she's underwater. She makes out fragments of conversation, some still in disbelief and some figuring out what they can do to help. She walks toward the stage, where Toby and Jake talk privately.

"You've got to understand my position here, Jake. If this baby's not hers, I'm not convinced Jackson is even still alive. You get what I'm saying?"

Crystal recoils, appalled. She's heard stories like that—of mothers whose children die unexpectedly and they steal another baby to replace it. But Bec isn't a child murderer. That much she knows. She steps onto the small stage, but Bec is gone.

A few people stop and stare up at her, as she has accidentally positioned herself behind the microphone. She crosses to the edge of the stage and shields her eyes as the last rays of the day drop from the flushed violet sky.

There.

Caroline is no longer shielding Rebecca from the crowd, and people swarm her. They offer help, sympathy, and fling questions at her like she's a celebrity. Crystal practically lunges off the stage and elbows her way through the neighbors. She struggles for breath, never one for crowds. Shouldn't Jake be with Rebecca? Where is he? She turns her head to see if he's still talking to Toby, but he's marching through the crowd too, which parts for him automatically. They reach Bec at the same time, and Crystal stops a few feet away. Someone else grabs her attention first: Pam.

Crystal grabs her elbow and steers her toward a tree. "What are you doing here? Where's Savi?"

Her red hair is in a topknot, and a few strands have escaped and gotten caught on her glossy red lips. She rips the strands free, and a smear of ruby drags across her cheeks like blood. "She's in the car." She points to Crystal's white Suburban that idles at the curb. From behind the tinted windows, Crystal can't see Savi.

"I really wish you wouldn't have brought her."

Pam points at the crowd. "What happened? What did they say?"

"I'll tell you at home."

Someone calls Pam's name and she waves and tells him to hold on just a minute.

Crystal assesses the guy: cute, young, tall. "Who's that?"

"Just a friend. Greg." Pam glances at her shoes and at Greg again. She bites her bottom lip and smiles. "I'll be right back, okay?" Pam tentatively approaches Greg and succumbs to a flurry of flirtatious behavior. Crystal sighs and retreats toward the car. When she turns back, she hunts for the red hair, but Pam has been sucked into the crowd.

Crystal curses under her breath. Should she go after her? She strains to find Rebecca, but she's vanished too. She raps on the window for Savi to roll it down.

"Where'd Pam go?"

"With a friend," Crystal says. She peers into the car, her daughter's large eyes worried. She jogs around to the driver's side. "I told you I wouldn't be gone long."

Savi points out the window. "But I wanted to see Ms. Rebecca."

"I know." Crystal buckles her seat belt and tentatively steps on the gas. "I do too." She inches forward as people flood the street. She hunts for Rebecca or Pam. Her mind is a vortex of jumbled facts and thoughts. Through it all, Rebecca's statement still roars in her ears:

His name is Oliver Watson. And he's not my son.

40

BEC

OLIVER WATSON. I CHEW OVER THE UNFAMILIAR NAME AND SIFT BACK through Chris's colleagues, his family, my family, and our mutual friends, but I don't know anyone with the last name Watson.

Jake drives us to the police station in silence. Everything's gone so fast since just a few hours ago, but I will never forget that pivotal moment when the nurse revealed who this mystery baby was. The absolute validation cascaded through my entire body: Oliver Watson.

Not Jackson Gray.

The nurse had cranked the screen to show Jake, and he'd confirmed. They'd both hunted through the rest of the file, but the electronic medical records hadn't told us the mother's name. Only the Department of Children and Family Services was listed.

My mind had exploded with possibilities. Was this baby put up for adoption? Was he a drug baby? Did he even have parents? How did he get to Elmhurst? Jake had contacted DCFS immediately, but had only gotten a voice mail. He'd been trying ever since to get someone active on the line, and now that Officer Toby is in my corner, I'm cautiously confident they'll figure out next steps.

"You okay?" Jake asks.

"Debatable." I'm still absorbing the crowd I just left, what it was like to stand behind a podium and verbalize the truth. I *wasn't* imagining things. Oliver *is* a different baby. Knowing I was right all along is still overshadowed by the truth: Jackson is out there. All the recent fears and mishaps haven't been because I'm too tired, paranoid, or grieving. He really is gone. Another baby really is in his place.

Oliver.

My heart jolts. "What's going to happen to him?"

"Oliver?" Jake flicks on his blinker and parks. "DCFS will probably take him."

I swallow the giant lump already forming in my throat. "What if . . ."

"You'd never be able to adopt him, Rebecca. Too many factors to name."

I nod again, gutted. Not that I want another baby, but I can't fathom handing him over to DCFS. I know what happens. My mother was a case worker for years. Oliver will be bounced from home to home until someone finally adopts him. My mother told me more horror stories around what happened to children in foster care than I can recount. Perhaps it wasn't a weak heart that had killed her after all, I realized. Maybe it was heartbreak.

"Ready?" Jake's words crack into my reverie about my mother.

"No." I unbuckle my seat belt anyway. I'd like to say that I am prepared for this, that finally, after days that feel like months, we are getting somewhere, but I have that feeling like I'm the one about to get fooled.

Jake grabs my arm, just as I situate Oliver into my arms. "Let me do most of the talking, okay?"

"I know."

Inside the station, it is abnormally quiet. No ringing phones. No inmates. No people waiting to bail other people out.

"Where is everyone?"

"Vigil," he says.

"Right." Only in Elmhurst would a police station clear out to go to a vigil. Talk about a supportive community.

Toby walks in a few moments later. "Sorry to keep you waiting."

I gauge his voice—calm and even—as he leads us back to his office. No stark interrogation room this time.

"Is this off the record?" I ask.

"You're not on the record, Bec. It's not an interview." Jake clears his throat. "So Oliver Watson. What do we know?"

"DCFS is on their way down. They're going to know more about this boy than we do. We're issuing the Amber Alert immediately for Jackson."

"You are?" A relieved hand flutters to my chest.

"Yes, immediately." He hesitates. "I'm sorry we didn't issue it earlier, Rebecca, but I'm following my chief's orders."

I know all about the chief's orders. He wants to present Elmhurst as a peaceful place—which it always has been. And now there's been nothing but chaos since my move back. We tidy up a few loose ends, and then the questions start. They're subtle at first—it must be hard raising a baby all by myself. How do I manage? How do I know when Jackson is sick? And that's when it hits me: Officer Toby is fishing.

"What are you getting at exactly?" I string his questions together in my head and form my own hypothesis. "Do you think I've harmed my baby and am trying to cover it up somehow?" I look between the two of them, turning their faces into angry black holes in my mind. "Why in the world would I go to all of this trouble? I've been trying to focus on *Jackson,* not this boy."

"I'm just asking, Mrs. Gray—Rebecca. Standard question."

I roll my eyes. "Right, right. Everything's protocol. Of course." Stillness stuffs the room until we're all ready to burst.

"Knock, knock."

Officer Toby shuffles to the door and excuses himself.

"DCFS?" I ask Jake.

"Most likely. Stay here."

I quiet Oliver who has just kicked it into a high enough gear that I can't overhear what's going on outside. "It's okay, little one." My voice catches. Are they going to take him right this second? I kiss the top of his head and sing, which quiets him. Where will they take him? Why can't he just stay with me until they locate his parents?

Worst-case scenarios shuffle through my mind, but I bury them. This isn't about Oliver—as much as I treasure him—it's about Jackson. What feels like an eternity later, Officer Toby, Jake, and a woman enter the room.

"Rebecca, this is Maya from DCFS."

I nod in her direction. "Are you going to ask me questions too?"

"Not my jurisdiction," she says.

I swallow. "Are you here to take Oliver?"

She's quiet.

"Verbal, please," Jake says.

"Oh, sorry. Yes, I am here to take Oliver."

"Where are you taking him?" Then I hold up my hand. "Actually, don't tell me. I can't think about it." I swallow and shush the baby. "Where are his parents?"

Jake slaps what sounds like a file against the desk. "Well that's the damnedest thing, Bec."

"What?" My heart lurches.

"We recovered the mother's name."

"And?" I ask. I brace myself for what he could possibly tell me. "Who is it?"

"Her name is Rose Watson. And she's dead."

41

CRYSTAL

CRYSTAL PULLS OVER TO THE SIDE OF THE ROAD, THEN TURNS AND CLIMBS into the back seat with Savi, who gives a surprised cry.

Savi looks to the third row behind them, shrouded in darkness, and up toward the now empty driver's seat. "What are you doing?"

"Talking." She takes Savi's hands, twists her body until she's facing her daughter, and looks into her eyes. "I want you to talk to me."

Savi pulls her hands away and folds her arms against her chest. "About what?"

"About Dad." She gestures toward the back seat. "About everything."

Savi's chin trembles only for a moment. "We don't ever talk about that."

Crystal closes her eyes. She's made so many mistakes. Sure, *she's* been in therapy, but what about Savi? After Dr. Gibbons saw her a few times, Savi begged not to go back and she didn't want to push her. But she should have. There was a window for grief—a window to deal with unhealthy thoughts formed about relationships, especially for kids. Why hadn't she fought harder these last few months to make sure she was getting the emotional support she really needed?

Savi uncrosses her arms and picks at a loose thread on the seam of her dress.

"That's my fault," Crystal says. "I want to talk about that. I want to know what you're going through, how you're feeling. Do you talk to anybody?"

Everything starts crashing into Crystal. Savi doesn't have a best friend here—or any friends, really. She turns to her cello in times of crisis, or to magic, or to Pam. Pam, who just disappeared in that crowd like a puff of smoke.

As if in confirmation, she shrugs. "I talk to Pam sometimes. But she doesn't know what it's like. And Ms. Rebecca. She makes me feel better."

Her heart wrenches. "It's important to share how you're feeling, even if it's not with me." She hesitates, unsure of how to frame her next question. "What about if we got you into some sort of group with other kids who've lost parents too?" She strokes her short brown hair.

Savi shakes her head, hardens again. "I don't want to talk to other kids. I just want . . ." Her voice fades and Crystal waits for her to say more.

"You just want what?"

Suddenly, the words explode out of Savi in a rush. "I just want you to pay attention to me!" Savi's voice trembles and she balls her fingers into tight fists. "I always try to make you happy, but nothing I do matters. Ever since Dad died, you aren't happy. You don't pay attention. It's like *you're* the ghost."

Crystal gasps. "What does that mean?"

Savi waves her hands in front of her face. "It's like you're here but you're not here. You don't care about me!" she howls. "You don't care about anything."

The admission blows her back. "That's not true." She fumbles for something more profound to say. Out the cracked car window, the sun has disappeared and the streets are pitch black and eerie. When is the last time she's even been out at night? Why doesn't she take Savi out into the world instead of staying in their house, night after night, like prisoners?

"Maybe I should just disappear too."

"Don't say that. Don't you dare say anything like that. I am your mother. Of course I see you." She reaches across the seat.

"Doesn't feel like it." Savi crosses her arms again and pulls away. Crystal closes her eyes and leans back. She struggles to rearrange the words in her head. A small click of an open door snaps her to attention.

"Savi?"

In one swift motion, Savi has opened the car door and taken off. Crystal catches only a glimpse of her blue dress fluttering in the inky night as she sprints away. "Shit." She wavers—probably a second too long—but she doesn't know if she would be faster on foot or by car. Savi could hide in the bushes or somewhere she can't drive. She rushes back into the driver's seat, starts the car, and takes a sharp right onto the nearest street. She rolls the windows down and begins screaming Savi's name. Real panic spreads through her chest. What if she can't find her? What if someone snatches her?

This is a safe town, she tells herself. *People are here to help.*

She circles the block and realizes they aren't far from Wilder. Maybe she went there? Or just ran home? She parks on the curb, hesitates, then locks the car and runs toward the playground. The stage is gone, wiped clean as if it never existed. She looks under slides and on every swing. She checks the trees, knowing how much Savi used to climb. Irritation gives way to real worry. No, Savi isn't a helpless child, but she is still ten. She knows her way home, and she can't get too far in the neighborhood without someone noticing or asking her where her parents are.

She walks briskly back toward the car, phone in hand. She dials Pam's number, but it goes straight to voice mail.

"Savi ran away," she says. "I need your help."

42

BEC

⠿⠐⠣⠿⠀⠐⠳⠐⠣⠿

"DEAD?" THAT WORD—A WORD I'VE BECOME SO FAMILIAR WITH—STILL
sticks on my lips. "Then how did Oliver end up here?"

Maya starts to speak, but Jake stops her. "I'll explain everything to
Rebecca. Why don't we just take care of logistics?"

I cling to Oliver. "What do you mean, logistics? If he doesn't have
parents, then where does he go?"

"I'm sorry, ma'am, but we have to take him."

Oliver starts crying again, and I gently shush and bounce his tiny
body while trying to think of ways out of this. They can't take him.
I'm not ready. Without Oliver, I have no one. "So you just take him
and then what? What am I supposed to do about Jackson?"

"We'll find Jackson," Toby interrupts.

I stop moving and grow still. "How can you possibly know that?"

"My boys are on it."

"Why isn't anyone telling me what's going on?" I demand. Pieces
click in my head, all of the events of the last few days building and
releasing. I laugh, a dry, sarcastic bark. "Because you think I'm
unstable. You think I'm somehow responsible for all of this, don't
you? That a blind mother who's lost everything can't possibly be in
her right mind or tell the truth, right? That she can't take care of
an infant, so you're not even sure you're going to give that infant
back."

"Rebecca, no one is saying that." Jake's large hand finds my shoulder, but I shrug it off.

"Don't touch me."

I unstrap the baby and gather him in my arms gingerly, even though I am boiling inside. I lift him up, a fuzzy halo in a green onesie—my very last memory. I bring him to my neck, nuzzle his soft skin, and kiss his cheeks. "I'm going to miss you so much, little guy." My voice breaks, and a well of emotion floods my chest. Tears slip silently down my cheeks, but I don't wipe them away. I hold him against my body one more time, gathering his legs in the crook of my arm. His sweet sigh cracks me apart. "You're going to be okay." I kiss his cheek again, memorizing him, and then Maya removes him from my secure grip.

The void is instant.

She steps from the room, and I immediately collapse back in my chair, smothering my sobs behind my hands. Another loss. Another person taken. Another life stolen.

No more.

"I need to use the bathroom," I say.

"It's just—"

"I remember," I tell Officer Toby. I grab my purse and cane and exit the room. In the bathroom, I strain for sounds of Oliver, but don't hear him. The tears well up, but before they can break free, I drown them. I have to be strong: strong for what happens next, strong for Jackson, and strong for Oliver. The void widens as I wash my hands and return to Jake and Toby. Now, I've not lost one baby, but two. Where is Jackson? What are they not telling me?

In the hallway, Jake intercepts me. "Hey, we're going to take it from here, okay? Why don't you go home and get some rest."

"What do you mean? Aren't we going to discuss what to do next?"

He steers me toward the entrance. "We are. But we need to do our end first. The Amber Alert is going out, which will drum up all sorts of media attention. We need to field it and figure out the facts. Set up a call center and tip line. This just became a real investigation. Okay?"

"Does he believe me?" I cock my head toward Toby's office.

Jake is silent.

"Got it." I hoist my purse strap and sigh. "Are you staying here?"

"For a bit. I'll be over once I'm done. Okay?"

I nod and see myself out. I make a left and then a right. My foot connects with a pine cone and the satisfying crunch explodes into my ears.

I must get my baby back.

Oliver. Jackson.

I face my mother's house, a trickle of sweat gathering between my breasts. I prepare to go in when something darts in the driveway.

"Bec, it's me. Sorry, I didn't mean to scare you."

Crystal. I press a hand to my chest.

"Where's Oliver?"

"DCFS." My voice is hollow. "They just took him." I stare up at my house. "I can't go in this house and be alone. I just can't."

"Hey, come here. Let's talk about it, okay?"

I nod, too drained to argue. She takes my keys and lets me inside. I remove my shoes, fold my cane, and shuffle toward the living room. She drops her bag on the side table and presses me into the couch cushions. "Sit, relax. I'll make us some tea." I almost joke and ask her if she and Beth are on the same "tea cures all" plan, but I don't feel like joking. I fear I might not ever joke again.

I tell Google Home to play music, not wanting to be alone with my thoughts for even a second longer than I have to. I close my eyes and try and assess what all this means. I know Jake will be coming here soon, and he will hopefully explain what's going on.

"Cream?" Crystal calls.

"Sure," I call back. "Thank you." I gently stretch my back, which still throbs from my earlier fall. In the kitchen, the kettle whines then dies. Teacups clink against porcelain.

"Okay, nothing a cup of tea can't fix." Crystal enters the living room, china tinkling.

My body loosens and slumps as she presses the warm cup into my hands. "How's Savi?"

I expect an obligatory response, but she sighs. "She ran away tonight."

I sit up, new adrenaline coursing through my system. "She what?"

"Don't worry. I found her. I think I scared her so much, she passed right out."

"Why did she run away?"

"She's just . . . sad, Bec. She's so sad."

I don't ask what she means. I know. I'm sad too—so sad that I literally can't wrap my head around one more night without my son. One more night without my baby in this house. It seems impossible. I set the cup down and tip my head back against the couch cushion.

"I'm so tired. I feel like I'm drowning."

"I know. I know you do." I sense there's more Crystal wants to say but doesn't. "Did Jake say what's going to happen now?"

"It wasn't Jake that was doing most of the talking. It was Toby. He said his men are on it, but I feel like he still doesn't believe me." My jaw hardens. "But I'm going to make sure whoever did this sees the inside of a jail cell, I can tell you that." I roll my head her way. "You know, I never pressed charges against the guy who killed Chris. But this time? There will be consequences." My voice trembles.

Crystal's arm is around me. "Hey, don't think about any of that now. Let's get you up to bed. How does that sound?"

I prepare to protest, but suddenly, my own bed is the only place I can bear to be. She guides me through the hall and up the stairs. The wood whines under our feet. At the landing, there's no comforting whoosh of Jackson's noise machine down the hall, no baby sounds echoing on a monitor.

"I can't live without him, Crystal. I can't." I mean every word. I've been able to survive so much else, but I cannot live without my son.

I know it as fiercely as I've ever known anything. If he does not come back, I will die.

"I know." She doesn't try to talk me out of it. In my bedroom, she draws the shades and pulls back the comforter. "Do you want me to stay with you?"

I nod and crawl into bed. My eyes close, drift open, and close again. Crystal sits behind me and strokes my hair, just like she did earlier today. Was that today? That feels like years ago. I wait for her to say something, to tell me some story of perseverance or resilience, but she doesn't. Instead, she lets me sit with my thoughts. We stay like that for quite some time, until I fall asleep.

43

BEC

⠃⠑⠉

A SHARP KNOCK ON THE FRONT DOOR WAKES ME.

My mouth is dry. My eyes flutter open. "Crystal?" I feel around on the bed, but she's not there. I rub a hand over my face and wait. There it is again, knuckles on hard wood. "Coming," I mumble to no one. Downstairs, the doorknob jiggles impatiently. A week ago, I would have been hiding in my closet. Now, I don't care. If I'm not protecting Jackson, then what does it matter?

I take the first step.

I'm not Chris's wife.

Another step.

I'm not my mother's daughter.

A few more in socked feet. I strangle the banister, not wanting to repeat my fall.

I'm not Jackson's mother.

At the landing, I unlock the door. Crystal must have locked it for me on her way out. I open it.

"Hey. Did I wake you?"

I turn away from Jake and walk down the hallway. I'm suddenly overcome with those early days when I was losing my sight. I'd stand at the end of hallways, capsized with fear about smacking face-first into a wall. That happened more times than I could count. It was like flipping the lights out in a room you'd been in a thousand times, and then suddenly, you were uncertain about everything.

Now, I'm certain of my steps and uncertain of everything else.

I stop in the kitchen. It's amazing how many hours of my life I've spent memorizing angles, so I don't make a fool of myself. So that I am capable. I use my affinity for math to calculate risk, and yet, look at where it's gotten me. I'm not like everyone else. I never was.

I fold my arms across my aching chest. "What's going on?"

"Alert is issued. Fielding calls."

I wait for more. "You know, I'm so sick of this babying act, Jake. I'm so sick of being treated like a fragile flower that will wither and die. I can handle the hard stuff, because it's my life. And regardless of what anyone believes, I was right."

"You were right."

A stab of longing hits me just below the heart. "Did they take him?"

"They did. Until they can get this sorted out."

"What's there to sort out?"

He groans, barely audible. "Everything."

I remember that groan, especially when he didn't want to tell me something. "What is it?" The outline of his face is so out of reach, even under the hot kitchen lights. I want him to tell me something I don't already know, something that will give me hope beyond the burning ache in my gut that my son is still alive.

"It's complicated."

"Bullshit." I slap my hand on the counter. I pace my own kitchen, the tile gummy beneath my bare feet. "Tell me something, Jake. If I could see, would any of this be happening?"

"Probably not."

"Exactly. You don't have any idea what it's like to be at the mercy of everyone else's *opinion* about you. To have everything you love snatched right from under your nose, but no one does anything because they don't believe you." Anxiety swirls in my chest. "I can't do this. I can't be jerked around anymore. I can't hear about false leads or babies with dead parents. I can't do it."

"I know you can't. Come here."

I fold into Jake's arms, but he's too heavy. I can't breathe. I push back. I know he's here to tell me something, and I know it's not good. I can tell by the way he holds me, and himself; the way he is tiptoeing around the truth. "Let's take a walk."

"It's late, Bec."

"I don't care."

I retreat down the hallway and slip on my shoes, grab my cane and keys, and wait for him. I'm halfway down the drive before I realize I don't have my phone again. "Shit."

"What?"

"Nothing." Jake lets me lead the way. I waver at the end of West St. Charles Road, somewhat placated by the sounds of the night—frogs and cicadas growing into that familiar vocal summer symphony— before starting the grid back to my house. I construct the map in my head—like a mouse in a maze. I've condensed my life down to this tiny patch. How did this happen? Before I lost my vision, I'd traveled all over the world for my music. Once I lost it, it's like I'd given up on travel altogether.

I sweep my cane along the path and pass something across the sidewalk. Chris used to jump up and down and shout "score!" if I got something good. He was such a good man, but underneath the surface, he still treated me gingerly. I stop in my tracks. Maybe that's what's bothering me about Jake. Not that he's not asked me how hard these last years have been for me, but that it doesn't make a bit of difference. Sighted or unsighted, he only sees me.

"Bec?"

I jump as Jake's voice echoes in my head. "Sorry. Lost in thought."

"Rightfully so."

"You know, it's crazy to me that just a few days ago, I was worried about being followed, and now?" I shrug. "Now, I feel numb. I'm not afraid of anything."

I ponder all of the recent events. How were they only a few days ago? Were they some weird premonition or sixth sense? Then I consider a harder question: didn't the incidents stop once Jackson was taken? I ignore that pinprick of fear that tells me I might not be thinking clearly and keep moving forward.

"I don't think that's unusual, given your circumstances."

I balk at the word *circumstances*. My whole adult life seems to be built on circumstances. The truth is I am exhausted by it all—tired to the depth of my bones. But I will not stop or settle until Jackson is in my arms.

"So Rose Watson."

Jake's change of topic throws me, but I listen. "What about her?"

"No father in the picture."

"Was Oliver awarded to the state?"

"No. She was on Medicaid and alluded to the fact that she wanted to give up the baby while she was pregnant. She had a meeting with the state, and DCFS was notified. Apparently she changed her mind by the time she checked out of the hospital."

"Okay." *Then what?*

We stop in front of my door. "Then she disappeared. Became a ghost. No sign of her. No sign of the baby."

My hand stiffens around my cane. "What does that mean?"

"It means that when Rose Watson died in Mexico two months ago, there was no sign of a baby. No one even knew she had a baby."

I find the house key. "Did she give the baby to a relative?"

"She has no living relatives."

My brow furrows. "How could she not have any living relatives?"

"Some people get the shit end of the stick, Bec."

I glare at him and forcefully twist the key. "No shit." I enter the house again.

"DCFS threw out the case, because they assumed she was raising him," he continues. "They didn't know she was dead."

"Have they done any digging into who her relatives were? Maybe some distant cousin or something?" I remove my shoes and rest my cane on the foyer table.

"Working on it now. Names will be released after they get clearance."

"Why do they need clearance?" I place my hands on my hips. I want to know and yet I don't want to know. What if one of her relatives is someone I know, or someone I don't? Which would be worse?

His cell phone chirps before he can answer. I almost beg him not to answer, but I know that's never an option when you're a cop. "Donovan." He waits a beat, then two. "Ten-four."

"Don't even say it."

"Sorry. Homicide on the South Side." He steps toward the door.

"When will we know anything?"

"Soon."

"Will you tell me the moment you hear?"

"I'll tell you when we have Jackson back, how's that?"

Rage erupts through my chest. "Jake Donovan, if you know who it might be, tell me right now."

"No." He says it simply, and for the first time in my life, I want to slap him. "If I tell you anything, you will take matters into your own hands, which could compromise the entire case. I'm not telling you anything until you have your son back in your arms. Then we'll talk."

I move a step closer. "Do you know where Jackson is?"

"No, but we're working on it. Hang on just a little longer, okay?" He opens the door and steps through. "Stay here until you hear from me or Toby. Promise me."

"You taught me not to make promises I can't keep, remember?" I firmly shut the door. A moment later, his engine revs and he peels out of the drive.

Inside my house, the silence consumes me. I walk through each room—the room where my father taught me piano, the room my mother spanked me in after I told her I hated her, the room where I used to make forts and eat popcorn. Now, they are different rooms: rooms where I rocked my son, rooms where I made my mother's funeral arrangements, rooms where the entire neighborhood came to pay their respects.

Once again, I replay the past week. The knife in the refrigerator. The footsteps. The bells. Was it all just imagined? I search my brain for answers it can't give and play each and every event on a loop. I call Crystal but her phone is turned off. I call Jess but it goes straight to voice mail too. I realize it's late—too late. I toss my phone in the dish by the door and pace my house until I can't take the silence. One hour bleeds into the next.

When my feet grow tired, I sit at my dining room table and repeatedly ask Siri what time it is. A few times, I swear I hear a baby crying from upstairs. Or the jingling of bells. Phantom sounds, like when people get limbs blown off and still experience the agony of that missing limb.

Jackson is my missing limb. And Oliver. Oliver Watson.

When the sun rises, I shower, make a fresh pot of coffee, and head out. The only person who might be willing to help is Crystal. I want to do some digging on Rose Watson. She can't be that much of a ghost.

I find Crystal's address and calculate the route: seven minutes. I put in my earbuds to hear the directions, the lovely morning sounds of an ending summer muffled instantly.

At her door, I lift my fist to knock.

I'm finding my boy today.

No matter what.

44

BEC

⠃⠑⠉

I WAIT ON THE FRONT PORCH. THE DAY IS CLEAR AND COOL, A REPRIEVE from the recent sweltering days.

The door opens. "Ms. Rebecca!" Savi flings herself into my arms. "Where have you been?"

I smooth my hands over her short hair. "I've had a lot going on lately. I'm so sorry I missed our cello lesson."

"That's okay. Can we play now?"

"Actually, I'm here to see your mom."

"She's next door talking to our neighbor. Design stuff."

I remind myself that Savi is ten, perfectly old enough to stay home alone, but with everything going on . . . "So Pam's not here?"

"Today is her day off. Come on. Let's go play!"

Despite my concern over her staying home alone, Savi's energy is infectious. In all that excitement, she probably doesn't realize I've only been here once. I close the door and lock it for good measure, then carefully follow her trail. The hallway is wide, and I use my cane for guidance.

"Where are the stairs again?"

She directs me from the second floor. "Stop!" She says as I nearly ram into the base of the spiral staircase. My hand glides over a polished banister as I curve up in a semicircle while Savi begins one of my favorite songs, Bach's Cello Suite No. 1. I listen to the bobbing broken chords and the tranquility that seeps through the entire piece. She fumbles through some of the progressions, but I applaud her effort, even from the top stair. It reaches its peak and then she finishes. I step into a room to my right and clap. "That was unbelievable!" I exclaim. "Do you know how hard that piece is?"

"I messed up a few times though."

Still, the pride is evident. I sit beside her on the small couch. "What room is this?"

"It's an office, but I use it as my music room. Mom says when I'm older, I can have a music studio."

"Good acoustics in here though."

"I know." To demonstrate, she plays another impossible riff. "The ceilings are really high."

I sit beside her. "I know people my age who can't play that well. You truly have a gift, young lady."

"Thank you. Can we play right now? I've missed it so much."

I hesitate. It's only been a few days, but she's right—it feels like ages since we last played together. Though I'm here to ask for Crystal's help, not play an instrument. But really . . . what will Crystal be able to do? Force the police to tell me what's going on? If Jake says they are getting closer, then I believe him. I have to believe him.

All leads take time, and time is literally my enemy. I need it to pass as quickly as possible. "I'd have to go get my cello."

"You can play this one. I have my old one."

"Wait. You got a new cello?"

"Mom got it for me yesterday. Here." She hands it over. I inspect every inch. It's a nice one—much too nice for a child.

"Is this a Cecilio?"

"No," she says. "It's a Holstein Bench Davidoff."

"What?" I calculate the price in my head. I've seen this go easily for eight thousand dollars, but I know Crystal doesn't have that kind of cash to throw at a new instrument. "Lucky girl." I sweep my hair over one shoulder. "What do you want to play?"

"Brahms?"

"Ambitious. I like it." I tell her to locate the Cello Sonata No. 1 and begin from memory. She joins, and we get swept away in the music. I detach from my role as a mother, a widow, and someone who's utterly lost. I find myself in my music. I've always found myself in my music. I close my eyes and sway with every chord progression. Savi struggles to keep up, and I slow the pace just a bit, but after a moment, she stops and lets me continue by myself. Everything builds: my passion, my pain, my agony, until I explode into the final few chords. Sweat trickles down the side of my face, mixed with tears.

"Ms. Rebecca, are you crying?"

I smile. "Sorry. Sometimes, the music moves me. Hazard of the profession, I'm afraid." I wipe my face with a sleeve. "Can I use your bathroom?" I lower my bow and carefully prop the cello against the couch.

"It's the first door on the right." She continues to read the music, hammering the same sections over and over until they are smooth and even. How had we gone from playing simple ballads like "My Heart Will Go On" to Brahms in a matter of months? It doesn't compute.

I slide my hand along the wall to find the bathroom. At the sink, I wash my hands and stare into the foggy mirror. My vision is getting so much worse. If I'd known I'd never see my own face again, I wouldn't have ever spent a second of my life disparaging my features. I would have memorized the exact color of my green eyes and thanked them. I would have worshipped my nose, my dimples, the curve of my mouth, my teeth, my jaw, my skin, all of it.

Instead, all I have is the *memory* of me, which is fading with every passing breath. I flip off the light, swat for the bathroom door, and unlock it. The notes stop. The scribble of a pencil makes me smile as I realize Savi is taking notes.

I step into the hall. A tiny noise, so slight you could miss it if you were breathing too heavily, comes from down the hall.

My head rotates so fast, my neck pops. My entire body hums. I hunt for the sound again and wonder if I imagined it . . . just as I've been imagining things at home. Savi begins playing Elgar Cello Concerto in E Minor. It's a joke in the music world that this piece makes the cello sound like a human voice. I listen wistfully, so taken by her talent but also wanting to know what I just heard.

I take slow, shaky steps down the carpeted hall. My fingers glide over textured wallpaper until I come to another door. It's at the very end of the hall, tucked away. I press my hands against the wood, then my ear. Silence.

"Ms. Rebecca?"

I move away as if I've been caught. "Sorry. I thought I heard something."

Savi's hazy outline floats down the hall. "That's just the guest room. Come play!"

I retreat down the hall, moving slowly, and join her, but my mind is somewhere else. It's on Jackson. And Jake. And sweet baby Oliver. It's on whatever Jake's keeping from me. It's on Officer Toby's lack of belief—because I'm blind. It's on my grief, coiled and bunched, hissing from the corner.

It's on Crystal getting home and being able to offer help.

Minutes later, I hear the door open and close downstairs, and then Crystal's footsteps. We finish the song, and I glance toward the doorway.

"Rebecca?" Crystal asks. "Hey. Are you okay?"

"Hi, sorry." I stand, suddenly embarrassed. How could I be focused on anything other than Jackson right now? What am I even thinking? "There's a break in the case, but Jake won't tell me exactly what it is. I thought you could help me research. I didn't know where else to go."

Crystal crushes me in her arms. "Of course I can help."

I pull back. "Thank you. I'm not really even sure how you can help. I just thought . . . I don't know what I thought."

"Where's Jake?"

"Chicago. Homicide."

"Shitty timing."

"Mom." Savi whispers. "Language."

"Sorry."

Will I ever raise a surly son who gives me a hard time for cursing? Will I ever get to hear him speak, tuck him into bed, or tell him good night? A sob ratchets through my chest, but I catch it and calm myself. One step at a time. Panic will not get me anywhere. I know that now.

"Unfortunately, I've got a client crisis I need to handle, but then I can come to your house right after?" Crystal asks.

"Can I go with Ms. Rebecca?"

Crystal hesitates, but I butt in. "It's totally fine. She can keep me company."

"Can I bring my cello too?"

"Duh," I tease. "Is that okay?"

"Please, Mom!" Savi begs.

"Just for a little bit. I'll be there as soon as I can, once I wrap things up."

"Take your time."

We all tread down the stairs slowly. Here I am, coming to Crystal for help, and I'm going to end up helping her. My ears prick for what I thought I heard down the hall, but I know it's my own wishful thinking. I can't fabricate a result. I can't make the police, DCFS, Jake, or Toby move any faster.

"Are you sure you don't mind if she comes over?" Crystal asks again. "It would help me out so much."

I don't ask about Pam, but instead nod. "Of course she can."

"Thank you. Let me just pack her a lunch and some snacks." On cue, her phone rings. "Crap. This is the client. Hold that thought and I'll get her stuff ready." She disappears out back. The sliding glass door opens and shuts.

Savi and I wait in the foyer. "Do you like living in this big old house?" I ask.

"Sometimes. I really miss my dad though."

"I'm sure you do." Savi doesn't often mention her dad, and I don't know whether to keep going or to let it die. "What do you miss the most about him?"

"I miss the way he used to take me places. We'd go to the museums or go walk by the beach."

"What else?"

"I miss his pancakes. He made the best pancakes."

"I bet he did." Chris was terrible at cooking. He would burn toast.

"I set fire to all his boxes."

Her admission startles me. "What?"

"My dad's stuff. It used to take up this entire room."

I try to conjure a room full of boxes. "Why did you set fire to them?"

"Because they were making my mom sad. I need to go to the bathroom before we go."

Once Savi is in the bathroom, I consider what she just said. Savi set fire to her dad's possessions? How much pain must she be in to do something like that? I realize that with all of my current drama, I haven't been here for anything Crystal might have been going through too.

As I pace the foyer, I realize Savi never brought her cello down. I tap the floor with my cane to be sure. I decide to grab her new one. I've already memorized my path. It's an obsessive habit that has paid off over the years. While I've always been meticulous, once you've injured yourself due to miscalculations, you learn to self-correct. I go over the math in my head now: twenty-four steps to the landing. At the top, the study is five steps to the right. Her cello is on its stand. I lower it carefully into the case, clean the bow, and place the music in the sleeve in case she wants to bring it.

And then, that noise again.

I step halfway into the hall, too afraid to breathe or move in fear of missing it. I slither against the wall and stay quiet. My body crackles while I strain to hear. I can't explain why the hairs on the back of my neck rise to attention as I get closer to the guest room.

My hand rests on the knob. I know once I open the door, I'll find a bed, dresser, drapes, dust. Nothing special.

I twist the knob. Instead of a stale guest room, there's the familiar scent of baby wipes and a diaper pail. An anticipatory breath shudders through my body. It's not a guest room—it's a nursery. Upon entering, the noise grows louder: a jingle.

The bells.

I charge through the room. My knee connects with something sharp before I bump into the rails of a crib. Another jingle—the same one I'd heard before—cracks through my heart like a bat. I would know those bells anywhere.

"Jackson!" I reach into the crib, hungry for my baby. My hands shake so much, I worry I might drop him before he's even in my arms. His sweet smell overwhelms all other senses. The bells fall from his tiny fingers.

It's him.

I traverse his skin: head, eyes, nose, mouth, the bumpy patch behind his ear, the notch in his collarbone, and sink to the ground. I smother him in kisses, my entire heart swelling with relief while I rock him against my chest. *My baby is alive. My baby is here. My baby is safe.*

I don't even have time to make sense of why Jackson is in this house. He's here, and that's all that matters. I gather my thoughts and then take out my phone. I snap photos of everything, wildly pointing and clicking to show that this is not my house. I place Jackson back into the crib for a moment, and he starts crying. I snap his photo, then shove the phone into my pocket before picking him back up. "I'm sorry, sweet boy. I just need proof." He settles, and I pause in the doorway. *Is there another way out?*

I take a breath and tiptoe back down the hall toward the top of the stairs. I pray he stays quiet so I can get down the stairs safely and outside.

I pause on the landing. Crystal is still on the phone. The sound of her voice ignites my fury. All of my senses rise and solidify: anger, fear, disbelief. I anchor Jackson in my arms and hesitate on the very top stair.

"Ms. Rebecca?" Savi's voice is incredulous from the first floor.

My body trembles until I am vibrating with rage. "Why is he here?" It is the only logical thing I can think to ask.

Savi runs away and calls for her mother. Her voice is as terrified as I feel.

I descend the steps carefully but quickly and almost ram straight into Crystal on the last stair.

"Please let me explain. Please." Crystal's voice tips toward hysterical. She reaches for me, and I claw at her hand like a wild animal.

"Don't fucking touch me. Don't you *ever* come near me again, do you hear me? You are going to jail."

"Mommy!" Savi begins to cry, and my heart aches for this child with such a duplicitous monster for a mother.

"Rebecca, please. I need to tell you what happened. I—"

I run out the door and trip on the stairs. I right myself, flick open my cane, and snuggle my child. My heart beats so hard, I'm afraid I'll collapse from a heart attack before I can get to the police station. I call Officer Toby, who answers on the first ring.

"I've got Jackson!" I scream. "He was at Crystal Turner's house. I took pictures. I found a nursery upstairs." I recite the address from memory. Officer Toby tells me to go to a neighbor's and stay put. In the back of my mind, I wonder if Crystal will come after me. I realize I have no idea what she's capable of.

I sink to the ground on the sidewalk and hold my baby against my chest. I thank God he's back in my arms. It's all I've wanted over these last few hellish days. I inspect every inch of him and make sure he's okay. Holding him makes me worry for Oliver. Who is

Oliver? Why was Jackson in Crystal's house? I sit in the dewy grass and wait for the police. I send an audio message to Jake and repeatedly kiss and rock Jackson on a stranger's lawn. As I wait, I forget the questions.

Now I want answers. And I will do anything to get them.

45

CRYSTAL

PANIC.

Crystal's entire life flashes before her eyes. Her in jail. Her without her daughter, without anything. She can't shake the image of getting handcuffed and being hauled away.

She looks at Savi, who appears as scared as she feels. "We've got to go." She softens her tone. The last thing she wants to do is scare her daughter further.

They hurry into the car and head to the police station. Crystal drives cautiously, searching for flashing blue lights at every turn. The way Bec had screamed at her, accusing her. She'd never forget that look. Everything she'd gained—all gone in a second.

She replays these last few months. How had they gotten so away from her? So many lies. So many half-truths. Her hands freeze on the wheel at the stoplight before the turnoff. She could go to the station and face the truth, or she could step on the gas and hide. Go somewhere else. Really start over. Leave Paul, Oliver, Pam, and every other sordid lie behind. The light turns green. Her foot itches to stamp the pedal and peel out toward the highway.

She glimpses Savi's reflection in the rearview: terrified, chewing her bottom lip, eyes large and glassy. No. She can't put her daughter in any sort of danger. She's put her through enough.

She takes a clotted breath and turns into the parking lot. She didn't think she could ever feel worse than after Paul died, but here it is. Betraying Rebecca, hiding such a big part of her life from everyone . . . But she has her reasons.

Once she's parked, she calls Pam, but gets her voice mail. Pam is the only other person in the world who knows some version of the truth. Not all, but enough.

"What's going to happen?"

Savi's voice shuttles her back to the present.

"I don't know yet." She's done lying to her daughter. She's done lying, period.

"Where are we?" Savi eyes the tidy row of cop cars in front of the brick building.

In their hurry to get out the door, she didn't even explain where they were going. "Mommy just has to answer some questions about Oliver."

"What about Jackson?"

"He's with Rebecca. Where he belongs."

Savi stares at her lap. "Will we ever see her again?"

Crystal shakes her head. "I'm not sure." She twists to face Savi. "It's all going to be fine though. I promise." Even as she says the words, bullets of panic ricochet through her gut. *Is everything going to be fine?* She unbuckles her seat belt.

They approach the doors just as Pam exits, giant movie star sunglasses perched over her startling doe eyes. Her signature red lips are wiped bare, and she looks washed out except for the spray of freckles across her face.

"Pam?" Crystal is confused. *Why is she here?*

"Hi," she says. She looks uncertainly between the two of them.

"What happened?" Crystal asks.

"They questioned me about Oliver," she says. "I've been instructed not to talk to you." She places a hand on Savi's shoulder. "Take care of yourself, Savi." Pam shoots a perplexed look at Crystal before heading to her car. She watches the young, naïve girl walk away from their family, perhaps for the last time.

A million thoughts fight for space in Crystal's brain. What did Pam say? How much trouble are they in? Crystal buries the fear and straightens her shoulders. "Come on," she says, more bravely than she feels.

She takes Savi's hand and leads her inside the station.

46

B E C

⠃⠑⠉

BEC WAITS FOR JAKE OUTSIDE.

"Bec!" His voice is swollen with relief. His footsteps pound the concrete as he jogs over. "Let me see."

I maneuver Jackson, not daring to loosen my hold for even a second.

He takes a moment and then exhales a shaky breath. "I really can't believe it. Come on. Toby's waiting."

I charge straight to the back of the police station, not bothering to tune in to sounds or hushed, excited whispers. No one believed me, but I never gave up hope. And because of that belief, my baby is back in my arms.

"Rebecca." Toby's voice is apologetic. Someone clears an agitated throat over his shoulder. A figure who's taller and more in charge from where he's positioned in the room.

"Chief Holbrook. Please let me apologize on behalf of Elmhurst PD for how this was handled."

I take his hand and squeeze it firmly—a trait my dad instilled in me from a young age. No limp handshakes here. I can sense he wants to say more by way of an explanation—that he didn't want to jump the gun, that they have to be certain before they make a missing-person case public—but I don't care. I want to know why Crystal had my baby. Was she the one following me? Had she been casing me this whole time? As the puzzle pieces start to slip and shift, I realize my cardinal mistake. I trusted her without ever really knowing her.

Mentally, I sort through the facts: I met her at a grief group. I assumed she was an interior designer, but did I have proof of that? She never invited me to her house, but she was always in mine.

I spew my thoughts into the police station, laying a track of her behavior. The men stay silent as I weave my supposed web, and then, finally, Jake interrupts.

"The nanny—Pam Booker—gave her statement. Gave us some insight into what's been going on." He rustles a piece of paper. "Apparently, Crystal hired her a few months ago for Oliver and had her sign a nondisclosure agreement."

I balk. "Why?"

"Paul was a lawyer. Crystal claimed it was standard. The girl is young, probably didn't want to lose the chance at the job," Toby explains.

I shake my head, confused. "What does a nondisclosure agreement have to do with anything?"

"It specifically states she is not to discuss the baby or anything that goes on in that house," Jake says.

I listen, dumbfounded. "What else did Pam say?"

"She said that in all her time working there, Crystal never paid attention to Oliver—she'd look right through him as if he wasn't there. Completely ignored him. Pam started to get suspicious that something was different about the baby a few days ago, but why would she think twice about some sort of swap?" Toby sniffs. "She thought maybe he was just outgrowing the colic, but when she saw the flyer for the vigil, she knew."

"So you're saying Pam had nothing to do with the swap?"

"Not as far as we can tell, no."

I adjust in my chair. "How is that possible? A nanny would know if they had a different baby."

"Like I said, she started to suspect something was off, but what was she going to do with that information? She signed that agreement. She wasn't even allowed to talk to her friends about who she was nannying for," Toby explains. "We checked her phone records, her texts. Nothing suspicious. Her version is that babies change almost daily. A little far-fetched, if you ask me. But we'll get to the bottom of it."

I sigh. "So what now?"

"Crystal just gave her statement," Jake explains. "She has taken full responsibility for swapping Jackson."

"What?" My entire body stills. Deep down, I wanted there to be some sort of massive misunderstanding . . . but I know the world doesn't work that way. Bad things happen to good people. Good people do bad things. Which one is this? "I thought she was my friend." The admission is pathetic, but the realization is crushing nonetheless. She never wanted to be my friend—she just wanted my baby. *But she doesn't like babies,* I remind myself. Or was that a lie too?

I smear away the unhelpful thoughts as if on a whiteboard. "Is she even a widow?"

"Yes. Her husband died months ago in a car accident."

"She told me."

"Did she also tell you about Evelyn?"

I shake my head. "Mistress?"

"Sister."

"Her sister?"

"No, her husband's sister. Rose Evelyn Watson. Rose is her legal name. She went by Evelyn."

The name clicks. "Rose Watson. Oliver's mother?"

"Yes."

So Paul's *sister* had given birth. Not Crystal. Oliver wasn't even her baby. "How did Crystal end up with Oliver?"

The chief exhales, remnants of tobacco on his breath. "After Paul died, Evelyn bounced from place to place. She was broke. Worked odd jobs. She gave birth in Chicago, but a month into it, she decided to leave Oliver on Crystal's doorstep."

The admission slaps me in the face. "She left Oliver on Crystal's doorstep?" A sickening sixth sense traverses my skin like a spider.

"Then she disappeared. Literally. Became a ghost. She met some guy, went to Mexico. Died in a boating accident. Drowning."

I shake my head. "But I don't understand. Did Crystal try to locate Evelyn?"

"She did, at least according to her statement. No dice. Evelyn didn't want to be found. I think Crystal was afraid if she went to DCFS with Oliver, they'd put him in the system. Or give him back to Evelyn if they located her. Same fear as you."

"So what? She decided to keep the baby a secret until she realized he was colicky and then made the swap? That doesn't make sense."

"It's an odd case, to be sure." He clears his throat again and waits for more questions.

"But where does DCFS come in?" I ask. "Why were they listed on Oliver's electronic medical records?"

"Evelyn talked about giving the baby up for adoption. She had no help, no family other than Paul, who'd just died. Paul and Evelyn's parents died when they were young, which is why Paul was so protective over her. A damned cursed family, if I've ever seen one," he mutters under his breath. "As far as the baby and Evelyn, DCFS is sometimes brought in with underage cases."

"Underage?"

"Evelyn was only seventeen."

I close my eyes and shake my head. "Seventeen? Jesus." I ransack my brain for clues of a baby in Crystal's life, but there are none. "Crystal never mentioned a baby. Not once." I think of Savi. "There's no way a ten-year-old could hide something like that. They're natural truth tellers."

"I think Crystal was worried about the legal ramifications of having a baby she had not reported. The longer she went, the more fearful she got. She made it very clear to Savi not to tell anyone, or she could get in big trouble. Savi just wanted to make her mother happy. You know how literal kids are."

"What about Pam?"

"The contract."

Right. The contract. The new information percolates in my brain but doesn't answer the big question: "But why did she swap Jackson?"

The chief sighs once again, and I imagine him ripping off tiny spectacles from bloodshot eyes. "That we don't know. Oliver is extremely colicky, so that's one possibility. Maybe Oliver reminds Crystal of Paul. Maybe she never wanted to be a mom again. Who knows?" His weight shifts. He groans and sits in the chair opposite mine. "Could she have been jealous of you or your baby? Did she ever say anything about how good Jackson was, insist on holding him? Things like that?"

Chills barb my skin. "She doesn't like babies. She had severe postpartum after Savi was born. Hardly had anything to do with her the first year. She definitely didn't take any interest in Jackson." Something still doesn't add up. Unless Crystal is the best actress in the world, then I totally misjudged her and our friendship. Jackson lets out a tiny cry and I snuggle and rock him. "What happens now?"

"We're going to continue to question Crystal. This isn't a standard case, but of course there will be consequences once you press charges."

Press charges. Instantly, I'm shuttled back to the man who hit and killed Chris. I didn't press charges then. Should I now? "But what about Oliver? And Savi?"

He sniffs and straightens a file on the desk. "They'll be awarded to the state temporarily."

Something buzzes in my head. "No." I grasp the edge of the table as my world tilts. "Absolutely not. Savi just lost her father. She can't lose her mother too."

"It's the law." He chews over his words. "And if the mother's unstable, then they'll be better off."

"No." I say it again, firmly. I hold my baby—a baby who is unharmed, a baby who is back in my arms, safe and sound. *This* is what I was after. Jackson back home. Not revenge to right some wrong I can't possibly understand. "I'm not going to press charges."

Three heads snap in my direction. "Rebecca," Jake urges.

I lift my hand to stop him. "That child will go home to her mother, as will Oliver. Get her supervision or help or whatever. But there will be no more disruptions in Savi's life or fear that her only other parent will disappear too. Absolutely not." I shake my head, more certain than I feel. Shouldn't Crystal be punished for what she's done?

I, more than anyone, understand that grief can make you do crazy things. Maybe she wasn't thinking straight. But I know she loves Savi. I know she can be a good mother to Oliver with the right help.

"Ma'am, we really don't advise that."

"Then let me talk to her." I shock myself with my own request. "And then I'll decide." I hitch my jaw in that stubborn way Jake knows he can't fix.

Jake whispers something into the chief's ear, and the two murmur back and forth. Officer Toby doesn't say a word. "Fine," the chief finally says. "But we'll be watching."

"I wouldn't expect anything less," I say. I hoist Jackson, pat his back, and mentally prepare to face her. "Lead the way."

47

BEC

THE INTERROGATION ROOM IS COLD. CRYSTAL GASPS WHEN SHE SEES ME. I sink into the metal chair across from her and grind my teeth to keep from screaming. The two-way glass is behind me, only Crystal's face visible for the viewing pit.

"Rebecca." Her voice wavers between fearful and remorseful.

I steel myself for whatever is to come, unbuckle Jackson from my chest, and twist him around to face her. "How could you?" My words are tiny, the meaning sharp. *How could you take something that doesn't belong to you? How could you betray me? How could you lie?*

"It's not what you think."

I laugh, surprising even myself with how unfamiliar that sound is to my own ears. "You have no idea what I think." All of my feelings just moments ago about not pressing charges and letting her go free evaporate as easily as they came. There is only one thing I feel: a mother's rage. And I will not leave without a clear answer as to why she's done this to me.

"I can't . . ." She loses her words, regains them. "I'm just so sorry."

I sit across from her, Jackson bucking his wild legs, pulling things off the table and wriggling in my arms. "How could you keep him from me?" I'm not sure if I mean Jackson or Oliver.

"I'm sorry." She says those same ineffective words again, her voice cracking open to reveal something I've not yet heard: vulnerability.

"I thought you were my friend."

"I am." Crystal leans forward. "I've always been your friend."

I move farther away. "Then tell me what happened."

She sighs and adjusts in her chair. "The night Paul died . . . I don't like to talk about it. His sister Evelyn had been calling him for months. He'd been secretly feeding her cash, sneaking away to meet her. I thought he was cheating." She snorts. "In some ways, that would have been better. I tried to get him to choose: her or us. But he couldn't. Paul was a loyal man. He was a family man. After his parents died, he felt an obligation to make sure his baby sister was okay, which I respected, of course.

"But she went too far. She always went too far. The night he died, she called in the middle of the night. She was stranded somewhere in downtown Chicago, and he told her he'd be right there. She didn't have any money for cab fare. I woke up, but I didn't tell him not to go. I was annoyed and didn't even say good-bye." She pauses. "If I'd just told him to stay, then maybe . . ." Her voice fades. "On the way there, he got hit by a drunk driver. Killed instantly."

Her admission drops to a whisper, and I strain to hear.

"I was so furious with Evelyn. I blamed her for Paul's death and told her I never wanted to see her again. But she was pregnant. She had no one. She disappeared after he died, and then two months ago, I open the door to find a baby on my doorstep. She left a note saying it's what Paul would have wanted and that I'd be a better mother than she ever would."

She laughs sarcastically. "Except she couldn't possibly know what a terrible mother I was to Savi as a baby, right? I was terrified of any baby, but especially one that wasn't mine. I didn't know what to do. So many days, I thought about dropping him on someone else's doorstep or putting him up for adoption—though I couldn't legally do that—but then I'd hear Paul's voice in my head . . . and I figured I just needed a little time to try and find Evelyn and get her the help she needed. So I hired Pam in the interim, who's sweet but clueless. She did what she was told."

"I still don't understand how you kept Savi and Pam from telling anyone you had a baby. Elmhurst talks."

She sighs. "They do, but not when you're invisible. Look, I'm not proud of it, but I told Savi we could get in real trouble if she uttered a word to anyone. I told her to just let me find Evelyn first, and then we'd figure it out.

"But Evelyn literally disappeared. I even hired someone to find her, but she didn't want to be found. I didn't know what to do. To make matters worse, anytime I stepped foot around Oliver, he cried. I thought it was my punishment."

"Punishment for what?"

"For being a self-absorbed wife. For not appreciating Paul when I had the chance. For making him choose between blood and us. And now this. I seem to sabotage anything good in my life. I never meant to hurt you, Rebecca. I swear."

My heart aches. "But you did. You did hurt me."

"I know."

I don't want her sob story or her apology, but I let her continue. She tells me that in her eyes, Oliver represents Evelyn. Evelyn represents Paul. Paul represents death.

"Paul was too loyal for his own good," she explains. "It was his loyalty that killed him." Her voice breaks.

I fish the pacifier from my pocket, freshly cleaned, and pop it into Jackson's mouth. I rock him as she talks—as though we are two friends spilling our guts and not two women facing off in a precinct.

"Why didn't you just get some help?" I ask.

She laughs again, a cold, hollow sound spilling from her lips. "I was a mess. Paul had just died. I couldn't even bring myself to unpack the boxes. I was drowning in debt. We'd just moved, I was trying to build my business, and then this baby appears . . ."

Silence fills the gaps.

"Oliver." Her voice hardens around his name. "It's not the baby's fault, of course, but I just couldn't believe that this child I wasn't related to was alive while the husband and father we needed in our lives was gone." She drops her head into her hands. "And I kept going over it and over it in my head. If I'd just stopped him from leaving in the middle of the night, maybe he would have stayed. Or left later and missed that drunk driver altogether."

Despite my anger, a familiar longing spreads through my gut. I know that *what if* game all too well.

"I just wasn't ready to be a single mother of two children *and* a widow. I couldn't handle it. I wanted to pretend none of it was happening. That's why Pam was a lifesaver. She took care of the baby while I searched for Evelyn and tried to figure out what to do next."

"Did you know Evelyn was dead?"

"I didn't." Her voice drops. "They just told me."

"So you just hired Pam and then what? Decided Jackson was a better baby and the poor blind woman wouldn't notice?" My rage bucks and revs again. "How dare you? How dare you take advantage of me like that?"

"I didn't take advantage of you." Crystal's voice is firm. "That's not what happened."

"I'm sure you saw the similarities between them, right? They must look alike. You began hanging around. You even made the comment that you've never heard him cry. I get it. Colic sucks. But here's what I don't get. When did you do it?"

That's the piece that nags me. That's the piece I can't figure out. Jake has interviewed the women at the park. If Crystal had walked up with a baby, someone would have noticed. Someone would have recognized her. I mull over the possibilities as Crystal lets me work it out for myself.

Jackson gives a sharp kick to my belly, and I gasp. My eyes search hers, a cloudy halo of frosty hair and white-hot skin.

"It wasn't you," I finally say.

Her silence confirms the truth.

I sit back, knowing exactly what that means.

48

CRYSTAL

CRYSTAL SEARCHES THE RECOGNITION IN REBECCA'S FACE. SHE CAN'T *TELL* her the truth—can't admit it here, with these men scrutinizing her behind protected glass—but Rebecca is smart enough to figure it out. She realizes she's ruined their friendship, that these last few days have fractured what they have so carefully built over all these months. Serves her right for not taking care of Oliver in the first place.

She can't explain that in these past three days, even with a blind, frantic, grief-stricken mother, Oliver was in better hands with Rebecca than with *her.* She can't tell her that she's literally held Oliver maybe twice since he was left on her doorstep. She can't tell her how, in her darkest moments, she's thought about shaking him to make him stop crying, how every time she looks into his innocent face, she thinks of how Evelyn ruined their family. She has to let go of these thoughts. Even Dr. Gibbons doesn't know. No one does.

Until today.

She can't tell her that the more she didn't mention having a baby, the more in control she really felt. Pam had the baby. Pam took care of the baby. Savi was like a big sister when Pam and Oliver were around, but with Crystal, it was just mother and biological daughter, as it should be. But she was even failing at that. Savi was acting out, vying for her attention. Nothing seemed to work.

Crystal had done everything she could about the colic. She'd taken him to a specialist. She'd called over a sleep guru, but nothing. And then, after only a few days with Rebecca, he was happy as a clam. Because she was a better mother than Crystal.

She watches Rebecca dismantle all of this across the table and waits for questions. When she doesn't ask any, Crystal finally speaks up. "Are you going to press charges?" They are the only words she can think of, and they are cowardly.

Rebecca drums her fingers on the table, those long, tapered hands that care for babies, play the cello, and hold the keys to her fate. Her glazed, jade eyes slide toward hers, and a chill slithers down her spine. Sometimes she swears Rebecca can see her. She could never admit it, but there have been so many moments in the last few months where Crystal has been envious of her friend's lack of vision. Crystal is so good at pretending things are invisible; sometimes she wishes they really were.

Suddenly, Rebecca stands, startling Jackson, who is nearly sound asleep against his mother's chest. His eyes jolt open and then settle as he sucks rhythmically on his pacifier.

"Bec?" She stands too and takes a step forward, then stops. "Are you going to . . . ?" She can't finish the sentence but she needs to know. She needs to know what's going to happen to her.

Rebecca knocks on the door and someone comes to get her—probably Jake. The moment Rebecca walks out that door, Crystal is on her own. Pam can't help. DCFS can't help. She has no real friends. All of this is her fault, but she can't do anything to change it. She can't go back. She can't undo her choices, as much as she wants to.

The door opens and closes, and then she's gone. She sinks back into the chair and folds her hands on the metal table. She stares into the smudged glass, which houses the firing squad on the other side. Her jaw sets, her eyes clear and unblinking. A single tear slips down her cheek at the thought of what Savi must be going through.

Her daughter, without her father.

Her daughter, without her aunt.

Her daughter, without her mother?

No.

She stands, and the chair topples backward with the force of her legs pushing away from the table. She knows what she is about to do is risky, but it's her only choice.

"Bring Rebecca back." She shouts it loud enough that someone must hear. "I want to tell her the truth. I want to tell her who really took Jackson."

49

BEC

⠃⠑⠉⠀⠞⠲

I'M ALMOST OUT THE FRONT DOOR OF THE PRECINCT WHEN JAKE STOPS ME. "Bec. Wait." I scurry out of his grip and push through the rotating glass to feel the sunshine on my face. I tip my chin skyward and resist opening my arms like some heroine in a novel. It's over. It's all over.

"You can't leave."

Not yet.

"Why not?"

"Paperwork. Just hang tight, okay?"

I rotate toward him—this man who's been here for me, even when he didn't fully believe me. This man, who stayed away for eleven long years, just so he wouldn't rock the boat and I could have a chance at happiness. All this time, I thought if Chris was out of the picture, then I had to do everything alone. I didn't see the point in getting too close to anyone, because people leave. That's what they do.

But Jake is here now. I walk forward and slide my hand down his arm and find his hand. "Thank you." I squeeze his fingers.

"For what?"

"For not giving up on me."

"Bec." He laughs, his voice projecting skyward. "I've never given up on you. Not then, not now. Not ever."

I want to ask what will happen when all of this is over. Will I see him again? Will we be those exes who get coffee once a year? The thought of him being removed from my life is agonizing. I haven't even gotten to enjoy his company. It's just been one crazy moment after the next.

"Will I see you after this?" I ask.

He steps closer to me. His body radiates heat, just a foot away. "I'm not going anywhere." He says the words, and I wish I could believe him. But he's a detective. I know the odds of staying safe in a job like his.

"You don't know that," I say.

He scratches his jaw. "You're right. I don't know that. But I do know I'm not leaving you again. I shouldn't have left all those years ago. And I'm certainly not going to leave now."

"Jake, Rebecca." Toby approaches, his steps quick. "Crystal wants to confess something."

"I don't want to talk to her."

"Bec, we really need to make this official. If she's got something else to say, it could help," Jake offers.

"I don't want to see her." I say it again, more adamantly.

"Look, we can't book her unless you decide to press charges or she confesses. The choice is yours," Toby offers.

The choice is yours.

That common phrase bounces around my head. I take a few steps away, turn back, waver. I'm not sure I want her booked, but I sure as hell don't want to go back in and listen to one more second of what she has to say. In the span of a few days, I've gotten my son back, but I've lost three people. A best friend, a child I adore like my own, and Oliver. "Do I really have a choice?" I ask.

Jake sighs. "Not really."

I nod. Toby holds the automatic door open long enough for all three of us to pass through. I walk back through the station, for what feels like the millionth time in a few days. Jake opens the door for me, and I sink back into the hard, metal chair across from my ex-friend, both hands resting protectively over my sleeping son.

"What is it you have to confess?"

But it's not Crystal's voice I hear: it's Savi's.

"Hi, Ms. Rebecca."

I lean back in surprise and close my eyes. *No, no, no. I don't want to hear this.*

"Go ahead, sweetheart." Crystal urges Savi in a stern but kind voice, but I don't need her to talk. I already know some version of what she's going to say.

"I just wanted my mom to be happy again." Her voice is tiny, and I can tell she's twisting something in her hands. "Oliver was always crying, and Mom never wanted to be at home. And Jackson is such a good baby. He never cries. So, I thought . . ." Her voice fades and I can hear her swallow. I resist the urge to bang on the glass behind me and request some water. "I just wanted to fix the problem."

The simplicity of a child's mind slams into focus: everything is black and white, cause and effect. The air bolts from my lungs. I realize what Crystal has been doing this whole time. It's not lying to everyone—it's protecting her daughter.

"I knew you liked to go to Wilder," Savi continues. "I always wanted to go there too, but Mom didn't want the baby going where you were. She didn't want you to know. She didn't want anyone to know. It was our little secret. And Pam's."

My gut twists at all the wicked ways to mess up a child, but I stay silent.

"And what happened that day at the park?" Crystal asks softly.

"I don't want to tell," she says.

"Savi. You have to. It's time to tell the truth. The real truth."

My breath swirls inside my chest until I feel light-headed. I vacillate between wanting to hear the truth and run from the room.

"Am I going to get in trouble?" she asks.

Crystal doesn't say anything, and finally, I speak up. "No, you're not," I say. "But you need to tell me exactly what happened, so we can all understand."

She takes a quaking breath. "Okay."

I sit back and prepare myself for the truth of what happened that day in the park.

50

BEC

⠃⠑⠉

"I DIDN'T MEAN TO," SAVI BEGINS. SHE TAKES A SHAKY BREATH. "I WATCH you in the park sometimes. From my bedroom window. I always see you on the same bench with the other moms. Jackson always seems so happy," she adds wistfully. "Mom never takes Oliver to that park because she doesn't want us to get in trouble."

I refrain from telling her what bullshit that is; that no one would assume anything other than she had a baby of her own, but Crystal's own warped paranoia has made Savi concoct a dangerous, inaccurate theory too.

"Anyway, that day, we were walking to the music store, and I saw you faint. I knew my mom didn't want anyone coming to our house—like *ever*—especially in case they saw Oliver, but he was finally asleep, because Pam had given him some Benadryl. I knew he wouldn't wake up and cry. It's the only time he doesn't cry."

I wait for her to continue.

"When you came back, I went upstairs to tell Pam what happened, but she'd fallen asleep. She takes naps in the music room sometimes when Oliver has had a really bad day. I heard Jackson fuss downstairs, but when I went to his stroller, no one was watching him. Mom was with you, and your friend was outside, so I decided to walk Jackson around to keep him company. I showed him my room and my cello and he was so happy."

She swallows. "Then I took him to Oliver's room. I couldn't believe how much they looked alike! They could have been twins. They were both wearing white onesies too." Her voice sounds incredulous, reminding me just how young she really is. "So I set Jackson beside Oliver. He was still sleeping. They looked exactly alike, except for Jackson's bells. I went to pick Jackson up, but then I thought about my mom. And how Pam is always so focused on Oliver. I thought it would be good to give them both a break."

I almost retort that Jackson isn't a toy but refrain. "Then what?" I ask instead.

"I picked up Oliver, and I rushed back downstairs and put him in Jackson's stroller. He was still asleep. Jackson didn't even cry. It's like he wanted to be with me!"

Her rationalizations are ridiculous, but I don't interrupt.

"Then you left. Mom had to go to work. Pam was still asleep. So I created a diversion to be safe."

Crystal sucks a sharp breath. "You mean the fire?"

Savi sniffles. "I didn't want to, but I knew Pam would find out what I had done, and I just wanted to keep Jackson for a little while. Just . . . just to see what it was like with a different baby. But when you fired her, I realized how lonely I would be. When she came back, she knew something was different. I was so afraid she was going to tell."

I attempt to wrap my brain around this story. So the swap didn't happen at the park. That was my mistake. It happened in the house where another baby was sleeping upstairs. The overlooked clue. The ultimate betrayal. The blatant lie.

I gather my words, unsure of what to say. "When did you know?" I direct my question at Crystal.

"I swear I didn't know until you showed up to the vigil and said Oliver's name. I knew things were quieter in our house and Pam said something seemed different, but I thought he might just be going through a new phase." She's quiet for a moment. "I guess I chose to believe what I wanted to believe."

"I thought if I had the *good* baby, then Mom would be happy again," Savi interrupts. "Everything was supposed to go back to normal. I didn't think you'd notice, but you did."

"Of course I noticed," I snap. "He's my *child*. I know the difference between my child and someone else's."

"But they look alike." Savi exudes such childlike innocence in that statement, but she's not innocent. Nothing about this is innocent.

Crystal sighs, and in that sigh are a thousand wrongdoings she can't correct. "When you first told me what you suspected happened, I didn't connect the dots, but at the vigil . . . I didn't know what to do. I didn't know if Savi had taken him or if Pam had, or what I was even dealing with. I knew I had to figure out a way to get him back to you. But I was so worried Savi or Pam would get in trouble—legally, I mean. Not only had I kept any knowledge of this baby from the world, but now he was involved in a swap? I was paralyzed with fear."

"How did you keep Pam from saying anything?" I ask Savi.

"She thought she'd go to jail."

"Look, Savi knows what she's done is very wrong," Crystal interjects. "Right, Savi?"

Savi says nothing.

"Oh, does she?" I look toward Savi. "Do you know you can't steal another woman's baby to make Mommy all better?" I hate how cruel I sound, but these aren't dolls we're dealing with—they're *humans*. "What you did is inexcusable, Savi. There are real consequences to your actions. Do you understand that? This isn't just a magic trick. This is real life."

"I know."

I address Crystal. "Are you even capable of taking care of Oliver? It's clear you don't want him." My heart lurches thinking about him.

"I don't know." Crystal's honesty rips away my righteousness. As much as I've been through, how would I feel raising another woman's baby after my husband just died? It's hard enough raising my own by myself. But then I straighten. We are mothers. This is what we *do*.

"I'm so sorry, Ms. Rebecca." Savi's voice wobbles, and the ice around my heart begins to thaw. But where can we possibly go from here? She *stole* my child. The preposterousness of the actual situation settles over me like a lead blanket. This isn't the stuff of fiction. This is my life. And here is a little girl crying for help from a mother who is oblivious to anyone's pain but her own.

The adrenaline dump from the last few days leaves me almost catatonic, and I can barely form the words to tell her she needs to get professional help—they all do.

"Do you forgive me?" Savi asks.

Do I forgive you? I think of all the people I need to forgive: Jake for taking that job so many years ago, Chris for dying, my mother for not taking better care of herself, Crystal for lying, Savi for taking my child. Can I possibly forgive her? And then I realize it's not her I need to forgive—it's myself.

The door opens before I can answer.

"Rebecca, we can take it from here." It's Officer Toby, not Jake or the chief.

I stand and comfort Jackson, who stirs on my chest. "I won't be pressing charges. Just make sure they get the help they need, please."

I resist the urge to give Savi a hug or tell Crystal good-bye. These two have been a lifeline for me over the past few months, but it was all a mirage. Crystal wasn't *really* my friend. Savi wasn't *really* my prodigious student. They are liars.

They are thieves.

As I step into the hallway, Savi bawls behind the heavy door. "I'm sorry, Ms. Rebecca!" she shrieks. "Don't leave! Please!" Tiny fists pound on the steel door, and I flinch. I hesitate, then force my legs to keep moving. It's not my job to comfort her. It's her mother's.

Jake meets me in the hall. "Do you need a minute?"

"I need to go home," I say. "I just want to go home."

"We need to clear a few things with DCFS first, take your final statement, and make sure you don't want to press charges."

"I don't."

"I know you say that, but just think about it before you decide."

"I've already decided." I just want this to be over and to move on with my life.

He ushers me down the hall. "You've got the whole damn town out there backing you, you know."

"I don't care about any of that," I say. I think of Caroline, Jess, Beth, Rob, and all the neighbors who attended the vigil. I don't want Crystal and Savi made out to be villains, but I know I have zero control over that. Unless I can get Caroline to do damage control. "This is all such a mess."

"You'll get through it." He claps a hand on my shoulder and squeezes. "You always do."

His hand is a welcome reminder. I *do* always get through it, but now I want to be past it.

I want to move on.

He holds the door open to Chief Holbrook's office, who offers me coffee and a warm seat. I sink into the chair, close my eyes, and realize this nightmare is almost over. I know the truth. I have my son.

I survived.

EPILOGUE

7 MONTHS LATER

⠈⠎⠀⠈⠇⠀⠘⠉⠀⠺⠀⠃⠀⠈

THE HARD, FRIGID WINTER HAS PASSED, AND THE FIRST HINTS OF SPRING
prick my senses on the walk to Wilder. I pass Mrs. Jansen's rosebush
and inhale. Jess chats noisily beside me, Beth on my other side. Jackson kicks in his carrier, so close to walking, he's eager to get down. I
grip the harness in my left hand. "Beethoven." My guide dog instantly
slows, and Jess laughs.

"Only you would get a dog named after a nineties movie," she says.

"It was meant to be." Beethoven had come from the B litter of
guide pups and was trained for eighteen months. He's now two years
old and ready to work. "You know you mention this every time you
see him."

"Naturally," she says.

Though I've only had Beethoven for a few months, he's the perfect
addition to our family. Jackson adores him, and I am thrilled my son
will grow up with a dog who not only knows him, but can protect
him too.

And me.

We turn left into the park, our pumpkin lattes clogging the air with
the last remnants of the season. I adjust the light scarf around my
neck and suck in the crisp air. Jackson's ankles jingle—now sporting
a bell for each foot as he prepares to move into the next stage of life:
walking.

"Wait, stop," Jess says. "I want to take a photo."

"It's not real unless you post it, right?" Beth jokes.

I know this is more for them than me, but I tell Beethoven to halt and hold my latte up in one hand and smile for the camera while Beth and Jess squeeze in. Me, Beethoven, and Jackson. One happy family.

We locate our familiar bench at the park, all of the incidents of the past months steadily draining with each passing day. Beth and Jess comment on the activities lined up for spring. Beth mentions her friend Crystal, who's on a committee for one of the charities she backs. The name twists in my brain.

Crystal left me a long voice mail after I decided not to press charges, but I deleted it without listening. I know through the grapevine that Savi is in therapy, that Oliver was returned to Crystal under strict supervision from the state, and that she's put her house up for sale. I'm not sure where they're going or when, but I hope it's somewhere they can start fresh. I don't tell the girls how much I miss all three of them, and how, even though I haven't yet forgiven them, I do want them to be okay.

We spend the morning talking as the kids play on a picnic blanket spread out in front of the bench. Jackson crawls at warp speed, and I lunge after him every few minutes, which constantly cuts into our conversation. After an hour of chasing and talking, I tell the girls I need to get Jackson home for a nap. I retrieve Beethoven's harness.

"Don't forget the nanny interview tomorrow," Jess trills.

"I'm looking forward to it," I say. "I've got so many music lessons lined up, I might hire her no matter what."

Jess set up a nanny interview for me after months of gentle prodding, and instead of saying no, per usual, I was ready to accept. I've realized help isn't a bad thing—it's necessary, and it doesn't make me a weaker person because of it. I've always been capable. I trust my intuition, and my intuition tells me it's time for help.

I'm finally listening.

On the way back, I think about how much my life has changed in less than a year. I'm sleeping. I've found a good, local therapist. I'm no longer paranoid or imagining things. I've even formed a group for vision-impaired mothers in surrounding areas. We meet once a month at the local community center.

At my front door, I disarm the alarm and stick the key in the lock. The house has received a modest renovation thanks to the help of a contractor Jake knows. It's nothing drastic, but it's enough to make it feel like my home—not my mother's.

As I turn the key, the hairs on the back of my neck prick to attention, and I rotate, key stabbing the air. My pepper spray hangs from my key chain, and I clutch it in my fist, ready to aim and spray. Beethoven barks in confirmation.

"Hey, it's just me. Sorry to scare you."

Crystal's voice barbs my skin, and I take a step back until I ram into the door.

"Why are you here?"

"I just wanted to say good-bye. We're leaving—moving. I'm . . . I just wanted to say I'm so sorry for everything that's happened." Crystal approaches and places something in my hands. "For you. Good-bye, Bec."

The opening and shutting of a car door sounds from the curb, and then an automatic window rolls down. "Bye, Ms. Rebecca! I'll miss you *so* much!" Savi's joyous voice blasts into the open space, and despite myself, I press a hand to my chest. It's been months since I've heard her sweet little voice. My eyes fill with tears, and I'm thankful for the sunglasses.

I offer a timid wave as they pull away, and something releases. Blame. Guilt. Anguish. That part of my life is over. This part of my life is what matters. Despite that reality, I still wonder how Oliver is doing. I never even got to say a real good-bye.

Once inside, I release Jackson to his play mat, and the mad jingle of bells makes me smile as he takes off in a loop around the first floor.

Beethoven follows. I drop my keys in the dish, remove my shoes, and cradle the envelope. I walk to the couch, curl my feet underneath me, and tear open the envelope to remove a few pieces of heavy paper. The letter is written in braille. I'm shocked by the effort. I take a breath, then my fingers begin to read.

Dear Rebecca,

Words cannot express how sorry I am. I can't imagine what we put you through when Jackson went missing, but please know—what happened forced me to look at my life and all the denial that had become a part of it. I was so afraid to face the world . . . and even myself.

I want you to know that Savi is getting the help she needs. I should have put her in therapy the moment Paul died, but she was so resistant, I let her guide me instead of the other way around. As her mother, I should have known there was a difference between acting out and crying out for help. I am the parent—the parent of Savi and the parent of Oliver, who, as it turns out, is a wonderful, inquisitive, amazing little boy.

He's changed the fabric of our lives, and it's not a bad thing. I'm not hiding anymore, and I really think this move will be our new beginning. I hope, with time, you will be able to forgive us too. And I hope, with time, I will be able to forgive myself.

We are moving to California. A little sunshine and ocean breeze are just what the doctor ordered, I think. There are some great music programs out there too. Savi is so excited. (Thankfully, she's outgrown the magic.)

I wish you luck, Rebecca. You are, by far, the most capable woman I have ever known, and the best mother a child could ever ask for. Believe in yourself.

I know we all do.

If you continue to do that, you will always have all the support you could ever need.

We will miss you.

Your friend (hopefully again someday?),
Crystal

The letter softens the last remnants of anger I cling to. I reread it, fold it carefully, and place it in a drawer in my desk. I walk to the dining room, where her braille art still hangs, and run my fingers over the quotes. All of the angst, frustration, and terror I've experienced . . . it's not all their fault. I wasn't taking care of myself back then either. I was so exhausted. I was drowning in grief. I was imagining a world out to get me.

I step away from the painting and realize, by some miracle, that we all got the help we needed. We all got a second chance.

I move through the rest of the day, preparing my interview questions for the nanny and my music lessons for the end of the week. At exactly six, the doorbell rings. Jackson is once again crawling through the house after a massive afternoon nap, his ankles like a Christmas jingle on repeat. Beethoven follows him protectively, the steady clop of his nails slipping on the refinished hardwood floors. The doorbell rouses his attention and he comes trotting to see who's there. I let him know it's okay. I'm smiling before I even unlock the newly installed screen door.

"There she is." Jake's arms are around me in an instant, and I surrender against his chest and breathe him in.

"Hi, handsome."

"Hi, beautiful." He tips my chin up and kisses me softly. Though his lips are familiar, they still electrify every part of my body.

He crosses the threshold and hangs his jacket on the coatrack. Beethoven wags his tail, and it thumps heavily against my leg. Jake crouches down to pet him before Jackson crawls into the foyer. He babbles and tries to form words. Jackson squeals as Jake picks him up and tosses him in the air.

"Careful," I warn.

"What's the fun in that?" He blows on Jackson's belly, which garners a round of insatiable giggles.

His presence fills my foyer—my baby in his arms, my dog obediently sitting by his feet. "Did you behave for your mother today?" he asks. "Were you a good boy?"

I follow my boys down the hallway. Jake flip-flops between baby talk to Jackson and baby talk to the dog. I roll my eyes good-naturedly and lean against the doorframe to the remodeled kitchen, arms crossed, to listen. It's not the ticking clocks and running dishwasher I hear: it's life.

Life is in my mother's house again.

Life is in *me* again.

Jake turns, noticing I've hung back. "You good?" he asks. I can tell his eyes assess me from head to toe, and I stand a little taller and smile.

"I'm great," I say. I repeat the words in my head—*I'm great.* Jackson lets out a giant belly laugh. Jake laughs too. Beethoven barks.

Life.

I push off the doorframe, uncross my arms, and happily join my family.

ACKNOWLEDGMENTS

Stepping into Rebecca Gray's world was one of the most humbling—and terrifying—experiences of my life. Creating a world for the reader when stripped of sight is no small undertaking, but it made me stretch, grow, and think about creating a story in a different way. I've always feared going blind due to my own astigmatisms, vitreous detachments, floaters, nearsightedness, and farsightedness, so it was empowering to realize you can still have a full, beautiful life without vision. Without a husband. Without a parent, or any kind of concrete help. I wanted to put an extraordinary woman in the toughest circumstances imaginable and see if she could endure.

I became a student of research and could not have constructed this character or world without the following people and institutions: the Tennessee School for the Blind, Dr. Alan Chase, Nick, and all of the other incredible visually impaired individuals who answered my questions and helped me understand what it's like to go through a daily routine without sight. A very special thank-you to Katherine Peterson, who served as my visually impaired beta reader at the eleventh hour and gave me some wonderful insight about guide dogs and all the fun gadgets for the blind.

Thank you to Adriana Aude Cook for being my go-to Elmhurst queen, letting us crash with you to explore the neighborhood in more detail, and to the tight-knit community of Elmhurst (and Chicago) who helped inspire the setting for this story (and will hopefully buy the shit out of this book . . . right?). Thank you to Adele Stein and Ben Prior for explaining in such beautiful detail what it feels like to play the cello.

Thank you to my early editorial guru, Cheryl Rieger, who makes such fabulous suggestions and always gives me the very best New York experience. To my infallible editor, Alexandra Sehulster, for the brilliant idea to make Rebecca visually impaired and then pushing me to take her to her brink and see what she's really made of. When I turned in my first draft and you said, "This book checks all the boxes, but I want you to be better," I panicked, ripped the book apart, and pieced it back together. Your belief in me makes magic happen. To my agent, Rachel Beck, who is a literal maker of dreams. You are always here—to answer questions, to step up to the plate, and to indulge all of my big career dreams. This career all started with a simple query letter to you, and it has changed the course of my entire life. Thank you.

To the entire team at St. Martin's Press and Macmillan Audio: no one gets to see what goes on behind the curtain, but without you, there is no book. I appreciate all of you. To Thomas Mis, who suggested Samantha Desz to narrate the audiobook of my first novel, then my second, and now my third. Samantha, your work is truly exceptional, and there's nothing more thrilling than hearing the interpretation of my work through your voice. A special thank-you to Erica Martirano and Mara Delgado-Sanchez—I hope this is just the beginning of working together. To the writers I've come to know over the last year or so: Kimberly Belle, David Bell, Emily Carpenter (who has the most amazing house I've ever seen), Wendy Walker, Zoje Stage, Kimmery Martin, Jeremy Finley, J. T. Ellison, Liz Fenton, Lisa Steinke, Ami McConnell, R. J. Jacobs, and so many others I've crossed paths with— thank you for the continued inspiration, advice, and conversation. And to all of the amazing authors who took the time to read and blurb this book—you rock. A special thanks to my media coach, Mary O'Donohue: everyone should be so lucky to work with a coach like you.

A special thanks to Jessica Zweig for braving her insane Chicago schedule to come away with me to the mountains so I could write the last forty thousand words of the first draft of this book in a single day—all of which were promptly trashed and rewritten, but still . . . Little did you know you were creating something spectacular that will soon live in the world too. Working with you for so many years has expanded me in ways I can't even articulate, but working *next* to you in the mountains was a revelation.

I must also extend a very special thank-you to JC Childree, childhood friend turned trusted cop, whom I bombarded with detective questions about this very "strange" case. You supplied hard facts for how Rebecca would be treated by her local precinct when dealing with a swapped child and zero evidence.

And a super special thank-you to the trusted beta readers who speed-read this and gave me incredible feedback: Andrea Nourse, Aimee Pinard, Missy Block, and my amazing Nashville writers group. Thank you to Joe Tower, for giving this the polish it needed and for your insightful, unparalleled eye.

I also want to extend a very special thank-you to the #bookstagram community on Instagram. This group of passionate readers has really made such a difference both personally and professionally, and every writer appreciates all that you do! Thank you to my publicity team, who works so hard to spread the word. Thank you to my trusted life coach, Elizabeth Pearson, who makes me believe I can do anything. Everyone should have a mentor in their life like you.

Lastly, I want to thank my family. My parents and brother for those last-minute pickups when I need them, a glass of wine, a good meal, and normal conversation. My husband, Alex, who is my truest supporter, my first reader, and my consummate rock. You are a creative genius and a wonderful man, and going through life with you makes everything possible. Let's keep dreaming our big dreams.

During the writing of this book, I was preparing to launch *Because You're Mine*. We'd just moved into a new house. I'd also made the monumental, life-altering decision to homeschool my child and take on twenty-two book proposal clients. To say I was "busy" was an understatement.

But now I realize there is no perfect "climate" to write books. There will always be interruptions, distractions, life changes, and things that pull you away (#election). But I'm glad I sat down and spent time in Rebecca Gray's world. A protagonist with a disability isn't something we see in "thrillers" often, and I think we should. It's the biggest challenge I've ever had writing a book, and I hope you—my amazing, dedicated readers—enjoy.

On to the next . . .

1. Does Rebecca's lack of people she can truly trust impact her ability to trust herself to find Jackson?

2. In *Until I Find You*, a mother's intuition is a central theme. Do you believe a mother's intuition is stronger than "logic"? Do you think people give the idea too much merit?

3. Would you have believed Bec?

4. Put yourself in Crystal's shoes. Would you make the same choices she does? Why or why not?

5. What does Bec's diminishing eyesight symbolize in her life? Do you think that ultimately, she's a stronger person having gone through so much loss? Why or why not?

6. Discuss Bec's relationship with Jake. Do we give too much power to the idea of the path not taken? Have you ever had to choose whether to follow someone and not done so?

7. What does it say that such surreal things can happen behind pristine suburban doors? Is there a level of distrust we always have for our community, even if we are active within it?

8. Bec sets out to raise Jackson completely alone while going blind. Do you admire her independence or think she should have put more support systems in place?

9. Explore the nature of the two infants and how they relate to their mother figures. Jackson is an easy baby, and Bec is a mother who will never give up on her child. Oliver is a fussy baby, and Crystal is willing to let him slide out of her life. How do we make these connections as a society: between happy babies and "good mothers," between challenging babies and women who aren't up to the task? How can we look to reverse this? Do you think it's accurate?

10. How would the book be different if Bec weren't blind? Would the other characters believe her more readily? Would you?

11. What would you have done if you were Bec?

ST.
MARTIN'S
GRIFFIN

ABOUT THE AUTHOR

© Vibe Tribe Creative

REA FREY is the author of three novels and four non-fiction books. She is also the founder and CEO of Writeway™, where aspiring writers become published authors. Learn more at reafrey.com or writewayco.com. She lives in Nashville with her husband and daughter.